"Let me go!"

" 'Tis too late."

"No!" She wriggled atop him, which only served to further inflame his desire.

"By heaven," he uttered huskily, "you will tempt me to madness yet."

He forced her head down to his, kissing her with such fierce, intoxicating ardor that she felt a familiar heat spreading throughout her body. She shivered as her breasts made contact with the bronzed, hard-muscled expanse of his chest again. With another moan of surrender, she became an active participant in the kiss, her long, unbound tresses cascading down about her face and shoulders to tease at his fevered skin. . . .

By Catherine Creel
Published by Fawcett Books:

WILD TEXAS ROSE
LADY ALEX
TEXAS WEDDING
WESTWARD ANGEL
WILDSONG
THE REIVER'S WOMAN

THE
REIVER'S
WOMAN

Catherine Creel

FAWCETT GOLD MEDAL • NEW YORK

A Fawcett Gold Medal Book
Published by Ballantine Books
Copyright © 1997 by Catherine Creel

http://www.randomhouse.com

Library of Congress Catalog Card Number: 97-90362

ISBN 0-449-18282-7

Manufactured in the United States of America

First Edition: September 1997

10 9 8 7 6 5 4 3 2 1

To Joshua, Amanda, Travis, and Katie. Your aunt loves you very much.

And to Penny Turner and Michelle Mountier. Dear friends, thank you for your kindness to this American in London.

Chapter 1

Northumberland, 1596

Lady Analise Hayward descended the turret stairs with an ill-disguised reluctance. Her spirits were low, a fitting match for the cold September wind that whipped across the hills and thrashed vengefully at the castle walls.

A sudden shiver ran the length of her spine. She cursed the day she had been summoned to this wild, inhospitable country in the far north of England. Truly fate had conspired against her.

"When has it not?" she murmured, her blue-green eyes clouding, albeit briefly, with painful remembrance as she reached the last of the narrow steps. Appearance would have it that her life had been one of ease and privilege these many years past, that she had known only happiness. Yet her heart told her differently.

For a moment, her gaze drifted to the high-arched window in the thick stones above. There was no sun to warm her with its benevolence, no laughter or friendly greetings to make her welcome. There was only this deep, unrelenting grayness and the mournful howl of the wind.

A wave of homesickness rose within her.

1

She quickly stifled it. She would not surrender to self-pity. No, by heaven, she would not. Though torn from both the safe and the familiar, she must nevertheless remain true to her avowed determination to make the best of things. How else could she hope to keep her wits about her in such a place?

Resolutely squaring her shoulders, she gathered up her long, full skirts and swept across the firelit splendor of the Great Hall to face the man who, until yesterday, had been known to her in name only. *Would that he had remained so,* she mused with an inward smile of irony.

"I began to grow impatient, dearest cousin," Simon Hayward drawled softly at her approach.

He was every bit as haughty and aristocratic-looking as his lineage would imply. Five and thirty years of age, he sported a tiny, pointed Spanish beard only slightly darker than his shoulder-length blond hair. The collar of his white linen shirt rose fashionably high with lace trim above his crimson brocade doublet, while his gray satin breeches were full and gartered below each knee. There were some who would call him handsome. There were others who would, perhaps even more readily, call him the devil incarnate.

Smiling, he rose from his seat near the brilliant glow of the flames. There was no trace of either affection or amusement in his pale gray eyes as they traveled over the young woman standing so proud and silent before him.

God be praised, he reflected with a keen, calculated satisfaction, she was at least a beauty. Her features were delicate, her thick, lustrous curls the color of burnished gold. Her emerald velvet gown, worn over the requisite farthingale, showed her slender curves to advantage. The low, square neckline of the fitted bodice offered a tantalizing glimpse of her full, creamy breasts.

His gaze flickered reluctantly back up to her face. He wondered if any man had as yet availed himself of the pleasure of tasting her sweet lips. Was it truly possible that she had spent this past year at court without enjoying any sort of the dalliances that even the Virgin Queen herself was said to encourage?

She had none of the world-weary air about her, he concluded, his eyes narrowing a bit now. It was, of course, lamentable that she should be possessed of such a headstrong nature, but no matter. He would bend her to his will soon enough . . .

Analise stiffened beneath her guardian's hard and discomfiting scrutiny. She was tempted to speak, to inquire angrily if he had requested her presence for no other reason than this ill-mannered inspection, but she said nothing. By all the saints, holding her tongue had never been easy.

"I trust you spent your first night here pleasantly enough?" Simon finally queried in a smooth, negligent tone. "It does not appear to me that you have suffered any ill effects as the result of your journey."

"I am quite well, thank you," she replied, her gaze avoiding the cold steadiness of his.

"I am pleased to hear it. For we are to entertain guests this evening."

"Guests?" Her spirits rose at the prospect. Since her arrival the day before, she had met with no one else but a handful of servants. Indeed, she had thought it strange that the castle, however gloomy, should be so thoroughly bereft of visitors.

"Beauford is not usually such a quiet place," advised

Simon, as though reading her mind. He folded his arms across his chest and leisurely advanced upon her now. "My recent appointment as Warden of the Middle March demands that I maintain a constant vigilance along the border. To that effect, it has been necessary for me to dispatch my deputies elsewhere on urgent matters of business. But they shall return before nightfall. And joining their numbers will be two gentlemen who are most anxious to make your acquaintance."

Analise tensed anew. There was something in his voice that sounded an alarm deep within her. Taking a steadying breath, she raised her eyes to his and tried to ignore the uneasiness that crept over her when he paused mere inches away. He was not so very much taller than she, yet she felt oddly threatened.

"I know little of the situation here," she confided with remarkable composure. "It was seldom mentioned in London. I should very much like it if you would explain—"

"You will soon learn, my dear Analise, that ignorance is both a woman's right and privilege," he interrupted brusquely, then allowed the corners of his mouth to turn up once more. His smile this time was full of derision. "Suffice it to say that those thieving, black-hearted savages north of the border shall soon answer to justice. If it were but my decision alone, I should make Scotland bleed for its many transgressions."

"I was not aware that the two countries were at war."

"You are as naive as you are beautiful." He raised his hand and idly fingered one of the silken curls that framed her face. "What a pity that your mother was French."

"On the contrary, sir, I consider it a most gratifying stroke of good fortune!" she retorted, her eyes flashing at the unexpected attack.

"We can at least give thanks for the fact that your father was clear-witted enough to place you within his sister's care following the death of your mother," Simon continued as though she had not spoken. "And your convent education can have done you no harm."

"Why did you send for me?" she demanded, her tone sharp and accusatory. "You have been my guardian these seven years past, yet you never once saw fit to acknowledge my existence. And though you are the trustee of my father's estate, you have shown little enough interest in it—save for the income it provides you!"

"Ah, but then I have had other 'interests' to occupy me. Besides, my uncle was scarcely known to me. No doubt your own memory of him is fading, given that he died when you were still but a child. Blood ties alone are responsible for my guardianship, an honor I neither sought nor happily embraced. In truth," he told her with little attempt to soften the blow, "I would have been content for the two of us to remain strangers. Yet I find that I have need of you now."

"Need?" She stared up at him in mingled surprise and puzzlement. "What possible need could—"

"All in good time."

He turned and crossed back to resume his chosen place of repose beside the fire. Analise watched as he sank down into the velvet-upholstered chair and took up the glass of wine he had been nursing prior to her arrival within the cavernous, richly decorated hall. It was clear that she had been dismissed.

Her temper flaring, she realized that her first impression of him had not been wrong after all. He was a remote and unsympathetic man, one who would prove to be considerably less than the friend she had prayed he would be.

"You may retire to your chambers once more," he instructed her, a discernible note of impatience in his smooth-toned voice. "It would serve my purpose if you were looking your best at the banquet tonight."

"Perhaps I shall be too wearied to attend," she threatened, her chin lifting in an unconscious gesture of defiance.

"That would be most ill-advised." His expression hardened while his eyes glinted malevolently across at her. "I can assure you, little cousin, that I am not a patient man."

"And I can assure you, *my lord*, that I am no weak and docile maiden to be ordered about at your pleasure!"

Simon offered no response, other than to raise the glass of wine to his lips with a slow deliberation. Analise might well have said more, if not for the fact that she sensed in her guardian a barely controlled violence. It was too soon to know what he was capable of. Perhaps, she realized, her yearning for excitement and adventure had led her into a situation even more precarious than she could have imagined.

Filled with a growing sense of dread, she turned upon her slippered heel and headed back toward the stairs. She could feel Simon's cold gray eyes upon her, and she silently cursed the trembling of her hands as she gathered up her skirts and ascended to the living quarters on the third floor. The eerie shadows within the narrow, stone-walled corridor seemed to taunt her, to offer a subtle promise of even further menace ahead.

An audible sigh of relief escaped her lips when at last she reached the safety of her bedchamber once more. Closing the door behind her, she leaned back against it and cast a swift, worried glance heavenward.

"Sweet mercy, what have I done?" she whispered, having cause now—yet again—to regret her own impulsive nature. If not for a desire to escape the suffocating, tedious confines of her life at court, she would never have so willingly obeyed the summons from her guardian. She could have appealed to the queen for help. And if even that had failed, she could have fled to France. Her mother's family would certainly have offered her refuge.

But she had chosen her path. And, at least for now, she must follow its course.

Heaving another deep sigh, she wandered to the tall, brocade-canopied bed and perched for a moment upon the edge of the mattress. The room, like the rest of the castle, boasted of expensive and finely detailed adornments—tapestries from the finest weaving houses in all of Europe, carpets so thick and sumptuous they concealed any trace of the stones beneath, and ornate, carved mahogany furniture that would have been far more suited to a palace rather than this ugly stone fortress upon the very edge of the frontier.

A well-tended fire burned steadily on the other side of the hearth. Yet, thought Analise, in spite of the blaze and the richness of the furnishings, there was no true warmth to be felt. Only the same coldness she had glimpsed within Simon Hayward's eyes.

Drawing herself up from the silken coverlet, she moved across to the window. Her brow furrowed anew as she distractedly fingered the heavy velvet draperies and gazed outward. The landscape below her was shrouded in mist at present, its rugged, fiercely varied expanse kept secret from all save those who had spent a lifetime upon the wooded valleys and thrusting green hills, peat bogs and spongy mosses, and vast, heather-covered moorland.

A curiosity rose within Analise. A sudden powerful yearning to know what manner of people would choose to live in the midst of such a rough and primitive country-side. Her friends in London had declared themselves horrified at the prospect of so much as a single night spent along the border. Indeed, she mused while her eyes sparked with a momentary flash of humor, it was difficult to imagine any of her acquaintances, however sweet-mannered, enduring either the journey northward or the sight of Beauford without voicing their complete and utter dismay. And, God knew, there was much by which to be dismayed.

Behind her the door opened, and a buxom, dark-haired young woman bearing a pitcher filled with hot water slipped tentatively inside the room.

"Begging your pardon, my lady. I did first knock, but there was no answer," the maidservant apologized. She gave Analise a deferential nod, hesitated a moment longer, then hastened forward to pour the water into a porcelain bowl atop a small round table near the fireplace.

"In truth, I am glad for the intrusion," Analise responded with a brief, preoccupied smile. She turned away from the window and surveyed the girl, perhaps only a year or two younger than herself, who had emptied the pitcher and now stood drying her hands on the apron that protected her simple, coarse brown woolen gown. "You are called Meg, are you not?"

"Yes, my lady."

"Have you been long at Beauford?"

"I was born in the village. I came to work at the castle but a fortnight ago when my sister was wed. Betty was chambermaid till then, and now I've taken her place. My mother was—"

Realizing that she was talking too much, she broke off guiltily, caught up the pitcher again, and set off toward the doorway.

" 'Tis to be hoped you will settle in soon enough, my lady," she murmured politely, preparing to take her leave.

"My name is Analise. And would that more than a day had already passed," said Analise. She was glad when Meg paused upon the threshold and cast her a sympathetic look.

"I fear you must miss London."

"More than I had expected." She folded her arms beneath her breasts and crossed to stand before the fire. Her eyes were full of a genuine appeal when she met the other young woman's gaze and suggested, "Perhaps the longing could be eased somewhat if you would agree to tell me more about this place I must now call home."

"What is it you wish to know, my lady?"

"Analise," she corrected gently, another faint smile touching her lips. "And I would know everything, Meg. I would know about life here in the castle, about the men and women in the village. I would know about those who live on the other side of the border. Do they—"

"May God save us from the Scots!" Meg suddenly gasped. Her blue eyes had grown quite wide, and she startled Analise even further when she put forth with a heartfelt emphasis, "The only thing you must know about *them*, my lady, is to pray they keep well away from these walls!"

"Why do you say that?" Analise demanded, much intrigued. She stepped closer, her own eyes bright with the curiosity that had so recently taken hold within her. "Are our two countries not at peace?" It was the same question she had earlier posed to Simon.

"The devil's peace!" replied Meg. She shook her head before asking in disbelief, "Have you truly heard nothing of the Reivers, then?"

"Reivers?" Analise echoed, turning the word over in her mind at the same time. She was purposely evasive when she admitted, "In truth, the sound of it is familiar— yet I am afraid my education upon such matters has been woefully inadequate."

"If it is an education you want, my lady, then you have come to the right place," Meg declared in a wry tone. She immediately grew serious again, her eyes searching Analise's face. "Do they not speak of the Border Reivers at court? Surely the queen's men warn of the many troubles here in the north, of those bloodthirsty heathens who would murder us in our beds!"

It was Analise's turn to remark with more than a touch of irony, "The queen's men talk of little save themselves." She unfolded her arms, lifted a hand to tuck a stray tendril of hair back into place, and glanced down at the flames. "I *do* know a little of the troubles here, but only a little. My guardian has proven himself unwilling to disclose the extent of his duties. And what I heard at court was only that the border is a land where violence and lawlessness rule." Her eyes were aglow with renewed excitement when they sought the guilelessness of Meg's again. "But I would hear more! Sweet heaven, Meg, I would hear what sort of men possess the ability to strike terror with such ease!"

"The sort who would as soon slit your throat as bid you good morn!"

"You have seen them?" Analise asked, her fingers now closing eagerly about the maidservant's arm.

"Yes, and more's the pity for the seeing. There are few of us here who have not suffered at their hands. They ride with the moonlight, from Michaelmas to Martinmas. Why, but only a week ago, my mother's brother did find himself lighter by some three dozen head of cattle!"

"Were the thieves apprehended?"

"No." Meg shook her head and explained, "Catching them is not so easy. Expert raiders they be, full of cunning, with horses that can find their way through even the deepest and darkest of the fens. Sometimes they go a-reiving with only a handful among them. But 'tis said they have ridden as many as a thousand strong!"

"And it is my guardian's appointed task to put an end to their plundering," noted Analise, half to herself. She turned slowly about to face the fire, and crossed her arms against her chest once more. "Perhaps he is the man to succeed where others have failed."

"Begging your pardon, my lady," Meg was emboldened enough to disagree, "but the failing has endured for nigh on to three hundred years. Were Sir Simon the hardest and cleverest of men, even so he could not hope to tame the Scots."

"Still, I wonder if he might not prove a fitting match for those who would set themselves above the laws of both God and man." Her gaze reflected the dance of the flames, and she caught her lower lip between her teeth as the unpleasant memory of her brief encounter with her cousin rose in her mind again. "Surely these 'Border Reivers' are nothing more than flesh and blood, with all the faults and weaknesses of ordinary men. They cannot be completely infallible."

"Many *have* found their way to the end of a rope," Meg allowed, then gave an eloquent sigh. "But the hanging of them has only made their clans all the more set upon revenge." A telltale blush stole up to her cheeks when she unexpectedly confided, "Evil, murderous rogues they may be, yet they have the devil's own way about them. They are a fearsomely handsome lot, big and strong, and can charm even the stoutest of hearts whenever it pleases them to do so. Yes, and more than one poor lass this side of the border has a swollen belly to show for it!"

Analise could not prevent herself from coloring at the bluntness of Meg's remark, but she quickly recovered and smiled again.

"I must confess that everything you have told me has only served to increase my curiosity."

"If that be the case," whispered Meg, flinging a wary, conspiratorial glance toward the doorway, "and if you are still wanting to see the spawn of Lucifer for yourself . . ."

"Yes?" Analise prompted.

"There is to be a Truce Day at week's end. 'Tis the one day of a month when the Scots and English can meet in peace. Oh, my lady," she exclaimed, warming to the subject, "never have your eyes beheld such a sight! Men and women will come from all over the land. Yes, and there will be peddlers and musicians and—"

She broke off with a gasp when the chatelaine, a tall, raven-haired woman named Lady Helena Montrose, suddenly appeared at the opposite end of the corridor. Lady Helena's heavy mauve silk skirts rustled a warning of her approach as she descended upon Analise and Meg.

"You've work to do, girl, and had best be about it if you have a care to your post!" she threatened Meg. She, too, was cousin to Simon. Yet she was well past thirty years of age, a fading beauty with both a sour, haughty disposition and a futile hope that Simon Hayward would one day make her his wife.

Meg paled and clutched the empty pitcher tightly to her breast. She exchanged one last frightened, speaking look with Analise, then spun about to flee from the room. In her wake Analise's blue-green gaze bridled with anger.

"Surely, Lady Helena, it was not necessary to speak so uncivilly to the young woman," she protested. "Indeed, Meg and I were engaged in a private conversation."

"A private conversation with a serving wench?" parried Lady Helena, her own voice dripping with scorn. The smile she offered did not quite reach the glacial azure of her eyes. "I must remember, Lady Analise, that you are as yet unfamiliar with our ways here in the north. In time, you shall learn the right of things." Without waiting for an invitation, she swept inside the bedchamber and coolly announced, "Sir Simon has instructed me to make certain you understand the importance of your presence at tonight's banquet."

"My guardian does me far too great an honor," Analise responded with a noticeable hint of sarcasm. She was not the least bit repentant upon glimpsing the answering flash in Lady Helena's gaze.

"Nonetheless, you will conduct yourself as befitting the ward of Sir Simon Hayward. And you will pay particular attention to Lord Walsingham and Sir Harry Claibourne."

"Why should I do so?"

"Because Sir Simon commands it!" Lady Helena snapped. It was obvious that she bore Analise no amount of goodwill. "Do not think me a fool," she warned, her eyes narrowing to mere slits in her sharp-featured countenance. "You are but a silly child, a spoiled and pampered girl who cares for nothing save her own selfish interests. Were it not for the use Sir Simon can make of you, you would still be among your perfumed dandies at court!"

"Pray, Lady Helena," Analise countered, struggling to maintain control of her temper again, "what possible *use* could I—"

"Do as you are told, and we shall all of us reap the benefits" was the woman's curt, enigmatic reply. "I have ordered a bath for you in but an hour's time. You would be well-advised to rest until then. I have little doubt that the night will be a long one—or that Lord Walsingham and Sir Harry would prefer you to remain awake throughout the festivities. It might interest you to know that they have looked forward to your arrival with great expectation. We must not disappoint them, for Sir Simon has chosen their favor from among the best in Northumberland."

"And if I choose to absent myself from the banquet?" It was a not-so-subtle challenge, and they both knew their resolve to be tested.

"We should be allies, not adversaries," Lady Helena said without conviction. Her smile this time was at once contemptuous and triumphant. "But you must believe me when I say that Sir Simon will tolerate no defiance. A few days spent locked within the confines of your bedchamber should school you to compliance. If not, then there are other methods—methods, I daresay, you would find not at all to your liking." With that, she took her leave.

Were it not for the use Sir Simon can make of you. The significance of her words had not been lost upon Analise. Outrage and apprehension burned within her as she glared after Lady Helena.

"So I am summoned here in order to be married off," she fumed aloud, the very thought of Simon's plan making her blood boil. Now it was clear to her why the summons had arrived after so many years of complete silence. And why Simon was so eager for her to look her best that evening.

Muttering a furiously unladylike oath, she closed the door and whirled about to return to her stance at the window. Her fingers threaded tightly within the velvet. Outside, the wind tumbled the mist about, the sun's rays trying in vain to make their way through the thick, swirling cover of clouds. Night would come soon enough, Analise thought unhappily . . . and with it the two would-be suitors, known to her as yet in name only, whose chances of winning her hand were bettered only by that of a handful of snow in the very depths of hell.

Her gaze sparked with the force of her anger and defiance. No matter how pleasing to the eye the gentlemen might be, no matter how wealthy or well connected, she would not wed either of them.

Lady Helena could threaten all she pleased. Simon Hayward could lock her away until the flesh dropped from her bones, and *still*, she would not marry. She had not avoided the oppressive bonds of matrimony these many years at court in order to have them thrust upon her now. Not when the long-held dream of adventure finally lay within her grasp.

"If ever I *do* wed," she renewed an earlier vow, her

fervent whisper drifting heavenward, "it shall be for love alone." She closed her eyes for a moment before adding impulsively, "And may God help the man who dares to woo me with little regard for my feelings in the matter!"

Her eyes flew wide again. She was startled when something Meg had said returned to echo within her brain.

They have the devil's own way about them.

"The Border Reivers," Analise murmured, releasing the draperies and wandering back to sink down upon the bed once more. Though Meg had told her little enough, her curiosity had nonetheless been increased tenfold. She longed to catch a glimpse of the notorious Scots. She longed to see for herself why, in spite of the violent, deep-seated enmity between the two countries, a goodly number of local women had willingly surrendered themselves to the outlaws.

Her face flamed at the wicked turn of her thoughts, yet still she could not be sorry for it. Heaven help her, would not even an "honest" rogue be preferable to the men of ambition and deceit she had encountered thus far?

There is to be a Truce Day at week's end.

It was the memory of those particular words that caused her pulse to take a sudden leap. And her gaze to sparkle with what should, if conscience be her guide, remain a forbidden determination.

Once again, however, curiosity emerged the victor.

She would find a way to attend the Truce Day. If necessary, she would steal away from the castle and go under cover of darkness. But go she would.

"Perhaps the summons was not so ill-timed after all." The prospect of a genuine escapade made her forget—at least temporarily—the plans her guardian had made for her. Finally, she mused with an inward smile of satisfaction, her life would begin in earnest.

Chapter 2

Anticipation burned strong within Analise. She could scarcely contain her excitement as she rode along, flanked by Lord Walsingham on her left and Sir Harry Claibourne on her right. Though she would have voluntarily claimed neither gentleman as companion, she had nonetheless been forced to swallow her distaste for their escort in order to gain permission to attend the Truce Day. It still infuriated her to recall Simon's visible gleam of satisfaction when she had agreed to his terms.

Indeed, there was little doubt that her cousin was immensely pleased with himself of late. In addition to urging her into the company of his two political allies for the past several days—she had stated, with considerable yet ultimately futile vigor, that she would much rather be confined to her room—he had decreed that she should make her choice of husband within the space of a fortnight.

A fortnight. The memory of his demand brought a renewed spark of fury to her eyes. She had once again proclaimed herself unwilling to marry at all, but Simon had countered with an awful truth. As her legal guardian, he had complete and utter control over her future. He could force her to wed any man of his own choosing.

Unless, of course, she would prefer the peace and solitude of a convent.

Either wife or nun . . . in truth, she had never considered herself as a likely candidate for the cloister, but even *that* would be preferable to marriage with a man she could not stomach. She cared for Lord Walsingham only slightly less than Sir Harry. The former was attractive enough yet boorish, while the latter possessed the unenviable ability to rattle on about his own achievements and connections without pausing to draw breath. The two of them had importuned her with their attentions ever since the night of the banquet. She would have surrendered to the impulse to send them packing if not for her secret, increasingly passionate desire to see the men whose very description had kindled her fascination more than ever before.

She had begun to think the appointed day would never arrive. But it had come at last, bringing with it an endless blue sky. The transformation was astonishing, Analise now marveled silently. Her turquoise gaze widened as it swept across the distant, rolling green of the Cheviot Hills. They were in Scotland now, only a few miles from the border. The countryside through which they had been journeying since well before dawn was punctuated by reminders of times both fierce and ancient—great, Iron Age hill forts, a towering wall built by the Romans in the vain hope of protecting them from the savages to the north, and massive stone castles, where Borderers, English and Scottish alike, had for centuries taken refuge from one another's hostilities. It was a wild and rugged and beautiful land. But within its beauty lay a danger, ever present, few could withstand.

Analise shifted in the saddle and gripped the reins more tightly, oblivious to the many admiring glances directed her way. Both her gown and overskirt were of fine emerald wool. A fur-lined, deep blue velvet cloak protected her from the chill of the morning breeze. She was grateful for the fact that no farthingale was required while riding; she would have been even more grateful if the rigid dictates of fashion allowed a lady to wear breeches. Her thick golden tresses had been confined in a silken net, which was in turn topped by a black velvet hat with a crimson plume and a jeweled band. Kid gloves and a pair of soft leather boots completed the ensemble. The sight of it had provoked a surge of jealousy within Lady Helena.

"We draw near to Windy Gyle," Lord Walsingham announced in his usual disinterested tone. A dark-haired man of both wealth and noble stature, Analise might have viewed him with at least some small measure of favor if not for his constantly bored expression.

"I pray that you will heed my warning, Lady Analise," reiterated the blond and much younger Sir Harry, his own manner of speaking far too emphatic. "Hang me if these Scots are not a barbarous, uneducated lot!"

"I am not afraid," Analise was quick to assert. But it was not entirely true. A touch of fear *had* crept forth to join with the excitement she felt, and she wondered if she had perhaps been a bit too impetuous.

"Sir Simon has charged us with your safety," Lord Walsingham reminded her, unnecessarily. "You must remain close."

"Yes, my dearest Lady Analise," Sir Harry seconded while sparing a swift, uncongenial glance toward his rival. "*I* shall give protection should any dare to offer you insult."

Though sorely tempted to voice a fitting retort, Analise

bit her tongue and looked to where her cousin rode at the head of the English cavalcade.

His slashed and brightly colored doublet showed beneath his armor, which glinted harshly in the morning light. Following close behind him were his several deputies. Their weapons, along with those of the dozens of soldiers in their wake, also caught the sun's rays and provided a none too subtle warning to any man foolish enough to consider breaking the truce.

Within a matter of minutes, the cavalcade topped a hill and drew to a halt. Analise's eyes grew round at the sight unfolding before her.

Spectators had converged from far and wide, making their way over the fells and moors while the countryside was still cloaked in moonlit darkness. Spread out across a gently rolling, heather-mantled river valley were the stalls of the peddlers and tinkers—"badgers and cadgers" to the local folk—who had arrived the previous evening in order to be ready to ply their wares. A carnival atmosphere already prevailed, with ale flowing freely in spite of the early hour, and musicians and traveling players lending their efforts to send a merry, echoing clamor throughout the clearing. The smells of food, wood smoke, and horses filled the air. And in the midst of such festivity, a great crowd of men and women from both sides of the border, dressed in their Sunday best, bargained and gambled and gossiped. For this one day alone, old scores would be forgotten or temporarily set aside, and old feuds kept waiting.

"One would think these brigands would at least have the presence of mind to wash," Lord Walsingham drawled, wrinkling his nose in disgust as he withdrew a handkerchief from his padded brocade doublet.

"Faith, man," Sir Harry remarked with a sneer of his own, "have you not heard? They never wash, for fear of weakening their 'powers.' Rather like Samson and his hair, I should think!"

Analise paid them no mind, for her attention had now been captured by the opposing cavalcade. Several hundred strong, the Scots sat astride their hardy, surefooted mounts on another rise just across the valley. Poised in watchful readiness, each man among them armed and silent, they looked for all the world like something out of a dream . . . or a nightmare.

They were not dressed in the fashionable silks and velvets, nor in the gleaming armor, chosen by their counterparts. Instead they wore quilted leather coats known as "jacks"—sewn with plates of metal or horn—over doublets of homespun linen, leather breeches, thigh-length boots, and gauntlets of steel and leather. On their heads were the infamous "steel bonnets" by which they had come to be known, helmets with a peak and a flared rim. Their weapons were also peculiar to their number— round shields called "bucklers" that were studded and covered with leather, well-tempered broadswords with barred protection for the knuckles, lances (or "long spears") nearly twelve feet in length, and wheel-lock firearms called *"daggs,"* which could be carried safely while primed. Even the poorest among them could lay claim to a small arsenal of weapons. Even the least skilled among them could kill an opponent swiftly and without remorse.

Analise felt a sudden, involuntary shiver dance down her spine. Sweet mercy, she thought while her eyes sparkled with the force of her mingled pleasure and excitement, *this* was what she had come to see! Bold, lionhearted men who knew what they wanted and let nothing stand in their way. Men who gave no quarter, and asked for none as well. Clean-shaven, clear-eyed, with faces that betrayed none of their bloodthirsty tendencies toward the English. Even from this distance, she could see that they were every bit as rugged and handsome as Meg had led her to believe. And perhaps most significantly of all, they provided a stark, telling contrast to the "civilized" men in whose company she rode.

Shifting her fascinated gaze back to Simon, she watched as he suddenly turned his head and signaled to three of his deputies. They maneuvered their horses to the front and, following an ancient custom—part of the same custom which required English wardens to cross into Scotland on the day of truce—obediently cantered down the hill and across the valley toward the opposing line of riders. They were met halfway by three of the Scottish deputies.

An abrupt silence fell over the crowd. Hundreds of pairs of eyes widened in apprehension—would the assurances of peace be exchanged? If so, then no man or woman present would have cause to fear for their lives until after sunrise of the following day. All would be able to reach the safety of their homes before the truce had expired.

Analise held her breath. She looked at the stoic, awe-inspiring multitude of Scots on the opposite rise, spared a glance toward Simon again, and remained blissfully unmindful of her two escorts. Never before had she been caught up in such a thrilling rush of expectation. In that moment she was glad she had left London. No matter what lay ahead, she knew that she would never forget what she had seen. Nor what she had felt. The great adventure for which she had yearned truly lay within her grasp now; she sensed that this one day would change her life forever.

At long last, the promise was given. Simon and the other warden responded by lifting their hands in a token of good faith. The day of truce had officially begun.

A loud cheer erupted from the spectators. Simon led his soldiers and remaining deputies down the hill. The Scots set forth as well, their horses treading lightly over the moist, grassy earth.

Still deep in thought, Analise was only dimly aware of the fact that her own entourage was on the move. She was finally drawn out of her reverie by the grating tones of Lord Walsingham's voice as he leaned close to pronounce, "We have no need to immerse ourselves within the *vulgaire*. I have taken the liberty of arranging food and shelter for us but a short distance from your guardian's assemblage."

"Unfair, Walsingham!" Sir Harry objected. He frowned and narrowed his eyes into an accusatory glare. "You knew I had done the same!"

"I do implore you to forgiveness, gentlemen," Analise exhorted with a feigned sweetness, "but I have every intention of going among the people here. Would you have me remain ignorant of their ways? I think not. Indeed," she concluded, adding a winning smile to temper her recalcitrance, "I do not believe myself capable of embracing this country as my own until I know more. Therefore—"

She gave them no time to argue, setting her heels to her mount and riding down into the valley in the wake of the English soldiers. That her gallant admirers would give chase, she had little doubt, but she was determined to elude them for as long as possible.

Approaching the outskirts of the vast collection of stalls and tables, she drew the horse beneath her to a halt and quickly dismounted. A rapid glance back over her shoulder told her that Sir Harry and Lord Walsingham were fast upon her. She wasted little time in securing the horse's reins to the branch of one of the trees alongside a wide, swiftly flowing stream. Gathering up her skirts, she hesitated but an instant before setting off to explore.

The sheer boisterousness of the proceedings overwhelmed her. As did the smells. She smiled to herself and plunged happily within the crowd. No one appeared to think her presence there anything out of the ordinary, even though she was the only highborn English lady in evidence. Her clothing was far more elegant than the simple woolens and linens worn by the other women, yet she attracted little notice as she wandered throughout what was in truth a country fair.

Officially, of course, the day had been appointed for the sole purpose of a wardens' meeting, as an opportunity to gain redress for grievances and to see justice done. To many in attendance, however, Truce Day was a social event and nothing more. With startling ease, the majority of people from both sides of the border were able to fraternize, to forget that they had suffered so terribly at the hands of the other. It was difficult to believe that these same folk would, on the morrow, suffer no pangs of conscience for trying to rob or injure or even kill the same men with whom they had drunk and talked so companionably. Save for these few hours alone, they were enemies.

Analise paid little heed to the question of politics and

alliances. She was as yet still ignorant of the true nature of the long-held enmity between the two sides. Reveling in her newfound freedom, however temporary she knew it to be, she made her way further into the whirl of merrymaking.

Her senses eagerly drank in the sights and sounds about her. The lilting melody of a reel, played on pipe and fiddle and borne aloft by the wind, added to the festive mood. Merchants who had seized advantage of the gathering in order to make a profit offered up an array of goods—"fairings" for the ladies, cooking utensils, spices, weaponry, animals, and even the services of a matchmaker (for which only half payment would be required if the union did not produce fine, strapping sons). Nearby a baby's cry of hunger pierced the din, while elsewhere a horse race was arranged for later in the day. Women shared stories of both joy and hardship, men alternated between discussions of the weather and the "plump, powdered weaklings" who governed in both Edinburgh and London, and children bobbed wildly through the melee. And all the while, the morning sun burned brighter and higher in the sky, sending its golden glow upon a land that was too often bereft of warmth.

Analise reached the far side of the clearing, and in so doing came unwittingly upon the very spot where her guardian sat at a table alongside the Scottish warden. She drew up short and hastily pressed back into the crowd, concealing herself so that she could eavesdrop upon the meeting.

The two wardens, she saw, were surrounded by their deputies. Two clerks sat at opposite ends of the table, preparing to record the judgment. A short distance away stood the men, from both sides of the border, who had

been summoned to answer charges against them. The
crimes of which they were accused ranged from kid-
napping and robbery and arson to outright murder. If
found guilty, they would be ordered to pay compensa-
tion. Or, providing they were judged wholly beyond
redemption, they would be taken away to be hanged or
beheaded. Truly it was a rough justice they faced. And
those who were dissatisfied with the outcome, and who
were still alive at the end of the day, might well decide to
seek revenge when next the moon was full.

Peering from behind the corner of a tinker's stall,
Analise ventured a glance toward the group of accused
men. Several, she noted with an inward shudder, looked
entirely capable of the most horrible of transgressions.
Some of them, however, appeared to be little more than
boys. Still others had an air of insouciance about them, as
if they were not in the least bit worried about their fate.
More than half within the group wore the identifying
garb of the Border Reivers. They had removed their helmets. Their swords gleamed in the morning light. Every
man among them seemed menacing, and ready to spring
into action at the first sign of a threat.

Another small tremor of fear coursed through Analise.
She turned away, intent upon immersing herself within
the crowd once more. But as she moved away from the
stall, her gaze suddenly encountered that of a man who
had materialized just beyond those waiting for the trial to
begin.

She stopped short, her breath catching upon a gasp.
Her heart gave a strange flutter within her breast. She
found herself unable to look away.

He was perhaps thirty years of age, tall and powerfully
built, his sleeveless jack and leather breeches molding

a body that was well muscled and unaccustomed to leisure. The sun lit fire in the thickness of his dark chestnut hair. His features were tanned and chiseled above his long-sleeved, homespun linen shirt. He was by far the most attractive man she had ever seen, albeit in a rugged, thoroughly masculine way. There was something almost otherworldly about him; more than any of the other men assembled, he looked as if he had stepped from the pages of a book offering up tales of romance and high adventure. And his eyes . . . his eyes were so deep a blue as to put the sky to shame.

They burned steadily across the clearing into the wide, luminous depths of hers.

He is one of the Reivers, her mind's inner voice saw fit to point out. One of the savages with the devil's own charm and the ability to make women forget he was the enemy.

She swallowed hard and instinctively lifted a hand to her throat. Dismayed to feel her cheeks turning rosy, she forced her gaze downward at last. Yet she was still acutely conscious of the Scot's hot, penetrating gaze upon her. In spite of the many layers of clothing she wore, she felt as though his eyes stripped her naked. Her instincts urged her to leave, to turn and flee as quickly as she could, but her legs refused to obey.

"Let us begin!" Simon's voice rang out, finally breaking the spell. Analise inhaled upon a gasp and momentarily transferred her gaze to him, only to note that his expression was one of cool disdain as he looked to the Scottish warden beside him. Her eyes moved with a will of their own back to the tall Reiver. The look he gave her sent a chill down her spine . . .

"I have chosen six of my men for the jury," continued

Simon. "You must now choose six of your own. We have more than four and twenty complaints to be dealt with before nightfall, so I suggest—"

"Did I not say to you, Hayward, that I would have a trial by honor this day?" the slender, redheaded Scot beside him interrupted, scowling darkly. He had been appointed to the post for that one day only, acting in his father's stead. It was well-known that he was an absolute scoundrel. Even his own men held little respect for him. Although not much above the age of twenty, he had already led a number of raids. And committed a number of murders.

"That you did, Robert Kerr of Cessford," Simon replied with a smile that was unmistakably patronizing. "Yet I place little faith in such methods. Nor will I make a judgment on either oath or avowal." His smile faded, and his eyes glittered harshly when he warned, "Take care. I am well aware of the fact that my predecessor, Sir John Forster, was a lamentably . . . shall we say 'inadequate' warden. Did he not have a reputation for executing the innocent and conniving against his queen? I intend to follow my own path."

"Aye, straight to hell!" one of the Reivers pronounced in a voice loud enough for all to hear. His remark elicited a burst of scornful laughter from his fellow Scots.

Simon's pale, aristocratic features hardened, but he maintained an outward show of calm. "We shall have a trial by jury this day."

"You are in Scotland, man, and we will abide by no *English* rules!" Robert Kerr ground out.

"The rules are not mine alone," Simon reminded him smoothly. His lips curled upward once more, this time in certain triumph. "I have heard it said that your father is a fair and reasonably minded man. Would he take pleasure in knowing that his son had broken the truce he has honored for so long?"

At that, Robert Kerr's freckled, sharp-featured visage became suffused with an angry color.

Analise caught her breath again, certain that she glimpsed a foreboding spark within the handsome stranger's gaze. She paled now. A tremor of fear coursed through her body as his face took on a grim look.

And then he stepped forward.

With deceptive nonchalance, he made his way easily through the assembly to the table. He paused close behind Robert Kerr. Analise, once again breathless and mesmerized, watched as he spoke a brief, private word in the younger man's ear.

Robert Kerr's expression remained mulish but a moment longer. With obvious reluctance he accepted the counsel of the other man and conceded tightly, "A trial by jury it will be, then."

The meeting began at last. Robert Kerr wasted no more time in designating six of his men to serve on the jury. At a nod from Simon, his clerk read out the name of the first Englishman to face charges of robbery.

Analise finally gathered up her skirts and whirled to seek refuge within the crowd once more. She was so preoccupied with thoughts of the Reiver, and still so gripped by a strange light-headedness, that she very nearly collided with the two gentlemen who had been conducting a frantic search for her along the many rows of stalls.

"You have led us a merry chase, Lady Analise!" Sir Harry admonished, his face flushed from his efforts and his forehead beaded with perspiration.

"You might well have been in danger," said her other

suitor. He took her arm and linked it possessively through his. "Refreshments await us."

Analise heaved a sigh of resignation. More affected than she cared to admit by what had passed between herself and the wondrously appealing Scot, she allowed Lord Walsingham to lead her away.

The remainder of the day passed with alternating pleasure and frustration. Though she had hoped to spend time among the other, "common" celebrants, neither of her gallant and damnably attentive companions would let her out of their sight. She was allowed to witness the horse race—with Sir Harry shouting encouragements so close to her ear that she winced—and Lord Walsingham was kind enough to escort her past the stalls again so that she could more closely peruse the goods on offer. Yet she longed to be on her own, to listen to the gossip and watch the bawdy antics of the traveling players. And, if she were but honest with herself, to risk another encounter with the man whose image had risen frequently within her mind in spite of her best endeavors.

Thus, when twilight approached with its gathering darkness and the promise of a clear, moonlit night, she decided to make a second bid for freedom.

It was not so very wicked a thing to do. Had she not sacrificed the entire day to an uncomplaining endurance of her suitors' company? Surely even her guardian would not begrudge her some small measure of liberty. She knew that Simon was still occupied with the wardens' meeting and would remain so until well after nightfall. If she only managed to escape for an hour or so, then at least she would be able to hold fast to the memory of what she had seen and heard.

She seized advantage of her opportunity when both

Sir Harry and Lord Walsingham, after quarreling over who should claim the honor, set forth on a quest to find her a sweet Scottish delicacy known as "Clootie Dumpling." Her gaze kindled with determination once they had gone.

She immediately leapt up from where she had been sitting upon a small, carved oak chair brought there for that purpose. Her long skirts swirled about her legs as she took flight. For the moment she would keep close to the perimeter of the festivities. She suddenly felt the need for a bit of solitude—no easy feat, she reflected with an inward smile of irony, since there were literally scores of other people about. Still, she would direct a course toward the trees that lined the stream, and would tarry there until darkness blanketed the countryside and better concealed her from Sir Harry and Lord Walsingham.

The sun was fast sinking below the horizon, turning the sky into a magnificent blaze of color. Music still filled the air, and the wind still carried the aromas and laughter and conviviality, which showed no sign yet of lessening. If tradition were followed, it would be long after midnight before the merrymakers sought the "comfort" of their makeshift beds upon the ground. For Simon Hayward and his entourage, of course, the relative luxury of tents and satin-covered feather mattresses awaited. The Reivers, on the other hand, were long accustomed to bedding down with nothing save a saddle beneath their heads and, if they were fortunate, a blanket to stave off the cold. They would have none of the fripperies and soft conveniences of the English.

Analise shivered a bit as the cool evening breeze swept across her. She was tempted to stroll near to one of the many fires burning brightly in the midst of the clearing.

But, spying the swaying branches of the trees silhouetted against the sky, she drew her cloak more securely about her and quickened her steps.

A number of people offered a friendly greeting to her, and she responded with a brief smile and a nod each time. But she dared not stop and speak, for she knew her gallant escorts would soon be in pursuit of her once more. If the prospect of marriage to either of them had been distasteful before, it was a hundred times more so now.

Distracted by such thoughts, she reached the cover of the trees. The solitude she had hoped to find there eluded her, for there were others congregating alongside the stream. Before she had even realized it, she had intruded upon a gathering of some seven or eight men. It was immediately apparent that they were Reivers—and that most of them had been drinking heavily.

"By the blood of the Virgin, what gift is this?" one of them loudly remarked, his voice holding both surprise and a pleasure that was far less than virtuous.

Analise gasped, stopping so suddenly that she very nearly lost her balance and tumbled into the water. Her eyes grew round with apprehension.

Firelight played across the solemn, roughly attired Scots' faces, giving them an eerie cast that only added to their look of menace. They slowly rose from where they had been seated upon the ground. Their own gazes held a predatory gleam, raking over Analise as she instinctively pulled the edges of her cloak together. She had removed her hat earlier; the fire's glow caressed the honey-gold richness of her hair and revealed the proud, delicate beauty of her countenance.

She was aware of an awful tension charging the air, and knew that danger lay close. The color drained from her face, while her blood pounded in her ears. The men stared back at her, some of them edging closer. She resisted the urge to scream.

"I—it was not my intent to intrude upon your privacy, gentlemen," she managed to proclaim, her outward show of composure belying the fear gripping her heart. She finally turned to leave, only to discover her path blocked by a dark, coarse-featured man whose demeanor was particularly threatening.

"Gentlemen?" he repeated, his mouth curling. His tone was both coaxing and derisive when he insisted, " 'Tis no reason to be in a hurry. We've not yet had the pleasure of your company."

"Och, Maxwell, let her be," growled the oldest among them, before dismissively resuming his seat in front of the fire.

"She is English," another declared, though without any real concern. He raised his cup of ale to his lips. "And highborn. Hayward's whore, no doubt."

"How dare you!" Analise cried, too outraged now to be afraid. Her eyes flashed hotly as she raised her head to a defiant angle and commanded the man who still blocked her way, "Allow me to pass, sir!"

"Speak the truth," he countered. He pressed his face close to hers. "Your intrusion was no accident. Mayhap you wish to know what it is like to have a real man between your legs, instead of those—"

"You are despicable!" breathed Analise, so furious she could scarcely speak. Clutching at the folds of her skirts, she tried once more to escape. This time, however, the man known as Maxwell did not merely plant himself before her. His hands shot out to curl tightly about her arms. He yanked her up hard against him.

"I'll wager, *my lady*, that your lips taste no sweeter than those of any other wenches!" he sneered.

"Release me at once, or I shall scream!" She struggled within his grasp, but his fingers clenched about her arms with bruising force.

"As you please." He gave a low chuckle. "The cry of a woman this eve will summon none."

Unable to believe what was happening, Analise prepared to give a belated call for help. Her captor raised his hand, clamping it across her mouth. She screamed low in her throat and intensified her efforts to break free. Balling her hand into a fist, she brought it smashing up against Maxwell's chin. Several of the men expressed grudging admiration for her spirit as Maxwell bit out a curse and cruelly twisted her arm behind her back.

"I think, Maxwell, you go too far." A fair-haired young man, not so much older than Analise herself, unexpectedly stepped forward to intervene. "English or no, the lady is unwilling."

"Hold your tongue, Jameson!"

"Come the morrow," one of the others put forth with a broad grin, "I suspect her 'objections' will be long forgotten."

Analise felt hot tears starting to her eyes. She offered up a silent, desperate prayer for deliverance. Surely, she told herself numbly, someone would witness the assault taking place and raise an alarm. Surely Lord Walsingham and Sir Harry would come upon her any moment now!

Without warning, Maxwell removed his hand and brought his lips slanting down upon hers.

Dear God, no! Her head spun dizzily while her stomach churned. Bile rose in her throat. Never had she felt so sickened, so utterly frightened and angry and revolted. Giving a low, strangled moan, she sought to raise her knee and deliver a blow to Maxwell's groin. But he was too quick for her. His fingers dug into the soft flesh of her thigh. His kiss grew harder, punishing . . .

And then, suddenly, she was free.

She stumbled backward, her skirts tangling about her legs while she clutched at a tree for support. Her breath was still ragged. Her long tresses had escaped from the confines of the silk net to tumble wildly about her face and shoulders, while her cloak hung in disarray. She looked to where her champion, after sending Maxwell crashing down beside the fire, stood ready to do battle.

Analise's gaze widened with incredulity. A sudden tremor raced through her body.

It was him. The tall, dark-haired Reiver she had seen at the wardens' meeting. Yet he looked so very different now, she noted dazedly. His handsome features were set in a grim mask of fury. His gaze smoldered with a murderous, white-hot rage she did not understand.

"Have a care, Maxwell!" a friend called out a warning. Maxwell climbed to his feet, his own expression one of vengeful fury as he fingered the bruised and bloodied skin of his jaw.

"Aye, lift your hand to an Armstrong and count it lost!" another Scot advised, though with equal parts of humor and solicitude.

"The matter was none of yours!" Maxwell accused the man who had easily sent him sprawling.

"*I have made it so.*" His voice was low, deep timbred, and splendidly resonant. Analise felt her heart stir at the sound of it.

"The woman—"

"She is not for you."

Their eyes locked in silent combat. It was obvious that Maxwell was considering retaliation. Still shaken, Analise swept the tangled mass of honey-gold curls from her face and looked back to her rescuer. *Armstrong,* she repeated his name inwardly. The taller and more lithely muscled of the two, he stood waiting with an impassivity that was in direct contrast to the violence within him.

"You would set yourself against one of your own to defend an *Englishwoman*?" demanded Maxwell, his tone harsh with scornful disbelief.

"I would set myself against any man fool enough to risk breaking the truce I have sworn to keep." For a moment his gaze flickered toward Analise. She hastily pulled the folds of her velvet cloak about her once more and sought to deny the way her pulse leapt.

"Heed me well, then, Ronan Armstrong," Maxwell bade him curtly. "I will not forget the insult you have shown me this day. You harbor a traitorous notion within your head. Aye, and one that will like as not bring you death!" He said nothing more, but directed one last inimical glare at Analise and stalked away into the gathering darkness. The others in his group hesitated only briefly before following after him. None dared to cross swords with Ronan Armstrong.

Left alone with the one man whose presence both alarmed and excited her, Analise stepped forward to meet his gaze in the firelight. She wondered why she had not run away when she had been given the chance. And why she did not do so now.

"My gratitude, sir, for your assistance," she murmured, tilting her chin up in order to face him squarely. He was a full head taller than she. His powerful frame made her feel incredibly vulnerable—and more feminine than she had ever felt before. Acutely conscious of his nearness, and of the heat emanating from his body, she found herself trembling. *Though not with fear.* She glanced away for a moment and drew in a deep, steadying breath before looking up at him again. "I do thank you," she reiterated in all sincerity.

" 'Twas not your gratitude I sought."

He did not smile. His eyes, every bit as blue and piercing as she had noted earlier that day, burned down into hers. It was difficult for her to think clearly, to remember that he was a Scot and therefore an enemy. Sweet mercy, she wondered as her head spun anew, was he a thief and a murderer like so many others of his kind? He was a Border Reiver, after all. A man who took pleasure in wreaking havoc upon the English. And yet . . . she sensed within him a gentleness, a compassion and understanding that set him apart from his fellow brigands.

Drawing in another ragged breath, and chiding herself for such fanciful rumination, she said with as much dignity as she could muster under the circumstances, "Nevertheless, Mr. Armstrong, gratitude is what I must offer you. But," she submitted at a sudden thought, "perhaps you seek a reward. If so, then, my—"

"Aye." He stepped even closer, so that only inches separated them now. The merest glimmer of amusement shone within his gaze now as it traveled over her bright, streaming locks and sadly creased attire. "You are at Beauford?"

"No," she was startled to hear herself utter the lie. She gently cleared her throat, her gaze falling beneath the intensity of his. "I—I am to stay amongst friends at Hexham."

"Then, it is to Hexham I will ride."

"You must not!" she gasped, her eyes full of trepidation as they flew back up to his face.

"Would it matter so much to you, then, if I were caught?" he challenged softly. The lilting quality to his voice was appealing in the extreme. Dismayed to feel her heart fluttering within her breast, she assumed an air of cool aplomb.

"You have shown me kindness. I would not wish you any misfortune." She swept the wayward tresses from her face once more and frowned. "Yet, in truth, did you not proclaim that you came to my assistance in order to preserve the truce?"

"I did." The ghost of a smile played about his lips now. "But you know it was more than that."

"Why, indeed, I have no idea—" she started to weakly protest.

"Do you not, lass?" He moved even closer, towering above her in the firelit shadows. The sounds of the ongoing celebration drifted to them on the cool evening breeze. To the right of them was the pleasant rushing of the stream, while to the left the fire crackled and hissed. Overhead, the sky had deepened, a host of stars already twinkling in its blue-black midst. The silvery radiance of the moon fell upon the countryside with a rare and wondrous softness. The night held magic.

Analise shivered again, but it was not from the cold. She searched for words with which to break the strange, highly charged silence rising up between herself and Ronan Armstrong. But he spoke again first.

"Tell me your name." It was a command. A surprisingly well-favored one.

"It would be better, I think, if my name remained a mystery." Her instincts warned her that danger was upon her once more. An altogether different kind of danger, one that might well leave her with a good deal more than a sense of wounded pride. She quickly gathered up her skirts and asserted in a small voice, "I must go."

"Not yet," he decreed, another faint smile tugging at his lips. "The night has scarce begun." He lifted a hand toward her. She tensed and took a hurried, instinctive step backward.

"There are others about," she reminded him, her remark sounding foolish even to her own ears. "This time, I shall not hesitate to scream!"

"Ah, but I mean you no harm."

"Do you think me easy prey because I am English?"

"I do not think of you as prey. And the fact that you are English is naught save a minor inconvenience to me."

"A minor inconvenience?" she echoed, not at all certain whether she should be insulted or flattered by such a pronouncement. "Pray, sir, what do you mean?" she demanded with a loftiness that provoked an unholy light within Ronan's gaze.

"From the first moment I saw you, I knew I would taste the sweetness of your lips." True to his word, his powerful arms came up about her and swept her close. And she was momentarily so shocked that she could offer little more than a halfhearted resistance.

"Release me!" she breathed, her hands lifting to push at the immovable force of his broad chest.

"No, lass." His eyes caught and held the flashing blue-green fire of hers. She suffered a sharp intake of breath and squirmed within his embrace. But she did not scream.

"Is *this* why you rescued me? So that you could accost me yourself?"

"My reasons were many," he replied with maddening equanimity.

And then he kissed her.

It was nothing at all like the kiss the man known as Maxwell had forced upon her. Instead of pain and revulsion, she experienced a pleasure so wicked, so utterly consuming, that she was in danger of forgetting all else. Ronan Armstrong's lips were warm and strong, gentle yet demanding. And, God forgive her, she could summon neither the strength nor the will to stop him.

Still, she blushed at the intimacy of their embrace, all too conscious of the feel of Ronan's hard-muscled warmth against her curves. Her traitorous arms stole upward to entwine about his neck. Her mouth responded to the sweetly savage onslaught of his. He urged her closer, his arms tightening about her until she felt her feet leave the ground.

His mouth virtually ravished hers, and all the while she was too caught up in the whirlwind of newly awakened passion to listen to that small voice inside her head warning of certain disaster. She had been kissed before, of course. Indeed, she had allowed more than one casual, insignificant kiss to be stolen by an admirer while playing games within the palace corridors. But no man had ever dared to kiss her like this. *Never like this.*

One of his hands moved downward to close about the

well-rounded firmness of her hips. She gave a low moan and wriggled in protest, but to no avail. Ronan held her captive with his intoxicating nearness as much as with his arms. She moaned again when his hot, velvety tongue plunged within her mouth. Startled to feel a strange, liquid warmth spreading throughout her body, she boldly kissed him back . . .

It was Ronan, finally, who put an end to the exquisite torment. Forcing his lips to relinquish hers, he lifted his head and gazed tenderly down into her flushed, upturned countenance.

"Though an Armstrong and a Scot, I am but human," he declared huskily. Again the sound of his voice caused her to melt inside. He allowed her feet to touch the ground once more, but did not yet release her. "I will ride to Hexham in two days' time," he vowed quietly.

"Wha . . . what?" stammered Analise, still reeling from their fiery embrace.

"I would strengthen our acquaintance. Aye, and defy the whole of England if need be."

"No!" Crashing back to reality, she shook her head and drew her arms from about his neck. "You cannot!"

"I can and will," he insisted. He raised his hand to gently cup her chin. "Do you think I would forget what has passed between us this day?"

"We have shared nothing but a kiss," she murmured without any real conviction.

"You lie." He released her now, though he did not step away.

"You took advantage of me!" It was not at all what she had meant to say. But an inexplicable fury suddenly took root within her.

"The advantage was not mine alone." His handsome features tightened. His eyes smoldered with ire as well as passion.

"I know that this should never have happened. And that it shall never be repeated!" She drew herself rigidly erect and, trying without success to ignore the way her whole body still tingled as a result of his kiss, met his gaze with a forced coolness. "I bid you good-bye, Mr. Armstrong. We will not see one another again."

"You are mistaken on that count as well."

"No, I am not!" Desperate to put some distance between them, she retreated, back to the edge of the stream. Nearby, the strains of a ballad rose to a stirring crescendo, but she took no notice of it. "Until but a short time ago, we were unknown to one another," she pointed out, snatching the edges of her cloak together. "It was wrong of me to—to tarry here with you. But *you*, sir, had no right to embrace me!"

" 'Tis a right I will yet claim."

She drew in her breath sharply. Her eyes widened with both incredulity and a pleasure she dared not acknowledge. Infuriated by her own weakness, and even more so by Ronan's presumption, she took refuge in her anger.

"So it is true then that the Scots are ill-mannered barbarians who do not hesitate to kill men and ravish women!"

"Aye." His mouth curved into a brief, humorless smile. Torn between the urge to turn her across his knee, and the much more agreeable desire to sweep her into his arms again, he did neither. But he slowly advanced on her now, his gaze searing down into hers. "Mayhap, sweet lady, you are in more danger than you think."

"I am not afraid of you!" Her eyes flashed as she gave another proud, defiant toss of her head.

"You have reason to be."

He loomed ominously above her. She blanched at the look in his eyes. Her throat constricted, and she felt her stomach knotting. In that moment she feared he would make good on the violent tendencies she sensed within him. Gone was her chivalrous defender. In his place was a grim, steely-eyed stranger who appeared all too capable of brutality. A man who would steal considerably more than a single kiss.

Her fingers shook as she gathered up her skirts and cried rashly, "Come near me again, Ronan Armstrong, and I shall see you hanged!"

"No doubt Ewan Maxwell would be glad to provide the rope." His tone held a note of mocking amusement. But there was no trace of humor when he frowned darkly and said, "You've a sharp tongue, lass. And a temper as hot as any spitfire's. Yet I'll not forget this night. No, and though I may have to ride to hell and back, I will find you."

"You dare to threaten me?" she gasped, edging away from him again.

"Not a threat." His gaze traveled over her with a bold, unnerving familiarity. *"A promise."*

His words, as much as the way in which he spoke them, caused her to shudder. She finally turned and fled. Her face was hot and flushed as she raced back through the trees. She was dismayed to feel a lingering warmth deep within her.

Furiously berating herself, she paid little mind to

where she was going. She thought only about what had just happened. Dear heaven, how could she have been so weak and wanton? It was humiliating to recall the way she had responded to the Reiver's kiss, the way she had allowed him to touch her.

But most disturbing of all was the memory of his vow to find her.

She cursed herself for a fool—and then gave thanks for the fact that she had neither revealed her name nor her true circumstances. Surely he would never learn of her identity. And, even if he somehow managed to do so, she was safe at Beauford. No Scot would dare to come near to the English warden's home.

"Please, God, I shall never see the man again!" she whispered fervently. The entreaty had no sooner rolled from her tongue than she spied Sir Harry and Lord Walsingham bearing down upon her in the moonlit darkness. Muttering an oath, she very nearly surrendered to the temptation to turn and run in the opposite direction. She was in no mood to endure their presence.

"Once again, Lady Analise, you have been—" Sir Harry started to chide, his voice booming above the others raised in song and laughter nearby. He broke off when he took note of her shocking state of dishevelment. "Satan's teeth!" he burst out, his eyes growing round as saucers. "What has happened? Have you suffered an injury?" He tried to slip an arm about her shoulders, but she was quick to move away.

"No," she assured him quietly, wishing for all the world that she could be alone. "I am unhurt."

"Has someone—" Lord Walsingham thought to demand. His eyes narrowed suspiciously across at her.

"No!" She shook her head in a vehement denial and

prevaricated with, "It was nothing more than my own clumsiness. I stumbled while enjoying a stroll. No harm was done. I shall be perfectly all right."

"Perhaps Sir Simon should know of this," Sir Harry pondered aloud.

"It *was* most regrettably unwise of you to wander about without an escort again," Lord Walsingham told her with his usual, condescending manner. "I think it best if you—"

"I care not what you think!" Analise retorted hotly, startling the two noblemen as well as herself. The sight of them prompted yet another stark contrast, bringing to mind the eminently more attractive vision of Ronan Armstrong. She felt a dull ache in her heart. And she was seized with the sudden, uncharacteristic impulse to burst into tears. As it was, her companions bore the brunt of her distress. "You have both plagued me with your fawning, bothersome attentions for these several days past! It was my guardian who sought your good opinion— not I—and I will not be persuaded to this false civility any longer!"

If not for the fact that she felt so utterly miserable, she might well have laughed at their openmouthed expressions of surprise and bewilderment. Later she would have cause to regret the outburst. It was not usually within her nature to be shrewish.

She said nothing more before hastening away to seek the privacy of her tent. Once there, she allowed the tears to come at last. She couldn't have said precisely *why* she wept. Nor why some small part of her wished she had not been so cowardly when in Ronan Armstrong's presence. The day had suddenly turned sour, and she could take no further delight in the merriment that only a short time earlier had held such fascination for her.

Chapter 3

Though she was determined not to do so, Analise found herself thinking about Ronan Armstrong with an alarming frequency throughout the next two days.

Her disloyal body warmed at the memory of his kiss. Her dreams were haunted by his devilishly appealing image. She wondered if he would make good on his promise to find her; whenever she approached a window, she could not prevent her gaze from searching the outlying hills and moors for any sign of a lone rider. One with a bold, commanding air about him and eyes that seemed capable of boring into a person's very soul.

But he did not come.

It was not the least bit surprising, of course. Even if he *had* discovered the truth, he couldn't possibly hope to reach her. Beauford was in England and heavily guarded. Besides, she reflected with a disappointment best ignored, he had no doubt forgotten all about her by now. He was a Scot, an insolent rogue accustomed to taking his pleasure where he would and suffering no unfortunate pangs of contrition afterward. He was a Border Reiver. And *she*, may heaven be merciful, was a foolish, highly impressionable young woman who had spent far too much time dreaming of adventure. The reality, thus far, had proven itself every bit as intriguing as the fantasy. Yet it was a false reality.

By the time the third day arrived, she had almost managed to convince herself that the entire episode meant nothing. She had attached far too much significance to the ungallant actions and empty threats of a man who, like as not, had spared little thought for her since the night he had held her in his arms. Truly she would never see him again. That particular thought should have given her a sense of relief. Why, then, did it not?

A sigh of mingled resignation and disquiet escaped her lips as she finally ventured downstairs to speak with her guardian. The morning sun was but a muted, straw-colored glow within the clouds. The air was cold and crisp, the wind a series of bone-chilling gusts filled with aromas both pleasant and not. She was suddenly reminded of Truce Day again. The celebration, she recalled, had lasted throughout most of the night, only to be followed at dawn by an event that still caused her to shudder in horrified disbelief.

Three men—all of them Scots—had been hanged. She knew that she would never forget the haunting sight of their bodies swinging at the end of a rope. And try as she would, she could not help wondering if the same terrible fate lay in store for Ronan Armstrong. Her eyes clouded at the thought, but she resolutely cast it aside and continued on her way down the steps.

Although the day's work had begun at first light for many of the castle's inhabitants, Simon had only recently dragged himself from the warmth of his bed. Analise discovered him waiting for her in the Great Hall. He was alone. And clearly in a foul temper.

"Congratulations, dearest cousin," he greeted her in a

tone laced with biting sarcasm. He pivoted from his
stance in front of the fire and subjected her to a narrow,
thoroughly malevolent glare. "You have succeeded in
chasing away the two most important gentlemen in all of
Northumberland!"

"Have I, sir?" she replied calmly, her gaze lighting
with satisfaction in spite of his anger.

"I have just this morning received word that the both
of them have gone from Northumberland. *Gone.* Sir
Harry to his estates in the west. And Lord Walsingham to
London. Ah, but did I not receive fair warning?" he furiously bit out. "Indeed, had it not already been made clear
to me that your behavior while in Scotland was remarkably ill-bred?" He advanced upon her now, his expression prompting her to tense. "I should never have
allowed you to accompany us there. Would that I had
paid heed to Lady Helena's objections!"

"It matters not." She clasped her hands together and
tilted her chin upward, her eyes daring him to strike her.
"I told you I would wed neither of them. Important in
your eyes or not, they were but poor copies of men—vain
and selfish and dull-witted! How could I ever choose to
become the wife of someone such as that?" It was on the
tip of her tongue to declare that she had been embraced
by a *real* man and could scarcely accept anything less
now. The impulse dismayed her.

"You little fool!" sneered Simon, unimpressed. "Do
you have any idea what an alliance with either of them
would have meant?" His mouth suddenly curled into a
smile that was both derisive and sinister. "Perhaps you
feel that you may count this as a triumph." When she did
not answer, he lifted a hand to caress the smoothness of
her cheek. He seemed to gain pleasure from the fact that

she recoiled in disgust. "I cannot believe you would prefer life within the walls of a convent."

" 'Tis true that I have never before offered it consideration." She drew herself even more proudly erect and avowed, "Yet if I must choose between that and a forced marriage, I shall not hesitate to choose the cloister!" She would in actuality choose neither, of course—it seemed that a secret, hurried flight across the Channel would be necessary after all.

"Such spirit must be rewarded," Simon told her, then smiled again. "We may yet find you a husband, my dear."

"Have you not heard—" she started to protest.

He cut her off. "You have defied me. You have proclaimed your refusal to obey, even though I have the right to command you." His eyes narrowed, and he moved so close that she caught her breath in alarm. "I will allow you one last chance. There are others in Northumberland, others with wealth and influence, who might yet be willing to overlook your damnably headstrong nature. Accept my choice, and all else will be forgotten."

"No!" She backed away and shook her head in a furious denial. "I shall not!" A loud gasp broke from her lips when his hand curled painfully about her wrist.

"You dare to defy me still?" he snarled, his features turning ugly again.

"Threaten all you please," she cried while struggling to pull free, "but know that the queen shall hear of your treachery!"

"Do you think I care what those weak, simpleminded bastards in London think? *I* rule at Beauford. Yes, and it is *I* who will yet control the whole of the border!"

Abruptly releasing her, he muttered a foul curse and sliced her a look that was downright murderous. "Stupid girl. You have sealed your own fate this day."

His words caused her pulse to leap in a very real dread, but she gave no evidence of it. Drawing an air of composure about her, she turned and gracefully swept back across the room to the stairwell. There were plans to be made, she realized, her mind already racing. She must leave at once, before the week's end. Before it was too late.

"You must wake, my lady!"

Analise stirred beneath the covers. Her eyelids fluttered open, and she slowly pulled herself upright in the bed. The room was dark, save for the soft, flickering light of a single candle. Morning had not yet broken.

"Meg?" She blinked up at the housemaid in surprise. "What is it? What is wrong?"

"You must dress and come below, my lady!"

"But . . . why?"

"Sir Simon bids you to come to the Great Hall. Now, hurry, my lady, else Lady Helena will turn me out!"

"Very well." She tossed back the covers and rose from the bed. Astonished by her guardian's summons at so late an hour, she quickly removed her nightshift. She drew on a delicate, embroidered linen chemise, a petticoat, black silk stockings, and a pair of kid slippers. Waving aside Meg's offer to help her don a farthingale, she pulled on an informal gown of emerald velvet. The color accentuated the green within her turquoise gaze, while the fitted bodice and low, square neckline revealed the shapeliness of her figure. But she cared little about her appearance at the moment.

"Have you any idea what Sir Simon requires of me?" she finally queried. Her hair was secured in a single long braid hanging down her back. Deciding to leave it as it was, she turned to face a strangely subdued Meg. "Did he perchance—"

"I cannot say," Meg whispered, her gaze falling guiltily. She said nothing more until Analise, catching up a lighted candle of her own, opened the door to leave. "God keep you, my lady!"

There was an urgency within her voice, a certain plaintive note that gave Analise pause. She offered a rather wan, puzzled smile in response. Apprehension rose within her as she slipped from the bedchamber and made her way downstairs.

The Great Hall, she soon discovered, was curiously ablaze with light. She expected to find Simon seated in his usual place before the fire. Thus, she was surprised when she saw that he stood, fully dressed and with a look of malignant satisfaction on his face, at the foot of the stairs. Two of his deputies were in attendance on the other side of the room. They were armed, their swords shining in the glow of the crystal chandelier hanging from the vast, beamed ceiling above. A third man, older than the others and unknown to her, waited beside the fireplace. He was attired in the somber black robes of the clergy. His countenance was grave, and his eyes seemed to hold an inordinate degree of pity when they briefly met hers.

Bewildered, Analise looked back to Simon. He came forward and tucked her arm within the crook of his.

"We began to grow impatient, my dearest cousin," he admonished her smoothly.

"Why have you summoned me here like this?" she asked. "Could it not have waited—"

"There is to be a wedding ceremony." He gave a soft, contemptuous laugh at her expression. "And no, it could not wait. Did I not caution you this very morning that you had sealed your own fate?"

"You—you cannot be serious!" she stammered. Her eyes widened with incredulity as the awful truth began to dawn.

"Oh, but I can assure you that I have never been more so." His arm clamped about her waist. He propelled her firmly across the room with him and directed a curt nod toward one of the deputies. "Escort the 'bridegroom' hither."

"Bridegroom?" echoed Analise, her voice quavering. She shook her head in a fervent denial, and prayed that she would awaken from the nightmare in which she had become lost. "I shall wed no one this night. No, nor any other night!"

"You will do as you are told," Simon decreed. It was said with a cold-blooded assurance that struck fear in her heart. She watched in growing dismay while the deputy left the room to do his master's bidding.

"You cannot force me to this, Simon Hayward!" she cried hotly. "I will have no part of this madness!" She set up a furious struggle, lifting a hand to strike out at him. But he was a good deal stronger than he looked. He seized both of her arms in a cruel, punishing grip and forced them behind her. Lowering his face close to hers, he gave her yet another slow, baneful smile.

"At this moment, *Cousin*, I would not hesitate to do you harm," he warned. "The time has come for you to pay for your defiance. If I am not to have the benefits of an alliance with either Lord Walsingham or Sir Harry Claibourne, then I will secure my position here by another means!"

"What are you talking about?" she demanded, twisting futilely within his grasp. "Who is it you—"

"You are to take as your husband a man who wields great influence on the other side of the border. Indeed, a man who could no doubt gather an entire army should he wish to do so." He unexpectedly released her, drawing away to make a great show of straightening the lace that trimmed the cuffs of his fine white shirt. "It might interest you to know that he is no more willing than you to enter the holy state of matrimony."

"Then, the wedding cannot take place!" Her eyes sparked with a desperate hope as she rubbed at her arms.

"It will take place. You see, my dear," he explained with an exaggerated patience, "he was offered a choice. A wife—or the gallows."

"You—you were going to *hang* him?"

"I was indeed. Mind you, he took his time when pressed for a decision. And even then, he stood within sight of the rope itself before choosing the much more agreeable prospect of marriage." He did not add that there was a second man who faced death. Nor that to force the match with the one, he had agreed to spare the other as well. "These Border Reivers are a peculiar lot. They thieve and murder, yet claim to hold honor above all else. I must confess, I would rather not align myself with such a scoundrel. But, through you, I will gain his fealty. And *that*, my dear, can be quite useful to me."

"You intend for me to wed a Border Reiver?" she gasped out, her head spinning dizzily.

"A true Scot," confirmed Simon. His tone was laced

with both scorn and amusement when he added, "Oh, but he is a fine specimen indeed. He was captured following a raid near Hexham some two days ago and has been enjoying the hospitality of my dungeon since then. To spare your more delicate sensibilities, he has been offered a bath and fresh attire. I cannot think you will be displeased."

Analise gazed at him in shocked disbelief. Panic rose within her. She whirled and hastened across to where the clergyman stood regarding her near the fireplace.

"Sir, you are a man of the cloth!" she said, her eyes glistening with unshed tears. "I entreat you to help me! Surely you cannot in all good conscience allow this—this *travesty* to take place?"

"Your guardian has the right to see you married to the man of his choice," the vicar declared, though not without some measure of kindness. In truth, he held sympathy for her and was a reluctant participant in the night's business. Yet there was nothing he could do. Sir Simon was his benefactor.

Analise spun about to direct a vengeful, searing glare toward Simon. Outrage, however, gave way to startlement when the door at the far end of the hall swung open. Four men entered the room.

The first to appear was the deputy who had been dispatched by Simon but a few moments earlier. Two of the others were in his employ as well. Both of them coarse-featured and brawny, they flanked the fourth man, ready to take hold of him should he decide to try and escape.

In spite of the fact that he had agreed to the marriage, there were chains about the prisoner's wrists and ankles. His face bore the marks of a struggle. He had disdained the clean garments offered him, and was dressed in the same jack and breeches that Analise remembered. His knee-length leather riding boots were caked with mud. Several drops of blood stained the open collar of his linen shirt.

Analise met his gaze across the room. A shiver coursed down her spine. Her legs suddenly threatened to give way beneath her. Unaware that her "bridegroom's" startlement was every bit as forceful as her own, she lifted a hand to her throat.

"You!" she breathed, paling at the gleam of white-hot fury in Ronan Armstrong's eyes.

"You have seen this man before?" Simon asked her, his own eyes narrowing in suspicion.

"No!" she was quick to deny. Still reeling, she looked back to Ronan and tried to ignore the way her heart thundered wildly within her breast. "I know him not. But I would—"

"Good," remarked Simon, his impatience visible. "Then, we may begin."

"Has this not gone too far already?" she appealed in growing desperation. She forced herself to face him calmly. "You offered me a choice between marriage and the convent. As God is my witness, I would rather live the remainder of my life in piety and seclusion than be wed this night!"

"I fear, little cousin," he replied caustically, "that you will find neither in Scotland." He took her arm again and led her back to where the vicar waited.

She was acutely, painfully aware of the moment when Ronan was escorted across the room to take his place beside her. He spared not so much as a single glance for her. She felt scorched by the heat of his body. She sensed in him an anger so deep, so foreboding, that she instinctively tensed in alarm. The sudden, unbidden memory of his embrace only served to heighten her agitation. She battled the impulse to turn and run. She would not show herself a coward before him, nor before Simon Hayward. But how on earth was she going to prevent this madness?

"There are no impediments to the marriage?" the clergyman inquired of Simon.

"None."

Unable to believe what was happening, Analise stole a look up at the tall, handsome Scot beside her. His countenance was dangerously grim, his gaze steadfast and smoldering. How incredible that this man, the same man who had refused to leave her mind these past several days, should now be the one designated to become her husband.

I will find you. His vow burned within her mind once more. Sweet heaven, she wondered dazedly, was she the reason he had been captured? He had ridden to Hexham after all. And now faced the prospect—a disagreeable one, judging by his tight-lipped visage—of becoming her husband.

"Do you accept this woman as your wife, sir?" the clergyman asked Ronan.

Analise held her breath. She closed her eyes and prayed that he would deny the marriage. Yet—would she wish to see him hang? No. Nor did she wish to find herself wed to a man who had found it so very difficult to choose between the gallows and marriage to her . . .

"Aye."

The sound of his voice, low and splendidly vibrant, caused her eyes to fly wide again. She trembled and felt the inevitable closing in upon her.

"And you, Lady Analise?" the vicar put to her now. "Do you accept this man as your husband?"

She did not offer an immediate response. Shocked at the temptation, however fleeting, to say yes, she swallowed hard and realized that there was no hope at all of dissuading Simon from the course he had set for her. Her eyes strayed up to Ronan's face again. He refused to look at her still.

"Lady Analise?" prompted the vicar a second time.

"I cannot!" she finally answered, shaking her head for emphasis. She surrendered to the impulse to flee now, but Simon caught her and pulled her back.

"She can and does," he decreed, frowning markedly at the vicar. "Under the law, *my* consent is all that is required."

" 'Tis true," the older man admitted with an obvious reluctance.

"Does it not matter to you that I am forced to this?" Analise pleaded with the vicar one last time. "And this— this gentleman beside me has agreed only because he faces the threat of death! If you will but offer him refuge—"

"Get on with it!" Simon ordered tersely, his fingers clenching about her wrist until she gave a soft cry of pain. He did not see the way Ronan's eyes darkened with a sudden, barely controlled rage.

"I do hereby declare the marriage valid," the clergyman pronounced.

Analise shook her head again, slowly and in benumbed horror. She did not notice when Ronan cast her a look full of anger and suspicion and—though he cursed himself for it—more than a touch of desire.

It was done.

"You will keep the bargain, Armstrong?" Simon demanded with an insulting, mistrustful air.

"I have given my word," Ronan asserted, his quiet tone belying the violence within him. He wanted nothing more at that moment than to kill the Englishman with his bare hands. But he was bound now, by honor as well as the ties of marriage, to keep the peace between himself and Simon Hayward. Still, he vowed silently, there would yet come a time for revenge.

"Remove the chains," Simon instructed his deputy. The man hastened to obey, and in a matter of moments had loosed the shackles. Ronan's burning gaze shot back to Simon.

"And Calum?"

"Is no doubt sampling the charms of one of your rustic little milkmaids by now." His mouth curled into yet another expression of pure, gleeful malevolence. "Your brother has been free these twelve hours past."

"By damn," Ronan ground out, a near savage gleam in his eyes, "you shall pay for your treachery!"

Bewildered by the exchange, Analise looked to Simon, then back to the man who was now her husband. *Husband.* God help her, she was married to a Scot.

"You will wish to tarry here no longer," said Lady Helena, surprising Analise as she swept haughtily across the room. Meg followed close behind, her eyes downcast and her arms laden with a large valise. She lowered the bag to the floor before scurrying away.

"A bride's wedding night should be spent within her husband's home," Lady Helena added. It was clear that she was delighted with the turn of events. Her eyes shining with a satisfaction to match Simon's, she lifted the heavy woolen cloak draped over her arm and prof-

fered it to Analise. "You must take particular care with
the cold in Scotland, my dear. I hear it can be quite
deadly. And I daresay you will have no need of the
remainder of your finery, for the Scots are a crude, hea-
thenish lot."

"I am not going to Scotland!" Analise dissented. She
met Ronan's gaze at last. "Surely you—"

"Enough," he said brusquely. He took the cloak from
Lady Helena, tossed it about Analise's shoulders, then
caught up the valise.

"I shall accompany you nowhere, Ronan Armstrong!"
declared Analise. Hot, bitter tears stung against her eyelids once more.

"You are my wife," he reminded her grimly. As if that
settled the matter, he returned to her side and sought to
take hold of her arm. She resisted, jerking away as
though the contact had burned her.

"No!"

She took a deep, steadying breath and implored him to
see reason, a task made all the more difficult by the fact
that his eyes held an inexplicable reproach. She could not
comprehend why he should be angry with her—it was
almost as if he blamed *her* for the night's misfortune.

"Like you, sir," she pointed out in a voice that was
remarkable for its evenness, "I did not willingly consent
to this charade. But now it is done, why should we suffer
further humiliation at my guardian's hands? He has
achieved his purpose—to force an alliance between us.
Very well. We are wed. Yet it must be a marriage in
name only. You have fulfilled your part of the bargain,
have you not? Seek the comfort of your own home and
allow me to do the same!"

"The marriage will be recognized by none if you do

not come with me." He said it quietly, his tone as level as her own, and seemed unmoved by the desperate appeal in her eyes. She could not know how his heart twisted at the sight of her distress, nor how much he wanted to believe she had played no willing part in Simon Hayward's villainy.

"Do we witness the first signs of marital discord, Armstrong?" Simon taunted. His remark earned him a deadly glare from Ronan.

"Have you not done enough harm?" cried Analise, rounding on her cousin. Her eyes were full of liquid fire, her beautiful face flushed and stormy. "You are my *kinsman*. How could you force me into a union with someone you have called enemy? I shall never forgive you for what you have done this night. And I swear by everything I hold dear that I will see you punished somehow. If you think to benefit from this ill-begotten alliance, then you are sadly mistaken!" She inhaled upon another ragged breath and turned back to Ronan. "Please, you do not understand!"

"Do I not?" he countered softly. His handsome features were still taut with fury, and it seemed to her that he battled more than one temptation of his own.

"I will not go with you." She lifted up her head to meet his gaze unflinchingly.

But Ronan had grown weary of her protests. He had grown weary of the misadventure these two days past had offered him. By damn, he swore inwardly, *he was married*. To the cousin of the English warden.

He was not a man to be forced into anything. Yet a wife had been thrust upon him this night. Never mind that it was the one woman who had stirred his blood like no other. The memory of her sweet lips beneath his, of her soft curves pressed against his body, only added fuel to the rage simmering so dangerously within him.

She had deceived him. No doubt she had thought to lead him a merry chase. It was even possible that *she* was responsible for both his capture and the marriage. More than one woman had sought to ensnare him, by means both fair and foul—did this woman's angelic beauty disguise the heart of a temptress? Were her protests nothing but a ploy to conceal her guilt? He swore to have the truth from her.

The look on his face as he closed the distance between them caused Analise to tremble once more. A sharp gasp escaped her lips when his hand shot out to curl none too gently about her arm.

"Come." There was no sign of mercy in him. No hope of reason or persuasion or sympathy.

A sudden lump rose in Analise's throat. She knew herself lost . . .

She offered no resistance this time. Ronan led her across the Great Hall, toward the door which would grant them access to the castle's outer stairway. Behind them, Simon strolled leisurely back to stand before the fire.

"We will meet again, Ronan Armstrong," he promised. "Indeed, you can be certain I will call upon the fealty you have sworn to me."

Ronan paused at that. He turned his head, his gaze searing across into the other man's.

"Honor compels me to spare you."

"You spare *me?"* jeered Simon.

The merest ghost of a smile touched Ronan's lips. "But even loyalty can be broken," he cautioned. "Aye, and will be done if you ever again offer my wife insult."

My wife. Analise's eyes flew wide in startlement once

more. As if in a daze, she allowed Ronan to propel her outside and down the steps. The cold night air was like a slap in the face. She caught her breath and looked to where a stable man waited a short distance away. He held the reins of two horses. The animals, already saddled, snorted impatiently in the flickering glow of the torchlight.

Analise stiffened when Ronan's strong hands closed about her waist. He tossed her effortlessly up onto the back of one of the horses, looped the handle of the valise across the saddle horn, then mounted the other horse. It was immediately apparent to her that he was a man accustomed to spending long hours astride.

"Where are you taking me?" she demanded, drawing the hooded woolen cloak about her.

"Home."

"And where is that?"

"Scotland." Refusing to elaborate further, he reined about and touched his booted heels lightly to the horse's flanks. Analise was infuriated by his reticence. She considered making a bid for freedom there and then. Casting a swift, encompassing glance about the courtyard, she clutched the reins more tightly and shifted in the saddle.

"Think not to escape me, woman," Ronan tossed the warning back over his shoulder. She started, guilty color staining her cheeks as she wondered how he had guessed her intent. Her eyes flashed as she watched him pull the animal beneath him to a halt. He turned his head to give her a hard look.

"We want none of one another, sir," she argued resentfully, "so why—"

"You are my wife. And I hold what is mine."

"But—did you know beforehand that it was *I* whom

you had agreed to wed?" She held her breath while waiting for his answer.

"No." His gaze darkened anew. "I did not."

Her heart ached unaccountably. With wrathful impatience, she dashed at the tears threatening to course down her cheeks. "All the more reason for you to let me go my own way!"

"We've a long ride ahead of us this night. Keep up, or else you'll share my mount." His magnificent blue eyes held the promise of retribution. "And that, *my lady*, is something neither of us desires."

With that final, bitter admonition, he set off again. Analise stared after him, wracked with indecision as well as anger. It was clear that Simon would not allow her to remain at Beauford. And she had not yet had time to make arrangements for the journey to France. In truth, she had little choice.

Cursing both fate and Simon Hayward—*and* the man who, at least for the moment, held her life in his hands— she followed in Ronan's wake, through the castle gate and onward to the mysterious, windswept darkness of the Border hills.

Chapter 4

Analise knew that she would never forget the ride that night. It was wild and hellish.

Except for the two brief stops made in order to rest the horses, her "husband" seemed almost oblivious to her presence. His discourtesy was of no real consequence, she told herself, for she had neither the will nor the inclination to engage him in conversation. Her outrage at the night's calamity was as acute as his own. And he was, after all, still little more than a stranger to her. She was completely at his mercy. Already England and Beauford—and, indeed, *civilization*—seemed far away.

She tried not to think about what would happen once she and Ronan Armstrong reached his home.

It required all of her strength to remain astride. The pace was relentless, the night air cold. The wind stung against her face and tore at the cloak she caught about her. Though she was scarcely of a mind to notice, the journey took them across countryside that was alternately bleak and lovely. Treacherous salt marshes gave way to green and wooded valleys. Rugged, rolling hills led down to rivers and streams that glistened in the pale moonlight, while ever present was a palpable tension.

Danger lay close. A danger within the land itself, and in the hearts of the men who would control it.

Recalling Ronan's threat to make her share his mount, Analise struggled to keep up. She wondered how he could find his way so easily in the darkness. Had she not heard it said that many riders had perished upon these lonely, untamed borderlands? Yet the man she had wed that night appeared familiar with every inch of the ground they traversed. He never faltered. He certainly never lost the masterful, commanding air she had noticed the first time she saw him. The animal beneath him was obviously his own. The Scottish "galloway" was not quite so large as the horses favored by the English, but it was agile and surefooted and could gallop swiftly across bog, moss, and moorland. Analise's horse, a roan mare, grew wearied long before the shaggy, light-colored gelding in the lead.

Time lost all meaning while they rode. Analise began to fear that the ordeal would never end. She was so very cold and tired, and her entire lower body ached with the effort of staying in the saddle. She flung more than one furious, indignant glare at Ronan's back. It was evident that he cared little for her comfort. No doubt, she mused resentfully, he would have preferred to leave her stranded upon the night-cloaked frontier. But honor, of course, would not allow him to do so.

Would that same honor prevent him from offering her insult of another kind? a small voice within her asked. Shivering, she groaned inwardly and chided herself for the thought. It would serve her ill to consider that—far better to occupy her mind with plans to escape. Even from Scotland, she would find a way to be free.

The hours flew past. And then, finally, just as the

heavens began to light with the first rays of the dawn, Ronan slowed the pace.

Analise straightened, her eyes filling with hopeful anticipation as she pushed back the hood of the cloak. She saw that they had drawn near to the surrounding defensive wall—a "barmkin" as it was called in the north—of a tower house. Built of stone and mortar, and topped by battlements, the five-storied house itself rose nearly sixty feet against the sky. A cluster of much smaller buildings, fashioned of roughly coursed rubble and red sandstone dressings, lay scattered about the grounds. Cattle slumbered in the center of a large enclosure. A millpond sparkled in the gathering light. There was as yet no sign of anyone astir.

Analise felt her heart sink at the sight of the place. It looked dark and cold and unwelcoming. Nothing at all like the comfort and elegance of Beauford.

"Dunslair," Ronan quietly told her its name. Her eyes flew to his face.

"This is your home?" she asked, scorning the unsteadiness of her voice.

"Aye. And yours."

She shivered anew. He led the way onward, to a gateway in the barmkin, where they were granted entrance by a young man who guiltily rubbed his sleep-drugged eyes before springing to his duty. He appeared both shocked and overjoyed to see the master of Dunslair come home in the flesh.

"We thought you dead, Mac Ghillielaidir!" he exclaimed, impulsively using the old, Gaelic form of Armstrong.

"Not dead, Lawrie," Ronan assured him with a faint smile. His gaze flickered toward Analise. "Though some would say my choice was ill made."

He dismounted and allowed Lawrie to take the reins. Analise, loath to accept his assistance, swung down from the saddle as well. A sudden grimace of pain crossed her face. Her legs buckled unexpectedly. She would have tumbled to the ground if not for Ronan's swift response. In an instant, he was at her side, his arms encircling her with their hard, sinewy warmth.

"You English are not a hearty lot," he remarked. His tone was underscored by a touch of wry amusement, but her temper flared nonetheless.

"Perhaps so, but at least we do not thieve and murder like the Scots!" she retorted. "Truly, you are savages, and—"

"Have a care, lady wife," he warned. His eyes burned down into hers, and his features were dangerously grim. "You know not of which you speak. And savage or no, I will have your loyalty."

"My loyalty?" she echoed in disbelief. Her weariness made her both brave and reckless. She pushed at his chest and vowed, "*You*, sir, shall have nothing save my contempt!"

"Flyte all you please in my company alone." He caught her up against him so abruptly that she gasped. "But curb your tongue when there are others about," he directed softly, "or else know my wrath."

"I do not fear your threats!" She struggled within his grasp. He held her easily. Tears of helpless, angry frustration gathered in her eyes again. "Release me!"

His only response was to scoop her up as though she were no more than a babe. She protested, squirming and twisting, but still to no avail. He bore her across the courtyard, to the narrow, iron-banded wooden doorway on the south wall. Another man, considerably older than the first, opened the door with a jubilant greeting for his laird. Ronan spared him but a curt acknowledgment before carrying his defiant bride through a second, open-barred inner gate of iron. It was unguarded; an angry Ronan made a mental note to demand why.

Analise finally ceased her struggles as curiosity (and exhaustion) got the better of her. Her eyes grew very wide once more, and she turned her head to see that she was within a vaulted, dimly lit basement. It was obviously used for storage, for there were a good many barrels and provisions stacked against the walls.

She ventured a glance at Ronan's face while he crossed to a spiral stairwell in the corner. His expression was stern, unapproachable, and she felt her stomach knot again. His arms were like bands of steel about her. She felt scorched by the heat of his body.

Still without a word, he climbed the steps, past the second story of the house—also for storage alone—to the third, where they emerged within the baronial hall. It, too, was vaulted, and served as the main room in the tower. A massive, rough-hewn table and chairs, along with only slightly more comfortable-looking wing chairs across the room, told of its function as both a living and dining chamber.

Ronan set Analise on her feet at last. She moved away from him with unsteady haste, her gaze anxiously sweeping the sparsely decorated hall. Windows, with stone benches below, offered much needed light from all of the walls save the north one. There, a great stone fireplace provided warmth from a blaze that was never allowed to die. Above the ancient, splintered mantelpiece, a length of cloth was draped—the Armstrong tartan, with black and red checks upon a green background. Fastened upon the wall to the left of the cloth was a large crest badge, showing, appropriately enough, a man's arm embowed. And to the right was a wooden plaque upon which had been skillfully carved the clan's motto.

"Invictus maneo," Analise murmured the Latin words she read.

" 'I remain unvanquished,' " Ronan supplied the translation for her, then allowed a smile of bitter irony to touch his lips. He moved across to stand before the fire. "Since we have arrived unexpectedly, none are here to greet us."

"You . . . you share your home with many others?"

"A brother. A few servants." He took off his jack and frowned at her before commanding, "Draw near to the flames. You look well chilled." He was surprised at the impulse to sweep her close again, to sit before the fire and cradle her upon his lap while she slept. Cursing inwardly, he flung the jack onto a chair and braced a hand upon the mantelpiece.

"I would prefer to seek my privacy," she declared in a tremulous voice, striving, without a great deal of success, to appear both queenly and composed.

"Food and drink are what you need."

"I want only to be alone."

"By damn, I'll not have it said that an Armstrong treated a woman ill. Once you have—"

"If I were not so weary, sir, I would make a greater point of declining your 'peculiar' brand of hospitality!" she stormed at him. She was perilously close to tears once again—*she*, who had always disdained such weakness—and wanted nothing more at that moment than to lie down and welcome the sleep beckoning her. Making her way over to a chair opposite the other, she clutched at its high back for support.

Ronan was irritated to feel a sharp twinge of guilt. He knew that he had driven her too hard. Treacherous or not, she was a lady, an Englishwoman. No doubt, she was accustomed to an easy life. Yet she had offered little complaint throughout the difficult journey. And she had never once asked for mercy.

His eyes glowed with a mixture of admiration, fury, and desire as they traveled over her. She stiffened beneath his scrutiny, her fatigue obvious but her beauty undeniable.

"Aye," he said curtly. "To bed, then."

Analise's throat tightened in renewed panic. She grasped at her skirts and cast a look full of desperation toward the stairwell. What escape could there be from such a place?

"And do you think, Ronan Armstrong, to share that bed?" she demanded, only to color hotly at her own bluntness.

"We are wed." He spoke the words with an indifference that belied the temptation burning deep within him.

"Our marriage was to be in name only!"

"I did not agree to that, Analise," he pointed out quietly. The sound of her name upon his lips set her heart wildly aflutter.

"Nor did *I* agree to come with you!" she reminded him. Raising a hand to sweep the bright, windblown curls from her forehead, she gave a ragged sigh and appealed, "If you possess one whit of decency or virtue, you will not force me to . . . to the duties of a wife." Her eyes met his again.

"Better hanged than ill married," he muttered, half to himself.

"If you believe that to be true, then why did you not choose the gallows?"

"Had it been only myself at risk, I would have done so." Refusing to consider the validity of that claim, he gripped the mantelpiece so hard that his knuckles turned white. "But my brother Calum was also a 'guest' in Simon Hayward's dungeon." The memory caused his eyes to darken anew.

"So it was *he* you—"

"Aye."

Stunned at the news, she looked toward the fire. She had never felt so utterly miserable. "My guardian is a cruel man," she remarked, her voice little more than a whisper. She hesitated a moment before adding in all sincerity, "I am sorry that you and your brother were caught within his trap."

Though Ronan yearned to believe her, he cautioned himself against it. Still, his heart stirred with compassion for her weariness. He sensed that her strength was ebbing fast.

"We will talk again once you have slept." He came forward, proffering his hand. "Come." Analise's gaze, narrowing in suspicion, flickered briefly downward before returning to his face.

"May I have your word that you will not—"

"Is the word of a Scot good enough for you?" he challenged dryly. Then frowning, he assured her, "None will disturb you."

She had to be satisfied with that. Too tired to argue any longer, she took his hand and allowed him to lead her back to the stairwell. They climbed to the fourth level of the tower house, and then to the fifth. At the far end of a narrow, torch-lit corridor, Ronan opened a door.

Analise pulled her hand from his and stepped inside a room that was small yet surprisingly comfortable-looking. A fire burned softly within the fireplace. A tall carved bed, hung with brocade curtains and covered with a plump feather quilt, beckoned nearby. There were heavy carpets upon the floor to warm the stones, and two large Flemish tapestries upon the walls. Atop a table beside the bed, a pitcher and bowl offered the opportunity to wash. The strengthening light of the new day streamed in through the panes of a single window.

A slight frown of bemusement creased Analise's brow. She turned to face Ronan again. "How is it that this bedchamber was made ready before—"

" 'Tis always so." He crossed the room and knelt to place another log upon the fire. "In the Borders, we are accustomed to visitors who arrive without advance warning."

"I see." She watched as he straightened again. Dismayed to find herself contemplating the easy, masculine grace with which he moved—and the well-muscled tautness of his hips and thighs—she assumed an outward air of composure. "Where are you to sleep?" Her cheeks flamed anew, and she folded her arms tightly across her chest in order to conceal the irregularity of her breathing.

"My chambers are directly below. Perhaps it would give you comfort to know that no other rooms upon this floor are occupied. And above you is naught save the battlements." He offered her another faint, mocking smile. "In truth, you are as safe as any bairn in her cradle."

"I did not doubt it," she lied, unconvincingly. Her eyes fell beneath the steadiness of his again.

"I will bid you good night, then." It was not at all what

he secretly wished to do, of course—by damn, was this not his wedding night? Yet, he was married, unwillingly, to a woman who professed to want none of him. A woman whose angelic beauty might very well mask the heart of a scheming, cold-blooded temptress.

He cursed the desire burning within him. And swore that his bride would not know how much he longed to stay.

"My things—" said Analise at a sudden thought. She cast a swift, anxious look toward the corridor.

"I will have them brought to you later," Ronan assured her quietly. He moved back to the doorway, his features inscrutable but his gaze as unsettling as ever. "Sleep well, my lady."

She could manage only a wordless nod in response. Once he had gone, closing the door softly behind him, she flew across the room to draw the bolt. Her breasts rose and fell rapidly as she turned and leaned back against the door.

"So. I am 'home.' " she murmured, her mouth curving into a humorless little smile while her gaze swept the room once more. Fraught with emotion, she crossed to the bed and began to undress. Her hands shook while she removed her gown. She cast more than one worried glance toward the doorway as she drew off her shoes and stockings and petticoat. Clad only in her chemise, she hurriedly washed, made use of the privy hidden in the corner, and climbed beneath the covers of the bed.

A deep, uneven sigh escaped her lips. Her eyes strayed to the doorway again.

I did not agree to that. She caught her breath at the memory of Ronan's words.

Sweet Mary, did he intend for her to forget that it was her cousin's treachery and not love that had brought them together? Was it possible that he would insist upon more than her respect?

"Enough," she whispered, aware of the fact that she could not think rationally at present. The day had been long, the night even more so. Once she had slept, she would go to Ronan Armstrong and demand that she be released from the vows forced upon her.

He would have to consent. He wanted the marriage no more than she. Had he not made that clear enough already?

Another sudden, inexplicable ache gripped her heart. Turning upon her side, she pulled the quilt up to her chin. Her eyes swept closed, and she surrendered to blissful unconsciousness at last.

She awoke to the sound of a knock upon the door. Her eyes flew open in startlement. With a gasp she sat bolt upright in the bed, hastily noting that the room was filled with the soft gray light of the afternoon.

"Yes?" she called out, unable in spite of her best efforts to keep her voice steady.

"Will you be wanting your *claes* now, Mistress Armstrong?" a young woman inquired from the other side of the door.

Mistress Armstrong, Analise's mind echoed numbly. The sound of it brought a vivid, painful remembrance of all that had happened. With an inward groan, she lifted a hand to her throat and replied, "I shall be but a moment!"

She flung back the covers and scrambled from the bed. Her gaze fell upon the crumpled, travel-worn velvet gown lying across the chair. Frowning at the sight of it, she pulled it on and hastened to open the door. She found herself facing a slender, auburn-haired girl of indeterminate years who bore a striking resemblance to the young man called Lawrie. And, for a fleeting second, she was also reminded of Meg. Yet *this* girl seemed to be offering her a wary appraisal instead of friendliness.

"The laird bids you to come downstairs to the hall at once," said the housemaid, giving Analise the valise which had been left outside. In her other hand, she carried a tray laden with a mug of fresh milk, a thick slice of oat bread, and a plate of cheese.

"The laird?" Analise repeated in puzzlement. She brushed several wayward curls from her forehead, and felt her stomach rumble at the bread's tempting aroma.

"Lord Ronan. Your husband."

"Oh, I . . . of course." She colored faintly and forced a rather wan smile to her lips before asking, "What is your name?"

" 'Tis Mairi." With a severe white cap upon her head and an apron tied over a shapeless gown of homespun linen, she looked a bit like a child playing at dress up in her mother's clothes. She eyed Analise dubiously and ventured a quick glance inside the bedchamber.

"Well, then, Mairi," said Analise, "you may tell the 'laird' that I shall join him when I am prepared to do so—within the hour."

"He will not be pleased with the hearing of it, my lady," Mairi cautioned, shaking her head.

"Perhaps not." She turned about and swept across the room, setting the bag atop the bed. "But I must insist upon the time to dress properly. Lord Ronan," she declared, wondering if the title was genuine or merely a token of reverence, "will simply have to wait until I am ready to join him." She had little doubt that he would be angered by her defiance. And she could not deny that the thought of it gave her a certain degree of satisfaction.

There was a spark of begrudging admiration in Mairi's brown eyes now. She watched as Analise opened the bag and began removing its contents.

"There are some who will not like it that an Armstrong has taken one of the English to wife," the young housemaid grew emboldened enough to remark.

"I do not like it myself!" Analise countered, then immediately regretted the outburst. She gently cleared her throat before explaining in a low voice, "The marriage was sought by neither of us."

"And so the laird was telling Calum but a moment ago."

"Calum?" Remaining baffled for only an instant, she recalled aloud, "Yes. He is Ro—*Lord* Ronan's brother."

"Aye." It was Mairi's turn to blush. She dropped her gaze, folded her hands together primly, and heaved an eloquent sigh. "Young Calum is a bonny wild one. We feared he would come to great harm. Seldom has he dared his brother's anger in such a manner—at least in these few years past. But, the saints be praised, he came home safe. And now Lord Ronan as well." It was on the tip of her tongue to add, "No thanks to those black-hearted devils across the border," but she swallowed the words before they could be uttered. Though the laird's bride was English, she was nevertheless the lady of Dunslair now and could not be given *too* much discourtesy.

"He dared his brother's anger?" echoed Analise, her curiosity piqued. She left off with the unpacking and moved back toward Mairi. "In what way did he do so?"

The young redhead looked quite happy with her superior knowledge of the situation. "Why, it was Calum himself who had gone a-reiving the night the two of them were captured. Lord Ronan gave chase as soon as Calum's plans were made known to him, for did he not know his brother's troublesome nature? But it was too late."

"I don't understand. How—"

"Calum was away to Hexham," Mairi told her with a slightly exaggerated patience. "Lord Ronan has long forbidden him to cross the border, yet he would do it." Her eyes lit with mingled excitement and approval when she proclaimed, "The blood of the clan does surely run strong in Calum Armstrong!" And then a sudden frown creased her brow. "Still, if not for Lord Ronan, Calum would now be dead. And good men along with him."

Analise's head spun, her own eyes clouding with confusion. She wanted to ask more, to seek a full explanation of what had brought about her guardian's startling, ultimately disastrous triumph, but Mairi made it clear that she would tarry no longer.

"Lord Ronan's temper is a thing to be feared," she advised gravely—and perhaps, with a touch of satisfaction. For the first time, she smiled. "You had best hasten yourself, my lady." With that, she handed Analise the tray and took her leave.

Carrying the tray to the bedside table, Analise took up the bread and milk and sank down upon the coverlet. She was as in much of a quandary as ever—more so, in truth, for now it seemed that Ronan Armstrong had not been caught as a result of trying to find her after all. No, indeed, the disaster had been provoked by his own brother's wild and lawless tendencies. Why, then, had he behaved as though *she* were somehow to blame? Was she not as much a victim as he?

She took a bite of the bread, then raised the mug to her

lips and drank deeply. Sleep had not given her the clear mind she had hoped for. And now she must once again face the man who, if it so pleased him, could try and keep her a prisoner in Scotland forever.

"Aye. The laird awaits," she murmured, the corners of her mouth turning briefly upward again. Heaving a long, disconsolate sigh, she rose from the bed and set about preparing herself for the ordeal ahead.

Within the firelit confines of the baronial hall, meanwhile, the discussion between the two Armstrong brothers had grown heated.

"Mind your tongue, Calum," Ronan warned, "or else feel the weight of my hand." His countenance was thunderous, his eyes glinting harshly as he turned away from the fire. He had allowed himself a few hours' sleep, had washed and donned clean clothing, then had broken his fast afterward with a hearty meal. But his mood remained dour. And his patience dangerously thin.

"You blether as easily as an Englishman!" Calum shot back, undaunted.

He was very much like Ronan, though his eyes were not quite so blue nor his stature so commanding. All the same, he was a handsome man, his dark brown hair waving rakishly across his forehead and his charm legendary among the ladies. Younger than his brother by eight years, he had benefited from Ronan's love and guidance since the death of their parents more than a dozen years earlier. Yet he was given to a recklessness that frequently plunged him into peril and earned him his brother's well-deserved fury.

"Aye," he now saw fit to add, "perhaps your bride will be swayed by your pretty words!"

"By heaven—" Ronan ground out, only to break off

and clench his hand into a fist while he struggled to control his rising temper.

"Would there not have been more honor in the gallows?" Calum demanded with all the impertinence of his youth. Instantly contrite, he shook his head and insisted, "I did not mean it, Brother. I would not see you dead. And I know too well that you did but place my life above your own." He suddenly muttered an oath and moved to stand before Ronan. "A curse upon my own wretched soul for riding that night! If I had but curbed my impulsiveness, you would not have been forced to this blasted mockery!"

" 'Tis done now," said Ronan. He frowned, his expression becoming more pensive than ireful as he looked back to the flames. "The bargain has been struck."

"Surely you do not mean to keep her?" Calum asked, his eyes widening in shocked disbelief. "Satan's teeth, man, you cannot be wed to Simon Hayward's kinswoman!"

" *'Tis done,*" Ronan asserted once more. His low, resonant tone was laced with steel, and his gaze hardened as it caught and held his brother's. "I gave him my word."

"That you did, but—"

"No, Calum." His visage softened a bit, and a telltale warmth crept into his voice. "No matter how it came about, she is mine. I'll not set her aside."

Calum's eyes narrowed as he studied Ronan's face closely. He scarcely managed to conceal a smile when he queried, "The Englishwoman is pleasing to the eye?"

"She is more than that," Ronan answered, half to himself.

"Ah, then, the marriage cannot be so loathsome. Though, has it not been said that fanned fires and forced love never did well?"

"You understand little."

"Indeed, Brother?" drawled Calum, his eyes holding a touch of mischief. He folded his arms across his chest and subjected Ronan to yet another affectionate scrutiny. "Perhaps my plea for forgiveness was not so necessary."

"Do you dare to jest about it?" Ronan charged with an all too visible anger. His hand shot out to grasp the front of his brother's shirt. "By damn, not only have you caused me to be bound to a woman who would as soon see me drawn and quartered by my enemies, but you have given Simon Hayward the means to make us bleed even more!"

" 'Twas not my intent!" Calum replied defensively, jerking free.

"Aye, but the results were the same."

Scowling, he pivoted about and crossed to take up a rigid stance in front of one of the windows. His gaze darkened anew as he stared outward. A mist had crept upon the hills now, the wind gentling as the air cooled.

"You can be certain that Hayward will take advantage of the alliance," he added, absently noting the familiar bustle of activity within the barmkin. "I do not doubt him capable of a treachery far beyond what he has shown thus far."

Behind him, Calum struggled with his own emotions. He was plagued by guilt, and desperate to make amends for what he had done. Yet he realized that such a thing was impossible. There was no way he could ever hope to compensate his brother for the loss of his freedom. Because of *his* foolish quest for adventure, Ronan had been forced into a loveless union with a woman who could bring him nothing but grief. Ronan, who had always valued his independence above all else. In truth, what had happened was unforgivable.

His manner much subdued, he slowly approached the window and asked, "What of the other clans? Do you think they will react favorably to the news of your marriage?"

"No," said Ronan, his features grim. "They will not."

"Aye," Calum acknowledged somberly. "Our blood feud with the Maxwells will no doubt be fueled by it." One Maxwell in particular rose in his mind . . . his eyes took on a faraway look at the thought of her.

"I will demand a meeting with Angus Maxwell in two days' time. He cannot refuse me."

"I will go with you."

"No, Calum." He turned to face his brother, the ghost of a smile upon his lips. "The sight of you would send old Angus running for his sword."

"Damn it, Ronan, did I not tell you that no harm was done to the girl?"

"Aye. But her kinsmen were not convinced." He wandered back toward the fireplace. "And Ewan Maxwell has declared his own hand against me." Recalling Ewan's mistreatment of Analise, he swore inwardly and vowed once more that his longtime adversary would pay for it.

"What—" Calum started to question, only to break off when Analise appeared at the foot of the staircase.

His eyes filled with no small measure of astonishment as they swept over her; she was far lovelier than he had expected. Swallowing hard, he looked to Ronan. His surprise deepened when he saw the look upon his brother's face. It held a tenderness he would not have thought possible under the circumstances.

"I ask your pardon, sir," Analise declared coolly, her gaze also fastening upon Ronan as she stepped forward. "I did not mean to remain abed until such a late hour."

Her pulse was racing, her every muscle tensed, but she concealed her nervousness well. She gave silent thanks for the fact that her bag had been packed with such unexpected care. The square-necked gown of soft crimson wool she had donned a short time ago was elegant and becoming, and made her feel better equipped for composure. Unfortunately, not a single piece of her jewelry had found its way into the bag. She could only surmise that Lady Helena, seizing an unfair advantage of the situation, had claimed it as her own.

But she did not think of that now. What did such things matter when her entire future was at peril? Drawing near to the fire's warmth—yet keeping a safe distance between herself and the husband she was determined to escape—she cast a brief, quizzical glance toward Calum and waited for Ronan to speak.

"You have recovered?" he asked, his gaze traveling over her with a boldness that made her catch her breath.

"Yes." She could not help noticing that he looked much better now that he had exchanged his dirty, days-worn clothing for a fresh linen shirt and breeches. Even at his worst, however, he had been devilishly attractive.

Would you continue a fool? she reproached herself. Her eyes fell beneath Ronan's, then strayed toward Calum again.

"My brother," Ronan finally disclosed.

"Welcome to Dunslair, my lady," Calum offered, his formality matching her own. Sauntering forward, he took her hand and raised it to his lips.

"Thank you." A faint blush stained her cheeks as she withdrew her hand and remarked on impulse, "You are very much like your brother."

"So it has been said," he answered wryly. He regarded her with what she considered to be an inordinate degree of amusement. Indeed, his eyes were virtually dancing as they flickered up and down the length of her body. She stiffened, her color deepening.

"Leave us, Calum," Ronan directed.

"But, I—"

"Now."

Calum appeared mutinous, but knew that it would be utter folly to try his brother's patience any further. Thus, he turned to Analise again and made her a gallant bow.

" 'Tis an honor to have you at Dunslair," he asserted smoothly. Ignoring the dark look Ronan sent him, he smiled at her once more and left.

Analise clasped her hands together in front of her and directed her gaze toward the flames. The firelight played softly over her face, and set aglow the single braid of golden curls hanging down her back. She looked quite young and vulnerable at the moment. And, to Ronan, incredibly beguiling.

He cursed the desire burning within him, cursed anew the fates for having seen him wed to a woman who was not what he had believed her to be the night they had shared a kiss. Recalling the way she had deceived him then, it suddenly occurred to him that she might not be as pure and virginal as she appeared. Perhaps other men had fallen under her spell. He had been told that she had but recently come from London—was it not well-known that the English court was rife with worldly intrigues? It was possible, then, that Simon Hayward had forced the marriage for more than one reason.

Though he was reluctant to admit it, the thought sent a hot, powerful surge of jealousy coursing through him. His features tightened angrily once more, and his gaze smoldered as it raked over his bride.

"No doubt you are hungry," he said tersely, breaking the silence between them at last. Analise suffered a sharp intake of breath at the sound of his deep, resonant voice.

"I . . . I have eaten," she stammered, furious at her own lack of composure. She raised her eyes to his face, only to pale at the unaccountable displeasure she saw there.

"Were you surprised, *my lady*, that I did not intrude upon your privacy?"

The question took her by surprise. "You gave your word, sir," she replied, her brows knitting together into a frown of confusion.

"Aye. But perhaps your trust has been misplaced before this."

"I do not understand your meaning!"

"Do you not?" He advanced upon her, his expression unfathomable yet his eyes holding menace. In that moment, she feared that he might strike her.

"I suggest, Ronan Armstrong, that we waste no more time on these 'pleasantries'!" she told him. Masking her disquiet well, she lifted her head proudly and met his gaze without flinching. As always, her pulse leapt at his nearness, but she was determined that he should not know of it. "We must set about righting the wrong my guardian has done to the both of us."

"Do you still insist the union was forced upon you?"

he demanded. Her trepidation would have increased ten-fold if she had been aware of the considerable effort it was costing him to keep his hands off her.

"Why, how can you ask it?" Indignant, she folded her arms tightly against her chest and flung him a resentful glare. "Indeed, when offered the choice between marriage and the convent, I did announce my preference for the latter!"

" 'Tis difficult to envision you within a nunnery." His eyes moved over her with an even bolder familiarity than before, then returned to linger upon the curve of her breasts swelling above the gown's low neckline. She blushed fierily and hastened to uncross her arms, at the same time plagued by a wicked, traitorous desire to feel the warmth of his lips upon hers again.

Alarmed, she swept past him and across the room to the same window where he had stood but a few moments earlier. She could feel his penetrating gaze upon her still.

"The marriage must be dissolved at once," she insisted. "I am certain that, given the circumstances, a special dispensation shall be granted."

"No. The marriage must stand."

"What?" she breathed in startlement, whirling to face him once more. "How can you say—"

"The bargain has been struck." He had told Calum the same, of course, but it seemed to gain an altogether different, stronger meaning now that he was with Analise again.

"I wanted none of this bargain!"

"Nor did I." He closed the distance between them. His face wore a look of grim determination as he towered above her. "We are man and wife, and will remain so."

"You cannot mean that," she replied, her eyes flashing up at him. She shook her head and argued, "Will you allow Simon Hayward the pleasure of—"

"By heaven, are your wishes to be placed above the lives of the innocent?" he cut her off sharply. She took an instinctive step backward while he pointed out in a low, furious tone, "Were this alliance broken, English and Scots alike would suffer. Do you not realize the power your kinsman calls his own? He holds the fate of too many in his hands. If I were to deny you now, he would send scores of his men across the border to kill and plunder at will. He would use *this* as an excuse to break what little peace exists. You must stay," he concluded with another severe frown, "or risk the consequences."

"I . . . I did not know." Feeling very foolish, she looked away and confided, "In truth, I know far too little about my cousin's duties. And about what is happening here." Recovering her spirit in the next instant, she tilted her head back to face him squarely, avowing, "Yet I cannot pretend that ours is a real marriage! We are faced with a dilemma neither of us courted, and must now settle upon the means with which to resolve it."

"The solution is clear enough."

"Pray, what—"

"Speak the truth, Analise," he ordered abruptly, his hands moving with a will of their own to close about her shoulders. "Confess your part in Simon Hayward's villainy!"

"Merciful . . . do you think . . . " she faltered, stunned by his accusation. She blinked up at him for a moment before his meaning sank in. Her beautiful, heart-shaped countenance grew stormy, and she reiterated, "I was *forced* to wed you!"

"Were you?" His fingers tightened about her, his voice holding an all too noticeable scorn. "You claim to have been an unwilling bride. Yet I recall that you were not so repulsed by me that night at Windy Gyle. You were as eager for the kiss as I, and now do shame yourself by denying it!"

She gasped as though she had been struck. The blood drained from her face, while her eyes sparked with both hurt and anger.

"I curse the day we met, Ronan Armstrong!" she cried feelingly. "Would that I had been bound to any man save you!"

"You shall have no other," he decreed, his own eyes holding a dangerous gleam. "No other man will claim what is mine."

"I am not yours!" She struggled to pull free, her hands lifting to push at his chest. But he was not of a mind to release her. Since the night he had held her in his arms, he had been taunted by the memory of her sweet response. The battle within him raged even more fiercely now that she was his for the taking. Scheming little vixen she might be, yet it was impossible to deny the way she stirred his blood.

"Do not think, Analise, that you will return to your London ways," he warned in a voice charged with simmering emotion. "Though the marriage be forced, I will demand your faithfulness. Cast your eyes elsewhere, and by damn, I will make you pay!"

"Despicable rogue!" Thoroughly outraged, she tried to strike a blow across his face. He seized her wrist and gave her a slow, mocking half smile that struck a chord of fear deep in her heart.

"Perhaps, lady wife, we are well matched." He caught

her none too gently up against him then, his arms encircling her with their strong, sinewy warmth. "Aye. Perhaps the bargain was not so tragic after all!"

She had no time to reply, for his mouth descended upon hers with a forcefulness that literally took her breath away. His arms tightened about her, molding her supple curves against the length of his hard-muscled body. She felt her senses reeling, but would not admit defeat. Furiously squirming within his embrace, she tore her lips from his, then raised her arm and landed a hard, stinging slap across the smooth-shaven ruggedness of his cheek.

He did not release her as she had hoped. Instead he swept her even closer while his eyes burned relentlessly down into the fiery, blue-green depths of hers.

"Do you not fear, my lady, that I will return the blow?" he challenged. His low and level tone belied the fierce raging of passion inside him.

"You would not dare!" she breathed, so shocked by the threat that she abruptly stilled within his embrace. "I am certain, however, that such . . . such savagery is not at all unusual among men of your caliber! You are, after all, a Reiver!"

"And you are a Reiver's bride."

"A grievous misfortune which shall soon be remedied!" She resumed her struggles with a vengeance, and would have struck him again but for the fact that he seized her arms and forced them behind her back. Painfully aware of the heat of his body against her breasts, she cried, "Let me go!"

Her wish might well have been granted—if not for the untimely rashness of her next words. Glaring up at him, she forgot all else save the desperate need to escape, to flee the disturbing, utterly sinful longings his touch provoked.

"I should not have been so ready to decline the affections of the *English* suitors my guardian pressed upon me!" she scornfully proclaimed. "They, at least, were gentlemen and would have treated me with kindness and respect. But you, sir, are naught but an ill-mannered ruffian who has in all likelihood bullied a great many people into surrender. Though I am perhaps ignorant of the ways between men and women in Scotland, I cannot believe chivalry is completely unknown. Whether that be true or not, I must assure you that *I* will not be so easily vanquished!" Her color was becomingly high as she finished, and she held her breath while waiting for Ronan's response.

His eyes filled with a hot, dangerous light as they narrowed imperceptibly. Once again, he was loath to admit just how much her words had affected him. His pride demanded retribution. His heart demanded much more.

"I would not have your opinion of me disappointed," he declared softly.

With a swiftness that made Analise's head spin, he took a seat upon the stone bench beneath the window and pulled her across his lap. One arm remained about her shoulders, while the other clamped across her knees.

"No!" she gasped, her throat constricting in dismay. She pushed at him weakly and squirmed atop the lean hardness of his thighs. "Release me!"

He paid no heed to her objections. She inhaled sharply again when, in the next instant, he lowered his head and pressed his mouth to the upper curve of her breasts.

Her eyes flew wide in startlement, her hands grasping

at his arms. "Do not!" she whispered. His lips roamed hungrily across her exposed flesh. She trembled and fought against the waves of pleasure washing over her, her skin branded by the heat of his mouth.

While she struggled to gather resistance, his lips trailed a fiery path upward along the graceful column of her neck. His hand closed upon one of her breasts. She was tempted to strike him again, but was indeed afraid of what he would do. Her struggles were entirely futile, it seemed, for he held her captive with very little effort. And when she opened her mouth to curse him for his devilry, he silenced her with another kiss.

A low moan rose in her throat. She grew still now, her eyes sweeping closed as her newly awakened passions flared to match his. Of their own accord, her arms crept up about his neck. Her lips, ever disloyal where he was concerned, were soft and welcoming beneath the masterful warmth of his, and she pressed instinctively closer.

The kiss deepened. Ronan's hand left her breast and began tugging her skirts upward. She was shocked a moment later to feel the rush of cool air upon her skin, and even more shocked when his hand suddenly closed about her naked hips. Her face flaming with embarrassment, she tried to push his hand away, but he remained oblivious to her protests. He caressed her with a bold possessiveness, making her gasp and squirm and blush even more hotly. And before she knew what he intended, his fingers smoothed across her belly, then lower to claim the moist, secret place between her thighs.

Her eyes flew wide. Shocked at the intimacy of his

touch, she tore her lips from his and pushed at him in earnest.

"Dear heaven, *no!*" she cried in a hoarse, breathless voice. Panic gripped her as she realized just how close she had come to a complete—and irreversible—catastrophe. She renewed her struggles, and would not admit that she fought against her own desire as well as Ronan's.

His arms tightened about her once more, his deep blue eyes aglow with a mixture of triumph and frustration. He ached to continue with the exquisite torment, to possess this proud, willful English beauty who had kindled the fire within him and then defied him to put it out. Never had he wanted a woman as much as he wanted her. His pride had rejoiced at her defeat. Yet it was that same pride which now demanded that he release her.

Would that I had been bound to any man save you. The memory of her words prompted his gaze to darken anew. Had she already given her heart to someone? he wondered. Had she given her innocence?

Breathing an oath, he stood and set her on her feet. She pulled away from him, furiously jerking her skirts down and adjusting her bodice. It was with an air of haughty outrage that she faced Ronan. Her cheeks were still warm, her eyes splendidly ablaze.

"You *are* a savage!" she pronounced.

"Were that true," he countered while his gaze seared down into hers, "I would have taken you and damn all else."

She blushed at his indelicacy. Filled with anger and humiliation and an acute, puzzling discontentment, she whirled about and fled back up the staircase.

Ronan stared after her for several long moments, his

brow creasing into a frown that was both ireful and pensive. And when a grinning, hapless Calum reappeared shortly thereafter, he had cause to regret asking his older brother if the new lady of Dunslair had indeed been swayed by his pretty words.

Chapter 5

Sitting alone in her bedchamber, Analise stared pensively at the bright, energetic dance of the flames. She dreaded the approaching night. Ronan would expect her to join him for the evening meal. And the prospect of seeing him again after what had happened was disagreeable in the extreme.

Her emotions were still in utter chaos. Her conscience had not ceased in its reproach for her weak and wanton behavior. She was sorely tempted to plead illness and stay within the sanctuary of her room, but was almost certain that her husband would assume (correctly, of course) that she was defiant instead of unwell. No doubt he would come himself to demand her presence. And *that* was something she must take care to avoid. The thought of being confronted by him within such intimate surroundings filled her with dismay.

She could not understand why he had been so determined to insult her—or why she had found it so difficult to resist him. Never before had she allowed such liberties. Never before had a man dared to take them.

Does he not have the right? a small voice inside her challenged. She frowned and rose abruptly from the chair.

"I cannot stay here," she murmured, then recalled Ronan's warning about what would happen if she left. If his words were true, then her only hope was to appeal to her guardian once again. Perhaps Simon could be persuaded that she need not be in Scotland in order to keep the alliance intact. Indeed, she would agree to remain wed to Ronan, yet live in France. She wanted no husband at all, so what did it matter if she was not free to marry another? A marriage in name only would be far preferable to spending years shut away within a convent. For, in spite of what she had said, she had little desire to embrace a life of poverty and seclusion. No, better to choose exile.

But first, she mused with a heavy sigh, she must find a way to return to Beauford . . .

The long afternoon wore on. Shortly after darkness began to fall, Mairi arrived bearing two buckets filled with hot water. Another housemaid, a shy brunette whom Mairi identified as her younger sister Flora, followed with a bucket of cold water, a bar of heather-scented soap, and a length of toweling. Lawrie was close upon their heels. He carried a simple wooden bathtub into the room and set it in front of the fireplace.

"The laird did say you would be glad of a wash," he explained, turning to Analise with a smile. His amiability toward her was a pleasant surprise.

"Thank you." She could not help returning his smile, but the smile faded when she saw that Mairi was regarding her with a baffling, ill-disguised resentment.

"Did you not think Calum Armstrong bonny?" Mairi demanded sharply.

"In truth, I had not given it much thought," replied Analise, wondering what had prompted such a question.

"It might please you to know that bonny Calum has given *you* thought enough!" Her eyes flashed, and she made no pretense at the courtesy she had earlier displayed. "Perhaps you have wed the wrong brother!"

"Mairi!" a shocked Flora admonished, glancing nervously toward Analise.

" 'Tis true!" said Mairi, unrepentant. "Calum did say that his new sister is the most beautiful—"

"Hold your tongue!" Lawrie cut her off. Visibly angered, he grabbed her arm and brought his face close to hers while hissing, "The sheep on the moors will sprout wings and fly before Calum Armstrong sets his eyes upon you!" He released her and turned back to Analise. "She does not truly offer you disrespect, my lady. 'Tis only that our Mairi has long held a false hope where the young master is concerned. She speaks with her heart, not her head."

Analise turned a gaze full of sympathy upon Mairi. She smiled softly and proclaimed, "He is a fine, handsome man, to be sure. Yet I can assure you that I gain no significant pleasure from his compliments."

"Aye," said Flora, widening her eyes at Analise. "With such a man as the laird for your husband, you've no need of any other's—"

"We'll be leaving you to your bath now, my lady," Lawrie broke in once more. He cast a severe, quelling frown toward the two sisters, then took up the buckets and quickly emptied their contents into the bathtub. That done, he told Analise, "When you've finished with it, my lady, I will come back to take it away."

"Thank you," she murmured again. She watched as Flora took Mairi's arm and led her from the room. Lawrie took himself off in their wake. It was clear from the look on his face that Mairi would bear the full brunt of his tongue once they were belowstairs again.

Analise bolted the door after the trio and hurried to undress. She had secretly yearned for a bath since her arrival at Dunslair—it surprised her that Ronan had thought of it. But, then, there were so many things about him that were surprising. And very, very alarming.

Flinging a distracted glance heavenward, she drew off the last of her clothing and finally eased her body down into the water. The tub was not overly deep, but she did not mind. A deep sigh of contentment escaped her lips, and she closed her eyes while the liquid warmth swirled about her aching muscles. Following several minutes of such sweet, languid repose, she took up the soap and scrubbed at her skin until she was convinced that no traces of the journey's dust remained. She stood and wrapped a length of soft wool toweling about her, then loosed her hair from its plait and knelt to wash it as well.

Feeling remarkably better afterward, she caught up a fresh linen chemise and slipped it on. She shivered and moved nearer the flames, all the while reflecting that Scotland was a good deal colder than London. Sinking down upon the rushes spread across the floor, she threaded her fingers through her damp tresses and leaned toward the fire in an effort to dry them.

A loud, insistent knock landed upon the other side of the door. Analise started, her fingers stilling and her eyes flying wide.

"Yes?" she called out, wondering if it was Lawrie, come to fetch the bathtub.

"I would have a word with you."

It was Ronan. The sound of his voice—edged with a noticeable, angry impatience—caused her stomach to tighten in alarm. She scrambled to her feet and gazed apprehensively at the door.

"I . . . I am occupied at present!"

"Now," he ground out.

"No!" she cried impulsively, her own temper flaring. "Am I to be denied even a brief moment's privacy?"

"Open the door, else I will break it down."

It was no idle threat, and she knew it. Mentally consigning him to the devil, she hastened to the bed to retrieve her gown. Her hands were shaking as she drew it on, and she had scarcely managed to tie the lacings when Ronan knocked again.

"I am coming!" she told him breathlessly. Opening the door at last, she paled beneath the thunderous look Ronan turned upon her.

"By damn, your kinsman has wasted little time in making the alliance known," he said, his tone full of barely suppressed rage. Pushing past her, he strode across the room to brace a hand upon the mantelpiece. He stared into the fire, his eyes holding a gleam that was a fitting match for the flames they reflected.

Analise took a deep, steadying breath and assumed an air of queenly composure. "Have you intruded upon me for no other reason than that?"

"I am summoned to Edinburgh to answer for my crime." His mouth curved into a faint, humorless smile as he turned to face her now. For the first time, he took note of her crookedly arranged gown and the wet curls streaming down about her face and shoulders. His body warmed at the thought of her in her bath. "Aye," he added wryly, "and to explain to the king how an Armstrong came to be caught in such a web."

"You . . . will be going away?" Her hopes leapt at the

prospect. She was certain that, if *he* were not at Dunslair, she could escape.

"I must leave at once." He came forward, his eyes traveling over her with such knowing intensity that her breath caught in her throat. "But do not think to take advantage of my absence," he warned. Observing the guilty, telltale flush that crept up to her face, he frowned and stopped mere inches away from where she stood so proud and angry and, unbeknownst to him, dismayingly weak-kneed. "Be assured, Calum will guard you well." Another brief smile of irony touched his lips when he murmured, "My brother owes me that much, at least."

"You cannot keep me a prisoner forever, Ronan Armstrong!" she asserted hotly, her eyes kindling anew. "Though I would not become the cause of bloodshed, I shall find a way to put an end to this—"

"Women of strong spirit have long been valued here." He stepped even closer, his features inscrutable, yet his deep-timbred voice laced with meaning. "To be sure, we Scots are a hardy and passionate breed. But take care not to go too far, Analise."

"Your threats are growing tiresome!" All too conscious of his nearness, she swallowed hard and lifted her chin to an even more defiant angle. "Do you expect me to quiver and quake every time you darken your brow? I am no longer surprised by your churlish behavior. In the short time of our acquaintance, you have proven yourself devoid of any true gallantry. Indeed, sir, I have not yet passed an entire day beneath your roof, yet already I have been the recipient of insults far beyond those offered by even the most ungentlemanly of men at court!"

"Have you forgotten?" he parried in a tone that was both low and dangerously even. *"I am no gentleman."*

She read the intent in his eyes. Her hands came up to push him away, but it was too late.

He swept her against him, his arms holding her captive while his lips claimed the parted softness of hers. She moaned in protest and recalled, with painful clarity, what had happened the last time he had kissed her. Furious with herself still, she summoned all her strength and jerked free of his embrace. But when she spun about to flee, her skirts tangled about her legs. A sharp, breathless cry broke from her lips as she lost her balance and tumbled downward.

Ronan's strong arm slipped about her waist, breaking her fall. He knelt upon the floor, turned her about so that she was facing him upon her knees as well, and gathered her close once more. Before she could renew her struggles, he captured her mouth with the skillful, sensuously persuasive warmth of his.

She moaned again, though in pleasure instead of protest, and found herself swaying against him. Her arms crept up to entwine about his neck, her lips moving beneath his. She suffered a sharp intake of breath when his tongue plunged within her mouth, and felt herself grow light-headed as the kiss deepened. Desire, even more potent than before, spread like wildfire throughout her body.

Ronan's hand moved to the fastenings of her gown. With a startling swiftness and dexterity, his fingers untied the laces. He tugged the square-necked bodice downward.

Analise's eyelids fluttered open. Shocked to realize what he meant to do, she pulled her arms from about his neck and tried once again to push him away. But he would not be denied. His arm tightened about her waist.

His mouth left hers, his lips trailing a fiery path across her face to tease at the delicate lobe of her ear, then down along the graceful curve of her neck. Ignoring her breathless and halfhearted protests, he impatiently swept the rounded neckline of her chemise lower.

Her breasts were bared to him now. His mouth closed about one of the rose-tipped peaks, his tongue flicking with short, tantalizing strokes while his lips sucked as greedily as a babe's.

"Ronan!" breathed Analise, hot color flying to her cheeks. Her hands curled tightly about his powerful, hard-muscled arms. She caught her lower lip between her teeth, her eyes sweeping closed as she trembled and gasped and instinctively pressed closer to the man who, scoundrel though he was, possessed the ability to make her forget all else save the pleasure his touch provoked.

The heat of the fire was a fitting match for the passion blazing between them. Analise threaded her fingers within the rich-hued thickness of Ronan's hair and strained upward while his hot, demanding mouth continued to ravish her breasts. She gave herself up to the sweet madness, her head falling back as a secret yearning built to a fever pitch within her. By the time Ronan's lips returned to claim hers again, she was perilously near to a complete surrender. She threw her arms about his neck, kissing him back with such innocent yet provocative fervor that he felt the last vestiges of his own self-control slipping away . . .

"Ah, so it is to be a rough wooing, is it?" Calum's voice, full of mocking amusement, reached out to them from the doorway. "Much the same as England with Scotland." He grinned as he watched Analise open her eyes in startlement and hasten to pull free. "Though, from what I see before me, with far more success."

Ronan ground out a curse. Reluctantly he let go of an embarrassed, fierily blushing Analise, and climbed to his feet while she snatched her bodice upward to cover her breasts. His gaze, hungry and smoldering, raked over her one last time before he turned to confront Calum.

"By heaven," he demanded in a tone that left little doubt of his anger, "do you forget yourself this day?" His body still burned—and his heart was filled with a pleasure far beyond what the embrace itself had given him. Offering up another silent oath, he glared vengefully at his brother.

"The door was open," Calum pointed out, without any trace of remorse. He had the audacity to smile again. "Aye, and you should be glad that *I* alone was witness to your wee bit of *hochmagandy*." His eyes twinkling, he looked to Analise and said, "My humblest apologies, dear sister. In truth, I did not suspect that your husband's leave-taking would be so 'thorough.' "

Her face flaming, Analise gave an inward groan and clutched the bodice of her gown even more tightly against her breasts. Her eyes strayed toward Ronan. She wondered how it was possible that she could profess to hate a man and yet find his kisses and caresses so utterly, sinfully intoxicating.

"Your horse has been made ready," Calum told Ronan. "And the hour grows late. Edinburgh is—"

"Leave us," Ronan commanded brusquely.

"But will you not—"

"Do you try my patience further?"

"No," Calum was quick to affirm, shaking his head. There was no humor lurking in either his voice or his gaze now. He obeyed his instincts and beat a hasty retreat.

As soon as he had gone, Ronan pivoted slowly to face Analise once more. Her eyes fell beneath his. She wanted desperately to forget what had just happened between them. Yet *how could she*? Her lips were still warm from his kisses. Her breasts still tingled from the moist, hotly possessive tribute he had paid them.

"I will be away for a day or two, perhaps longer," he advised her. His impassivity belied the white-hot desire still thundering within him.

"And would you have me wish you Godspeed?" she shot back, glancing up at him.

"I would have you as you were before Calum came." His deep blue eyes gleamed with triumph at the sound of her gasp. Too well, he remembered the willing sweetness of her lips, the taste of her soft, beautiful breasts. If not for the king's summons—and the lingering soreness of his pride—he might well have taken her there and then. The thought made his loins tighten anew.

"You are without conscience!" Analise declared in reproach. Her hands trembled as she pulled the bodice higher.

"Aye," conceded Ronan, his voice splendidly low and vibrant.

There was no warning this time. He caught her up against him, kissed her with a fierce, heart-stopping mastery, and released her so suddenly that she very nearly lost her balance again. Then, while she stood flushed and breathless, he strode from the room.

"Sweet Mary, how much more can I endure?" she whispered, moving to grasp at the chair while her head swam. There was no use in trying to deny the wicked, powerful attraction between herself and Ronan any longer. And, if drastic measures were not taken, it would most assuredly prove to be her downfall.

I hold what is mine. His words returned, unbidden, to taunt her. Mayhap that was true enough as things were now, she mused disconsolately, yet there would be no chance of freedom if she became more than a wife in name alone. Of that, she was certain. Once she had shared Ronan Armstrong's bed, he would never let her go.

An involuntary shiver coursed down her spine. Panic rose within her once more.

She could wait no longer! She must get away at once, before Ronan returned. Before it was too late to prevent something that could only bring disaster to the both of them. He did not want a wife who was English and high-born and headstrong. He did not want a wife at all. And she . . . dear heaven, how could *she* ever hope to find happiness with a man who was arrogant and overbearing and little better than a savage?

Sudden, inexplicable tears gathered in her eyes. She dashed impatiently at them and hurried to close the door. Drawing the bolt, she squared her shoulders and took a deep breath. Her features were set in a look of determination as she began lacing up her dress. Crossing to the window, she arrived just in time to see Ronan swing up into the saddle and ride away. She bade him a silent farewell—and was startled to find herself wishing they had met under different circumstances.

The night, a typical one in the Borders, was deep and cold. And bereft of moonlight.

Thankful for such mercy, Analise stole out of her bed-chamber and crept toward the staircase. Her heart was drumming loudly in her ears, and her every muscle was taut with anxiety. But she would not be swayed from her resolve.

The house had grown quiet more than an hour earlier, long after she had eaten the evening meal alone in her room. Calum had generously granted her the request. Though he had declared himself responsible for her welfare (and for her captivity) during his brother's absence, he had done so with such amiability that she had suffered a sharp pang of guilt for what she was about to do. She knew that he would bear the full force of Ronan's anger once she was gone.

"Forgive me, Calum," she murmured underneath her breath as she began descending the stone steps. If not for the torches kept burning day and night, she would surely have stumbled. She gathered up her skirts more securely, and, lamenting the fact that she had left her bag behind— it would be far easier to travel without it—continued down through the winding, narrow passageway.

She passed the next floor, and then the next. The baronial hall was empty. She spared it only a cursory glance before climbing down to the second story. It, too, was dark and deserted, and more cluttered than she had remembered. Her trepidation increased as she reached the foot of the staircase, for she knew that once she had crossed through the storage area before her, she would have to slip past the men posted at the two doorways which led to the courtyard outside.

Her pulse racing, she made her way slowly across the room. Her eyes adjusted to the darkness as she kept a vigilant gaze upon her surroundings. She spied the open-barred iron gate ahead and approached it cautiously, looking for the watchman. However, just as it had been upon her arrival, the gate was unguarded.

She breathed a sigh of relief and hurried to open it. Once through, she crept on toward the next exit. Her throat constricted in renewed apprehension. She remembered the older man who had greeted Ronan with such warmth. Would he be at his post still? Surely fate would not be so kind as to grant her a second miracle.

Good fortune followed her still. She saw that the guard was there—but fast asleep. It was a different man, a younger one with amber-colored hair and a face marked with a profusion of freckles. He was in a sitting position, propped up against the stone wall, his hand resting upon the hilt of the dagger sheathed at his waist.

Analise's eyes lit with mingled satisfaction and amazement. She held her breath and raised a hand to the latch, fervently praying that the door would not be locked.

It was not. Her fingers trembling, she eased the door open and cast one last glance down at the sleeping guard. He did not wake. She stepped carefully, slowly through the doorway. Emerging into the courtyard, she moved a goodly distance along the inner wall before pausing to release another sigh of relief.

"Now to the stables," she whispered. Her gaze swept the courtyard. She saw no one. But the barmkin, the last barrier remaining, rose before her. She felt her courage falter. Even if she managed to find a horse, how could she possibly get past the guard at the outer wall?

It was too much to hope that he, too, would be remiss in his duty. No matter, she told herself sternly. She would find a way.

Drawing her resolve about her once more, she scurried across the courtyard to begin her search for the stables.

Her eyes darted warily about as she wandered through the cluster of outbuildings. The cold night air was suffused with the smell of wood smoke. The faint bleating of sheep drifted on the gentle, mist-filled breeze. She inhaled deeply and continued toward the farthest corner of the grounds.

Finally her efforts were rewarded. Guided by the telltale scent, she flew inside the building of wood and stone. She allowed her instincts to lead her to one of the horses, and guided the snorting, dun-colored mare from its stall. Speaking soothingly to it, she looked for a saddle and bridle. But, realizing that she had little experience with such matters, she decided to settle for the bridle alone. Catching one up from a peg upon the wall, she slipped it over the mare's head and led it outside.

"Please," she murmured softly, praying now that the mount she had chosen would not prove too spirited. She gathered up her skirts again and, with some difficulty, managed to climb upon the horse's back. Though it whinnied in protest and pawed impatiently at the ground, it did not attempt to unseat her.

Holding the reins in a tight grip, she touched her heels gently to the horse's flanks and rode across the courtyard. Her body tensed as she neared the outer gate, her eyes falling upon the man who stood at attention beside it. He frowned and stepped forward at the sight of her.

"You cannot ride, my lady," he declared, making it clear that he was aware of her identity. Much taller and burlier than Lawrie, he looked entirely capable of stopping her. She lifted her head to a proud angle and fixed him with what she hoped was an imperious glare.

"Am I not the mistress of Dunslair?" she challenged haughtily.

"Aye. But the laird—"

"Awaits me but a short ride from here," she lied. Warming to the story that took root in her mind, she added, "My husband expects me to join him. He wanted none to know that I would accompany him to Edinburgh. Thus, the lateness of the hour."

"I was not told of this," the man grumbled, visibly wavering between disbelief and duty.

"If you doubt my words, you've only to seek confirmation from my husband's brother. He alone knows of the plan." She directed a look back at the tower house, then leaned forward to proclaim in a low, conspiratorial voice, "I am English. It was thought best that my journey remain a secret. My husband has many enemies who would break the alliance."

"I must speak to Calum." Still eyeing her dubiously, he asked, "Will you dismount and come with me, my lady?"

"No." She shook her head and announced, "I shall remain here."

Her reply threw him into a quandary. Unaccustomed to dealing with a woman of authority, and not at all certain how to respond to her demands, he could not deny his own suspicions about the situation. Still, he told himself, he dared not accuse her of speaking falsely. The laird would have his head for that. No, better to ask the young master.

"You will not leave until I return?" he demanded of Analise. He had to be satisfied with her silent nod of agreement. Though reluctant to abandon his post—even for a brief time—he finally chose his path and strode purposefully across the courtyard toward the house. Analise watched him until he had disappeared inside the first doorway.

She felt another twinge of guilt, but cast it aside. Aware that she had scant enough time, she quickly slid down and hastened to raise the smaller of the two gates. It required all of her strength to turn the wheel. Once the gate had been lifted, she looped the rope into place about the thick wooden stake and climbed upon the horse again. With her heart pounding, she urged the animal forward through the opening.

Once outside the wall, she hesitated, uncertain which way to go. She knew that Calum, once apprised of her escape, would ride after her. Yes, she told herself, but he would expect her to head south toward Beauford.

Cursing her unreliable sense of direction, she set what she hoped was an easterly course across the rugged, night-cloaked hills. She gathered the folds of her cloak more closely about her and urged the horse into a gallop. With Dunslair soon nothing but a speck in the distance, she found herself thinking of Ronan.

She would never see him again.

A sudden, unaccountable ache took hold of her heart. Both confused and dismayed by an acute feeling of loss, she bent lower over the horse's mane and endeavored to turn her thoughts to the impending audience with her guardian. But it was no use. Ronan's face swam before her eyes. Her ears burned with the memory of his voice. Her lips recalled too clearly the warmth and pleasure of his kisses . . .

She did not know how long she rode. Her backside soon enough regretted the lack of a saddle. And the cold mist stole beneath her cloak, making her shiver and wish she had donned another layer of clothing. She took little notice of the countryside, intent only upon enduring the journey and avoiding capture.

Venturing frequent, worried glances back over her shoulder, she wondered what Ronan's reaction would be when he discovered her gone. He would be furious, of course. Furious with Calum, who had been foolish enough to leave her unguarded, and furious with the watchman who had unwisely trusted her. His anger toward *her* would be fearsome, indeed . . . how fortunate that she would not be there to witness it.

No doubt, she mused with a curious lack of triumph, he would vow to bring her back. Yet would it be his sense of honor alone that suffered? Was it possible that he valued her as something other than the means to prevent bloodshed? If he had known *she* was to be his bride, would he have been any less reluctant to agree to the marriage?

The questions tumbled about in her mind, prompting her to mutter an oath and shift uncomfortably upon the mare's back again. Her eyes drifted toward the vast, starless horizon, then narrowed as they caught sight of what she soon realized were several horsemen bearing down upon her.

"Dear heaven, no!" she breathed in alarm. Incredulous to think that Calum had found her so quickly, she reined about and urged her mount into another gallop. But the group of riders, nine of them in all, had already spotted her. They gave chase, their horses' hooves thundering across the darkened moors.

The lead rider closed the distance in a matter of seconds. He skillfully maneuvered his horse close beside hers, and with remarkable ease, snatched her from the mare's back. She gave a sharp cry of outrage and struggled in the man's grip, heedless of the fact that she could fall and be trampled.

Her captor swiftly pulled his mount to a halt. He lowered her to her feet. She jerked the edges of her cloak together and swept her tumbling curls from her face. Her turquoise gaze, aflame with all manner of emotion, flew to the eight other riders who drew rein before her. She battled a fresh wave of panic and peered back up at the group's leader.

Her eyes widened in stunned disbelief. She took an instinctive step backward, her hand fluttering to her throat.

"You!" she gasped. Even in the darkness, she recognized the swarthy, coarse-featured man who had dared to accost her at the Truce Day. He wore the familiar garb of a Reiver.

"Ewan Maxwell at your service, my lady," he pronounced, swinging down from the saddle now.

If not for a hardness—indeed, a sense of cruelty—about him, she might have thought him handsome. His lips curled into a sneer, his dark, hawkish gaze traveling over her with such menace that she blanched.

"How is it an Englishwoman rides alone, at so late an hour and so far from the border?" he demanded.

"I—I am but returning home!" She folded her hands tightly together in front of her and sought to control her deepening fear. All too conscious of the eight other pairs of eyes fastened upon her, she offered up a silent, desperate prayer.

"By the Virgin's blood, I will have the truth!" snarled Ewan.

"I have given it!" Her whole body tensed as he stepped

closer and fixed her with a look that made her catch her breath in dismay.

"Who are you?"

"I am Lady Analise Hayward," she declared, fervently hoping that the truth would ensure her safety.

"Hayward?" His eyes narrowed, his features drawing together into a scowl. "You are from Beauford?"

"Yes." She lifted her head proudly and tried to keep her voice steady. "My guardian is Sir Simon Hayward."

"And your husband is Ronan Armstrong."

The color drained from her face again. She read the anger and hatred in the Scot's gaze, and feared that he meant to harm her. It occurred to her that he and his men had probably been on their way to raid across the border. They would not hesitate to add yet another crime to the list.

"I am—" she started to explain.

"You are a runaway bride," Ewan finished for her, with another faint smile of derision.

"If you will take me to Beauford, I will see you handsomely rewarded!"

"I will have my reward." He lifted a hand to finger one of the silken, honey-colored tresses that had escaped to fall across her cheek. "I will have it when your husband comes to ransom you." He drew his hand away and gripped the hilt of his sword, his expression growing deadly. "Aye, I have sworn revenge on Mac Ghillielaidir."

"No!" Analise cried in horror, her concern no longer for herself now, but for Ronan. "Please, sir, I implore you to consider—" She broke off with a gasp when his arm suddenly shot out to curl about her waist. He yanked her up hard against him.

"Was Armstrong not man enough to please you?" he

asked contemptuously, his face so close to hers that she shuddered in revulsion. "Married but a day, and already you would break your vows." His eyes glinted with lust. "If you were mine, I would keep you abed too often to think of escape."

"Let me go!" She struggled, but knew it was futile. She was completely at his mercy.

"Though I would tarry here," he told her huskily, "we must be away before the break of dawn." He drew his arm from her, yet maintained a secure grasp upon her wrist.

"Where are you taking me?"

"To Longcroft. The hold of the Maxwells."

While her pulse raced and her heart filled with trepidation, he pulled her along to where her horse, recovered by one of the other men, waited beside his own. He seized her about the waist and tossed her onto the mare's back.

"If you harbor but a spark of compassion toward Armstrong, my lady," he advised, taking obvious pleasure in her distress, "pray for his soul."

"You would do well to pray for your own, Ewan Maxwell!" she countered in a low, simmering tone. With far more bravado than she actually felt, she warned, "You know the measure of my husband. He will kill you for this." In truth, she did not doubt it ... if only Maxwell did not kill Ronan first. The thought caused her such pain that she had to close her eyes against it.

Smiling in malevolent satisfaction, Ewan swung up into his saddle and snatched up the reins of Analise's horse. He spurred his mount forward. The mare hung back for only a moment before obeying the tug on the reins. Close behind rode the other Reivers, none of whom had dared to interfere with their leader—though several of them wanted no part of his scheme. They, too, knew of Ronan Armstrong's strength and fierce, iron-willed character. He would swear revenge of his own. And the blood feud between the clans would flare once more.

Not yet fully aware of the terrible events she had set in motion, Analise clutched at the horse's mane and battled the faintness that threatened her. *Ronan.* His face swam before her eyes.

"Dear God, what have I done?" she whispered, a sob rising in her throat. Her eyes swept closed again as she felt a misery far beyond what she had ever known before.

The journey was mercifully short. Well before the first light crept over the land, the group reached Longcroft. They rode through the open gateway of the defensive wall and drew their mounts to a halt in the muddy, rock-strewn inner courtyard.

Analise gazed at the tower house rising so ominously before her. It was larger than Dunslair. But, whereas Ronan's home had been well kept through many generations of Armstrongs, the Maxwell hold suffered from visible neglect. The battlements were crumbling, the grounds were littered with refuse, and the air was heavy with the smell of the slops emptied day and night from the windows above.

She battled a new attack of fear and nausea. With an angry roughness, Ewan pulled her down from the mare's back. She offered little resistance when he led her through the entrance and into the house. Her legs threatened to give way beneath her, but she managed to keep her footing as she was forced up the steps to the topmost floor.

Finally she was thrust into a room that was cold and

damp and lit only by the flickering glow of a candle. A narrow bed sat in one corner. An ancient chair rested beneath the single, uncurtained window.

"You'll get bread and wine," Ewan told her gruffly, his eyes following her every move as she folded her arms across her breasts and turned her back upon him. "I'll order the fire to be lit. No doubt your English blood is too thin for Scotland. And I would keep you alive." He moved back to stand framed within the doorway. "But cause trouble," he warned, "and Armstrong will have naught save a corpse to warm his bed."

"He will make you pay for this!" she promised, rounding on him again. Her eyes were magnificently ablaze, her beautiful face flushed with anger. Ewan felt a renewed surge of lust. He began slowly advancing upon her.

"Dead men cannot seek vengeance."

Analise gazed at him in horrified disbelief. She backed away while stammering, "If you . . . if you dare to harm him, I will see you hanged! Indeed, I have little doubt that the others of his clan and even my guardian—"

"Simon Hayward would readily exchange *this* alliance for another," Ewan remarked with a gesture of disgust. "Aye, and the Armstrongs have been our sworn enemies for hundreds of years." A smile of malicious intent played about his lips as he drew closer. "It puzzles me, this concern for a husband you deserted. In truth, my lady, you would do well to look to your own peril."

He raised his hands to grip her shoulders. She jerked free and sped back toward the doorway.

"Touch me again, you loathsome, black-hearted swine, and I will kill you myself!" The threat was uttered with far more conviction that she actually felt. Was it possible that she could take a man's life?

" 'Tis time we finished the embrace Armstrong interrupted," decreed Ewan, his dark eyes filled with a hot, predatory gleam. He lunged for her, his hands once again reaching for her. She cried out sharply when he drew her against him. Certain that he would force more than a kiss upon her, she lifted her arm and brought her fingernails raking down across his face.

Biting out a curse, he shoved her away from him. She scrambled to the far corner of the room, holding her breath as she watched him lift a hand to where blood seeped from four narrow, ragged furrows in his cheek.

"Your blood will be the next to run!" he vowed, his face a mask of vengeful fury as he strode toward her. Panicked, she sought to flee the room. But he caught her, his arms tightening about her with such force that she was sure she would be crushed.

"Release her!"

Analise's startled, pain-filled gaze flew to the doorway. The man who stood there was very tall and broad-shouldered. His weathered features, and the gray hair streaming wildly down about his shoulders, gave evidence of his nearly sixty years upon the earth. Yet there was an air about him that was as strong and vibrant as that of a man half his age. Scowling across at Ewan, he stepped inside the room.

"Obey me," he urged grimly, "else draw your sword."

The threat sent a tremor of alarm coursing through Ewan. Though his expression remained both angry and mutinous, he released Analise and grumbled, "She is *my* prisoner, Angus. You have no right to interfere!"

"Am I not still the chieftain?" Angus Maxwell challenged. His eyes, so much like the younger man's, glittered hotly. "Aye, and will remain so long after you rest within your grave!"

"Were my father still alive," muttered Ewan, "you would not—"

"Guard your tongue, Nephew," Angus warned, his countenance dangerously solemn. "Someday, you will go too far."

Analise, watching from where she had fled behind the chair, shifted her bright gaze from one man to the other. She trembled at the look Ewan suddenly turned upon her.

"You will yet be repaid!" he swore. Flinging one last belligerent glare at his uncle, he pushed past him and strode from the room.

Angus turned to Analise and assured her quietly, " 'Tis not the custom of the Maxwells to make war upon women. None will insult you again, lass." He frowned at the sight of her noticeable weariness. For only an instant, his expression softened. "I will send a maidservant to tend you."

"Thank you," she murmured, her eyes falling beneath his. He left her alone then, closing the door behind him.

She released a long, ragged sigh and collapsed down upon the chair. Her nerves were still raw, and her body still ached from the ride as well as from Ewan Maxwell's brutal touch. Blinking back tears, she stared into the cold, blackened depths of the fireplace and allowed her thoughts to drift back over all that had happened.

The past four and twenty hours had been the most eventful and dramatic of her life. Married against her will. Forced to accompany her husband to Scotland. Subjected to a "rough wooing," as Calum had so appropriately termed it. And now imprisoned by an evil rogue who would see her made a widow.

Fate had proven itself more than capricious.

"Ronan," she whispered, her heart twisting anew. She knew that he would come for her—and in so doing would plunge himself into mortal danger. She told herself that the anguish she felt stemmed from nothing more than a sense of guilt, and from a compassion she would have demonstrated toward any other man.

Heaven help her, how could she bear it if she were the cause of his death? If only there were some way she could warn him. If only she had not run away . . .

The bargain has been struck. Strangely enough, she drew comfort from the memory of his words. She yearned for the feel of his strong, capable arms about her. And, in that moment, she would gladly have traded any chance at freedom to be back within the towering stone walls of Dunslair.

Chapter 6

Another night approached. Analise stood at the window, her eyes clouded with worriment, her stomach knotted with an awful anticipation.

The hours had crawled by with a merciless unhaste since her arrival at Longcroft. She had spent the day shut away within the shadowy confines of her prison, her solitude interrupted only by the silent maidservant who brought food and drink. She had eaten little. Her appetite had fled the night before—along with her peace of mind.

"I cannot bear much more of this waiting!" she lamented in an uneven whisper. Whirling about, she crossed back to stand before the fire. But its warmth failed to offer her any comfort. Her mind was filled with thoughts of Ronan . . . with thoughts of Ewan Maxwell's thirst for revenge.

Without warning, the door swung open. She started, her gaze kindling with a mixture of alarm and hostility as she watched her captor step into the room.

"May it please you to know, my lady," said Ewan, his mouth curling into a sinister smile, "your husband has arrived."

"Ronan is here?" she gasped, unable to believe that he had come so soon. Her pulse leapt wildly. Torn between a profound relief and a dismay that wrenched at her heart, she trembled and raised a hand to the chair beside her.

"Aye. He must value you greatly." His tone was full of derision. He moved closer, his eyes flickering hotly up and down the length of her. Even in her distress, she was beautiful. The soft emerald wool of her gown clung to her supple curves. Her long, honey-colored tresses had now been tamed within a plait. And the expression on her face was as proud and defiant as ever.

He scowled darkly, his blood fired anew at the memory of her lips beneath his. If not for the fear of his uncle's retribution, he would have taken her already. Soon enough, he promised himself, she would be his. He would kill her husband. And then he would make her beg for mercy.

The prospect was so pleasurable that he was tempted to claim a kiss beforehand. But he knew that Angus would become suspicious if they did not soon appear. And he was anxious to settle the score with Ronan Armstrong.

"By the morrow," he predicted, "you will call me master."

"Never!" she told him, shaking her head in a vehement denial.

"As a widow, you will need 'comfort.' " He smiled as her eyes filled with horrified disbelief.

"You cannot truly mean to—"

"Ronan Armstrong thinks to take his bride from Longcroft. But he comes to meet his death."

"No!" A violent tremor shook her.

"Come," Ewan ordered tersely, moving forward to seize her arm.

"Do not touch me!" she cried. Instinctively struggling,

she suffered a sharp intake of breath when his hand moved to cup her chin.

"Hold your tongue," he bade her in a voice laced with mingled desire and contempt. *"Or I will cut it out."*

She paled at the sound of his threat. He yanked her roughly over to the doorway and out of the room. She offered no further protest as he led her down the steps. Her throat constricted with dread as they approached the main hall, and she briefly closed her eyes to offer up another desperate prayer—for Ronan's deliverance as well as her own.

Ewan pulled her into a cavernous room that was ablaze with the light of a dozen torches. In spite of the fire crackling and hissing beyond the stone hearth, the cold and damp had taken hold. The air was filled with a palpable tension. A group of six men stood assembled in front of the fireplace. Angus Maxwell and five others of his clan. Their features were quite grave. Their gazes, dark and steady, fastened upon Analise.

She felt her legs weaken. Then, gathering her courage about her, she pulled away from Ewan and swept forward. Her eyes searched for Ronan.

She drew up short at the sight of him. Her breath caught in her throat. And her heart turned over within her breast.

He stood silent and grim-faced a short distance away from the other men, looking entirely like the powerful, battle-hardened warrior he was. His eyes glowed hotly when they met hers—whether with anger or joy (or both), she could not tell. Yet never in the entirety of her life had she been so glad to see someone.

He had come for her. Her wide, luminous gaze remained fixed upon him for several long moments. She longed to race across the room and cast herself upon his chest, to feel his strong arms closing about her.

She knew that he would rescue her. Or die in the attempt.

Shuddering at the memory of Ewan's threats, she now saw that Calum stood in the shadows just beyond his brother. He, too, appeared ready to fight.

She cast a swift, wary glance toward the Maxwells. Ewan had crossed to stand beside his uncle. His hand was resting upon the hilt of his sword.

Paling anew, she stiffened. Her gaze flew back to Ronan.

"It is a trap!" she warned, her voice sharp with fear. "They mean to—"

"What foolishness is that?" demanded Angus. He scowled darkly at her.

" 'Tis true!" Analise exclaimed. She gathered up her skirts and hastened forward to appeal. "You must listen to me. Your nephew has sworn to murder him this day!" She came to a halt directly before Angus, her eyes glistening with sudden tears. "He has come in peace. Would you dishonor yourselves and betray his trust?"

"The woman is *glaikit*," Ewan remarked scornfully. In truth, he had expected her warning. "She was wearied by the journey and does not yet think clearly."

"Do you call her a liar, then, Ewan Maxwell?" Ronan challenged in a voice of deadly calm. His eyes gleamed with both rage and suspicion as he took note of the marks upon the man's face. Slowly and purposefully, he began advancing upon Ewan. "If you have dared to touch her, I will kill you."

"Perhaps your bride has not been so unwilling a

captive," Ewan taunted, mistakenly believing that it was safe to do so.

Ronan's eyes darkened. With lightning swiftness he closed the distance between himself and Ewan, and pulled his sword from its sheath. He pressed the point of the blade to Ewan's throat.

"Hold fast, man!" thundered Angus. When the other Maxwells would have drawn their swords as well, he shook his head and ordered them to keep back. Calum, meanwhile, edged closer to where his brother stood battling the urge to run Ewan through.

Wide-eyed and breathless, Analise looked to her husband. She knew that if he killed Ewan, his own death would be a certainty.

"Please, Ronan, *do not!*" she implored him, moving to his side. She placed a hand upon his arm and insisted, "He has done me no harm!"

Ronan's furious, smoldering gaze shifted to her face. She felt her heart give another wild flutter.

"Truly, I am uninjured," she reiterated. Her fingers tightened about his arm, her eyes holding a desperate plea for reason.

Finally he relented. Stepping away from Ewan, he sheathed his sword. He startled Analise by briefly lifting a hand to the smoothness of her cheek. She shivered, her breath catching in her throat again as she watched him turn back to confront Angus.

"We are well acquainted with one another, Angus Maxwell. Aye, were you not once a friend to my father?" His gaze burned with a bitter reproach, and his tone grew harsh. "Though there is a blood feud between our two clans, it has been a long time since the peace was broken.

You have offered me an insult I cannot ignore. Why have you done so?"

" 'Twas none of my doing," the older man proclaimed, frowning as he shook his head. "Ewan must answer for his own misdeeds." He folded his arms across his chest and charged, "But what of the bargain you have made with the English warden? Was that not an act of treason?"

"No. I did not seek the alliance." His eyes strayed back to Analise. "Yet I cannot regret it."

"Can you not?" Angus parried angrily. "By the Virgin's blood, Armstrong, have you forgotten that marriage to one of the English can mean a sentence of death?"

Analise gasped, her eyes flying to Calum. He gave her a faint smile of reassurance.

"I have not," Ronan answered.

"Mayhap he considers the risk worth it," one of the Maxwells near the fire suggested.

"Aye," said another, with a mocking smile. "Those of us who would claim wives so becoming as *his* should make for the border this very night."

"Silence!" Angus ground out. His brow creasing into another deep frown, he told Ronan, "I will not press for any punishment. The law has been called upon seldom enough these many years past. But I must have your word that you will never use the alliance against us—that you will never gather the English to ride upon Longcroft."

"I do swear it." His features tightened with a grim determination once more. "Still, my wife must be avenged."

"Aye," Angus concurred, his gaze moving to his

nephew. "You must settle the matter between the two of you alone."

"You would trust the word of an Armstrong?" Ewan demanded resentfully. "Will you not stand with me?" He sliced a malevolent glare toward Ronan and fought against his rising fear. "I have done naught save avenge *myself* for the many insults I have suffered at his hands!"

"Indeed?" murmured Angus, his loyalty once again put to the test. For too long, his nephew had stirred up trouble throughout the Borders. He knew that Analise had spoken the truth—Ewan would have killed Ronan, probably in an ambush once beyond the gates of Longcroft. And if he had succeeded, many from both clans would have died. "If that be so," he concluded soberly, "then you will be glad of this chance to settle the score."

"You know I cannot fight him alone!" protested Ewan, panic bringing his cowardice to the fore. His eyes darted anxiously to Ronan again. "None have ever bested him in combat!"

"Should you not have thought of that before carrying his wife here?" one of his own cousins put forth.

"I tell you, the woman was running away when I came upon her!" he argued in his own defense.

"Aye, but the right to stop her was not yours," Angus pointed out. "Though you be of my own blood, I am ashamed to call you kinsman." He muttered a curse, his voice edged with contempt when he denounced, "Weak-livered fool! Did you think I would let you kill the man and steal his wife?"

Ewan offered no immediate reply. Nothing had gone the way he had anticipated. *Nothing.* He recognized the defeat bearing down upon him. For a moment he considered making an attempt to seize Analise and thereby force Ronan to surrender his weapon. But he sensed that, for now at least, his best hope lay in retreat.

"It has come to this, then?" he accused Angus, his body tensing in readiness. "You would see a Maxwell cast upon whatever mercy an Armstrong chooses to give?"

"I would see you behave like a man."

"Someday, Uncle, I will have the pleasure of cutting your throat!" he vowed. Seizing his opportunity, he spun about and fled toward the stairwell. Three of the Maxwells started after him.

"Let him go!" Angus commanded, halting the chase. His voice held a weary resignation when he decreed, "He is a Maxwell no more." At a signal from him, his men left the room.

Relief flooded Analise. She felt the warmth of Ronan's hand slipping about hers. Looking up at him, she was surprised, and confused, by what she saw. Though the expression on his face was inscrutable, his deep blue eyes were aglow with a mixture of tenderness and desire—and something else she could not put a name to.

"There will be an end to this now," sighed Angus, a shadow crossing his swarthy, weathered visage. "The ransom has been paid."

"It cannot end," said Ronan, "for I must yet claim the debt Ewan owes me."

"Aye." The older man turned his dark, penetrating gaze upon Calum now. "Did I not forbid you to come again to Longcroft, Calum Armstrong?" he demanded gruffly.

"That you did, Angus Maxwell," Calum replied, his own voice low and level. His eyes met Angus's squarely.

"But, since it was my negligence that led to this, I would repay my brother. With my life, should the need arise."

"It does not surprise me to hear that *you* are to blame," Angus muttered, leaving little doubt of his opinion. "Were you but half the man your brother is, I would not be so opposed to the match you desire."

Calum's eyes flashed, his countenance growing angry. He shook his head and stepped closer to Angus.

"I am not my brother. Nor will I ever be. Yet I am no less worthy of your daughter's hand."

"You are young and ill equipped for marriage."

"Why not allow Dierdre to decide for herself?"

"I will not see her wed to a man who cannot keep his breeches about his backside!" snapped Angus. He glowered at Calum, his face reddening. "Aye, you would remain faithful for no more than a fortnight. Are your rutting ways not well-known?"

"Well-known. Yet greatly exaggerated."

"Exaggerated?" His eyes narrowed. "The truth, then, boy. How many bastards have you fathered—on *both* sides of the border?"

"None," Calum answered in all honesty. "And if you will but give me the chance, I will prove myself constant."

"What do you say of this?" Angus demanded of Ronan now. "Do you share your brother's high opinion of himself?"

" 'Tis true he is young," Ronan allowed. His eyes met Calum's. "But if Dierdre holds his heart, I have little doubt that he will be calmed."

"You speak from experience, do you?" the older man asked, his own gaze lighting with a trace of wry amusement as it moved to Analise.

"Perhaps."

"Aye. Perhaps." He turned back to Calum and released another heavy sigh before telling him, "Even if I were to offer my blessing for the match, there are those who would not see a Maxwell given to an Armstrong. The blood feud is long-standing. And though our clans have fallen into an uneasy peace of late, a marriage such as this would only stir the troubles again."

"But would it not serve peace if—"

"No," Angus cut him off. "She must wed none save a Maxwell."

"How can she do so?" said Calum, his voice full of pain. "From the time we were children, we have been pledged to one another."

"You had no right to make the pledge."

"You cannot keep us apart!"

"By damn, I am her father and will do as I please!" Angus bellowed, then shook his head and said more calmly, "I will hear no more upon the matter, Calum Armstrong. Dierdre is not for you."

Calum's mouth tightened into a thin line of anger, his eyes ablaze. He gave Angus a curt, silent nod, then strode from the room.

"He loves the girl, Angus," Ronan attested. Beside him, Analise felt heartsick on his brother's behalf. She was not yet well acquainted with Calum, yet she had been able to sense the depth of his pain.

"He will recover," contended Angus. He wandered back to stand before the fire. "Does the king yet know of your marriage?"

"Aye. I had been in Edinburgh but a short time before I made for Longcroft." He did not add that, when he returned to complete his audience with the king, he would take his errant bride with him. His hand tightened about hers. She raised her eyes to his and felt her pulse quicken anew.

"No doubt the English queen will take pleasure in the news of this well-favored union," Angus remarked dryly, staring into the flames. He murmured something underneath his breath. When he looked to Ronan again, it was clear that he was of a mind to put an end to the meeting. "Away with you," he directed. "Take your wife and go home."

"Farewell, Maxwell," Ronan bade him quietly.

"Farewell, Armstrong."

Analise cast the man a look of gratitude as Ronan led her from the room. Still shaken by the ordeal, she was glad for her husband's hand about her arm. She knew that she would have to face his wrath once they were back at Dunslair, but at that moment she did not care.

Yet I cannot regret it. Her body filled with an inexplicable warmth at the memory of his words. She stumbled upon one of the stone steps. Ronan's arm was about her waist in an instant. She gasped softly and opened her mouth to thank him, only to fall silent at the look in his eyes. He said nothing before guiding her onward.

At that same moment, Calum was in the midst of a secret rendezvous with Dierdre Maxwell. He pressed her farther back into the shadows of the courtyard, his tone urgent and his arms tightening about the woman he had sworn to make his own.

"An elopement is the only way," he decreed.

"An elopement?" Dierdre echoed, her green eyes round with surprise. A full head shorter than Calum, she was a pretty girl, not yet twenty, with thick raven locks and a sweet yet spirited disposition. She had loved

Calum Armstrong her whole life. Yet how could she defy her father?

"Angus will never grant us permission to wed," Calum told her, then ground out the oath. " 'Tis my own fault! If not for—"

"No, Calum," Dierdre was quick to disagree. "Were you a saint, his decision would remain as it is now."

"To be sure, I am no saint." His eyes glowed irrepressibly while a crooked grin spread across his face.

"Nor would I wish you to be." She pulled his head down to hers and kissed him. They swayed against one another, their passion flaring and their hearts soaring. Finally Calum forced himself to put an end to the delectable torment.

"I must go," he whispered hoarsely.

"Aye." Flushed and breathless, she gave him a smile that made him yearn even more for the day when she would be his. "I will be in Jedburgh at the week's end, at the house of my mother's sister."

"Then, I will ride to Jedburgh." He could not resist the temptation to claim her lips in one last, wondrously intoxicating kiss. And when he let her go, his eyes gleamed hotly down into hers. "Until week's end," he promised.

"Aye, my love." She watched as he strode away, toward the front of the house. With his kiss still burning upon her mouth, she gathered up her skirts and hurried back inside the house.

Ronan had already swung up into the saddle when he took note of Calum's approach. He frowned, for he knew what his younger brother had been about.

"Take care," he cautioned solemnly. "Else Angus will have your head."

"My gratitude for your advice, Brother," Calum replied, mounting his own horse. "But I believe you ill-qualified to speak of avoiding risks worth taking."

Ronan's only response was to smile faintly. He reached down for Analise and, with masterful ease, pulled her up behind him. She settled herself upon the horse's back, and was acutely conscious of her husband's warm, hard-muscled body before her.

"Did you truly have to pay a ransom?" she suddenly thought to ask, cursing the telltale unsteadiness of her voice.

" 'Tis the custom." He tightened his grip upon the reins and instructed her to place her arms about his waist before adding, "And the reason we must ride double."

"What do you mean?"

"The mare that carried you to Longcroft was part of the payment."

"I . . . I am sorry. Someday, I shall repay you."

"Aye." He tensed at the feel of her breasts pressing against his back. With his eyes darkening, he urged his horse forward. Calum was close behind as they rode through the gate.

By the time they reached Dunslair, the moon had broken through the clouds to cast its rare—and some would say magical—glow upon the land. Analise stifled a groan when Ronan pulled her down from the horse. She ached all over, and the soreness of her bottom gave evidence of the discomfort she had endured these past three nights. Fervently wishing she could remain afoot for the rest of her life, she caught her lower lip between her teeth and made her way slowly toward the house.

Leaving Calum to see to the horses, Ronan caught up with her. Fury still simmered within him, yet he felt a twinge of sympathy nonetheless. Just as he had done on their wedding night, he swept her up in his arms and bore her inside.

"A hot bath will ease your pain," he said. His low, vibrant tone sent a pleasurable shiver down her spine.

"I am little accustomed to riding," she murmured, content to rest within his arms.

"You will get used to it soon enough." He said nothing more as he carried her up the stairs to the topmost floor. Setting her down at last, he opened the door to her bedchamber and led the way inside.

She moved past him to stand before the fire while he closed the door. Feeling guilty and ill at ease, she took a deep, steadying breath and crossed her arms beneath her breasts.

"I know you are angry with me," she began in a small voice. "I—it was not my intent to cause trouble. Yet I told you I would not remain at Dunslair!" Whirling about to face him, she inhaled sharply at the expression on his face.

"Were your backside not already burning," he avowed with deceptive calm, "I would turn you across my knee."

"How dare you!" she breathed indignantly. Hot color flew to her cheeks. "I am not a child!"

"Damn it, woman, did I not command you to stay?" His rugged features grew taut with the effort it was costing him to keep his temper in check. "Rest assured, the ease of your escape did not go unnoticed. My brother has been made aware of his negligence. And the others as well."

"Truly, it was not their fault!" she hastened to proclaim. "I employed dishonesty, and—"

"Do you not realize what could have happened?" he

ground out, his blood boiling at the memory of Ewan Maxwell's hand upon her. "The Maxwells have long been enemy to the Armstrongs. Old Angus, for all his turn to peace this day, might well have chosen to support his nephew's treachery. He has done so often enough in the past. Thanks be to God his mind was not upon revenge. If it had been, you might now be the widow Ewan desired you to be!"

"I did not think . . ." Her voice trailed away as she dropped her gaze toward the flames again. Ronan's eyes traveled hotly over her. When he had received news of her capture, his heart had twisted as never before. He had feared for her safety alone. The thought of her in the clutches of the Maxwells had filled him with a murderous rage. And had caused him more pain than he would have thought possible.

"If you had come to harm—" he muttered, only to break off and clench his teeth. When he spoke again, it was half to himself. "I am certain Ewan would have done his worst."

"My death would have given you your freedom," Analise pointed out in a tone that was scarcely more than a whisper. The firelight played over her face, setting her bright hair aglow and deepening the remorseful, blue-green luminescence of her gaze. "You would not have been blamed for it. The alliance would have remained unbroken."

"By heaven, do you truly believe I would take pleasure in your death?" He closed the distance between them in two long strides, his eyes kindling with renewed fury as he towered above her. She gasped in alarm and instinctively retreated a step, but his hands shot out to close about her shoulders. "You little fool!" he said, his deep-timbred voice raw with emotion. "Do you understand nothing?"

"What is there to understand?" She swallowed a sudden lump in her throat and tried desperately to ignore the way her whole body warmed at his nearness. "You married me against your will. No doubt you hoped to install someone else as mistress of Dunslair."

" 'Tis true that I did not seek the marriage," he conceded. "But I did not know *you* were to be my bride." He frowned and drew her closer. "There are no others I would have wed."

"Perhaps not," she replied, her hands trembling as she raised them to his chest and battled a wave of lightheadedness. "But what does it matter? You do not wish to be a husband. And I do not wish to be a wife."

"Yet fate has willed it so."

"Then, we must defy fate!"

"No, Analise."

"I cannot stay!"

"You can and will."

"You have no right to—"

"I have every right."

With an oath, he swept her up against him. She tried to pull free, and trembled while offering up a weak, breathless protest. But it was no use. This time, his determination was too strong to resist.

Anger helped to fuel a long-simmering passion, a passion sparked the first time he had held her in his arms. Pride be damned, he told himself. *He could wait no longer.*

He kissed her deeply and ardently and with such skill that her blood became like liquid fire within her veins. And then, while she felt herself torn between defiance and surrender, he scooped her up in his arms and carried her to the bed.

"No!" she gasped, a fiery blush stealing up to her face when she realized what he meant to do. Panicking, she renewed her struggles with a vengeance. "I will not allow you to . . . sweet mercy, you seek to punish me! If you think that by this *villainy* you will somehow lessen my intent to leave, then you are most grievously in error!"

"You know little of men," he parried, his voice low and resonant, his gaze full of an intoxicating mixture of tenderness and desire. He placed her upon the bed. She rolled to her side in a desperate attempt to flee, but he drew her back and lowered his own body atop hers. Seizing her wrists, he pulled her arms above her head.

"The devil take you, Ronan Armstrong!" she cried furiously, all too conscious of the heat and virility of his powerful, hard-muscled body as she writhed beneath him. "Are you so lost to decency that you would force yourself upon me?"

"You are my wife, Analise." His eyes bored relentlessly down into the wide, stormy brilliance of hers. " 'Tis time you were made to know it."

"I will never be yours!"

"Aye." He gave her a look that struck a chord of fear deep in her heart—and sent another secretly pleasurable shiver dancing down her spine. *"You will."*

With that whispered promise, he set about the belated, oft-anticipated seduction at last. Everything happened so quickly . . . there was no time to resist, no time to appeal to reason or heed the emphatic warnings of her conscience.

There was only Ronan. Only this tall, devilishly handsome Scot who could set her aflame with his very touch.

His lips descended upon the parted softness of hers once more, his hot, velvety tongue plunging within the moist cavern of her mouth. A moan rose in her throat, and she felt her head spinning. He released her wrists. Her arms came down about his neck. She began to return his kiss with an innocent fervor, her own passion spiraling upward to meet his.

His hand moved to the front of her gown. Impatiently he loosed the lacings there, swept the edges of her bodice aside, and tugged the neckline of her chemise lower. She gasped against his mouth when his hand closed upon her naked breast. His fingers caressed her with a hunger and boldness that made her tremble anew. Branded by his touch, she strained instinctively upward beneath him.

And then his mouth left hers, trailing fierily downward to where her full, creamy breasts rose and fell with each shuddering breath she took. His lips closed about one of the satiny globes, sucking gently, while the wet heat of his tongue swirled about the delicate peak. Analise bit at her lower lip, assaulted by so much rapture and longing that her fingers curled almost convulsively about his arms.

His own desire flaring hotter and hotter, Ronan entangled his hand within the skirt of her woolen gown and drew it upward. Analise gasped at the rush of air upon her feverish skin, and she squirmed in protest. But Ronan would not be denied. His hand swept downward, smoothing over the firm, saucy roundness of her naked hips before moving purposefully to the triangle of soft golden hair at the apex of her thighs.

"No!" she breathed, her eyes flying wide in shock. She pushed at him, painfully aware now just how close disaster lay.

It was already too late, of course. Disregarding her objections, Ronan caught her lips with his again. He kissed her until she was quivering and near to begging for mercy. His warm, knowing fingers insinuated themselves within the silken flesh between her thighs, claiming the tiny bud of her femininity.

She suffered a sharp intake of breath, another low moan rising in her throat. White-hot pleasure, more intense than she had ever known, streaked through her. She squirmed anew, her slender thighs parting wider of their own accord as Ronan stroked her with a mastery and tenderness that left her breathless. Desire built to a fever pitch within her. Dear heaven, she was sure she would go mad with it . . .

Finally Ronan himself could bear no more. He raised his head and unfastened his breeches. His hand delved beneath Analise's hips, lifting her slightly. She opened her eyes, and shivered at the look he gave her.

"You are mine," he vowed huskily.

Though he would have been gentle, he burned to possess her. He eased himself forward. His eyes glowed with delight when he felt the barrier of her maidenhood—she was an innocent, after all.

He could hold back no longer. Analise grasped at his arms, a sharp cry breaking from her lips when his manhood plunged within her virgin softness.

Her eyes clouded with remorse, only to sweep closed as the pain quickly gave way to passion once more. Ronan's hips masterfully tutored hers, his thrusts growing deeper and more demanding. She felt her senses reeling, felt a yearning so acute that she feared she would be consumed by it . . .

Then *fulfillment.* She cried out softly as pleasure exploded within her. The sensation was unlike anything she had ever known before. Every inch of her flesh tingled, while her heart soared heavenward.

In the next instant Ronan tensed above her, flooding her with the liquid warmth of his seed. She gave another gasp, and struggled to regain control of her breathing while he rolled to his side in the bed, pulling her close.

Stunned by what had taken place, she lay pliant and still against him for several long moments. She was filled with a profound sense of contentment. And she was conscious of Ronan's heart beating strong and steady beneath her cheek as she rested her head upon his chest.

But then her conscience sprang to life again. Guilt washed over her. How could she have been so weak and foolish?

Groaning inwardly, she pushed away from Ronan and scrambled from the bed. He watched as she snatched the edges of her bodice together and hastily smoothed her skirts down into place.

"This will make no difference!" she asserted, her proud, indignant manner in stark contrast to the dishevelment of her appearance.

"Has it not already done so?" He climbed from the bed and fastened his breeches. His eyes, glowing with triumph, traveled possessively up and down the length of her.

Her color deepened. She wanted to strike him. Instead she took refuge in her anger.

"You arrogant, ill-mannered scoundrel!" she fumed, her gaze full of fire. "No doubt you are pleased with your . . . your *ravishment*!"

"Aye," he admitted, thoroughly unrepentant. "And so are you."

She gasped, bitter tears starting to her eyes as he drew

closer. It was impossible for her to ignore the way his proximity affected her. Confused and angry and still plagued by a lingering satisfaction, she glared resentfully up at him.

"How I hate you," she declared in a low, tremulous voice.

"Hate me if you will." His expression grew quite solemn, and his eyes held a foreboding gleam when he cautioned, "But know that you belong to me now."

"You do not own me, Ronan Armstrong!"

"Do I not?" He caught her roughly against him, his mouth crashing down upon hers. She struggled in his embrace, but his arms tightened about her while the kiss sent passion thundering through the both of them once more. When he reluctantly set her away from him, he frowned and told her, "Were I the barbarian it pleases you to think me, I would take you again now."

She suffered another sharp intake of breath. Her eyes grew very round, her pulse leaping in alarm. She gripped the edges of her bodice more tightly and retreated toward the fireplace.

"If you dare to try—"

"The hour grows late." He turned and crossed to the door. Opening it, he paused to offer softly, "Sleep well, Analise."

His voice made her heart flutter. Speechless, she watched as he left. A sudden lump rose in her throat. Her emotions tumbled into utter chaos.

Moving back to the bed, she sank down upon the rumpled linens and closed her eyes. "Heaven help me, what have I done?" she whispered brokenly. With a ragged sigh, she turned and lay down upon the mattress, burying her face in the pillow.

The truth, however, was unavoidable. In every sense of the word now, she was Ronan Armstrong's wife. She knew that his determination to keep her would be even stronger than before—and that it was only a matter of time before he exercised his husbandly rights again.

Hot color flew to her cheeks, while at the same time a tremor of excitement shot through her. She cursed her own weakness. But no matter how hard she tried, she could not deny how much Ronan's fierce, wickedly capable lovemaking had pleasured her. It occurred to her that he possessed a great deal of experience in such matters. Indeed, she told herself, he had probably gained the knowledge through an "acquaintance" with a goodly number of women on both sides of the border.

The thought filled her with an inordinate amount of displeasure. Rolling abruptly to her side, she allowed her troubled gaze to drift toward the window. Yet it was Ronan's face she saw. It was Ronan's kisses and caresses that still burned upon her skin . . . and made sleep impossible until long after moonlight had faded.

Chapter 7

She awoke to the sound of voices in the courtyard below. Her eyelids fluttered open, and she saw that the room was filled with the soft gray light of morning. After stretching languidly, she flung back the covers and climbed from the bed.

"Sweet mercy!" she gasped, catching her breath at the unexpected stiffness of her muscles. She ached in places she hadn't even known to exist before. Realizing that the telltale soreness had less to do with the ride home from Longcroft than with what had happened afterward, she gave a low groan and folded her arms beneath her breasts.

The embers glowing within the fireplace offered her little warmth, but she drew near to them and wondered when she would see Ronan again. Her dreams had taunted her with memories of his lovemaking. And, in truth, her body still warmed whenever she thought of it.

"Have you become a strumpet, then?" she murmured in self-deprecation, still smarting from her own lack of control. She shivered and hurried to exchange her thin chemise for more substantial attire.

"My lady?" she heard Mairi calling from the other side of the door now. A knock followed. "Are you awake?"

"Yes," she replied, catching up the quilt from the bed and flinging it about her shoulders. "Come in." She had not bolted the door; what good would it have done?

Mairi opened the door and paused just beyond the threshold. Her eyes held both amusement and curiosity—yet no true rancor—as they flickered over Analise.

"Are you not cold?" she asked.

"A bit," Analise admitted. A faint blush crept up to her face. She pulled the quilt more securely about her and looked toward the fireplace again.

"Then, you will be glad of a hot bath."

"I shall, indeed." She had hoped to enjoy the benefits of a bath the previous night . . . there was even more need of one now.

"Aye," said Mairi, a mischievous smile playing about her lips. "It awaits you in the laird's bedchamber."

"In the laird's bedchamber?" She frowned in puzzlement. "Why have you—"

"Lord Ronan says you are to share his quarters now."

"*What?*" Puzzlement turned to shocked disbelief. She shook her head while her pulse leapt alarmingly. "He cannot force me to such a thing!"

"Are you not his wife?" Mairi pointed out, gaining a certain, perverse satisfaction from Analise's distress. "I know little of the ways between men and women in England, but in Scotland, 'tis the custom for married folk to sleep in the same bed."

"I will not . . . " Analise breathed, her voice trailing away at the memory of Ronan's triumph. *You are mine.* Dear heaven, she fumed inwardly, did he think that because he had taken her virginity she would now become docile and submissive, that she would so easily bend to his will? The thought provoked a torrent of indignation within her, and made her eyes blaze vengefully once more.

"Your bath grows cold, my lady."

Her fiery gaze shot back to Mairi. "Very well," she declared, for the moment accepting the inevitable. Once she had bathed and donned a fresh gown, she would be ready to do battle with her husband. "I must first dress and gather my things."

"I will bring them," offered Mairi. "And there's little need of getting dressed. None will see you. Lord Ronan and Master Calum have gone riding." She smiled before directing, "Your husband's bedchamber is on the floor below, the first along the corridor. I have left the door ajar. You cannot mistake it."

"Thank you," Analise murmured. She hastened from the room and down the hallway to the staircase, casting a wary glance over her shoulder to make certain she was seen by no one. When she reached the fourth floor, she had no difficulty finding the bedchamber Mairi had indicated. She held her breath as she stepped inside.

Her eyes grew very wide as they traveled about the room. It was nothing at all like she had imagined—warm and comfortable and undeniably masculine, it spoke well of its occupant.

The first thing to catch her notice was a massive, carved mahogany bed. Hung with heavy, dark red brocade curtains, it dominated the room. Tapestries covered the walls. Thick carpets were spread across the floor. A great wooden chest sat at the foot of the bed, while a table and two chairs had been pulled into place beneath the single, multipaned window. On the wall opposite the bed was the fireplace, almost as large as the one in the baronial hall. Steam rose from the bathtub waiting in front of the fire. Several shelves stretched on either side of the rough-hewn mantelpiece. Each was lined with books.

"He is an educated man?" Analise whispered to herself in surprise. It was difficult to envision him as a child, learning his letters and subjecting himself to the whims of a tutor. Had he been as proud and overbearing as a young man? Had he known the love and tenderness of a mother?

Frowning, she closed the door now and drew the quilt from about her. Tossing it to land atop the bed, she glanced anxiously toward the door one last time and pulled off her chemise.

She lowered herself into the bathtub, her eyes sweeping closed as the hot, soothing liquid swirled about her aching body. Moments later she took up the cake of soap and began to wash. Desperate to remove all traces of Ronan's possession, she scrubbed at her skin so hard that it glowed hotly. Then she loosened her braid. The long honey-gold locks cascaded down about her face and shoulders, darkening as they tumbled into the water. She closed her eyes again and slid farther down into the tub.

Without warning the door swung open.

Analise gave a soft cry, her eyes flying wide. She looked to where Ronan stood framed within the doorway.

"How dare you!" she stormed, furious at his presumption. "Get out!"

He said nothing, but a faint smile touched his lips as he closed the door and crossed to the bed. His hair was still damp from a bath in the cold waters of the nearby river, and he smelled pleasantly of leather and soap. He spared

Analise what seemed to be only a passing glance before he took a seat and began tugging off his boots.

"Will you not allow me to finish, sir?" she demanded, shivering in spite of the water's warmth.

Still silent, he stood again and drew off his jack, allowing it to fall to the floor. His shirt had soon joined it.

"Wha . . . what are you doing?" stammered Analise, her startled gaze traveling over his naked chest. His arms were hard and sinewy, the smoothness of his broad chest marked only by a jagged scar below his collarbone.

She swallowed hard and felt her heart pound in both alarm and excitement as she watched him unfasten his breeches.

"I thought you gone!" she accused in a highly unsteady tone. "Why have—" She broke off, her breath catching in her throat when he removed his breeches.

Though she would have looked away, she could not. Her eyes filled with wonderment as they took in the sight of his nakedness. She had never seen a man unclothed before. Yet she knew that *this* man was magnificent. There was not an ounce of fat on his body. A trim waist tapered down into narrow yet slightly rounded hips. His thighs were lean and rock-hard, his legs long and muscular. But it was the evidence of his arousal, springing from the cluster of tight curls between his thighs, that made her tremble.

There was little doubt what he intended. With a whispered oath, she climbed from the tub and snatched up the length of toweling beside it. She draped it across her body, leaving a trail of water as she raced for the doorway.

Ronan was upon her in an instant. He seized her arm, whirled her about, and gathered her close.

"No!" she cried in protest, struggling against herself as well as him. "Why, 'tis broad daylight!"

"Aye. And I would see what manner of woman I have married." She gasped when he yanked the towel free. His burning gaze raked over her with a boldness and intimacy that made her head spin. While she sought to cover her breasts, he pulled her down with him to the carpet before the fire.

"Let me go!" she choked out.

"Never." He captured her lips with the firm, compelling warmth of his and kissed her until very nearly all thought of resistance had fled. The next thing she knew, she was being turned facedown upon the soft woolen carpet. She gasped, her face flaming when Ronan's mouth roamed hot and wet over the well-rounded curve of her bottom.

"Stop!" she breathed, trying to rise. But he pushed her down once more and continued with the embarrassing yet wickedly pleasurable tribute. She squirmed restlessly, her fingers curling about the edge of the carpet.

When he urged her onto her back again, his lips trailed upward along the inside of her thigh. She shuddered and pushed at his shoulders. He relented—for the moment—and transferred his sweetly savage attentions to her breasts. His mouth teased and devoured. She arched her back, unable to suppress a moan.

And then his strong hands were about her thighs, impatiently spreading them apart while his head lowered to the soft, silky triangle of golden curls.

"Ronan!" Her eyes widened with shock when his mouth touched her *there.* She tried again to rise, tried to close her thighs against this most intimate, sinful caress, but he held fast.

He showed her no mercy. She closed her eyes tightly and threaded her fingers within the damp, rich-hued thickness of his hair. Passion flared so hotly within her that she forgot all else. Her thighs spread even wider of their own accord, her hips straining instinctively upward while Ronan seduced her with a hell-bent determination.

Her soft cries, her gasps and moans, fueled his own blazing passion. Finally he could bear no more. He raised his head. Analise's eyelids fluttered open. She trembled at the look on his face. His gaze burning down into hers, he slipped his hands beneath her hips. He thrust forward, his pulsing hardness sheathing to perfection within the moist, velvety warmth of her feminine passage.

"Sweet heaven!" she exclaimed in a hoarse whisper. She met his thrusts eagerly, her eyes sweeping closed again as her legs entwined about his hips. Desire, near painful in its intensity, raced like lightning throughout her body. She grasped at Ronan's shoulders. Her head spun, her senses reeled . . . and all the while Ronan loved her fiercely.

She gave a sharp, strangled cry, her nails digging into the hard-muscled expanse of his back when ecstasy, deep and heart-turning, shook her very soul. Ronan took his own pleasure in the next moment. With a low groan he tensed and filled her with another forceful, dizzying burst of warmth.

Several long seconds passed. Analise, breathless and trembling with wonderment, finally stirred beneath Ronan. He reluctantly left her, rising to his feet and gazing down at her with such steady regard that she blushed. He offered her his hand, but she would not take it. She climbed to her feet now as well, her wet hair streaming wildly about her as she retrieved the towel and hastened to wrap it about her body.

"Do you not think it a bit late for such maidenly modesty?" Ronan challenged softly. He made no attempt to cover his own nakedness.

"Am I never to be free of your presence?" she retorted, trying without success to keep her eyes from straying to his manhood.

"No." He caught her against him. "You are not."

"Release me! By all that is holy, have you not done enough?" She squirmed within his grasp, but was hampered by the fact that she did not want to loose her hold upon the towel. The thought of standing naked before him again made her groan inwardly.

"Analise."

She stilled at the sound of her name upon his lips. Looking up at him, she saw that his eyes were aglow with tenderness. A sudden lump rose in her throat. Her fingers curled more tightly about the edge of the towel as she held it to her breasts.

" 'Tis time, I think, for a confession," said Ronan.

"A confession?"

"Aye." He gave her a faint, quizzical smile, his hands closing gently about her shoulders. "Had I known you were at Beauford, I would have come for you."

"Why, you—you would have been killed!" she stammered, her eyes growing very round. "And why would you have risked your life in such a way? We had but met once."

"It was enough to know that you were mine."

She opened her mouth to offer a denial, but no words would come. Ronan smiled again.

"When I believed you at Hexham, I made plans to ride there as I had promised."

"But I thought you were captured because of Calum." Her brow creased into a frown of perplexity.

"Aye. Calum has long held a talent for upsetting my plans," he remarked wryly, then sobered. "If Simon Hayward had not forced me to the marriage, I would have sought it nonetheless."

"Why do you tell me this?" she demanded, his words throwing her into confusion. "What purpose can it serve now? You *were* forced to it, and—"

"Do you not understand?" His gaze darkened, his grasp upon her almost punishing. "I love you."

Stunned, she shook her head in disbelief. Unwilling to acknowledge the way her heart took flight at his words, she tried to pull free.

"That cannot be true!"

"Why can it not?"

"We are too different!" she declared vehemently, almost as if she were trying to convince herself. "I am English. You are a Border Reiver, a man who thieves and kills and willfully sets himself above the law!"

"Och, woman, do you think the English do not raid?" he countered with a scowl. "Aye, the Scots are no more guilty than your own countrymen."

"You lie!" she charged, then inhaled upon a gasp when he yanked her up hard against him.

"Do I?" His expression was one of barely controlled anger. "But for a few years in Edinburgh, I have lived here at Dunslair. I have seen the English cross the border to do their worst. I have heard the screams of women and children, and have watched helplessly as their homes were burned about them. No, Analise," he concluded grimly. " 'Tis not the Scots alone who wreak havoc upon their enemies."

"Even if that is true, it . . . it cannot excuse your own misdeeds." Her gaze fell beneath the piercing intensity of his. She was still acutely conscious of the intimacy of their situation. Indeed, it was difficult to think clearly when he stood before her in all his masculine glory and she was clad in nothing save a towel. The memory of what they had just shared could not be so easily cast aside.

"You think me a villain, then?" His tone was underscored by reproach.

"Is that not what you are?" She raised her eyes to his face again. "Do you not prey upon those weaker than you? Do you not steal away in the moonlight to take what others have worked hard to gather?"

"No." His hands held her lightly now. "When I was younger, I did go a-reiving with my father. But no more."

"Would you have me believe—"

"Believe what you will." He let her go, moving away to retrieve his clothing. Her thoughts and emotions in utter turmoil, she watched as he drew on his shirt and breeches. When he turned to face her again, she felt herself strangely tempted to approach him.

"Someday, perhaps, I will tell you more," he said. His eyes glinted dully, like cold steel. "Until then you must learn to trust me."

"Trust you?" she echoed, unable to believe what she had heard. "I cannot trust a man who cares so little for my feelings!" She sucked in a deep, ragged breath before vowing, "I *shall* find a way to leave."

"No, Analise." He closed the distance between them again. "If you are foolish enough to try," he warned, his countenance grave as his gaze locked with hers, "you will know the weight of my hand."

"Save your threats, Ronan Armstrong!" she cried, with a great deal more bravado than she actually felt.

With a swiftness that surprised her, he yanked the towel away once more. She gasped, but had no time to struggle before his arm slipped about her waist to pull her close. A startled, breathless cry escaped her lips when his large hand descended upon her naked bottom. He clasped her hard, his fingers digging into her flesh.

"Do not try me," he advised quietly, "for I am a man of my word."

He released her again. Though her pride hurt a great deal more than her backside, she was filled with indignation.

"You *are* a savage!" she seethed, her beautiful eyes furiously ablaze.

"Aye. Yet a savage who will be obeyed." Though he wanted nothing more than to tarry—and, in truth, to tumble his spitfire bride into bed—he knew that he had business elsewhere. Business that could be postponed no longer.

He moved to gather up his jack and boots as Analise covered herself again. She flung him a look full of outrage and resentment. Unscathed, he crossed back to stand before her.

"I spoke the truth when I said I loved you. But I will be master of my own household."

"I do not wish to *be* within your household," she proclaimed in a low, simmering tone.

"I must go now. But I will return before nightfall," he told her. Opening the door, he allowed the ghost of a smile to touch his lips. "This time, Calum will guard you well." He left her then.

She released a long, uneven sigh. Dropping the towel, she climbed back into the tub. The water had cooled by now, but she took little notice of it. Her skin endured yet another vigorous scrubbing.

I love you.

Remembering those words, she felt a splendid warmth stealing over her again. Had he meant them? she wondered dazedly. Was it truly possible that he could care so much for her after a few days' acquaintance?

"No," she murmured, rising so abruptly from the tub that water puddled upon the floor. She told herself that he had declared his love for one purpose alone—to coax her more easily into his bed.

Her eyes clouding again, she wrapped the towel about her body and sat down to wait for Mairi to bring her clothes.

A short time later, after she had dressed in a gown of soft crimson wool, braided her hair, and consumed most of the hearth cakes and milk Flora had brought in Mairi's wake, she ventured downstairs to the hall.

She was pleased to discover her brother-in-law draped negligently across a chair in front of the fire. He stood and welcomed her with a smile that put her to shame.

"Good day, Sister."

"I should like to offer you my apologies, Calum," she told him as she drew close. Tilting her head back to face him squarely—for he was almost as tall as Ronan—she clasped her hands together in front of her and felt a dull flush rising to her face. "You suffered for my defiance."

"Do you think me so fainthearted that I would tremble at my brother's wrath?" Calum responded in mock displeasure. "Had I been in your place, I would have done the same. Aye," he added, his blue eyes dancing, "though

I would have first made certain none witnessed my escape."

"I have your forgiveness, then?" she asked, her eyes searching his face for any lingering reproach.

"You do, indeed." He proffered his arm, suggesting, "Perhaps, my lady, you would care for a turn about the grounds."

"I should like that very much, thank you." She took his arm and gathered up her skirts. "I have seen little of Dunslair—save for the bedchambers." She blushed at the sound of his soft, mellow laughter.

"My brother would keep you to himself. And by the saints, I cannot blame him."

He led her down the winding stairs to the ground floor. When they emerged outside, Analise inhaled deeply of the cool, heather-scented air and allowed her gaze to sweep across the courtyard.

"Do all of your clan live at Dunslair?" she asked. Calum gave another low chuckle.

"That would be impossible. Aye, for there are near as many Armstrongs in Scotland as sheep upon the hills." He urged her farther, away from the house and toward the row of buildings where the tenants and their families lived. All of the cottages were neatly kept, all had smoke curling from their stone chimneys. A short distance past the cottages stood the smithy and the kennels, the laundry and the cookhouse, the stables, and the mill. Beyond the barmkin, sheep and cattle grazed.

Dunslair, Analise realized, was like a small village, or even a kingdom of sorts. And Ronan Armstrong was its king. Her eyes kindled at the thought.

Strolling alone with Calum, she was aware of the many curious gazes directed her way. Men stopped briefly in their tasks to watch her. Women whispered to one another, some in complaint that the laird had married her, others in admiration for her beauty and bearing. A few of the children at play near the stables cast her smiles that were tentative, yet friendly.

She felt confused. The scene before her was pleasant, peaceful—and completely at odds with the bloodthirsty reputation of the Scots. Perhaps, she reflected, they were not all the same. Just as there were men both good and bad in England, so must there be among the people in the Borders. Yet, had not Calum himself been setting out to raid the night he and Ronan had been captured?

"Why do you ride across the border?" she asked, turning to him with a frown of puzzlement as they paused beside the millpond. "Surely there is no need for you to steal. And why would you wish to do harm to those who, but for the misfortune of being born in England, have done naught to earn your hatred?"

" 'Tis the way it has always been," he answered. "For hundreds of years, on both sides of the border. England would subdue us. We will not surrender. They attack us. We seek revenge. There cannot be an end to it until we are left to govern ourselves. But I tell you, Analise," he said earnestly, "I have never taken the life of an innocent. Nor has Ronan. Those we have killed, we killed in defense alone. Or in battle."

"And you think to bear no guilt because of that?"

"I can only hope for the mercy of Providence." His mouth twitched, and his eyes were brimming with humor. "Once, when a vicar from Hexham came upon a group of Scots, he asked if they were true and faithful believers. Their reply was, 'No, sir. We are Scots.' Some believe it impossible to be both."

"Do you hold that belief as well?"

"No. I do not."

"Your brother claims that he has set aside his reiving ways," she then remarked, surprised at how much she wanted it to be true.

"Aye. Yet he still—" He broke off, catching himself in time. He did not know how much Ronan had told her. And no matter how tempted he was to confide in her, he must guard his tongue.

"Calum?"

"Come," he told her, smiling again. "A ride should bring color to your cheeks. There is a ruined abbey nearby. And beyond that, a village."

"I am certain there are other things that demand your attention," she declined reluctantly, feeling another twinge of guilt.

"None that would give me as much pleasure."

"Very well. But I should much prefer to walk." The thought of being astride a horse again filled her with dismay. Her backside still ached—most of all, she mused irefully, from Ronan's touch. "If you will allow me to fetch my cloak, I—"

"You have not yet grown accustomed to our fine Scottish weather?" he teased, his hand clasping warmly about hers.

"How can you bear it with so little clothing?"

"Our blood runs hot." His mouth curved into a grin. "Aye, but you would know that already."

"Do you speak so plainly with your ladylove?" she parried, cursing the warm color staining her cheeks again.

"Whenever I have the chance."

She noticed the shadow crossing his face. Her heart filled with compassion. She raised her other hand to his arm.

"Perhaps her father will change his mind," she put forth hopefully.

"He is not so easily persuaded." He shook his head, his eyes gleaming with determination. "But I will yet claim Dierdre Maxwell for my bride. With or without her father's blessing, she *will* be mine."

Analise caught her breath, for in that moment he reminded her far too much of his brother. She lapsed into thoughtful silence while he led her back toward the house.

Soon they were on their way across the green-mantled hills, heading eastward beneath a sky that offered only an occasional glimpse of the sun. Analise was glad of the cloak she wore. Calum had disdained the use of one for himself, but had buckled on his sword and slipped a dirk into the belt at his waist.

"Were the distance not so insignificant," he revealed, "we would not go afoot. Nor alone."

"Surely there is no danger—"

"There is never a lack of it." A brief smile of irony touched his lips. "In truth, we 'quarrel' with one another as often as we do with the English."

"Are there so many feuds, then?" she asked, recalling what Ronan had told her about the long-standing trouble between the Armstrongs and the Maxwells.

"Aye, many. Most began before any of us were born. But they can only end with bloodshed."

"Then, why did Angus Maxwell allow us to go free?" She shuddered at the memory of her time at Longcroft.

"Perhaps he does not want an end to it. It is said that hatred can keep a man alive."

"I do not understand the Scots at all," she sighed,

treading carefully over the rocky soil while the wind tugged at her skirts.

"Ah, but that will take a lifetime."

He changed the subject then, and set to regaling her with a number of stories about the area's history—as colorful and violent as the rest of Scotland's. She realized that she felt perfectly at ease with him. He possessed both a ready wit and an infectious sense of humor. But none of his brother's mystery.

They spent a pleasant hour exploring the ruins of the abbey, and after that the village. Analise was enchanted with the latter in particular. Called "Bairnkine," it was very picturesque, a storybook collection of vine-covered stone cottages, a tiny church with the rarity of a bell tower, and one of only a handful of schools between the border and Edinburgh.

"Once I was a pupil there," Calum told her, eyeing the ancient, one-room schoolhouse with a trace of nostalgia.

"And Ronan as well?" Analise queried impulsively.

"No. He was sent to Edinburgh. And when older, to Europe." For a moment he looked wistful. "Our father believed it necessary for only the eldest son to receive such a thorough education. He knew that Ronan would one day take his place as laird."

"Of course." Strangely enough, she felt a mixture of pride and pleasure at learning that her husband was no ignorant savage. Indeed, he was far more a man of the world than she could ever have imagined.

"My father died when I was still but a boy," Calum went on, finding it easy to talk to her. "My mother, heartbroken, followed him within a year. It fell to Ronan to look after Dunslair, and me as well."

"I, too, am an orphan," murmured Analise, her heart aching at the thought of his and Ronan's pain.

"So that is why you are ward to Simon Hayward."

"Yes. But I had never even made his acquaintance until I came to Beauford." She frowned, her fingers clenching within the folds of her cloak. "Though he is a kinsman, I cannot hold any affection for him."

"Nor should you. The man is even worse than you think him, and—" Again he left the sentence unfinished. He met her gaze and offered sincerely, "I can tell you this alone—Simon Hayward is not a man to be trusted."

Intrigued by his words, she would have pressed for more. But he set to his storytelling once more, this time confessing his part in a boyhood prank that had sent the young, superstitious schoolmaster running back to Edinburgh. Analise could not help but laugh at his account. For the first time in many days, her spirits began to lift. And, oddly enough, she found herself wishing that her husband would confide in her as his brother had done.

Once she and Calum had returned to Dunslair, she convinced him to grant her a turn about the grounds without an escort. She was reluctant to return inside the house. Idleness had never held any particular appeal for her. It held even less now, with the prospect of Ronan's return never far from her thoughts.

She enjoyed a leisurely stroll across the courtyard, then wandered toward the millpond again. All about her, life continued as usual. Men and women worked, children played. Everything was simple, uncomplicated. London seemed a million miles away.

A sudden yearning rose within her, a yearning to belong somewhere as these people did. Each of them had a place and a purpose. Was it possible that she could ever think of Dunslair as her home? Even more importantly, was it possible that she could ever freely accept Ronan Armstrong as her husband?

Once again the memory of his lovemaking sent a slow, pleasurable warmth stealing through her. She moved closer to the pond, until the water offered up the sight of her reflection. Her own eyes stared back at her. She crossed her arms against her chest and flung a perplexed look heavenward.

"Unlike the English, *we* have little time for leisure," Mairi remarked pointedly as she rounded the corner of the mill and approached Analise. She carried a basket full of apples, newly delivered from Edinburgh. "Aye, any who were useless and lazy would feel an empty belly."

"I was . . ." said Analise, her voice trailing away. She flushed guiltily and dropped her gaze. "In truth, I have been accustomed to servants performing most tasks for me."

"You are the laird's wife. Were I in your place, I would look to the household myself." She frowned and shifted the basket to her other hip. "You will lose your husband's respect if you cling to your English ways."

"Would you not be glad of that?" Analise demanded, stung by the woman's words.

"I am an Armstrong," replied Mairi. "Though I cannot pretend any among us were pleased with the laird's choice of a bride, I would not see him dishonored by you."

Analise caught her breath when a sudden, inexplicable ache gripped her heart. *Dishonored,* her mind echoed. No, she could not wish for that. Whatever he had done, however much he had bedeviled (and seduced) her, she held no true desire for revenge.

The realization was surprising. She slowly shook her head and looked back to her reflection.

"You were with Master Calum this morn," Mairi now said, her voice edged with accusation.

"Yes. He was kind enough to show me Bairnkine."

"Did he speak of Dierdre Maxwell?"

Analise was caught off guard by the question. She hesitated, her gaze falling again.

"Should you not ask him yourself?"

"I cannot," Mairi replied. Her expression grew pained. "I know that he would wed her. It has been so since we were young. Did you not see her when you were at Longcroft?"

"No," Analise was able to answer truthfully.

"She is a beauty. Aye, yet Calum would look upon her just the same." She heaved a sigh before murmuring, "Lawrie calls me a fool."

"Lawrie is your brother?"

"My brother?" Mairi repeated, then allowed her mouth to curve briefly upward. "No. A kinsman, though. He wishes to marry me."

"Does he?" Analise responded in surprise, for she recalled the brusque manner in which Lawrie had treated the young woman. "And do you feel any affection for him as well?"

"How can I look upon another man when Calum Armstrong is about?" exclaimed Mairi. She heaved another sigh and declared unhappily, "I have spoken too much of it already. There is work to be done. I must be away to the kitchen." She would have set off then, but Analise placed a hand upon her arm to detain her.

"I should like to help." Though the offer was made on impulse, she knew that she meant it.

"You would not know your way about a kitchen."

"Perhaps not, but I am willing to learn." She smiled and argued, "I am certain the laird would be pleased."

"Very well," Mairi agreed with obvious reluctance. "But some will not feel it right to have the mistress of Dunslair at work beside them."

"Then, they must not think of me as the mistress of Dunslair." Another soft smile of irony played about her lips. "It will give them the chance to treat me ill."

She followed as Mairi led the way across the courtyard to a small stone building only a short distance from the house. It was warm inside. A fire blazed heartily beneath a great iron cauldron. The mingling aromas of fish and onions and potatoes hung in the air. Two women sat chopping vegetables at a table near the fire, while two others kneaded the lumps of bread dough they had made with the wheat ground at the nearby mill.

They eyed Analise warily. She held back only a moment before sailing through the doorway to greet them with a smile and an offer to submit herself to their instruction. Within a short time, her gown was covered with flour and her face was flushed with effort. Yet she reveled in the experience. And in the chance to keep her mind, temporarily at least, from Ronan.

After more than an hour spent in the kitchen, Mairi agreed to show her the laundry. She tarried there as well, learning how to wash the endless mountain of clothing and linen. Again the work was hard yet rewarding, and she gained a further appreciation for the army of servants who had toiled at court. Never again would she take such things for granted.

By the time she joined Calum in the hall for the noon meal, she was tired and a bit stiff, but filled with a sense of satisfaction. Calum, taking note of the discomfort of her movements, frowned in disapproval.

"I was told that you had joined the women in their work today," he disclosed.

"Yes." She eased herself down into the chair and arranged the skirts of the clean, emerald brocade gown about her.

"Ronan will not like it."

"Why not?"

"Because the laird's wife is neither a laundress nor a kitchen maid."

"Am I supposed to sit idle, then?" she challenged indignantly. "Do women in Scotland do so? Indeed, do they occupy their time with nothing save their embroidery and occasional turns about the courtyard?"

"No, but 'tis not the same," he insisted.

"How so? I am the mistress of Dunslair, am I not? The household is now my responsibility. Even in England, the wife—" She broke off with a sharp intake of breath as the significance of her words sank in. Dear heaven, she wondered in dismay, why had she not once thought of escape that day?

"I am glad you begin to think of Dunslair as your home," Calum remarked, his eyes lit with amusement.

"It is not my home," she stubbornly dissented. "But I will not remain a prisoner inside the house."

Flora entered then, bearing a tray of food. She ladled the fish stew—"Cullen Skink," Mairi had called it—into the bowls and poured red wine into the large pewter goblets. After setting a plate of bread upon the table, she gave Analise a companionable smile and left the hall again.

Analise was relieved that Calum was not inclined to

tease her anymore. They spoke little throughout the meal. Calum seemed preoccupied, while she forced her mind to try and make new plans that would see her away from Scotland and across the Channel to France. The situation, she conceded with an inward sigh, looked more hopeless than ever. How could she escape when Ronan knew of her every move? Even when he was away, she felt his presence . . . and tried not to think of what would happen upon his return.

The remainder of the day passed quickly enough for her. Late in the afternoon, a mixture of restlessness and curiosity led her to explore the house. She was allowed to do so alone, though Calum did warn her that there were "eyes within the walls." Wandering about the two upper-most floors, she discovered Calum's bedchamber (as untidy as she might have expected) and the room shared by Mairi and Flora. It was at the far end of the corridor, and was by contrast both clean and orderly. Save for Lawrie's quarters, the other rooms were unoccupied.

She found herself wondering if their former, long-ago occupants had been happy there. Had they endured an abundance of hardship and tragedy? Had their misfortunes been softened by love? Surely they were not so different than those who now lived at Dunslair, she reflected as she strolled back along the corridor to the stairwell. It was even possible that once there had been another Armstrong bride who had been less than willing to surrender. The thought gave her little comfort.

Still feeling uneasy, she gathered up her skirts and climbed the winding, narrow stone steps to the very top of the house. She emerged outside onto the battlements, only to shiver when a cold gust of wind swept across her. Folding her arms tightly across her chest, she moved closer to the edge of the parapet. Her gaze drifted out across the rolling countryside. Night was fast approaching. Already the sheep and cattle were settling upon the hills. The people in the courtyard below were returning to the warmth of their cottages. The sky had darkened to a deep and remarkably cloudless blue.

Analise raised a hand to the top of the parapet. Once again she was struck by the wild, unexpected beauty about her. Dunslair was like no other place she had seen . . .

"Have a care, Analise."

The sound of that familiar, wondrously resonant voice filled her with emotion. Torn between the impulse to flee and the desire to hear Ronan speak again, she turned to face him. His clothing was dusty from his long ride. His hair was windblown, his boots caked with mud. But his eyes were as clear and penetrating as ever. She warmed beneath the look he gave her.

"I would not have you tumble to your death," he declared, stepping forward to take her arm.

" 'Better hanged than ill married,' " she retorted, trying to ignore the way her pulse leapt at his touch. "Is that not what you said when first we came to Dunslair?"

"Aye. But the words ring as false now as they did then." His arm stole about her waist. "Will you not greet me with a kiss?" he asked, his tone laced with desire and a trace of amusement.

"No!" She pushed at him, and was startled when he let her go. Unaware of the battle raging within him, she clutched at the stones again and lifted her chin to a proud angle. "Did you ride to Edinburgh?" The question sounded lame, even to her own ears, yet she could think of nothing else.

"No." He frowned then, his gaze searing down into hers. "Have you troubled Calum this day?"

"Indeed, sir, I have not!"

"Could it be, then, that you have accepted your fate?" he challenged softly.

"Never!" she denied, her eyes kindling. She was surprised again when he gave her a faint smile and turned away.

"Come. We have guests for dinner this night."

"Guests?"

He opened the door to the stairwell and waited for her to follow. "John Beattie and his wife would meet you. He is an old and trusted friend." He did not tell her that John's help had proven invaluable of late, that the two of them together had accomplished even more than he had hoped. By heaven, he swore inwardly while his eyes darkened, he would yet see both Simon Hayward and Robert Kerr pay for their crimes.

Analise hesitated. The thought of meeting her husband's friends filled her with apprehension. What if they did not like her? What if they found fault with either her appearance or her behavior? She told herself that their opinion should not matter. Yet it did.

"I . . . I must make ready first," she stammered, slowly moving toward Ronan now.

"And I." The corners of his mouth turned briefly upward as his gaze traveled over her. "Were our guests not awaiting us, I would share a bath with you."

Her cheeks grew hot, yet she offered no reply. Sweeping past him, she hastened down the steps to the floor below. But when she would have turned to approach her old room, he seized her arm in a firm, albeit gentle, grip.

"No, lady wife," he said quietly. "Do you not remember? 'Tis my bed you sleep in now."

"Have you not taken enough?" she flung at him. "Must you take my privacy as well?"

"I would have all of you." He drew her close, his eyes holding a promise of passion. "Body and soul."

"You shall not have that!" Her heart pounded with both fear and excitement. Murmuring another vehement denial, she jerked free and continued down the staircase. Ronan followed, though unhurriedly. When he entered his bedchamber, he saw that she stood before the mirror, smoothing the folds of her gown and tucking several wayward strands of hair back into place. She spared him only a brief, resentful look as he closed the door.

"John and Sarah are in the hall below," he told her, shrugging out of his jack. "Go to them. I will come once I have washed."

"And what am I to say to them?"

"As the mistress of Dunslair, it falls to you to make them welcome."

"So I am expected to behave as though we are any other man and wife?"

" 'Tis your duty."

"Dear heaven, when will this end?" she uttered in exasperation. Whirling to face him, she furiously blinked back sudden tears. "I beg of you, Ronan Armstrong—let me go! I will never belong here. I am English. What do I know of Scotland, of the people and their beliefs? You need a wife who understands your ways. I cannot—" She broke off and shook her head while a sob rose in her throat.

Ronan's heart stirred at the sight of her distress. He was across the room in two long strides, his arms encircling her with their strong warmth. She did not resist. She closed her eyes, resting against his broad chest while the tears spilled over from her lashes. For too long she had sought to hold her emotions in check. So much had happened so quickly. Her entire world had been turned upside down. And her heart was in grave danger of being captured as surely as her passions had been.

She cried until she could cry no more. After the storm of weeping had passed, she lifted her head and raised a lace-edged handkerchief to her nose. Her eyes, still glistening, traveled up to meet Ronan's.

"I am sorry," she murmured. "I—I am afraid your shirt is wet."

"No matter," he assured her, a soft smile playing about his lips.

His own eyes were glowing warmly, and he wanted very much to kiss her. She had never looked as beautiful as she did now. But he fought against the desire burning within him. At the moment she needed tenderness and understanding. He was willing to give her both. Never before had he experienced such a fierce surge of protectiveness.

His hand came up to gently cup her chin. "Know that I love you, Analise," he said in a tone so low and vibrant that it made her knees weaken. "One day you will admit that you love me as well."

"No," she breathed, her eyes growing very wide. "I do not . . . I cannot!"

" 'Tis already too late."

She stared up at him in confusion and disbelief. Finally she drew away. Drying her eyes, she turned back to the mirror to tidy her hair again. She was painfully conscious of Ronan's gaze upon her, and she cursed the fact that her fingers trembled.

"I shall go below now," she announced with deceptive calm.

"Analise."

"There is nothing more to be said between us," she told him, though without much conviction.

"Analise."

She felt her heart flutter wildly. Pivoting to face him again, she caught her breath at the love reflected in his magnificent blue eyes.

"In time, you will come to regard Dunslair as your home. You possess both a strong spirit and a keen mind. Aye," he asserted solemnly, "you will soon learn what you need to know."

Though she would not tell him so, his words filled her with a surprising amount of pleasure. She swept across to the door and opened it, her gaze straying back to Ronan.

"Do your friends know that our marriage was forced?" she asked, then wondered why she had done so.

"No." He closed the distance between them again. His hands curled about her shoulders. "I have told them the truth—that I am in love with my bride."

"By all the saints, I do not know what is true any longer!" she sighed, her eyes clouding in perplexity. "Only a few days ago, I was at Beauford, quarreling with my guardian about the men he would see me wed. Never did I dream it possible that I would soon be *here* with *you*." She looked up at him and felt her head spinning anew. "Perhaps you have bewitched me, Ronan Armstrong. Indeed, I have heard it said that the Scots consort with witches and wizards!"

"If that were true, then your surrender would have been complete the first time I held you in my arms."

Reluctantly he set her away from him. "Now, go. I will join you soon enough."

She could refuse to do his bidding, of course. She could declare herself unwilling to play the part he had set for her. Yet she found herself inclined to obey. What harm would it do? she reasoned. It would be good to talk to someone other than Calum and Ronan. Yes, and to learn more about the man she had married.

With that thought in mind, she left the room and descended the stairs. In her wake Ronan's eyes lit with satisfaction, and he smiled to himself as he began stripping off his clothes.

Chapter 8

The evening proved to be far less of an ordeal than she had anticipated. John Beattie, a great bear of a man with hair much the same color as red wine, was by turns gregarious and reflective. He told her that he had known Ronan since childhood, and was therefore the one man whose opinion should be sought if ever her new husband "troubled" her. John's blonde wife, Sarah, pretty and plump and a full head shorter than her towering mate, was possessed of such a kind and agreeable nature that it was impossible not to like her. In spite of the vast difference of their backgrounds, Analise sensed in her a kindred spirit, a woman who, for all her amiability, would not hesitate to defend herself against tyranny.

Indeed, Analise had soon concluded, neither of the Beatties seemed to offer her judgment—only a ready friendship. She could not help but warm to them. Her spirits lifted considerably again, and she was all too willing to forget her earlier disquiet.

When Ronan finally joined the trio in the hall, he took pleasure in the sight of his wife's smile. He moved to her side and slipped a possessive arm about her waist. Though she did not draw away, she was struck by the absurdity of the situation. To the Beatties, she and Ronan no doubt gave the appearance of typical, devoted newlyweds—little did they know that she was determined to leave Scotland and never return, that she was a captive bride instead of a willing one.

She was glad when Mairi entered the hall to announce that dinner was ready. The meal that followed was delicious, yet she found that her appetite had fled once more. Conversation, though pleasant enough, was by turns enigmatic, with Ronan and John frequently speaking in lowered voices and Sarah exhorting them to set aside their matters of business. Analise was frustrated in her efforts to hear what was being said. She could have sworn, however, that she caught the name of her guardian.

Afterward the Beatties retired to the room Flora had prepared for them upon the topmost floor. Analise was reluctant to bid them good night, for she had enjoyed their company immensely. And, in truth, she dreaded the moment when she and Ronan would be alone again.

Her nerves were as tight as a bowstring when she preceded him into the bedchamber. She crossed to stand before the fireplace, the dance of the flames reflected in her eyes while Ronan closed the door and began to undress.

"Why did Calum not join us tonight?" she asked in a small voice, desperately trying to postpone the inevitable.

"He is away to Jedburgh. We will join him there on the morrow."

"We?" She turned to face him, only to blush and hastily avert her gaze when she saw that he was unfastening his breeches. "You intend for me to go as well?"

"Aye."

"I have no wish to ride again." Her stomach knotted at the prospect.

" 'Tis not far," he assured her. Naked, he slipped

beneath the covers of the bed. "Come, Analise." His tone
was low, laced with desire. She drew in a sharp breath
and met his gaze.

"I do not—" she started to protest.

"Come."

She had no choice, of course. There was nowhere to
run, no hope of avoiding her husband's embrace. As she
knew too well, he was a man who could not be swayed
from whatever he had set his mind upon. He was a
Reiver in every sense of the word, she mused crossly.

It would do her little good to attempt modesty. With
hands that were once again unsteady, she removed her
gown, then took a seat upon the chair in order to draw
off her shoes and stockings. She stood, clad only in her
linen shift, her head lifting proudly while the firelight
revealed the seductive, well-rounded suppleness of her
figure.

She approached the bed. Ronan's eyes caught and held
the soft brilliance of hers. She joined him beneath the
covers, her pulse racing in expectation. He pulled her
close. She inhaled upon a gasp as her thinly attired
curves molded to perfection against the length of his
naked, hard-muscled warmth.

"Good night, my love," he bade her softly, then
dropped a light kiss upon her forehead. She raised her
head and saw that he had closed his eyes. Did he not
mean to take her? she wondered in bewilderment.

She dared not ask him. A long, quavering sigh escaped
her lips as she rested her head upon his chest again and
felt his arm urging her even closer. Relief and disappointment warred within her. She cursed herself for a
fool and closed her eyes, drifting off to sleep while
Ronan's heart beat strong and steady beneath her cheek.

* * *

The next morning she learned that the Beatties were to accompany them to Jedburgh, and that she and Ronan would spend the night in the town. He had not yet told her the reason for their visit. And though she would have been glad to learn of it, her mind was at present occupied with thoughts of the journey she would have to endure.

"Must I go?" she appealed again as she laced her gown. Though dawn had scarcely broken, Ronan had awakened her with a kiss and a threat to tumble her from the bed if she did not arise. "If you have business there, would it not be—"

"Do you think me fool enough to leave you here unguarded?" he cut her off, battling the urge to sweep her into his arms and carry her back to the bed. He had suffered immeasurable torment already; aye, it had been hell to hold her close and do nothing else. But he would have her know his love to be true. He would have her know that he could be merciful.

"With Calum away as well, I can trust no others to watch you," he maintained, tugging on his boots. His gaze lit with wry amusement when he stood and added, " 'Tis time you saw more of our rough paradise."

"It can be no rougher than its men," she retorted, then felt her heart turn over in her breast at the sound of his quiet laughter. She assumed an air of wounded dignity. "How long will you keep me a prisoner? Is it not time that we—"

"The battle is within yourself alone, Analise." He pulled on his jack and thrust his sword into its sheath. His countenance was grim, his eyes glinting dully now as he moved toward her. "Do not think to try and escape when we are in Jedburgh," he warned. "There are some who would use you to force the hand of Simon Hayward. *Or mine.*" He thought of Ewan Maxwell, and felt murderous rage burn within him again.

Analise paled at the look on his face. Turning about to catch up her cloak, she sought to keep her voice steady while asking, "Why do we go to Jedburgh?"

"I must meet with Robert Kerr," he answered, but did not tell her that it was upon the king's orders.

"Robert Kerr?" She frowned pensively, for the name sounded familiar to her ears. "Is he not the man who was with you at Truce Day?"

"Aye. He is a Scottish warden. Of the Middle March, the same as your kinsman serves for England." And with the same mind to treachery, he added silently.

"Simon Hayward has not yet called upon his alliance with you," she pointed out as she flung the cloak about her shoulders. "Perhaps our marriage was for naught." She looked away, dismayed by the feeling that she had somehow betrayed herself with such words.

"He will make use of it yet," Ronan assured her quietly. His arm came about her, and his mouth curved into a faint smile of irony as he drew her close for a moment. "I would kill him for his methods, yet thank him for the outcome." His fingers trailed across her cheek in a light, sensuous caress. He kissed her then, his lips at once gentle and demanding upon hers. She was flushed and breathless when he released her, and he was sorely tempted to continue the embrace. But he knew that John and Sarah were waiting for them. And that, if he tasted her lips a second time, he would not stop at a kiss.

He led her downstairs and outside into the gray light of the cold October morning. The Beatties, who, like them, had breakfasted in their room, were standing ready beside the horses. They both smiled a greeting.

" 'Tis not like you, Mac Ghillielaidir, to stay so long abed," John opined, a broad and knowing grin on his face.

"Hold your tongue, John Beattie, or else your own bed will grow cold this night," Sarah threatened with wifely sternness. Her eyes were full of sympathy when she took note of Analise's embarrassment. She hastened forward to suggest, "Perhaps, once your husband has completed his business in Jedburgh, he will bring you to Hawkfield. My four sons would be pleased to welcome you. And, I must confess, with so many men about the house, I am too often lonely for the company of another woman."

"I should like to come," Analise told her truthfully. She would have said more, but Ronan was at her side now, his hands closing about her waist. He lifted her up to her horse's back, and lingered for a moment.

"Should you be plagued by soreness again," he offered in a voice meant for her ears alone, "I will be glad to provide a remedy."

"Indeed, sir, I shall require no remedy!" she whispered, fiery color staining her cheeks. She was unaccustomed to his teasing, and was alarmed at the way it made her feel. Gathering up the reins of her mount, she watched as Ronan swung up into his own saddle. John and Sarah followed suit, and the four of them rode across the courtyard to the gate.

The journey was, mercifully, unlike the others Analise had endured of late. As Ronan had said, the ride was not a long one, nor a difficult one. Nevertheless, she was relieved when they came upon Jedburgh. She reined her mount to a halt upon the crest of a heather-covered hill while the others did the same.

Her gaze widened with surprise and pleasure as it swept across the town below. Located on the banks of the River Jed, Jedburgh was dominated by the massive ruins of both an abbey and a castle—the former destroyed fifty years ago when the town had been under siege by the English, and the latter demolished long before that so it should not fall into English hands. It was still an important market town, with people often traveling a considerable distance in order to purchase whatever they needed in the shops or at the market held each day in the town square. The streets were narrow and lined with stone buildings both new and ancient, the air filled with the sounds and smells peculiar to such a bustling settlement.

Analise shifted in the saddle and felt a smile tugging at her lips. "Why, 'tis a lovely place," she murmured to no one in particular.

"I have always believed it so," Sarah replied, then announced, "We must leave you now. Hawkfield lies but a short ride farther." Casting a fond yet reproachful glance toward Ronan, she appealed to Analise, "Your husband will not agree to sleep at Hawkfield this night. Will you not convince him? Aye, for our beds are far softer than what you will find at the inn, and—"

"We stay in Jedburgh," Ronan decreed once more, though he tempered it with a brief smile.

"And *we* must be away to home," said John. He gave Analise a nod before turning to exchange a few last words with Ronan.

"Perhaps, we may come another time," Analise told Sarah. On impulse she placed a hand upon the other woman's arm and declared earnestly, "Thank you for your kindness, Sarah Beattie."

"Have you known so little of it, then?" Sarah asked,

half in jest. Glimpsing the shadow that crossed Analise's face, she was instantly contrite. " 'Twas not my wish to sadden you. In truth, you invite kindness." She covered Analise's hand with the gentle, affectionate warmth of her own. "Farewell, Analise Armstrong."

"Farewell."

John and Sarah rode away, leaving Analise to wonder if she would ever see them again. Her path would most certainly not cross theirs if she succeeded in escaping.

"You have gained a friend," Ronan commented, urging his mount close to hers.

"She does but show me charity," insisted Analise, but knew it was not true.

"Aye." His eyes caught hers, while a tenderly mocking smile played about his lips. "As do I." He set his heels to his horse's flanks and set off down the hill. Analise stared after him for a moment, once again disarmed by his raillery. Her heart taking a strange tumble, she gathered up the reins and followed after him.

Soon they were making their way through the crowd, vying with the other horsemen and wagons and people afoot who would crisscross the muddy, cobbled lanes. Analise felt exhilarated by the melee about her. She had never taken any delight in it while in London, yet it was different here. Not only was everything on a much smaller scale, but there was also a pervasive vitality, a particular joie de vivre she had never sensed elsewhere.

Ronan drew his mount to a halt before a building, near the ruins of the abbey, which rose three stories tall against the cloud-choked sky. He swung down, and was at Analise's side as she prepared to dismount. Though she allowed him to assist her, she hastily pulled away once her feet had touched the ground. Her eyes lifted to the sign hanging above the doorway before her.

"The Spread-Eagle Inn," she read aloud.

"The finest in Jedburgh," Ronan put forth, his gaze warming with a spark of humor. Retrieving the small valise from behind his saddle, he looped both sets of reins over the post and took Analise's arm to lead her inside. She hung back momentarily.

"Are you to meet Robert Kerr here?" she asked, at the same time recalling how a brief word from Ronan had persuaded the man to calm his temper during the wardens' meeting at Truce Day.

"I am not." He would say no more. While her eyes flashed at his maddening reticence, he propelled her up the steps.

Minutes later, they stood within a small, firelit room furnished only with a curtained, three-quarter oak bed, a wash table, and a single chair. There were no rushes or carpets to warm the cold floor, no tapestries upon the walls. Analise reflected that Ronan's bedchamber at Dunslair was far more comfortable. She wandered across to the window and gazed outward at the towering remains of the abbey.

" 'Tis said that Mary Stewart once lay with her lover, Bothwell, within these walls," Ronan disclosed with a faint, wry smile as he came up behind her.

"Was the queen not another man's wife?" She turned to face him.

"Aye." His visage grew solemn now. "And if she had been mine, I would have killed her lover and locked her away so that she could never again look upon another man." With a startling roughness, he caught her against him and pressed a hard, almost punishing kiss upon her lips. She was appalled to feel herself responding, yet she could not keep her mouth from welcoming the rapture of his, nor her arms from stealing up about his neck. And when he finally released her, she searched in vain for words of defiance.

They left the inn soon thereafter. Analise's fascinated gaze traveled to and fro as Ronan led her through the streets. She smiled to herself at the sight of the market, crowded with every manner of person and goods, and peered curiously up at the figure of a piper carved into the gable of a narrow, very old house near the public wells. The town was particularly busy, for it was Saturday, the day when provisions were purchased and stored for the week ahead. A festive atmosphere prevailed. Somewhere, a fiddler played, the joyful strains of his music carried on the wind. Laughter rose in the air, along with the appetizing aroma of the traditional "haggis and neeps." Inhaling deeply, Analise felt her stomach rumble in protest of her less than hearty breakfast.

At last Ronan drew to a halt in front of what appeared to be a friary. It was quite small, and looked deserted, though a number of rosebushes and pear trees about the grounds offered evidence that someone still cared for it.

Ronan's fingers tightened upon Analise's arm, his expression grave as he commanded her, "You must keep silent."

"Would you not prefer my absence?"

"Aye." The merest ghost of a smile touched his lips. "But if I were fool enough to allow it *now*, I might well find myself enduring it forever." He quickly sobered again. His right hand moved to rest upon the hilt of his sword while his eyes darkened. "I must keep you close, for Robert Kerr is often of two minds." He raised his hand and knocked hard upon the door.

It was opened by a slender, bearded man with dark hair and a jagged scar across one side of his face. His gaze flickered hastily over Ronan, then shifted to Analise.

"You were to come alone, Ronan Armstrong," he grumbled, scowling.

"My wife is to be trusted." Something in his voice warned the other man against further objections.

Though he muttered a curse, the man turned and led the way through a narrow, darkened corridor. Analise grew more and more uneasy. She instinctively pressed closer to Ronan, who clasped her hand while casting a wary eye about him.

At the end of the hallway, they came to another door. It was opened to reveal a room where Robert Kerr sat waiting at a table before the fire. Three of his men, each armed and watchful, stood nearby. Ronan's eyes made a broad, encompassing sweep of the room as he entered with Analise.

Robert Kerr stood and offered him a manner of greeting. "Ah, so the Armstrong has come at last." His tone was smooth, mocking. He looked to Analise. His lips curled into a sardonic smile when he added, "And he has brought his English bride with him."

Analise tensed beneath his scrutiny, but met his gaze unflinchingly. He was even more sinister-looking than she had remembered. Indeed, there was a hardness about his mouth, a feral light within his eyes, that testified to his reputation as a monster. And it was obvious that, although he had allowed Ronan to exert some influence over him before, he despised him for being the better man.

"Perhaps the Armstrong thinks to hide behind the woman's skirts," one of the trio beside Robert Kerr taunted unwisely.

"You are free with your opinion, Alan Ridley," Ronan told the man in a voice of deadly calm. "Aye, and were my wife not present, *I* would be free with my sword."

"By the Virgin's blood, man, you dare to speak of killing?" Robert demanded angrily. "I summoned you here to tell me of your alliance with Simon Hayward." He came forward, his gaze raking over Analise once more. " 'Tis easy to see how you were led into such treason," he remarked with a sneer.

"Aye, for you are a traitor and deserve to rot in hell for it!" Alan Ridley exclaimed. This time Ronan was not so forgiving. With lightning swiftness he was across the room, his sword drawn and the tip of it pressed to the man's throat. Analise gasped, her eyes widening as she remembered how he had done the same to Ewan Maxwell. She looked to Robert, only to pale when she saw him draw his own weapon. His other men stood ready to do the same.

"Will you join me in hell this day, then?" Ronan challenged Alan in a low, deceptively even tone.

"Sheathe your sword, Armstrong, or know the feel of mine!" Robert warned him.

"Ronan!" Analise cried out impulsively.

He met her fearful, anguished gaze. In spite of the danger, his heart soared. He stepped away from Alan and plunged his sword back into its sheath.

"Ask me what you will, Robert Kerr," he said, a faint smile playing about his lips as he returned to Analise's side. "But should any of your men offer me insult again, I will not be swayed."

"They will hold their tongues," Robert assured him. He sheathed his sword now as well and shot Alan a furious, quelling glare. "In truth," he said, looking back to Ronan, "I am glad you have brought the woman. She can be of use to us."

"No," replied Ronan. His eyes darkened again, his countenance grim. "She has no part in—"

"She is kinswoman to Simon Hayward!"

"She is my wife."

"You would set her above our cause?" Robert asked in disbelief.

"I would set her above all else." His hand rested upon the hilt of his sword again. Analise's throat constricted in alarm, while at the same time Ronan's words echoed within her mind. *I would set her above all else.* Dear heaven, was it possible that she meant so much to him, then?

"Damn your eyes, you *do* speak treason!" charged Robert, his face reddening with anger.

"I am no traitor," Ronan denied quietly. "Yet I will not see her involved." Aware of the growing tension in the room, he sought a return to reason. " 'Tis true that my marriage has brought an alliance with Simon Hayward. And though he has not yet called upon it, I must honor the tie."

"That, too, might well be used to our advantage," said Robert, his temper momentarily cooling. His brow creased into a thoughtful frown as he turned and strolled back to his place behind the table. "Even Beauford itself is no longer safe, not with Ronan Armstrong to clear the path."

"You mean to attack Beauford?" one of his men queried, visibly taken aback at the thought.

"Why not?" He sank down into the chair and folded

his arms across his chest. "The king would not know of it until—" He fell abruptly silent, his eyes narrowing up at Ronan in suspicion. "Perhaps you are here as the king's spy." he put forth, then demanded, "Well? Are you?"

"Were you half the man your father is, you would have no need to ask it," Ronan declared, his voice edged with contempt.

"My father is a weak, spineless old fool!" snarled Robert, leaping to his feet. "Aye, he would speak of peace while all of Scotland burned!"

"And you would bring the English across the border with your raids."

"Do we not all want to make war upon them? Do we not all want to see them bleed?"

"No," answered Ronan, shaking his head. "Your father is right. The time has come for us to speak of peace."

"Peace brings naught save poverty and dishonor," Robert insisted with a dismissive wave of his hand.

"You have lined your pockets well enough."

"Have you become both a traitor *and* a coward?" sneered Robert, moving to stand close before him. "Mayhap you should prove yourself worthy of our friendship."

"Friendship, unless freely offered, means little," Ronan parried solemnly.

Analise caught her breath when Robert turned his malevolent gaze upon her again. She looked up at Ronan, and prayed that they would leave soon.

"I think the best proof lies here," drawled Robert, giving a curt, significant nod toward Analise. "Aye, mayhap *she* can force a return to loyalty."

"By damn, you will not take her!" Ronan ground out, his visage dangerously grim.

"Will I not?"

At a signal from Robert, the four other men in the room drew their swords. They advanced upon Ronan, while their leader smiled and retreated behind the table once more.

Analise's gaze filled with horror. She watched as Ronan prepared to fight. His own eyes held a savage gleam, his fingers clenching about the hilt of his sword so tightly that his knuckles turned white. She trembled at the look on his face.

"If you would die to keep her, then so be it!" Alan Ridley pronounced with a mind to revenge. He was the first to make a strike. His blade glinting in the firelight, he lunged at Ronan. But the thrust was deflected with such mastery that Alan nearly lost his balance. He tried again, only to give a sharp cry of pain when Ronan's blade tore through the flesh of his right shoulder. His weapon clattered to the floor as he stumbled back against the wall.

The other three men circled Ronan, each intent on avoiding their comrade's fate. Analise felt her heart twist painfully. She could not bear the thought of seeing Ronan harmed—*or killed*. Stifling a scream as the men closed in upon him, she looked desperately about for some way to help. Her eyes fell upon Alan's sword.

Without pausing to think, she flew across the room and knelt beside it. She had never before held a sword; it felt heavy and strange. But she managed to lift it nonetheless, and started to make her way back toward Ronan.

Robert Kerr swore when he saw what she was about. He hastened to intercept her, one hand seizing her arm in a brutal grip while the other twisted the sword from her grasp. A breathless cry escaped her lips, and she struggled with all her might as he attempted to force her to the door.

"Release her!" Ronan thundered, a murderous fury firing his blood. He would have gone to her, but the men before him prevented it. With a cry of rage, he launched an attack, his sword finding its target. The unfortunate man collapsed to the floor, clutching at the wound to his chest. Sparing him only a brief glance, the other two now lunged at Ronan in unison.

"No!" Analise gasped. She lifted her hand and struck a hard, stinging blow across her captor's face, then followed it with a forceful kick to his shin. Robert bit out a curse and loosed his hold upon her. Gathering up her skirts, she raced toward Ronan again.

Suddenly Calum burst into the room. His sword was already drawn, and he grinned at the look of surprise upon the faces of the men who were trying to kill Ronan.

"My apologies, Brother, for so late an arrival!" he declared, then immediately set to engaging one of the men in battle.

Within seconds, the last of Robert Kerr's lieutenants had joined the others upon the floor. Robert stared down at them. His features grew ugly with anger and defeat. He gripped the hilt of his sword.

"Draw it," warned Ronan, "and I will kill you." His eyes smoldered. His expression was grim, bloodthirsty. Shuddering, Analise lifted a hand to her throat. Calum moved to her side and gave her a faint, reassuring smile.

"I will have my revenge—" growled Robert, but lowered his weapon.

"Vengeance will be *mine*," Ronan vowed, still battling the urge to kill him. "Look to your back, Robert Kerr.

Someday, I will make you pay for the insult you have offered my wife."

"The king will hear of this!"

"Aye. And of your treachery."

He sheathed his sword now. His eyes met Analise's. She caught her breath, startled by the depth of her feelings.

He came forward, his hand curling gently about her arm. Still shaken, she allowed him to lead her from the room. Calum followed close upon their heels.

Once they were outside, Ronan turned to his brother with a frown. But before he could speak, Calum pointed out glibly, "You had no need of my assistance. Aye, you would have defeated them all easily enough on your own."

"You are ever late," Ronan complained, though, remarkably, without any true anger.

"Did you ... sweet heaven, did you expect something like this to happen?" Analise asked, her mind spinning anew.

"Always. Only a fool would trust Robert Kerr." His hand smoothed down along her arm, as though to reassure himself that she was unharmed. "It was not safe to leave you at the inn. And if you had remained at Dunslair, Kerr might well have taken advantage of my absence. Our marriage is known by all now."

"Could you not have told me of the peril?" she accused, her eyes flashing up at him.

"Did you think to defend me with Alan Ridley's sword?" he suddenly asked, ignoring her question in lieu of his own. She colored beneath his tender, amused gaze.

"I did not wish myself to be taken captive!" she proclaimed defensively.

"Aye." He slipped his arm about her waist and gave

her such a warm look that she melted inside. "Did I not say we were well matched?"

"If you have no further need of me . . ." said Calum, smiling indulgently at the two of them.

"You have done as I asked?"

"Do I not always carry out your orders?" Calum retorted in mock affront.

"Then, 'tis time you returned to Dunslair."

"I mean to ride soon." He hesitated for a moment, and it was obvious that he was undecided about something. His eyes met Ronan's again when he declared, "Never have I meant to cause you trouble."

"What has happened?" Ronan demanded, immediately suspicious. He drew his arm from about Analise, who listened to the exchange in growing curiosity.

"Nothing," replied Calum. "Not yet, at least." He looked away again. "I am no longer a boy, Ronan. And I must choose my own path."

"Aye, but I would have your choice be the true one." Though his brother's words filled him with no small measure of alarm, he revealed none of it. "What is it you plan?"

"Were I to tell you, you would seek to dissuade me."

"By all that is holy, Calum, if you—"

"You must trust me, Brother," Calum insisted, then forced a smile to his lips and changed the subject. "Will you return to Dunslair today?"

"No."

"Till the morrow, then," Calum offered in farewell. He smiled again at Analise before striding away, back toward the center of the town.

"He means to do wrong," Ronan murmured, his voice low and edged with anger.

"How can you be certain of that?" Analise queried. She felt compelled to rise to Calum's defense. " 'Tis true that he is young, and perhaps a bit willful, yet—"

"I know him well, Analise." His brows drew together in a frown, his eyes glinting like cold steel. "Once more, he allows his heart to rule his head."

"If he is in danger, then we must go after him." Genuinely worried, she placed a hand upon her husband's arm. "At once, Ronan!"

"Aye." His mouth curved into a faint smile of irony. "We are of the same mind." He took her arm again, and they set off in pursuit of Calum.

It did not take long to find him. Emerging from the crowded market, they watched as he climbed the steps of a small, square building with a simple wooden cross upon its roof.

"Why, 'tis a church!" Analise remarked in surprise.

Ronan said nothing, but urged her along with him as he gave chase. They entered the church, arriving just in time to observe Calum and Dierdre Maxwell joining hands before an elderly, black-robed clergyman.

Calum tensed at the sound of their approach. Pivoting to confront his brother, he was at first infuriated by the intrusion. But he quickly set his anger aside. In truth, he had secretly wished to have Ronan there. He had very nearly confessed his plans earlier. And he was not too surprised to discover that he had been followed.

"Come, Ronan," he exhorted, his features set in determination. "I would have you witness the ceremony."

"You cannot do this, Calum," Ronan warned him, drawing closer while Analise remained near the doorway.

"I can and will," said Calum. He heaved a sigh before finally admitting, "We were joined in handfast a year ago. Aye, and we would now gain the blessings of the church." He cast Dierdre a tender smile, drawing her arm through his again. She looked pale and nervous, yet happy. "I did but convince her of it this very morn."

"I will not allow it," Ronan decreed. "Angus Maxwell will have your head if you dare to wed her without his consent."

"Then, he will leave his grandson fatherless," Calum replied. He had the grace to look remorseful, but guilt was swiftly replaced by pride. "Aye. Dierdre carries my child within her."

Analise gasped, her eyes growing very round as she watched the telltale blush stain Dierdre's cheeks. She glanced at Ronan. He appeared ready to strike his brother.

"By damn," he ground out, "do you think the Maxwells' swords will be stilled by that? You have given them reason enough already to kill you. If you repeat the vows of marriage this day, your bride will be a widow before nightfall." Breathing another oath, he abruptly turned his hot, angry gaze upon the clergyman now. "Your own life is in peril if you perform the ceremony. The girl's father has made his objections known."

"They are handfasted," the somber, gray-haired reverend pointed out. He clutched the Bible in his hands more securely and frowned at Ronan. "God has blessed their union. And the child must have a name."

"If I must die for it, then I am ready!" Calum proclaimed stubbornly.

"No, Calum!" cried Dierdre, her eyes glistening with tears. She raised her hands to his chest, and gave him a look of such sweet appeal that he felt his resolve wavering. "Your brother is right. I must tell my father of the child first. I must persuade him—"

"You know well enough that he will not listen," Calum protested. He covered her hands with the warmth of his own. "We must be strong, my love. We can allow none to keep us apart."

"That is not my intent," Ronan assured him quietly. "The marriage will take place. Soon. I will go myself to speak with Angus Maxwell."

His words filled Analise with dread. She hastened forward now, her own eyes pleading for caution.

"You cannot ride to Longcroft alone!" she protested.

" 'Tis the only way. Were Calum to set foot there, Angus would strike without delay." His mouth curved into a crooked half smile when he asked her softly, "Do you still have so little confidence in my abilities, then?"

"You are no less human than any other man!"

"Aye. And no less determined to prevent bloodshed." Turning back to Calum, he bade him, "Go home. In three days' time, I will seek Angus's consent once more."

"And if he does not give it?"

"Then, we will appeal to the king himself."

"Do you truly think he—"

"He would," Ronan answered with a calm certainty. His eyes held his brother's. "You must trust me, Calum."

Calum knew that he must comply. Exchanging a look of hopeful longing with Dierdre, he reluctantly drew away. Dierdre blinked back her tears. Calum's features grew taut with the effort it was costing him to postpone the claiming of his bride. Watching the two young lovers, Analise felt her heart stir with compassion—and an understanding she did not know she possessed.

Calum turned to the clergyman. "There will be no wedding this day." His tone was one of sadness and resignation.

"I will speak of this to no one," the man promised in earnest, then took his leave.

"Will you grant us a brief time alone?" Calum appealed to his brother. He reached for Dierdre's hand.

Ronan gave him a curt nod, and led Analise from the church. They waited upon the steps outside, taking little notice of the fact that the sun's rays had broken through the clouds to warm the air.

"Would Angus Maxwell truly have killed Calum if you had not put a stop to the wedding?" Analise asked in a small voice.

"Aye. No man would see his daughter taken to wife without his consent."

"Yet you yourself might well have faced death as a result of *our* marriage," she pointed out. "I know that it is forbidden for English and Scottish to wed."

"Yet 'tis done often enough," he remarked, his eyes aglow with wry humor. "The laws were made long ago, to prevent the mingling of enemies. They have ever failed. And unless I lose favor with the king, I am in no danger of losing my life."

"You are friend to your king," she noted, recalling his promise to intercede on Calum's behalf.

"I serve him gladly." He smiled briefly before revealing, "The king would have me bring you to Edinburgh soon. He has made known his wish to set eyes upon the woman who has tamed the Armstrong."

"Tamed the—" she echoed, only to break off and color warmly. Her gaze fell beneath the loving intensity of his. "Such a thing is impossible."

"Is it? Perhaps, in fifty years' time, you will have succeeded."

"Why do you pretend that our marriage will endure?"

she suddenly demanded in exasperation. Though she did not know why, her emotions felt raw. She cursed the tears starting to her eyes, and was furious at the unsteadiness of her voice. "In spite of . . . of all that has happened, I am still determined to be free!"

"Never have I known a woman as headstrong as you," Ronan declared with mingled impatience and affection. "Nor as maddening."

She would have offered a suitable, defiant retort, but Calum joined them now. His pain was obvious. He looked to his brother and disclosed in a voice that was barely audible, "Dierdre will not leave until we have gone. None should see us together."

"Does she return to Longcroft this day?" Ronan asked.

"No. On the morrow." He frowned darkly, his eyes full of reproach. "Though I should thank you, I cannot do so."

"Aye." It was clear that he understood.

"You must not despair, Calum," Analise advised him, impulsively lifting a gentle hand to his arm. "I am certain that her father will be persuaded."

"Would that I held your optimism," he murmured. Clasping her hand for a moment, he drew himself rigidly erect and announced, "I ride homeward now."

"Take care, Brother," Ronan cautioned, his expression quite solemn. "Keep within the walls at Dunslair. If word of this should reach Longcroft—"

"By damn, I wish that it would!" Calum burst out. Flinging Ronan one last resentful glare, he strode angrily down the steps and disappeared into the crowd.

"Should we not accompany him to Dunslair?" Analise suggested, worried for Calum's safety.

"No," answered Ronan. "He is of no mind to allow it."

He shook his head, his gaze unfathomable when he added, "And I cannot yet leave Jedburgh."

"Why not?"

"Another meeting awaits me this night." His hand closed about her arm once more. "Until then we will tarry within the town."

"And what shall we do here?"

" 'Tis time, I think, that you had clothing more suited to Scotland." With a faint smile, he confessed, "Though you did not know it, my lady, you have married a wealthy man."

"A wealthy man?" she repeated, her eyes widening in surprise at the news.

"Aye. Wealthier than both of your English suitors put together."

"Do you think, Ronan Armstrong, that such knowledge would have made any difference?" Her eyes now kindled at the thought.

"No. I do not." His own gaze filled with satisfaction, he urged her down the steps with him.

Chapter 9

Though she was determined not to do so, Analise took delight in being fitted for several new gowns—all of them well-suited to the unpredictable, often chilling Borders weather. Ronan was content to watch her. She was dismayed to find herself tempted to consult him about the styles and fabrics, as if he were indeed any other husband. And she felt guilty, for she knew that her intention was to wear the clothes in France, not Scotland. Still, she allowed him the pleasure of his generosity—and was secretly thrilled by the approval and desire in his gaze.

By the time darkness crept over the town, she was happy to retire to their room at the inn. The day had been long, and far more eventful than she had expected. She shuddered at the memory of Robert Kerr's treachery. And her heart grew heavy again when she thought of Calum's pain.

Noting her disquiet, Ronan approached the fireplace. His eyes softened as they traveled over her face. She sat before the flames, her arms folded together in her lap and her long braid hanging over one shoulder. To him, she had never looked so beautiful. Nor so young and vulnerable.

"My uncle should arrive soon," he remarked. He braced a hand upon the mantelpiece and gazed down at her.

"Your uncle?" Her eyes flew up to meet his.

"Aye. He lives but a short distance from Jedburgh." He frowned, his grasp tightening upon the carved, splintered wood. " 'Twas necessary for him to wait for the cover of darkness."

"What is happening?" she demanded, abruptly rising from the chair. "What reason did you have for meeting Robert Kerr? Why do you now wait for your uncle?"

"I can tell you only that my reasons are many. And must, for now, remain a mystery to you."

"Sweet heaven, I have endured far too much *mystery* since the night we were wed!" She heaved a long, ragged sigh before accusing, "You do not trust me. 'Tis because I am English and—"

"No," he denied, moving closer. His hands lifted to her shoulders, his eyes burning down into hers. "I am sworn to a manner of secrecy. Yet, I would have you know that what I do, I do for peace alone."

She had to be satisfied with that, for she knew she could pry no more from his lips. Sinking back down into the chair, she inhaled upon a soft gasp when a knock sounded at the door. She watched as Ronan answered it.

"I fear I am late," said Thomas Armstrong, stepping inside the room. He was nearly as tall as Ronan. With graying auburn hair and a face that was still handsome in spite of more than fifty years spent amid the brutal Scottish elements, he looked very much like an older version of his nephew. Indeed, the family resemblance was undeniable.

Thomas gripped Ronan's hand, then turned his clear

blue gaze upon Analise. She stood once more, and colored faintly beneath his scrutiny.

" 'Tis a pleasure to make your acquaintance, Analise," he declared, offering her a gallant bow and a smile. "I have longed to bid you welcome to the Clan Mac Ghillielaidir."

"I thank you, sir," she murmured, unable to keep a smile from her own lips.

Ronan closed the door and drew his uncle to the far corner of the room. They began to speak in hushed tones, leaving Analise to wrestle with her curiosity. She did hear the king's name mentioned, along with that of Robert Kerr, and even John Beattie. It was apparent to her that Ronan was involved in some sort of political intrigue. The thought filled her with trepidation, for she realized that her husband was very likely plunging himself into further danger. Had she not seen evidence enough of that already?

Finally the men ceased their clandestine discussion. Thomas drew away from Ronan, offering Analise another warm and paternal smile as he moved back to take her hand.

"Already I must bid you farewell. Yet I have charged your husband with the duty of bringing you soon to Edinburgh."

"You . . . you are at the court, then?" she stammered, for it occurred to her now that he, like Ronan, might have the king's ear.

"Aye," replied Thomas. "And 'tis not often enough we are graced with beauty such as yours." He raised her hand to his lips, then turned to Ronan again. "If you will, tell Calum that when he next crosses my threshold, he must tarry for longer than a night alone. My daughters would see their bonny cousin more often."

"No doubt, it would serve him well to go to Edinburgh," Ronan allowed, a pensive frown momentarily creasing his brow.

Thomas took his leave then. Once the door had closed behind him, Ronan pushed the bolt into place. Still preoccupied, he returned to stand before the fireplace. Analise folded her arms beneath her breasts and fixed him with an angry, censorious look.

"You will not tell me what you are plotting, yet I have this day been privy to conversations that point to an involvement in a perilous undertaking." Her fiery gaze met squarely the deep, piercing steadiness of his. "Was I not at the court in London? Indeed, I have heard other men scheme, men who would betray their rivals or gain favor with the queen."

"It matters to you that I am in danger?" Ronan challenged, his voice laced with tender amusement.

"I . . . would not see you dead," she faltered, hastily looking away.

"You must trust me."

"You still speak of trust?" She raised her eyes to his again, only to suffer a sharp intake of breath when his hands closed gently about her arms.

"I would have us live in peace, Analise," he told her in earnest. "Aye, and school our children against murder and thievery."

"Children?" She paled, her head spinning. *Children.* Sweet heaven, she had not thought of that . . .

"Perhaps, lady wife, you already carry our bairn within you." He smiled softly and encircled her with the loving, hard-muscled warmth of his arms. "But if not, we will make certain of it soon enough."

"No!" she breathed, shaking her head as she lifted her hands to push at his chest.

"I grow weary of the battles between us, Analise," he advised, his eyes darkening.

"Then, release me! Set aside our marriage and—"

"By damn, woman, you try my patience sorely."

He lowered his head to kiss her, but she was not of a mind to surrender so easily. She twisted from his grasp and sought refuge behind the chair. Her breasts rose and fell rapidly with the force of her indignation, while her eyes were ablaze with emerald fire.

"Keep your distance, Ronan Armstrong," she bade him. "I shall not submit myself to your lovemaking this night!"

"So," he remarked with only the hint of a smile, "I must woo you still."

"I will not be wooed at all!" She did not understand the ache in her heart. Nor the accursed tendency to burst into tears again. But she knew that her husband was to blame for her turmoil. Yes, and that he would not stop until, true to his vow, he possessed all of her. Body and soul.

Alarmed, she cried rashly, "If you *must* ease your passions, I am certain there are women in Jedburgh who would welcome you to their beds!"

"You cannot mean that." His expression was quite grim, his gaze glinting harshly.

"Can I not?" she retorted, yet knew that it was the last thing she desired. In truth, the very thought of him in another woman's arms sent a sharp pain burning through her.

"Once, I might have done as you suggest," he admitted,

drawing closer. "But that was before we were wed. Henceforth, there will be no other women. I have given you my heart, Analise. And once given, it cannot be returned."

She could find no words with which to reply. Her pulse leapt wildly as he stopped before her. The chair remained between them; she clutched at the back of it and lifted her chin to look up at him.

"Why has this happened?" she whispered brokenly.

" 'Twas meant to be."

"No." She shook her head, all the while fighting against the temptation to return to the strong, protective circle of his arms. "No, I cannot believe—"

The sentence remained unfinished as, once again, she attempted to flee. Ronan's hand shot out to seize her wrist. She fought him, with such vigor that her long skirts became entangled about her legs. A strangled cry escaped her lips as she lost her balance. Ronan broke her fall, his arm slipping about her waist and hauling her back against him.

Wide-eyed and breathless, she stared up at him, expecting him to sweep her up in his arms and carry her to the bed. But he did not. Instead he set her away from him. His expression was cold, impassive, offering no hint of the anger and desire burning within him.

"Go to bed, Analise," he commanded in a tone that was very low and level. He turned back to the fire. His eyes stared deeply into the flames.

"You do not mean to—" she began to question in stunned disbelief.

"To bed."

Her breath caught in her throat again. She whirled about, hurrying across to the far side of the bed. Her eyes strayed frequently to Ronan as she removed all of her clothing save her shift. And when she climbed beneath the covers and lay down, she half expected him to join her.

He did not.

She watched as he took a seat before the fire. Though tempted to ask him when he would come, she bit her tongue and lowered her head to the pillow. An inexplicable misery took hold of her. She closed her eyes, her throat constricting as she rolled to her side and pulled the covers up to her chin. Acutely conscious of Ronan's presence, she was certain she would not be able to sleep. Yet it wasn't long until she drifted into unconsciousness, with Ronan's words echoing in her mind. *I have given you my heart* . . .

She was dreaming.

The dream was sweet, satisfying. She gave a soft moan and stretched languidly. Her lips beckoned the warm pressure of her husband's, her body molding against the length of his. Naked flesh met naked flesh. She trembled with pleasure. Ronan's hand glided upward, over the curve of her hip to the rose-tipped fullness of her breast. He caressed her gently, provocatively, while his kiss, deep and hungry and masterful, set her afire.

She moaned again, her arms urging him even closer. Her hands smoothed across his back, lowered to his buttocks, then moved with a will of their own to the hardness between his thighs. Her fingers did what they had secretly longed to do—they closed about his pulsing manhood, exploring and tantalizing with a bold yet seductive innocence.

Ronan groaned, his whole body tensing while passion blazed wildly through him. His mouth ravished hers with even more hot, merciless hunger. His strong arms wrapped tightly about her. He rolled to his back in the bed.

It was no dream.

Her eyelids fluttered open. She came fully awake now, her mouth falling open in startlement when she saw that she was lying atop him. He had managed to remove her shift without waking her. The dwindling firelight revealed all.

His eyes smoldered up into the beautiful, sleep-drugged softness of hers. She blushed fierily.

"Unconscionable knave!" she sputtered. "You would take advantage of me in such a way?"

"Aye. Though my pride would have kept me from you, I could not obey." A faint smile of irony touched his lips. "Your slumber was all the sweeter for your boldness."

Her color deepened. Indignant, she attempted to rise. But he easily held her captive, his arms like a vise about her. Her gaze kindled.

"Let me go!"

" 'Tis too late."

"No!" She wriggled atop him, which only served to further inflame his desire.

"By heaven," he uttered huskily, "you will tempt me to madness yet."

He forced her head down to his, kissing her with such fierce, intoxicating ardor that she felt a familiar heat spreading throughout her body. She shivered as her breasts made contact with the bronzed, hard-muscled expanse of his chest again. With another moan of surrender, she became an active participant in the kiss, her long, unbound tresses cascading down about her face and shoulders to tease at his fevered skin.

Moments later she was disappointed when his mouth left hers, but disappointment gave way to delight as he urged her farther upward in his embrace. His lips and tongue paid moist, loving tribute to her breasts. His hands glided downward to grasp the well-rounded firmness of her bottom. She clutched at his shoulders and shivered anew, so swept away by passion that, once more, all else was forgotten.

Ronan's warm, skillful fingers insinuated themselves within the silky triangle of curls at the apex of her thighs. Her own fingers dug into his arms as she gasped and squirmed and felt the now familiar, rapturous yearning spark and blaze deep within her.

She was long past any measure of resistance when he lifted her hips and brought her down upon his throbbing manhood. She inhaled sharply, her eyes flying wide as he sheathed to the hilt within her soft, velvety warmth. Certain that he touched her very womb, she closed her eyes again and instinctively arched her back. Her hips met the rhythm of his, her breath catching in her throat with each thrust. His hands left her hips to close upon her breasts. She leaned forward again, her fingers curling about the powerful, rock-hard smoothness of his upper arms. Unaware that Ronan watched her, and that his magnificent blue eyes burned with love and triumph as they raked over her, she gave herself up to the sweet madness.

And then came the explosion of pleasure, hotter and more satisfying than ever before. Analise gave a soft, breathless cry, her body tensing atop Ronan's. He sought his own release in the next instant.

In the aftermath of their tempestuous union, she lay against him, her head upon his chest and her heart filled with the strange, heart-stirring contentment she felt whenever in his arms. He gathered her even closer. His hand trailed downward to smooth possessively across the curve of her hip.

"You know the truth, Analise," he remarked in a quiet, resonant tone. "Never will I let you go."

"I know only that I am weak and foolish," she replied tremulously.

"Do you truly believe that to be the reason your blood stirs?" He entangled his hand within her thick golden curls now and gave a firm yet gentle tug so that she was forced to look up at him. She warmed beneath his tender gaze. "No, sweet lady," he told her, his voice laced with affectionate humor. "You are no wanton. 'Tis love alone that prompts you to surrender. Aye, and prompts *me* to want you near me always."

"I cannot love you," she sighed, her beautiful eyes clouding with confusion again. "I wanted none of this marriage. Indeed, I—I was determined to seek refuge with my mother's kinsmen in France."

"It matters not how we began. Nor that you would have fled." His hand cupped her chin, while his mouth curved into an indulgent smile. "Have I not told you that Providence decreed our marriage? By all the saints, lass, I knew it when I first saw you at Windy Gyle. And our fate was sealed the moment our lips met."

"You were with Robert Kerr that day," she recalled aloud, another sigh escaping her lips as she lowered her head to his chest once more. "I thought him your friend."

"He was never that, though an ally. His father is a good man and was friend to mine."

"Yet the son is both evil and ruthless." She shuddered anew at the memory of Ronan's danger, as well as her own.

"Aye. And will be made to answer for his crimes." He changed the subject then, his mind gladly returning to more pleasant thoughts. He wrapped his arms about her and buried his face in the fragrant softness of her hair. "Were I made of stone, I would still find it impossible to keep my hands from you."

"Does it not trouble you that I am English?"

"No."

"In London, we were told that the Scots were men without either conscience or mercy." She frowned, her hand smoothing across the hardness of his belly. "And I am now the wife of one of those savages, a Border Reiver who kills men so easily yet shows me tenderness. I will never understand you, Ronan Armstrong."

"In time, you will," he insisted, her touch igniting his desire once more. "We have been wed but a few days."

"No doubt you think me well and truly conquered!" she accused in sudden resentment. Her eyes flashed down at him as she raised her head. "I am not. No, for my heart is my own to give!"

"I have it already." While she grew visibly angry at his presumption, he rolled so that she was beneath him. His hands caught her wrists and forced her arms above her head. She squirmed in protest as the length of his muscular, virile body pressed her supple curves down into the mattress.

"Will you never cease your barbarous ways?" she stormed.

"No, my lady. I will not." He gave her a quick, thoroughly disarming kiss. She struggled for breath when he raised his head and moved one of his hands to her breast. His arousal was evident against her thighs. Her eyes widened in startlement and disbelief.

"But we have just—"

"Aye. And will again." His countenance was forebodingly solemn, his gaze searing down into hers when he vowed. "I mean to love you well this night, Analise. Until we can both bear no more. *Until I hear you say that you are mine forever.*"

He swallowed her gasp as his lips descended mercilessly upon hers again. She moaned, arching beneath him, furious with herself yet unable to extinguish the fire he alone could kindle within her . . .

They set out for Dunslair the following morning. Analise avoided her husband's gaze, and was glad that he spoke little as they dressed and made ready to leave.

Once away from Jedburgh, she groaned inwardly, her cheeks growing hot when she remembered the wild, passionate night she had shared with the man who rode beside her. He had kept his promise. And she . . . heaven help her, she had told him what he had vowed to hear.

Shifting uncomfortably in the saddle, she felt as though every square inch of her skin had been branded by his touch. Her pride stung as much as her body warmed at the memory of his fierce, hotly pleasurable lovemaking. She closed her eyes and offered up a desperate prayer for reason.

The sun's rays caressed her face. Though clouds had gathered upon the horizon, the day promised to be considerably milder than usual. The wind was gentle, fresh and scented with wildflowers, while the sweet, distant song of birds filled the air. Analise found her disquiet lessening. Her gaze swept across the rugged beauty of the hills, and she ventured a glance at Ronan. His eyes caught hers. She hastily looked away.

Soon they were drawing near to Dunslair. She was surprised at the way her spirits lifted when she caught sight of Dunslair's towers silhouetted against the endless blue of the Borders sky. It was as though she had come home. *Home.* The thought was puzzling, pleasing, and she wondered how such a thing had come to pass.

Calum was there to greet them. He spoke briefly to Analise, then drew his brother aside.

"Simon Hayward has sent word at last," he revealed quietly.

"He bids me ride to Beauford?" queried Ronan, his own voice low.

"Aye."

"Then, I must go at once." His gaze moved to Analise, who stood watching them a short distance away. He frowned before directing Calum, "Summon our nearest kinsmen. Dunslair must remain well guarded in my absence."

"Do you think Robert Kerr would dare to strike while you are gone?" Calum asked worriedly.

"We must take no chances." His features were quite grim, his eyes darkening when he added, "Were he to take Dunslair, Analise would become his captive."

"I would lay down my life to protect her."

"I know," said Ronan, lifting a hand to his brother's shoulder. "As would I."

Analise knew that something was amiss. A lump rose in her throat as she looked at Ronan's face. He left Calum and returned to her side.

"I must leave you," he announced. His reluctance to do so was obvious.

"Where are you going?"

"To Beauford. Simon Hayward would speak with me."

"You cannot go alone!" she protested, the color draining from her face at the thought of his peril. "You know that he is not to be trusted. Indeed, what if—"

"He will not seek to do me harm," Ronan assured her. "My death would see an end to the alliance he was so anxious to claim." He lifted a gentle hand to the smoothness of her cheek. "Calum will guard you well. Aye, and others of our clan will gather at Dunslair before this night." Slipping an arm about her waist, he pressed a quick, sweetly compelling kiss upon her lips, then promised, "I will soon return."

She watched as he mounted a fresh horse brought to him and rode back through the gate. Her eyes followed him until he was out of sight. Heaving a ragged sigh, she turned and wandered toward the house.

"No man is better able to look after himself," Calum declared, joining her now.

"He is but flesh and blood," she murmured.

"Aye." He gave her a faint smile. "To love another often brings pain."

She could not think of a response. Yet his words remained with her as she entered the house. And throughout the day, when she would have kept thoughts of Ronan from her mind.

* * *

More than thirty Armstrongs answered the call of their chieftain. The baronial hall at Dunslair was filled with the sounds of talk and laughter that night, with the light of blazing torches and the smell of leather. Every bedchamber had been prepared; those who had not drawn the comfort of a bed would content themselves with sleeping upon the floor near the fireplace in the Great Hall.

Though tempted to remain upstairs, Analise ventured among the guests. All treated her with reverence. They were tall and hearty men, men who were rugged yet not without social graces. And their affection and loyalty toward Ronan was evident whenever they spoke of him.

By the time she retired to her husband's bedchamber, Analise was both weary and restless. She undressed and climbed beneath the covers of the bed. Her eyes strayed to the empty place beside her. With a sigh she reached for Ronan's pillow and hugged it close.

You know the truth, Analise. Her breath caught in her throat at the memory of his words, of his splendidly resonant voice and his deep, penetrating blue eyes. Never before had she known a man like him. Never before had she been loved as he professed to love her.

Flinging a distracted look heavenward, she thrust the pillow away and tossed back the covers. Her bare feet padded swiftly across the cold floor, her fingers grasping at the curtain when she moved to stand at the window. She gazed out upon the rolling, moonlit countryside and wondered if Ronan would return that night.

"Please, God, keep him safe," she whispered.

Her heart took a wild leap within her breast. Her eyes grew very round as a sudden tremor shook her.

Was it truly possible that she loved Ronan Armstrong?

"No," she gasped, shaking her head. "It cannot be!"

She whirled about and returned to the bed. Lying down, she yanked the covers up to her chin and determined to think of Ronan and her feelings for him no more.

Her efforts met with little success, of course. And when she awoke the next morning, her mind burned with memories of her dreams. Dreams of the life she could enjoy with Ronan, and of the happiness they could share if only her love were as strong as his own.

She dragged herself from the bed. Once dressed, she hastened downstairs to help Mairi and Flora serve breakfast to the dozens of hungry Armstrong men. They were grateful for her help. She was grateful for the opportunity to occupy her mind.

Morning drifted into afternoon. The hours crawled past. By the time twilight approached, Ronan had still not returned.

"Perhaps 'twas necessary for him to ride elsewhere after Beauford," Calum suggested to her as they took a turn about the grounds.

"Could he not have sent word?" she replied, drawing her cloak more securely about her. Darkness was fast closing in. The air held a chill, the sky promising another clear night.

"Aye," said Calum. His eyes twinkled with humor. "But you know him well. He was ever a man of few words."

At that, her mouth curved into a soft smile of irony. She looked to the gate again, her smile fading. No matter how desperately she tried, she could not shake her apprehension. *Something was wrong.*

Sleep did not come easily to her that night. She tossed and turned, plagued by horrifying visions of Ronan lying dead upon the windswept moors. She would not ask herself why she should care so much. But her dread was real, and keenly felt.

It was long past midnight when a knock sounded at her door. She awoke with a start, her eyes flying wide. She scrambled from the bed and flung her cloak about her shoulders.

Opening the door, she was startled to find Calum supporting a strangely pale and stoic-faced Ronan. Her gaze fell upon the spot where blood had soaked through both his shirt and his jack.

"Sweet mercy!" she breathed in dismay.

"He is weakened by loss of blood," Calum told her. He half carried his brother into the room and laid him upon the bed. Analise was immediately at her husband's side. He was barely conscious. Her hands trembled as she leaned over him and began easing his shirt upward to examine his injuries. "What happened?" she asked in a small, uneven voice.

"Ewan Maxwell," answered Calum, his eyes gleaming vengefully. "He and his men ambushed Ronan. 'Twas four against one. Aye, yet Maxwell did pay for his treachery. He dances with the devil this night."

"He is dead?" At Calum's wordless nod, she turned back to Ronan and paled as she bared his chest. A sword had pierced him just below his rib cage. "The wound is deep," she noted, her dread returning to hit her full force.

"Heat the poker within the flames," Ronan instructed,

his voice raw. His eyes met hers now. "Calum will hold me. You must burn the wound."

"I cannot!" she choked out.

"You can," he insisted. In spite of his pain, a wry smile hovered briefly about his lips. "Aye, my headstrong bride can do whatever she pleases."

She swallowed hard. Her bright, distressed gaze moved to Calum. He turned and crossed to the fireplace.

"We must not delay," he decreed grimly. "The bleeding must be stopped."

A shiver ran the course of Analise's spine when Ronan's hand closed about hers. She looked deeply into his eyes. And felt her very soul stir with an emotion so intense that it left her shaken.

"None must know of my return yet," he cautioned her in a hoarse whisper.

"Oh, Ronan," she breathed tremulously. "I . . . never would I have thought to see you like this."

"Did you not once proclaim me mortal?"

He sucked in his breath, a grimace of pain crossing his features. She caught her lower lip between her teeth and felt hot tears start to her eyes. Calum returned with the poker. The end of it glowed red with heat.

"It must remain upon the wound for no less than the count of three," Calum directed. He pressed the length of iron into her reluctant, uncertain grasp, then moved in position to hold Ronan. "Bear it well, Brother," he exhorted with deceptive nonchalance, "for it would, in truth, require ten of me to force you to stillness."

Analise's eyes were wide with fear and anxiety as they flew back to Calum. He gave her a curt nod. She offered up a silent prayer. And lowered the glowing metal to Ronan's wound.

He ground out a curse. His jaw clenched, his eyes closing while his whole body tensed upon the mattress. It required all of Calum's strength to prevent him from rising.

Analise, filled with anguish at the thought of what he suffered, forced herself to keep the rod still. When she drew it away at last, Ronan's skin was blackened. The bleeding had been stopped.

She heaved a long, shuddering sigh. Her legs threatened to give way beneath her, and she scarcely realized that she still held the poker.

"Well-done," murmured Calum. He straightened, his expression grave as he stared down at his brother. "We must now bind the wound. And pray that infection does not set in."

"Should we not summon a physician?" she asked, her voice quavering.

"He would do naught save what we have done." He searched about, finally settling upon the clean toweling he spied upon the bedside table. He began tearing it into strips.

Ronan opened his eyes. It was clear that he was still in considerable pain. Yet he managed another faint smile.

"Mayhap you took pleasure in that," he accused his wife, though without conviction.

"I swear to you that I did not!" she was quick to deny. She finally spun about and returned the poker to the hearth. Her face was pale, her hands shaking so much that she folded them together. "I will fetch some wine to dull your pain," she told Ronan.

"Remember," he cautioned again, his tone quite low as he closed his eyes and leaned heavily back against the pillow. "My presence here must remain a secret."

Though tempted to ask why, she did not. She nodded her head in mute agreement, then hastened forth to make good on her promise.

Once she had gone, Calum moved back to Ronan's side with the bandages. He carefully pressed them to the wound.

"The king will not be pleased to hear of Maxwell's death."

"Aye," said Ronan, gritting his teeth while Calum wrapped a length of the toweling about him to secure the bandages. "The feud will be renewed. Blood must be met with blood." He caught his brother's hand with his own, and offered him a somber look. "Once Angus learns of what happened this night, he will not be of a mind to heed me. You and Dierdre—"

"By damn, the fault was not yours," Calum declared with a scowl. "If 'twas *you* lying dead beneath the moon, I would now be riding upon Longcroft with every Armstrong in Scotland!"

"The Maxwells may well do the same."

"Then, why must we not yet inform our kinsmen below? If there is the danger of attack, should we not make ready?"

"There will be no attack. None yet know that Ewan Maxwell died at my hands," Ronan explained. Inhaling sharply as another spasm of pain struck him, he balled his hands into fists and waited for it to pass. "I killed all four. And will not deny it when asked."

" 'Tis true enough that Angus will suspect you," Calum allowed quietly. He drew away from Ronan and wandered back to stand before the fire. "Yet, will he not be persuaded against revenge when he hears that you were ambushed?"

"Aye, if he were a man of reason. It matters not that Ewan had been cast out, nor that it was his own treachery caused his death. Angus will demand blood for it."

They fell into silence then. Ronan closed his eyes and battled a wave of light-headedness. Calum stared pensively into the flames. He cursed his own heartache. Though glad that his brother lived, he feared that Dierdre would now never be his.

Analise returned, closing the door behind her. She carried the wooden goblet filled with wine to the bed. Her eyes, still clouded with great worriment, traveled over Ronan's face.

"You are in much pain?" she queried softly.

"Enough." He took the goblet from her, raising his head to drink deeply of the wine. When he was finished, she set the goblet on the table and perched carefully upon the edge of the mattress. Her hand moved to Ronan's forehead. She breathed an inward sigh of relief for the lack of a fever.

"God willing, Ronan Armstrong, there will be no infection, and you shall recover quickly."

"And if I do not?" he challenged, his voice raw with a pain that had little to do with his wound. She was startled to realize that he was in earnest. A gasp broke from her lips when his hand shot out to capture hers. "Will you grieve for your husband, or dance merrily upon his grave?"

"You will not die!" she exclaimed feelingly. *"You must not!"*

He appeared satisfied with that. She shivered as he released her hand. Her eyes grew wide with incredulity.

"What of Simon Hayward?" Calum now thought to

ask. He came forward and frowned down at his brother. "You met with him?"

"Aye," Ronan answered. "He has called upon our bond." His gaze sparked with irony before he added, "He bids me gather the Armstrongs to join him in a raid upon Longcroft."

"What?" Calum breathed in disbelief.

"He would break the Maxwells. And foolishly believes we would be glad to ride with the English against them."

"What did you tell him?"

"That while honor prevents me from raising my sword to him, the alliance does not hold me to make war upon fellow Scots without reason. My words did not please him," he recalled dryly. "Aye, he would have thrown me into the hell of his dungeon again, save for his reluctance to lose my influence." He frowned darkly, tempted to confide all. But he did not. If Calum knew that Hayward meant to proceed with the raid without their help, and that *he* had given his promise to send no warning to Longcroft . . . by all the saints, there had to be a way to keep his honor and yet guard the safety of the woman his brother loved.

"I think," said Calum, " 'tis time you were left to your sleep. We will speak of this again on the morrow." He eased off Ronan's boots and drew the covers over him.

To Analise, meanwhile, their voices sounded strangely distant. Her head swam as the truth dawned at last.

She loved Ronan.

She could deny it no longer. She was in love with her husband, and had been so from the very first. All was made clear to her now—why she thrilled to his touch, why she yearned to know everything about him, why the thought of losing him was so completely unbearable.

Her heart soared with the knowledge. She stood and crossed to the window, still dazed, still wondering how she could have been so blind.

She loved him.

"Do you stay, Analise?" Calum asked her as he moved to the door.

"Yes." She turned to face him, and cast a swift glance toward Ronan. "I . . . I shall watch over him."

"I have little doubt of it." He smiled briefly, then left them alone.

Analise was all too aware of her husband's eyes upon her. She was not yet ready to confess her love to him. The realization was still too new, too startling. She would keep it to herself for a while yet. Until he was better. Until she was prepared to hear him boast of how he had always known.

Her gaze sparkled at the thought. But her throat tightened again in the next instant, for she knew he was not yet out of danger. She drew in a ragged breath and returned to hover anxiously over him.

"Come, lass," he commanded, his hand closing gently about her wrist. "Lie beside me."

"You must rest," she insisted. "Your wound—"

"Will heal much faster if you are near."

She could not summon the will to argue. Slowly removing her cloak, she tossed it aside and moved to the opposite side of the bed. She climbed beneath the covers, careful not to brush against him.

"You are warm enough?" she queried, searching his face for any sign of discomfort. "Is there anything you require? More wine, perhaps? Or—"

"I am no bairn, woman," he grumbled.

"Yet you are at my mercy until you are well enough to

leave this bed." She released another sigh before whispering, "Sleep now, Ronan."

"Aye."

Though pain seared through him, he pulled her close. She settled her head upon his shoulder and closed her eyes. Silently imploring God to heal the man she loved, she felt a deep, wondrous sense of peace. She knew that Ronan would live . . . and that he would soon claim his triumph.

Chapter 10

Ronan made a swift and truly amazing recovery. Within the space of a single day, he was sitting up in the bed. And complaining that he was being treated like an invalid.

Analise paid little mind to his crossness. She brought him a bowl of thin beef broth to eat, along with a cup of milk. He protested that she was determined to starve him. She would not be swayed. He accused her of vengeance. She merely smiled and reminded him that he was completely at her mercy.

He had slept often throughout the day, his body fighting to heal itself and reclaim the hours of rest lost to the journey. More than once, Analise had been tempted to tell him of her regard, to admit that she loved him more than she had ever thought possible. But she had remained silent on that score, for the time had not seemed right. And she would have it so.

Come nightfall, she was relieved that Ronan's wound still showed no sign of infection. She declared her intention to bathe him. His eyes lit with a roguish gleam, prompting her cheeks to warm.

"So," he put forth softly, "my bride grows less virginal now that I am injured."

"You are a wicked man, Ronan Armstrong," she retorted, folding her arms beneath her breasts as she stood beside the bed. Though she assumed an air of righteous indignation, her heart stirred at his teasing. "Perhaps *you*, sir, will be less arrogant and overbearing as a result of this."

"Aye. And no doubt a lifetime with you will bring me to virtue."

She stifled a laugh and drew the covers back. With Ronan's help, she eased off his breeches, then his jack and shirt. It was impossible to ignore the way the sight of his nakedness affected her. Her willful gaze strayed to his manhood, and she swallowed hard before turning to fetch the water she had heated a few minutes earlier. She returned with the bowl, setting it atop the table. Her hand closed about the cake of soap, and she rubbed it across the cloth she dipped within the water.

"I shall try not to cause you further pain," she promised earnestly.

"I trust you." Another crooked smile played about his lips.

Her gaze fell beneath the amused tenderness of his. She leaned closer, her hands trembling slightly as she smoothed the cloth down across his right leg. She did the same to the other leg, afterward rinsing and soaping the cloth again. Taking care to avoid his cauterized wound, she washed his chest and his arms. She scrubbed a bit harder when she moved on to his face and neck. Then, she prepared the cloth once more, squaring her shoulders before turning her attention to the cluster of tight, dark curls between his thighs. She swept the cloth over him—and caught her breath when she saw the undeniable evidence of his arousal.

Her eyes flew to his face. His teeth were clenched, his gaze smoldering.

"I am but wounded, lass, not dead," he ground out.

"I am sorry!" she breathed. "Truly, I did not—"

"Unless you mean to torment me, you must allow me to finish."

A dull flush crept up to her face as she handed him the cloth and turned away. When he was done, he pulled the covers over his nakedness. His wound was sore, but he was most pained by the desire burning within him.

"Soon, Analise," he vowed huskily, "you will be at *my* mercy."

"Is that a threat, my lord?"

" 'Tis a promise."

His words set her pulse to racing. She very nearly pressed a kiss to his lips. But a quiet knock sounded at the door. Answering it, she stepped aside so that Calum could enter. She closed the door behind him and watched as he crossed to stand beside his older brother.

"You look well enough this night," he pronounced with a brief, preoccupied smile.

"What has happened?" Ronan demanded, immediately sensing his disquiet.

"I have received a message from Dierdre." He frowned and shook his head. "God only knows how she managed to send it. She has told her father of the child, but would not reveal the name of her lover. And now she has been sent to a convent within Edinburgh so that none should know of her disgrace."

"All the better," said Ronan. At Calum's expression of surprise, he smiled faintly and pointed out, "It will be far easier to take her from that place than from the tower at Longcroft."

"You think I should—"

"Once I am able to ride, we will go together."

"But what of Angus Maxwell? If we bring Dierdre to Dunslair, he will surely lay siege. And," he charged, his eyes full of reproach, "were you not the one who advised against a marriage without her father's consent? If not for you, we would have been wed by now!"

"Things have changed," Ronan decreed solemnly.

"Aye," Calum agreed with a sigh. "We must now take our chances as they come." His gaze lit with hopefulness. "Perhaps Angus will yet give us his blessings. Once he learns that we were handfast, and that the child is mine, he might well see the right of it."

"If not, you must take flight and wait until the bairn comes. The sight of his grandchild should soften Angus Maxwell's heart."

"You can live at my father's estate in the south of England," Analise stepped forward to offer. " 'Tis beautiful and peaceful there. None will trouble you."

"I thank you, dear sister," Calum replied. "But not even to save my life will I live in England. Nor see my child born there." He turned back to Ronan. "Should the need arise, we can seek refuge with our mother's kinsmen on the Isle of Skye."

"So be it," Ronan concluded. "In a day's time, we will ride to Edinburgh."

"You shall not!" Analise was quick to object. She balled her hands into fists and planted them on her hips. " 'Tis much too soon."

"My wife would have me dance to her will," Ronan opined wryly to Calum.

"Your wife would have you live!" she parried.

"Then, I am pleased at her concern." His deep blue

eyes caught and held the fiery turquoise brilliance of hers. "Still, I will go."

"Was ever a man so infuriating and headstrong?"

"Have I not said we are well matched?"

Watching them, Calum hid a smile. "Will you still keep the news of your return from the others?" he now asked Ronan.

"Aye, for I would not yet have Angus Maxwell know where I am. And I would have no man speak falsely because of me. Except, of course, for my own brother," he amended with a swift glance at Calum. "*He* is well accustomed to it."

His gaze darkened as, once again, he recalled Simon Hayward's plan to ride down upon Longcroft. At least Dierdre would be safe, he mused, then offered up a silent curse. Because of his alliance with the English warden— a man who, though sworn to uphold the law, sought every opportunity to set himself above it—he must now turn traitor against his countrymen. The Maxwells were no friends or allies. But they were not as hated as the scoundrels across the border. By damn, he would yet find a way to give warning . . .

"Dunslair will remain well guarded while we are away," Calum assured Analise. "Should trouble come, every man worthy of the name Armstrong will strike in your defense."

"I do not fear for my own safety," she murmured.

"Aye." Another knowing smile tugged at his lips. He nodded down at his brother. "Again I bid you good night."

"Good night," Ronan uttered in return, then urged, "You must have faith, Calum."

" 'Tis easy enough to say when the woman you love shares your bed each night."

He turned and left, softly closing the door. Analise wandered back to the hearth. Her brow creased at the thought of Calum's heartache, and she released a sigh as she knelt and placed another log upon the fire.

"You have no other family save Simon Hayward?" Ronan queried, watching her every move.

"No." She straightened and dusted her hands together. "I am alone in the world."

"No, Analise," he corrected. *"You have me."*

His words filled her with joy. She pivoted about to face him, her eyes softly aglow.

" 'Tis time you slept again," she told him, though it was not at all what she wanted.

" 'Tis time you came to me." His penetrating gaze drew her closer. His splendid, deep-timbred voice sent warmth stealing through her. "I will be all to you," he vowed in earnest. "Husband, friend, lover. Let me love you as I would, Analise. Let yourself see the happiness we could share."

She stood close beside him now. Her eyes traveled over his face, her hand reaching with a will of its own to smooth over the clean-shaven ruggedness of his cheek.

"Aye," she answered, her mouth curving into a thoroughly winsome smile. "I shall."

"And will you give yourself freely to me?" he demanded. His hand captured hers. "Will you learn to love me as I love you?"

"I do love you," she finally confessed. Sudden tears of happiness gathered in her eyes. "In truth, my lord, I have loved you from the very first. Yet I did not know it until but a few hours ago, when I feared you would die." She released another soft, quavering sigh. "I love you, Ronan Armstrong. I give you my body, my heart . . . my soul."

Ronan stared up at her in mingled astonishment and exaltation. His heart soared heavenward. He smiled and tightened his hand upon hers.

"Then, I do offer you the same." He pulled her nearer, and it was clear that he meant to kiss her.

"Your wound!" she protested, her eyes growing wide.

"I will kiss you," he decreed in a tone laced with passion, "and damn my wound."

She had neither the will nor the inclination to stop him. Careful not to cause him pain, she sank down upon the edge of the mattress and lowered her mouth to his. The kiss they shared was sweet, heart-stirring, and left them both impatient for his recovery. When Analise drew away, she was flushed and breathless, and absolutely certain that there was no other man who could made her feel the way he did.

"Do not think," she warned him with mock severity, "that my love will force me to weakness or ready submission."

"Never that," he murmured wryly. His hand roamed downward, lingering at the saucy roundness of her hips while his lips nuzzled her silken throat.

"You must not ride to Edinburgh tomorrow." She stood and fixed him with a stern look. "You will not be strong enough."

"You cannot dissuade me." He frowned and heaved a sigh. "Calum loves Dierdre Maxwell, much the same as I love you. How can I deny him the chance to have her with him?"

"If you would but wait—"

"We cannot wait. There is no time."

"What do you mean?"

His features became a grim mask, his eyes smoldering with barely controlled rage. "Simon Hayward will soon ride upon Longcroft. Because of the alliance, I cannot send word of it to Angus Maxwell. I have given my promise and will not break it."

"So," she breathed, "that is why he summoned you to Beauford." Her eyes filled with horror. "Oh, Ronan, we cannot allow him to attack without warning. People may be killed!"

"Aye." He gave a faint, humorless smile. "The plan no doubt includes murder."

"What are we to do?" Gazing down at him, she shook her head. "What does your promise matter if it allows innocent people to be slaughtered?"

"There are very few innocents at Longcroft." He frowned again. "You do not yet understand the ways of the Scots. Always, we set honor above all."

"I understand well enough," she insisted, angrily folding her arms across her chest. "You will do nothing because the Maxwells are your enemies. I know that you are involved in some manner of intrigue. Does it make you content to do nothing while warfare rages along the border?"

"No," he denied, but would not elaborate.

"What of Dierdre? How can she hope to find happiness with a man whose brother allowed such treachery against her family? And why must you bring her to Dunslair *now*, when—"

"I have a plan," he finally confided. A grimace of pain crossed his face when he raised himself farther upright in the bed. "As soon as Dierdre is safe within these walls, I will send word to her father that we have taken her from Edinburgh."

"But he—he will come to demand her release," Analise stammered in disbelief.

"Not if I give him reason to think I plan an attack upon Longcroft. I will tell him of Ewan's death at my hands, of the abduction of his daughter, and I will lead him to believe that the Armstrongs will ride upon Longcroft before he can seek his revenge. The Maxwells will make ready to defend themselves. Simon Hayward will not be able to claim the advantage of surprise."

"And you will not have broken your promise," she noted, then sank disconsolately back down upon the bed. "My cousin is charged with upholding the law, yet would defy it easily enough. How can he do so?"

"He is no worse than Robert Kerr," Ronan told her. "Both grow rich from the misfortune of others. And both will answer for it."

"You are right. I do *not* understand you." She inhaled upon a soft gasp when his arm slipped about her waist.

"I will teach you what you need to know," he promised. "Aye, for have you not already proven yourself an apt and willing pupil?"

She colored beneath the loving amusement in his eyes. Though she would have risen, he held fast.

"The hour grows late," she observed, her voice underscored by a telltale breathlessness. "You must rest."

"I must first have another kiss."

"Only if you agree not to ride to Edinburgh on the morrow."

"Take care, lass," he cautioned in a low, vibrant tone that sent pleasurable chills down her spine. "The Reivers invented blackmail. And know how to use it to get what they want."

"You do not frighten me."

"Such is not my intent." His magnificent eyes lit with desire. "But I would love you well. Aye, and *will* once I am healed."

"Again, Scotsman, you offer empty threats," she retorted saucily.

"Do I?" He caught her against him, pulled her head down to his. She smiled before their lips met in another deep, intoxicating kiss, and silently vowed to love him as well as he loved her. Dunslair would in truth be her home now. She was determined to fill it with happiness . . . and children.

Another day passed. Another cold and moonless night was fast closing in when Calum came to collect Ronan. He was dressed for traveling, his sword buckled at his waist and his jack buttoned on over a thick woolen shirt.

"You are certain your wound—" he started to ask his brother.

"Aye," Ronan cut him off. He donned his own jack and sat down upon the bed in order to draw on his boots. Aware of Analise's eyes upon him, he turned his head and gave her a brief, bolstering smile. "Do not worry, lass. My life has been spent upon these hills. The way to Edinburgh is well-known to me."

"I do not fear that you will become lost," she told him, her eyes clouded with apprehension, "but that you will suffer another attack. Indeed, Robert Kerr did threaten revenge. And what if Angus Maxwell rides before he receives your message?"

"No disaster will befall me," he assured her firmly. Standing, he moved to pull her close. His eyes burned down into hers, his arms tightening about her while he promised, "I will return before the break of dawn."

"And if you do not?" she challenged, her voice edged with both anger and trepidation. She tensed within his embrace and tilted her head back to offer him a stormy, reproachful look. "If you truly loved me, Ronan Armstrong, you would not seek to cause me such distress."

"I must do what I think best." His own gaze glinted dully now. "And though I love you more than life itself, I will not become less of a man for it."

He released her and turned away to retrieve his sword. She stood battling tears, wishing for all the world that she had not been granted the misfortune of falling in love with such a proud and obstinate man. Calum sympathetically raised his hand to her arm.

"I swear by all that I hold dear," he vowed, "I will see him safely home again."

She could only nod in response. Her eyes followed her husband as he started for the door.

"How shall you leave without those below seeing you?" she asked, desperate to postpone his going.

"There is a secret passage beside the stairwell," he answered. Offering her one last hot, compelling look, he left. Calum followed, closing the door softly on his way out.

Analise stared after them for several long moments. Her heart felt unbearably heavy, and her mind was filled with horrifying visions of the dangers that could threaten Ronan. She released a long, quavering sigh and sank down into the chair before the fireplace.

Thus, the agony of waiting began. She slept little throughout the night. Her eyes strayed frequently to the door, and she repeated, over and over again, a prayer for her beloved's safety. Just as often, she cursed his stubbornness, his seeming belief that he was invincible ...

yet knew that, in truth, she would not have him any other way.

The hours crawled by. Her stomach knotted in alarm when, crossing to the window yet again, she observed the faint glow of a new morn teasing at the horizon.

And but an instant later, her ordeal came to an end. She whirled about, her eyes flying wide when the door opened and her husband stepped inside the bedchamber.

"Ronan!" she breathed. She was across the room and in his arms, her whole body flooded with relief. He held her close and pressed a gentle kiss to the top of her head.

"Did you doubt I would keep my promise?" he accused teasingly.

"The dawn has already broken," she pointed out, raising her head to eye him narrowly.

"Aye," he replied with a brief, crooked smile. "The good sisters at Our Lady of Mercy did protest with a good deal more earthly vigor than we had expected."

Calum had slipped into the room by now, with Dierdre at his side. Analise drew away from Ronan and hastened to clasp the other young woman's hands in welcome.

"No doubt you are weary from your journey," she remarked solicitously. "Come and sit. I shall go below to fetch you food and drink."

"Thank you," Dierdre murmured, her green eyes full of gratitude. She needed no further encouragement to take a seat. Calum led her to the chair, then dropped to one knee beside her. He lifted a tender hand to her cheek, smoothing a stray tendril of midnight-black hair into place behind her ear.

"You are well?" he queried softly, anxious about her health as well as the babe's.

"Aye, Calum." She placed her hand atop his and smiled. "Now that I am with you."

Analise moved back to Ronan. He had set aside his weapons and taken off his jack. She carefully tugged his shirt upward in order to examine his wound. He clenched his teeth when she probed gently at his skin.

"There has been no bleeding," she announced with another sigh of relief.

"And no sword thrust within my heart." His eyes glowed warmly at her concern. "Did I not tell you I would return safely?" He would have captured her hand, but she evaded his grasp and crossed to the door. Slipping from the room she crept down the stairs to fetch some wine and bread. Yet when she returned, it was only to find that Calum and Dierdre had gone.

"Where—" she started to question in puzzlement.

"They have retired to Calum's bedchamber," Ronan informed her. He came forward and took the tray from her hands. His mouth twitched when he added, "Their hunger was not for bread."

"But Dierdre will require nourishment."

"Aye. Calum will see to her." He set the tray atop the table. The firelight played softly over his face, the dwindling blaze reflected in the fathomless depths of his eyes. "On the morrow, I will summon a clergyman to perform the wedding."

"Yes," she agreed with a pensive frown. "The child should have its father's name." Her gaze widened as she watched him advance upon her now. His stride was slow, purposeful, his expression all too familiar. "Are you not fatigued?" she asked in a small, uneven voice. "Indeed, I do not doubt that you are sore and in need of sleep."

"I am in need of *you*." He paused to tower above her,

his eyes traveling over her with such bold, loving intensity that she felt her knees weaken.

"I . . . I should still be angry with you," she faltered.

"If it pleases you." Though he had not yet touched her,
she felt scorched by the heat of his body.

"It does."

She did not know why, but she turned away. A soft
cry broke from her lips when Ronan's hands seized her
about the waist. He took a seat in the chair before the fire,
settling her upon his lap. He smiled, his mouth descending
toward hers. She was sorely tempted to welcome the kiss,
yet told herself that she could not. She loved him with all
her heart, and it would be so very easy to surrender to
him. But did loving him mean that she must have no
pride? Sweet heaven, did it mean that she must forfeit
everything?

"No!" she murmured. Stirring within his arms, she
sought to rise.

But Ronan would not allow her to go. Though
admiring her spirit, he was bemused by her resistance.
He knew that she loved him. He knew that she wanted
him as much as he wanted her. And he was determined to
make her admit it. For three long days, he had burned to
make love to her. The ride to Edinburgh and back had
only fueled his desire. He would have her. Now. In spite
of her anger. In spite of the dull ache of his wound.

Analise's pulse raced at the look in his eyes. Before
she quite knew what was happening, he had turned her
about to face him. She was straddling his hips, her skirts
raked up about her pale, slender thighs.

"*Ronan!*" she gasped, her face flaming. She tried
again to rise, but to no avail. Ronan's hand moved to the
laces on the front of her gown.

"You have beautiful breasts, lady wife," he pronounced in a soft, vibrant tone. "And I can wait no longer." The laces were untied now. Sweeping the edges of her bodice aside, he allowed his lips the pleasure of exploring the ripe, creamy fullness of her naked breasts.

Analise felt her whole body tremble and grow warm. She squirmed restlessly atop her husband's thighs, her hands clutching at his powerful, hard-muscled upper arms. Another gasp escaped her lips when his hand delved beneath her bunched-up skirts to claim the silken, moist pink flesh between her thighs. Her eyes swept closed, and her head fell back as her desire flared to match his.

His lips trailed hotly upward to capture hers. She kissed him back with all the fire and passion he had created within her.

And then he was unfastening his breeches, his hands closing about her hips to lift her slightly. He brought her down upon his rigid, fully aroused manhood. She gasped against his mouth, shivering as her body accepted the wondrous, heart-stopping invasion of his.

Instinctively she began to move atop him. His lips returned to her breasts, his fingers curling about her waist. She wrapped her arms about him and was certain that she would faint with the sheer, heavenly pleasure of their embrace.

His thrusts grew harder, faster. She gave herself fully, all else forgotten. And when the ultimate ecstasy came upon them, she gave a faint, strangled cry and buried her face in his shirt.

Afterward he cradled her upon his lap again. She rested pliantly within his arms. Her face was flushed, her eyes softly aglow. And she had never felt such sweet contentment.

"By heaven, woman, you will kill me yet," Ronan murmured, though without any true complaint. Indeed, a smile lurked about his mouth.

"You are in pain?" Worried, she hastily sat upright.

"A little. But not enough to stir." He gathered her close once more. "Aye, for I find that I am well satisfied to remain thus."

She released another sigh of utter satisfaction and stared into the quietly dancing flames. But in the next instant, her brow creased into a frown. "Ronan?"

"What is it, my love?"

"Do I . . . do I please you?"

His lips curved briefly upward again. "How can you doubt it?"

"You know a good deal more than I about such things," she remarked, a flash of jealousy coursing through her at the thought.

"In the beginning, perhaps," he conceded. "But I think you capable of tutoring me now." His eyes twinkled roguishly down at her when she lifted her head to peer up at him.

"Then, you *are* pleased?"

"Aye. More than I could have dreamed possible."

Her heart soared at his words. She lowered her head to his shoulder once more, at the same time offering up an earnest prayer that they would always love one another as they did now . . . and that they would live in peace.

Chapter 11

Later than same morning, Ronan finally made his presence known to his kinsmen. He was greeted with much affection, and assured that, should he still have need of their help, they would remain at Dunslair. Thanking them for their loyalty, he bade them return to their homes. And promised that he would do everything in his power to ensure they suffered no further raids by the English. It was a nearly impossible task, and he knew it, yet his determination did not waver.

He and Calum accompanied the departing Armstrongs outside, leaving Analise to sit with Dierdre before the fire in the baronial hall. The two of them passed the first several minutes in silence. Then Analise stood and wandered nearer to the roaring blaze. The day had dawned cold and damp; winter would soon be upon them. She folded her arms against her chest, her mouth curving into a tentative smile when she turned to face the other woman again.

"It is my hope that you and Calum will know happiness together," she offered sincerely.

"I thank you for that, my lady," replied Dierdre.

"*Analise.*"

"Aye." She smiled as well now, her emerald gaze sparkling.

"I must confess, it will give me pleasure to share this house with another woman. I . . . I have longed for a sister."

"I, too," Dierdre told her. She rose to her feet, her deep blue woolen skirts rustling softly as she moved to Analise's side. "Calum loves you already. And so will I."

"Calum is a good man. As is his brother," Analise put forth. "Still, they are both proud and headstrong—and, at times, infuriating. Indeed, it will ever be difficult to persuade them to *our* minds."

"Ah, but we have our ways, do we not?"

Analise's eyes widened in surprise. She gave a soft laugh and held her hands toward the fire's warmth.

"You are not so very different," Dierdre concluded aloud.

"Nor are you." She clasped Dierdre's hand with her own now. "I think that if women from my country and women from yours were to meet often enough, there might well *be* no more warfare."

"Perhaps. But 'tis the men who make it." She drew away and resumed her place in the carved wooden chair. Analise watched her, and grew concerned at her paleness.

"Is there anything you require?" she asked.

"No," answered Dierdre, then managed a rather wan smile. " 'Tis only a touch of the sickness brought on by the babe. Aye, it will pass soon enough."

"I know little of such matters," Analise confessed. She sighed and moved back to take a seat in the chair opposite Dierdre's. "There were few children at court, and I fear I am sadly lacking in experience with them."

"You will learn," Dierdre predicted with another faint

smile. Her eyes clouded momentarily. "Calum and I would have waited. But I cannot be sorry for what has happened. Though Angus Maxwell may call me his daughter no more, I would risk all to be with Calum."

Analise nodded in understanding. Her eyes strayed to the stairwell. She felt her heart flutter at the sight of Ronan. He crossed the room toward her, while Calum hastened to drop a tender kiss upon Dierdre's forehead.

"The parson comes from Bairnkine this morn," Calum advised his betrothed.

"This morn?" she echoed, her eyes growing very round. "But I must have time to—"

"You have had nigh on to a year," he pointed out indulgently.

"Come," Analise said as she urged Dierdre to stand and go with her. "We shall make ready."

"Mayhap," Ronan suggested wryly to Analise, "we should speak *our* vows again—willingly this time."

"In truth, Ronan Armstrong," she replied, "we cannot be any more wed than we are now." Her cheeks grew warm at the sound of his quiet, mellow chuckle.

"Aye. We have made certain of that."

Casting him a stern look, she led Dierdre across the room and up the stairs. They were soon in the bed-chamber she shared with Ronan, pulling the gowns from the great wooden chest in the hope of finding one suitable for a wedding.

An hour later, Analise reappeared in the hall. Dierdre was close behind. She looked positively radiant in a bor-rowed gown of soft, pale green silk. Her raven tresses were loose and flowing about her shoulders. She trembled with joy when her bright gaze met Calum's.

He came forward, possessively tucking her arm

through the welcoming crook of his. Together they approached the parson. Analise assumed her place on the other side of Dierdre, while Ronan stood beside his brother. The book was opened, the encouragement to true faithfulness offered.

During the ceremony, Analise looked to her husband. His eyes told her all she needed to know. Her breath caught in her throat, and she found herself silently responding to the clergyman's sober questions.

And then it was done. The parson took his leave. After a brief toast to the newlyweds' happiness, Calum grasped his bride's hand and led her upstairs. Analise smiled as she watched them go.

"Perhaps your brother will forego his wild and wicked ways now that he is wed," she remarked with an arch look at Ronan.

"An Armstrong is not so easily tamed," he countered, his arms encircling her with their hard warmth. "Though you might well succeed."

"Never." Smiling again, she tilted her head back and offered on impulse, "Might I tempt you upstairs as well, my lord?" She blushed at her own audacity.

"Och, woman," Ronan charged huskily, "the very sight of you is a temptation." He kissed her, a deep and lingering kiss, then reluctantly set her away from him. "I must ride to Jedburgh once more."

"Now?" she asked in mingled surprise and disappointment.

"Aye. My uncle would meet with me this day."

"Why? What can be of such importance that—"

" 'Tis time you knew," he decreed solemnly. He raised his hands to her arms again and met her puzzled gaze. "By the king's command, I have played the spy Robert

Kerr accused me of being. The man has committed treason in his post as warden. As has Simon Hayward, with *his* crimes against your queen. Their treachery has long been known, yet they have powerful allies. Never was there enough evidence to bring them to justice."

"And you have enough evidence now?"

"I am near to it." He frowned before explaining, "My uncle uses his influence to protect me where he can, as does John Beattie. Without their help, I would long ago have been more than suspect. Aye, and perhaps dead."

"I see," murmured Analise, her head spinning as she looked away. A moment later her eyes flew back up to his face. "But what will happen when the truth becomes known?" she demanded anxiously. "Will your countrymen care that you sought justice? Will they not judge *you* as a traitor?"

"All of Scotland bleeds for what Robert Kerr and Simon Hayward have done," he told her, his features grim. "Any man who desires peace will not offer me judgment. And the others . . . by all the saints, they, too, will be made to pay."

He turned about and strode toward the stairwell. Analise hurried after him, her throat constricting in dread.

"But your wound has not yet healed completely!" she protested.

"I am well able to ride," he assured her, the ghost of a smile playing about his lips.

"Yes, but I—Oh, Ronan, I cannot bear the thought of you in danger!"

"Do we not live in dangerous times, my love?" He cupped her chin gently, his gaze holding the luminous blue-green of hers. "You must have confidence in me. For I *will* grow old with you."

He brushed her lips tenderly with his one last time, then disappeared into the shadows of the stairwell. She wanted to go after him, to plead with him to have a care for his safety. But he would not thank her for it. No, she told herself with an inward sigh, and neither would he be swayed from his purpose.

Again she could do nothing more than wait. It was easy enough to fill her time, for there was a good deal of cleaning to be done now that the many guests had gone. She performed her tasks with a vengeance, desperate once more to keep her mind from her husband's peril.

Calum and Dierdre emerged from their bedchamber in the early afternoon. Analise was happy to offer them a meal. She felt her spirits lift, a trifle at least, in response to Calum's reassurances that his brother would not take unnecessary risks now that he had a wife.

The three of them ventured outside afterward. Calum left the two women to investigate a problem at the stables. Dierdre, determined to forget her own troubles, linked arms companionably with Analise and spoke of how she had watched Calum change from a boy savage to only a slightly more civilized young man. They spent a pleasant hour strolling about the grounds, until the chill crept beneath their cloaks and chased them back inside.

Soon enough twilight deepened into a clear, starlit night. Sitting alone before the fire in her bedchamber, Analise could no longer keep her fears at bay. She muttered an oath, wondering if she would spend the rest of her life agonizing over her errant husband's fate. She admired his quest for justice, yet cursed the fact that he would plunge himself into such danger. Resentment joined with apprehension. Her eyes flashed as she snatched up her cloak again and flew down the stairs.

She was allowed to pass from the house to the court-yard, for the men who stood watch had been advised by Ronan that she could now freely travel about the grounds. A gust of cold wind tugged at her skirts as she wandered away from the house. Pulling her cloak tightly about her, she headed toward the far side of the compound.

All was quiet now, save for the rustling of the leaves on the trees and the soft, plaintive lowing of the cattle. Analise shivered a bit and raised her eyes toward the sky. Gazing at the stars, she was well and truly struck by the fact that she would never return to London, nor travel across the sea to France. Scotland was her home now. Yet, she realized, any place where Ronan was would be home. *Anywhere in the world.*

"Oh, Ronan," she sighed, drawing her gaze back down to earth. Her steps were aimless, leisurely, and she soon found herself beside the mill. Absently noting the way the pond glistened beneath the stars, she gathered up her skirts and approached the steps of the tall stone building where the wheat was ground.

Her eyes flew wide, her heart leaping in alarm when a large hand suddenly clamped across her mouth. A strong, hard-muscled arm slipped about her waist, and she was pulled back against a body that was undeniably mascu-line. A scream rose in her throat. She began to struggle, her hands lifting to strike at the face of her captor.

"Do you not yet recognize the touch of your husband, my lady?" a familiar voice murmured close to her ear. Fear turned to relief, then indignation. Her captor relaxed his grip. She spun about, her eyes bridling as they moved over his face in the silvery darkness.

"Does it amuse you to frighten me so?" she stormed, for the moment forgetting how glad she was to see him safely returned.

"You should not be outside at so late an hour," Ronan parried with maddening equanimity. "There are many dangers about."

"So you thought to teach me a lesson!"

"Will you not offer me a proper welcome?" He wrapped his arms about her again, his deep blue eyes warmly aglow. She stiffened within his embrace and raised her hands to push at his chest.

"No, my lord, I will not!"

"Aye. Then, I will claim an improper one," he declared. She suffered a sharp intake of breath when he released her. His hand grasped hers in the next instant, and he pulled her along with him to the steps of the mill. Once they were inside, he moved to light the torch hanging beside the doorway. The flame flickered and blazed, sending a soft golden glow throughout the building. The millstone sat in the center, while bags of newly ground wheat rested against the wall. In the far corner was a huge wooden barrel filled with grain. The scent of it was strong, albeit pleasant.

Analise tugged her cloak about her again and watched as Ronan closed the door. Though she longed to cast herself upon his chest and confess her joy, she felt a sudden attack of shyness. She told herself that such a thing was absurd, especially after the intimacy they had shared as husband and wife. Still, she could not help it.

"I . . . I thought you would return before nightfall," she faltered, her gaze falling beneath his.

"My journey took me beyond Jedburgh." He drew closer and gave her a faint smile before confiding, "I find that I cannot be away from you even an hour's time without misery." His eyes gleamed with an intoxicating mixture of tenderness and desire.

She gently cleared her throat and looked up at him once more. "Should we not retire to the house? Indeed, I am certain you are in need of rest, and your wound—"

"Pains me little," he insisted, his low, resonant tone sending a pleasurable tremor through her. She took a deep breath and hastily moved away. Her hands trembled as she raised them to the coolness of the millstone.

"I fear I am doomed to spend the remainder of my days at Dunslair worrying if you will even return at all," she lamented. "Have I not told you that I am unaccustomed to your ways? Indeed, Dierdre was born here and accepts the worry easily enough. Yet I find it difficult to endure."

"God willing, there will soon be no need for me to leave you." He came up behind her now, his hands closing about her upper arms while he buried his face in the fragrant, honey-gold thickness of her hair. "The smell of you stirs my blood. Aye, and the sweet taste of you as well." His fingers swept aside her tresses, his warm lips nuzzling the back of her neck. She moaned softly and felt her own blood turn to liquid fire within her veins. Her eyes swept closed as she swayed back against him.

"Heaven help me, for I become weak and feeble-minded whenever I am in your arms," she whispered. A shiver danced down her spine at the sound of his quiet laugh.

"You are never that." He turned her about, his arms encircling her while his mouth descended upon the willing softness of hers. She entwined her arms about his neck and did not protest when his hand tugged up her skirts to caress the delicate and wondrously sensitive flesh between her thighs. Leaning back against the millstone, she moaned and trembled anew.

Passion swiftly intensified. Analise was near to begging for mercy. Ronan burned to take her. With dizzying impatience, he unfastened his breeches and raked her skirts farther upward. His hands filled themselves with the pale, well-rounded firmness of her bottom. Her arms tightened about his neck when he lifted her higher in his embrace. His lips left hers to roam hotly across the swelling curve of her breasts.

In the next moment his throbbing hardness plunged within her. A soft, broken cry escaped her lips. She felt her whole body heating as his fingers commanded her hips to undulate with a slow, tantalizing seductiveness ... and then faster. She struggled for breath. He fought to postpone his release until she had found hers.

When it came, it was near painful in its intensity. Analise's head fell back, and she stifled a scream. Ronan was granted an equally pleasurable fulfillment. A low groan rose in his throat, his fingers digging into her bottom as he filled her with the life-giving warmth of his seed.

The remained together, breathless and sated, for several moments longer. Finally Analise stirred. She pulled her arms from about Ronan's neck and clutched at his shoulders while drawing her hips away from his. He seized her about the waist to lend assistance, his mouth curving into a wry half smile as she hastened to smooth her skirts back down into place.

"You have eased my hunger for now, lady wife," he pronounced while his loving, possessive gaze traveled up and down the length of her, "yet I would have you naked beneath me. Aye, and *will* before this night is through."

"No," she dissented firmly. Still a trifle breathless, she pulled the edges of her cloak together and did her best to look prim—no easy task, given that her hair was tousled and the bodice of her gown sadly askew. "You have ridden to Jedburgh and back this day. *And* elsewhere. 'Tis time you sought your rest."

"I am no weak young stripling, Analise." He smiled and suddenly grasped her hips, bringing her up against him. "We could tarry here awhile yet. Aye, and I could show you still another way for us to join together."

"Absolutely not!" she gasped. Determined not to surrender to her own quickly renewed yearning, she pushed at him and squirmed free, then assumed an air of composure. "Come. Calum and Dierdre will grow worried at my absence."

"Calum and Dierdre are concerned with other matters." He reluctantly acquiesced, taking her by the arm and leading her back to the doorway. "Though I am loath to admit it, you are right. We must sleep, for we are away to Edinburgh on the morrow."

"To Edinburgh?" She stopped abruptly, her eyes widening in surprise as they lifted to his face. "I am to go with you, then?"

"Aye. The king would speak with me. And I will not leave you again." A smile of irony tugged at the corners of his mouth, and he smoothed a gentle hand across her cheek while predicting, "Once they see you, my friends at court will understand how I came to claim an English-woman as my wife."

"You did not know of my identity when we were wed," she saw fit to remind him.

"Still, I would have found you." Catching up the torch, he opened the door and drew her outside with him. She slipped her hand into the strong warmth of his and cast another glance heavenward, giving silent thanks for the blessing of Ronan Armstrong's love.

They left at first light. Once again Calum was charged with the defense of Dunslair should there be an attack. It was expected that the Maxwells would be too concerned with their own preparations to ride forth, yet Ronan cautioned his brother to remain watchful. And to summon the others of their clan at the first sign of trouble.

Analise lifted her face to the sun's warmth as she rode beside her husband. It was a beautiful, clear day, and she was so grateful for a respite from the cold and the gray that she did not mind being astride. Her gaze swept frequently about the countryside, and she listened with great interest whenever Ronan offered her information about the land itself, or about the castles and tower houses they passed. She recalled how Calum had told her that the Scots fought one another with nearly the same vigor that they fought the English. Her eyes clouded as she wondered if her wish for peace would ever be granted.

Because Ronan had set an easier pace in order to spare her, it was quite late in the day when they reached the outskirts of Edinburgh. She caught her breath at the sight of the castle looming ominously over the city. Built atop a massive, jagged hill of volcanic rock, it was both impressive and frightening, yet another reminder of Scotland's turbulent past and present.

" 'Tis much larger than I had expected," Analise murmured, her fascinated gaze traveling from the castle to the myriad of slate-roofed stone buildings below. An ever-present cloud of smoke hung over the city.

"Aye, and you can see for yourself why it has long

been called 'Auld Reekie,' " said Ronan, his tone laced with humor. "Save for his own home, Edinburgh is the dearest to the eyes of a Scot." He touched his heels lightly to his horse's flanks again and led the way along the well-trodden road.

Soon they were in the very midst of the city. The sounds and smells were much the same as in London, though with a distinctively Scottish touch, and Analise took pleasure in them. As in Jedburgh, she sensed a certain vitality, almost a joyfulness, and wondered how it could thrive in what Ronan had told her was often as not a cold, windy, and rain-soaked place.

The streets were crowded with every manner of person and means of transportation. Analise found it difficult to guide her own mount through the jumble of horses and carts and wagons. She was glad when Ronan caught up her reins and urged her horse along behind his.

The clouds had returned to obscure the fast fading sunlight by the time they arrived at their final destination. Analise was astonished to learn that they were to stay within the king's palace.

"Holyrood," Ronan told her its name. Her eyes grew very round as he lifted her down from the horse. She gathered up her skirts, wandering closer to the front of the long, light-colored stone building while Ronan gave the care of their mounts into one of the king's stable men.

It was much smaller than the grand and sprawling royal abodes of England, yet it was beautifully fashioned and enjoyed a magnificent setting amid the hills at the end of a mile-long lane flanked by churches and shops and public houses. Analise turned slowly about, her gaze widening once more when she saw that the castle itself stood guard at the opposite end.

"No doubt you are weary," said Ronan, his hand closing about her arm. "I must have a word with the king. You can bathe and dine while I am gone. And upon my return, I will escort you to the king's chamber."

"Oh, Ronan, must . . . must I go before him today?" she asked. The prospect filled her with anxiety.

"He will treat you with naught save kindness," he assured her. Though she still appeared uneasy, he gave her a brief smile and led her across the grounds to a doorway where the guard—familiar with the tall, blue-eyed chieftain of the Armstrongs—allowed them entrance.

As Analise soon discovered, the interior of the palace had been furnished with a mind more to comfort and economy than elegance. Still, the tapestries and paintings were fine enough, she mused, and the heavy carved furniture was far more pleasing to *her* eye than the delicate and virtually useless pieces she had often noticed at court in London. She saw few people as she and Ronan made their way through the various passages and hallways, and she surmised that the men and women of the court were likely in the process of sharing the evening meal.

Finally, at the end of a narrow, candlelit corridor, Ronan opened a door and ushered her inside a room that was not overly large yet decorated in pleasing shades of crimson and gold. A fire burned comfortingly across the room from the curtained bed, and there was a bathtub already waiting in the corner. Two silver goblets had been filled with wine and placed atop a claw-footed table. A plate of bread and fruit sat beside them.

"I will see that a maidservant comes to assist you," Ronan promised. He lingered a moment, his mouth pressing a tender kiss upon hers. "Rest, my love. And stay within this room."

"How is it we are allowed to move so freely and without escort here?" she asked, her brow creasing into a frown of puzzlement. "Are there not men who would seek to harm the king? Yet I have seen but a handful of guards. And where are the courtiers? In the queen's palace, there were always scores of richly dressed men and women to—"

"Aye. 'Tis different here. Your queen both needs and fears her own subjects. Our king fears little. Nor does he stand upon ceremony. He surrounds himself with few courtiers—only those whose company he enjoys. The majority of his stewards and advisers have quarters at the castle." He opened the door again now and told her, "I must go. No doubt, it will be past darkness when I return."

She opened her mouth to offer a reply, but he was already gone. With another frown she drew near to the fire and stared deeply into the flames. Scarcely a minute had passed when a maidservant knocked at the door. The slender young woman wearing a mobcap was all that was gracious and respectful. Announcing that the water for the bath was on its way, she flashed Analise a tentative smile and insisted that she call upon her for anything she desired. Analise thanked her sincerely, but declared that she wanted nothing more than the bath.

"Will you not want a hot meal, my lady?" the maidservant queried in surprise. "Aye, you must have meat, and perhaps some potatoes and a bowl of Cock-A-Leekie."

"I fear my stomach has been unsettled of late," confided Analise, recalling the baffling attacks of queasiness she had experienced the past two days. The discomfort had never lasted more than a few minutes each time, and she told herself that it no doubt owed its origin to every-thing that had happened since she had come to the north. Indeed, she thought wryly, marriage to Ronan Armstrong had turned her world upside down.

Two footmen arrived, carrying buckets full of water for the bath. They emptied the buckets into the tub, then swiftly took their leave again. The maidservant, who had by now revealed her name as Elspeth, left soon thereafter, but not before trying one last time to persuade Analise to eat a more substantial meal. She was unsuccessful.

Analise did not realize how tired she was until she began to remove her clothing. The bath she took was warm, soothing. And once she had dressed again and eaten, she felt remarkably better. She plaited her damp tresses, and stood before the mirror to make certain the square-necked bodice of her heavy, emerald brocade silk was arranged properly. Her brows knitted together when she saw that the décolletage revealed a good deal more of her bosom than she had remembered, but the only other gown in her possession was the one she had worn during the journey.

Releasing a faint sigh of resignation, she turned away from the mirror. Her eyes flew toward the door when another knock sounded. Believing it to be Ronan, she gathered up her skirts and hastened to answer it. But it was not Ronan whose face she discovered upon opening the door.

"Why, Sarah Beattie!" she breathed in surprise.

"Did your husband not tell you that we were here at the palace as well?" Sarah asked. Without waiting for an answer, she remarked knowingly, "Aye, 'tis like a man to forget such a thing."

"Will you not come inside?" Analise bade her.

"No, I cannot at present. I must away to the queen's chamber. Prince Henry is a wee bit unwell. His poor mother would have my advice, since my own four sons are hale and hearty and nearing manhood already." She took Analise's hand in a warm grasp while adding, " 'Tis hoped that we can meet later this night."

"Yes," Analise replied with a smile of genuine affection. "Once I have been presented to the king . . ."

"He has been most anxious to make the acquaintance of the woman who did succeed where all others failed." Sarah's eyes lit with fond amusement. "In truth, many a heart was broken when Ronan Armstrong took you to wife."

"So I have heard," Analise murmured, her own gaze sparking with jealousy.

"Aye," said Sarah, "but 'tis *you* he loves." She embraced Analise warmly before setting off to speak with the queen.

Ronan declared himself in need of a wash and a meal when he finally returned. Analise warned him that the water had cooled, but he nevertheless stripped and bathed. Her eyes were full of love and admiration as they traveled over his bronzed, unmistakably virile body, and she found herself wondering if she would ever grow accustomed to seeing him in all his masculine glory.

Rising from the bath, he drew on fresh clothing, then drained the goblet of wine and ate a generous portion of the remaining food. Analise endeavored to remain patient. But when he took her by the arm and decreed it time to go, she could contain her curiosity no more.

"Why has the king summoned you here?" she demanded, hanging back. "What has happened?"

"He has received word that Robert Kerr plots to gain

control of the Borders. And worse, that Kerr means to lead an army against those who oppose him."

"But, that—sweet mercy, would he truly murder his own countrymen?"

"Aye." His handsome features grew taut with barely controlled fury. "He would."

"You are among those who oppose him," she pointed out in a small voice. Her throat constricted with dread. "Oh, Ronan, he will try to kill you!"

"I do not fear Robert Kerr," he proclaimed grimly. "Nor will I allow him to succeed in his treasonous intent."

"What are you going to do?"

"John Beattie and I must tarry here for a day or two longer. Then we will arrange a meeting with Robert Kerr—at his stronghold, so he will not suspect an ambush. You will remain at the palace while I am away. I must know that you are safe."

"You cannot go to meet with him!" she protested. "What is to prevent him from doing you harm while you are in his midst?"

"I do not think him prepared yet to murder me, or John. Still, I have sent word to my kinsmen to gather at Dunslair once more."

"But can I not return there as well? I should much prefer to wait—"

"No." He shook his head, his gaze softening as it met hers again. "The trouble comes to a head now, Analise. Until there is an end to it, we must take care."

She wanted to offer another argument, to declare that she was sick of waiting and would face any danger at his side, but she knew it would avail her nothing. It was with a heavy heart that she went to meet the king. She and Ronan walked together in silence, passing along a maze of corridors until they came at last to the king's private chamber.

James Stewart (or King James VI as he was known more formally) was not at all what Analise had expected. Slender and bearded, perhaps thirty years of age, with the flame-colored hair of his mother. He looked decidedly *un*-king-like. His clothing was plain, almost common, and his eyes held good humor instead of either hauteur or superiority.

He greeted her with an amiable smile. She felt her misery lifting temporarily as she moved forward with Ronan. The room was warm and cozy, not much larger than the bedchamber to which it was connected. Though tapestries adorned the walls and carpets covered the floor, the furnishings were a match for the king's love of simplicity.

"So this is the English bride," James remarked, rising from his seat before the fire. He took Analise's hand and raised it gallantly to his lips. "Aye, I can well see why the Armstrong allowed himself to be caught."

"I thank you for the compliment, Your Majesty," she replied. He released her hand and motioned her to sit in the chair beside his. No longer feeling nervous, she sank down and watched as Ronan took a seat opposite.

"Tell me, lass, what do you think of Scotland thus far?" King James inquired.

"It is very cold," she answered, then was surprised when he threw back his head and laughed.

"By heaven, 'tis *that* right enough," he allowed. He cast a look of mock severity toward Ronan before asking her, "Have you any complaints against this rough-mannered husband of yours? Does he treat you with all the care and respect you deserve?"

"He is all that is good and kind, Your Majesty." Though she did not smile when she said it, her beautiful eyes sparkled irrepressibly.

"Are you certain we speak of the same man?" King James teased. Sobering, he looked to Ronan again. "You have told her that she is to be our guest for a few days longer?"

"I have," confirmed Ronan. His own eyes gleamed warmly when they met Analise's. "And she is grateful for your hospitality."

"I am indeed," Analise interjected, then raised her chin to a stubborn angle. "Yet is a wife's place not at her husband's side?"

"Aye," James seemed to agree, "but not when he faces danger and needs his wits about him. No, my lady, you will serve your husband better if you remain under my protection here at Holyrood."

"Is that what your wife would do in these circumstances, Your Majesty?" she challenged.

"Analise," Ronan scolded in a quiet, commanding tone. The king, however, apparently took delight in her boldness.

"If not for her duty to our children, I fear that my own dear wife would protest the same as you are doing," he conceded with another smile. His response prompted Analise to raise her eyebrows at Ronan in a gesture of both defiance and triumph. He made a silent vow to take her to task for her sauciness once they were alone again.

"Now that I think of it," King James pondered half to himself, "my Anne would scheme to go with me." He brought his attention back to his guests and stood to tell them, "The hour grows late, and I do not doubt you are wearied. We shall speak again on the morrow."

"Aye," said Ronan. He stood as well, and took Analise's arm. She stiffened beneath his hand, before making a slight curtsy to the king.

"Good night, Your Majesty."

"Good night, Lady Analise." His mouth twitched when he confessed to Ronan, "I envy you your slumber, Armstrong."

Ronan said nothing, but gave the king a nod and led Analise from the room. Once they were back in the privacy of their bedchamber, she pulled free of his grasp and drew near to the fire's warmth.

"Perhaps I can persuade the king that I should accompany you when you ride to meet Robert Kerr."

"Dare to try," Ronan warned softly, "and by damn, I *will* turn you across my knee."

"But I can be of use to you!" she insisted, whirling about to confront him. "As kinswoman to Simon Hayward, I might—"

"You will remain here." It was clear from the tone of his voice that he would brook no further defiance. She, however, was not of a mind to be intimidated.

"I cannot sit and do naught while you ride into danger once more!"

"And I cannot keep my mind on my duty if I must worry about your safety." He frowned, his gaze darkening as he closed the distance between them and raised his hands to close about her shoulders. "You are my wife, Analise. You will do as I say."

"Again, my lord, it seems you would prefer me docile—indeed, *witless*," she accused hotly.

"Aye, if it means you stay alive."

"Then, you would have done better to marry one of your Scottish strumpets!"

Though her words displeased him, he could not ignore the way her outrage served to heighten her beauty. Her face was becomingly flushed, her body trembling with the force of her emotions. His gaze dropped to where her breasts threatened to spill out of her low-cut bodice. He offered up a silent oath when he recalled how the king's eyes had not been able to refrain from straying to her well-displayed charms.

"Fatigue has stolen your reason," he pronounced, his voice edged with a hazardous combination of anger and desire. His arms fell back to his sides. "Go to bed, Analise."

"You dare to send me to bed as though I were a child?" she demanded in furious disbelief. "I am a grown woman, Ronan Armstrong, and I shall *not* be treated with such disesteem!" She inhaled upon a gasp when his hands shot out to take her arms in a hard, near bruising grip.

"Do you not understand?" he ground out, his gaze searing down into hers. "I have a duty to my king. And you have a duty to your husband."

Hurt and angry—though she did not truly understand why—she assumed an air of cool, distant composure. "I did not know when I married you that I would spend each day fearing your death. Perhaps ... perhaps it would have been better if I had never learned to care for you."

"You do not mean that." Other than a darkening of his eyes, he gave no evidence yet of how much her words had pained him.

"Do I not?"

"By heaven—"

He got no further, cut off by the sound of a knock at the door. Muttering a curse, he cast one last narrow, ireful look at his wife before turning away.

Analise felt bitter tears starting to her eyes as she

watched him cross to the door and open it. He moved out into the corridor to speak quietly with someone. She attempted to eavesdrop, but could hear little. Her heart was pounding quite erratically when Ronan stepped back inside the room and closed the door.

"John and Sarah Beattie would have us join them for a late supper," he informed her in a tone that was very low and level.

"Are we to go, then?" she asked, folding her arms tightly beneath her breasts.

"No." He advanced upon her again, and it was clear from his grave expression that he was still troubled by what had been said between them. "I told them you are unwell."

"Why, you had no right—"

"We must quarrel no more, Analise," he decreed, his touch gentle this time when he reached for her. "If I am to face danger, then let it be with the memory of your kiss upon my lips." He drew her close and lowered his head toward hers. But she surprised him by pushing at his chest and squirming out of his embrace. She fled to the far side of the bed, where she stood glaring vengefully across at him.

"From what I have heard, my lord, you are no doubt well accustomed to ending quarrels by such methods!" Though confused by this sudden urge to do battle with him, she could not seem to help it. Her emotions felt raw, her nerves strung tight. And she was sorely, inexplicably tempted to strike the man she loved more than anything in the world.

"While I cannot deny I take some pleasure in your jealousy," Ronan said with a soft smile of irony, "in truth there is no need for it."

"I wonder, sir, if you would hold to that same opinion if *I* had given myself so freely before our marriage?" she challenged rashly.

"No, by damn, I would not!" All traces of humor were gone now as he strode toward her. Tensing in alarm, she searched for a means of escape. The only way open to her was across the bed. She climbed atop the mattress, intent upon fleeing the room, fearing her own response as much as her husband's.

As always, however, he caught her easily. He pulled her back to the center of the bed. Lying facedown, she could do little more than kick and writhe in his grasp. But her struggles were futile.

She gave a sharp gasp of startlement when he gathered her skirts and tossed them above her head.

"No!" she cried in a strangled voice. Thinking he meant to make good on his threat to punish her for her defiance, she tried once more to scramble free. Still, he held fast. And then, instead of striking her, he began to kiss her. She was shocked when his warm lips descended upon her naked backside.

"Ronan!"

He paid little heed to her objections. His mouth roamed boldly, hotly across her well-rounded bottom. She gasped and trembled and squirmed, her fingers entangling within the covers while the familiar heat stole throughout her body.

With humiliating swiftness, she was past all thought of resistance. She did not protest when he pulled her upward and back against him, nor did she think to deny him when his hand stole between her thighs. He caressed her with a sweet, breathtaking mastery, while his lips trailed fierily across the silken curve of her neck and shoulder.

She was on fire. And so was he. Her eyes fluttered open when he unfastened his breeches, and she waited for him to turn her around and lower her to the bed. But he did not.

"Ronan?" she whispered in bafflement, wondering what he was about.

Her question was answered, most satisfyingly, in the next moment. He urged her onto her hands and knees. And then he took her from behind, his manhood plunging within the moist, velvety warmth of her feminine passage.

Her breath caught in her throat. She gave a low moan of pleasure. He pulled her back against him again. She lifted her arms and curled her hands about his neck, while her hips matched the rhythm of his. His right hand returned to the secret place between her thighs, his left sweeping upward to close upon her breast. His thrusts grew deeper, swifter. She felt as though her very soul took flight.

Together, they reached the pinnacle of fulfillment. And were left shaken by its intensity.

While Analise stretched out upon the mattress, Ronan climbed from the bed to strip off his clothes. He smiled down at her, his blue eyes splendidly aglow.

"Perhaps the quarrel was worthwhile, lady wife."

"Oh, Ronan," she sighed, drawing herself up into a sitting position. Her own gaze was soft and earnest, her beautiful face still flushed. "Truly, I did not mean to be so prickly. 'Tis only that, since we were first wed, I have been fraught with worriment on your behalf."

"Aye." Naked now, he took a seat beside her and

began untying the laces on the front of her gown. She
trembled anew when his fingers brushed against her
breasts. "Though I cannot explain how, I know that I will
emerge unscathed from all that is to come. Perhaps even
a savage can lay claim to the protection of angels," he
remarked teasingly.

"Please," she implored, her voice quavering, "promise
me that you will be on your guard against Robert Kerr."

"You have my word upon it." He tugged her gown up
over her head. Her linen shift soon joined the gown upon
the floor, and then her shoes. With tantalizing unhaste, he
rolled down one of her fine black woolen stockings, his
lips following its progress downward. She gasped and
closed her eyes. A delectable shiver ran the length of her
spine. And by the time he had done the same with the
other stocking, she was warmed with desire once more.

"Do all Reivers possess such a . . . a ready passion?"
she asked.

"Aye, we are a hot-blooded breed," he answered with a
brief, thoroughly disarming smile. He smoothed his
hands over the satiny curve of her hips and slid upward,
lowering his body atop hers. "I could not be otherwise
with a defiant, sharp-tongued temptress like you to share
my bed."

"Would you love me so well if I were very thin, or
fat, or—"

"I would love you even then," he vowed in all honesty.
His eyes gazed deeply into hers. She felt her heart give a
wild flutter.

"Never would I have thought it possible," she
declared, her fingers threading within the rich-hued
thickness of his hair, "that I could care so much for a man

who threatens me one moment and loves me with such tenderness the next."

"As I have noted before, you will lead me a merry chase. Aye," he added huskily as his mouth neared hers, "but I would want it no other way."

She beckoned his kiss. He was happy to oblige. And soon enough, their bodies were entwined once more, their hearts beating as one.

Chapter 12

Two days later, Analise rose just after dawn and hastened to dress. Though Ronan had left her with a tender kiss and a promise to return soon, she was determined to bid him one last farewell. She flung her cloak about her shoulders and raced outside. Bravely blinking back tears, she flew across to where he and John Beattie were preparing to mount their horses. He frowned at the sight of her.

" 'Tis cold, Analise, and you should be abed," he scolded, his gaze flickering over her. In truth, he was heartened by her show of regard.

"I had to see you again," she proclaimed. "And to tell you that I will wait forever if need be." She threw her arms about his neck and strained upward to press her lips to his. A low groan rose in his throat as he swept her close. He kissed her deeply, hungrily, before forcing himself to set her away.

"By all the saints, woman, you make it no easier for me to leave you," he grumbled, though without any true anger.

"I do not want it to be easy!" she countered, then watched as he swung up into the saddle.

"I will look to his back, my lady," John Beattie

promised her. She cast him a faint smile of gratitude and drew her cloak about her once more. Ronan gazed down at her with such warmth that she caught her breath.

"Entrap no other men while I am away," he directed, his eyes lighting briefly with humor.

"In truth, my lord, I am not the least bit tempted to do so."

She managed another smile as he reined about and rode away. Her eyes followed him until he and John were out of sight. Until she gathered her wits about her and returned inside to the comfort of her bed. She suddenly felt very tired . . .

The remainder of the day passed with agonizing unhaste. She was glad of Sarah Beattie's company, and of the kindness of the king, who summoned the two of them to share the noon meal with him. Queen Anne was present as well. Analise liked the Danish woman very much, and enjoyed listening to her tales of maternal woe. Prince Henry, it seemed, was a particular trial to her.

"You have a son yourself, Lady Analise?" Queen Anne queried with a smile as she lifted a goblet of wine to her lips. She sat at a square table of inlaid brass, with her husband on one side and Sarah on the other. Analise was seated opposite.

"I do sincerely doubt it, my love." King James was the one to answer. "Did I not tell you that the Armstrong took her to wife but a short time ago?"

"Oh, yes," recalled Queen Anne. Her upswept blond curls glistened in the firelight, her very full bosom swelling above the low neckline of her primrose satin gown. She smiled at Analise once more. "I think, with such a man as your husband, it will not be long until you are with child."

"Aye, but there is no hurry," Sarah hastened to come to a blushing Analise's rescue. "John Beattie and I had been wed for nearly five years' time before our first son was born." Her eyes were full of understanding when they met Analise's. "Besides, is it not best for a man and wife to become well acquainted first? Such familiarity can only strengthen a marriage."

"Perhaps," the queen thoughtfully conceded, then heaved an eloquent sigh. "So long as one is not married to a king."

She rose from the table and glided across the room to the window. Sarah felt obliged to join her, leaving Analise to answer the king's questions about her former life in London. He proved to be a skilled conversationalist, and was far more intelligent than she had first thought him. But, then, she had already discovered that the Scots were not at all the uneducated heathens she had once believed them to be.

When night came, she sat alone before the fire in her bedchamber, a quilt wrapped about her shoulders. The queen had desired her company for supper, but she had pleaded a headache. In truth, she was sick with worry. She had expected Ronan to return before darkness fell. Sarah had warned her, of course, that the meeting might have been delayed for some reason, or that their husbands could have found it necessary to ride elsewhere.

Sarah was well accustomed to the waiting, Analise mused with another sigh. Would *she* ever become like her new friend? Could she learn to bide the time without dread?

She desperately longed to see Ronan again, to know that he was safe. Heaven help her, why could she not have fallen in love with a parson or a farmer . . . or with one of the foppish, powdered dandies who would no doubt faint dead away at the first sign of trouble? *They* would not ride off into certain danger and leave her to agonize over their fate. No, but she could not love a coward. She could not love anyone other than Ronan.

The hours crawled by. It was very late when she climbed beneath the covers of the bed. She slept fitfully for a while, her dreams once again haunted by visions of her beloved in peril. Prayer after prayer fell from her lips, each heartfelt and each offered up on Ronan's behalf.

Finally she drifted into a deep slumber. . . .

Her eyelids fluttered open. Something had awakened her. A sound, a sense of trouble. She sat up in the bed, her gaze hastily sweeping the darkened room.

"Keep quiet, and you will not be harmed," a man's voice hissed close to her ear.

She paled, her heart twisting in alarm. In spite of the threat, she opened her mouth to scream. A hand clamped across her mouth to silence her. An arm tightened about her waist with such force that she struggled for breath. Her unknown assailant dragged her from the bed and held her captive against him. Shocked and frightened, she could do nothing more for the moment than remain still within his grasp.

"Tell the Armstrong that he must never more turn his hand against Robert Kerr," the man instructed her. "Tell him that if he keeps to the path he has chosen, he will find himself mourning the English bride he holds so dear!"

His words filled her with dismay. Sucking in a deep breath, she came to life now. Her fingers clawed at the hand across her mouth. She fought him with such vehemence that he bit out a curse and loosed his grip. While she tumbled to the floor, he hastened across the room to the door.

"Persuade him," he cautioned one last time, "or else know yourself lost!"

Analise staggered to her feet and tried to summon enough voice to cry for help. But the man was gone.

Flying across the room, she locked the door, then leaned heavily back against it while her legs threatened to give way beneath her. She was quite shaken by what had occurred, and was now thrown into a horrible quandary.

Know yourself lost. The man's words burned within her mind.

"No!" she whispered brokenly. Dear God, what should she do?

The answer came, clear and indisputable.

She would not tell Ronan.

He would be enraged if he knew, she told herself. He would seek revenge.

Her breath caught upon another gasp as she realized that Robert Kerr wanted him to do just that. Indeed, Kerr no doubt longed for an excuse to kill the man who knew him for what he was. And if Ronan rode forth to challenge Kerr on his own, without the protection of the king, he would surely die.

A sob rose in her throat, and she crossed back to sink down upon the bed. Her fear was not for herself, but for Ronan. She knew that he would keep her safe. And knew just as surely that she would give her own life to save his.

Climbing beneath the covers, she heaved a ragged sigh and gathered the pillow to her chest.

Sleep would not come again that night.

She was still abed a full hour after the sky had been set

aglow by the first, muted rays of the dawn. Her eyes strayed to the window, then clouded when she felt her stomach churn. The wave of nausea passed as quickly as the others. Still, she wondered if, in part at least, it had been caused by the night's terror.

Her ears suddenly caught the sound of the door slowly swinging open. With a sharp intake of breath, she came bolt upright in the bed. Her gaze was wide and startled, her heart racing as she watched someone enter. She was certain that she had locked the door.

Sweet mercy, she thought in growing panic, had the villain come to offer more threats? She prepared to scream.

A familiar face turned toward hers. A face that was ruggedly handsome, in need of a shave, and the dearest thing in the world to her.

"Ronan!" Flooded with joy and relief, she flung back the covers and sprang across the room. His strong arms came about her. "Thank heaven you are safe!"

"Aye." He held her as though he would never let her go. She closed her eyes and rested her head against his chest, inhaling deeply of the scent of leather and wood smoke that hung about him. "The meeting with Kerr did not go well," he informed her somberly. "We found it necessary to leave in haste."

"Then, why are you so late in returning?" Lifting her head, she tilted it back to look up at him. She yearned to confide in him, to reveal what had happened, but she did not. She had made her decision and must keep to it. "Where have you been?"

"To Hawkfield."

"Hawkfield?" She frowned in confusion. "I do not understand."

" 'Tis feared that Kerr will soon ride against the Beatties. John has remained there, and gathers his kinsmen in readiness. I have sent word of the danger to Calum as well."

"Should we not return to Dunslair at once?" she suggested anxiously. "If there is to be an attack—"

"I ride there this day, after I have given my report to the king." He released her now and crossed to the table. Pouring himself some wine, he lifted the goblet to his lips and drank.

"I?" Analise echoed behind him. Her gaze filled with disbelief. Clad only in her shift, she shivered at the cold while demanding, "Surely you do not intend that I should remain in Edinburgh!"

"Aye," he confirmed, his expression grave. "You will be safe here."

"No!" She shook her head in a vehement denial, hastening forward to confront him. Her eyes were gloriously ablaze. She did not think about the threats she had been offered, but only of her need to be with him. "I shall not stay behind this time. My place is with you at Dunslair, and that is where I shall be!"

"Sarah is to remain at the palace," he said by way of comfort. His efforts met with little success. Frowning, he sought to draw her close again. "Have we not endured this quarrel already?"

"That was different!" she cried hotly, eluding his grasp. She stood before the fire and folded her arms against her chest. "Dunslair is my home now as much as it is yours. 'Tis where I belong." She lifted her chin to the proud, defiant angle he knew so well. "And I swear by all that is holy, Ronan Armstrong, if you dare to leave me behind, I will find a way to follow you!"

"You speak foolishly," he ground out, his own temper rising. He had not slept for more than a day, and was in no mood to argue. His eyes smoldered down into hers. "By damn, woman, will you never learn to obey me?"

"Will *you* never learn that I am no weak-willed little maiden who trembles in fear at your anger?" she shot back, unflinching beneath his gaze.

Ronan knew that her threat to follow him was all too real. He wanted her with him. God knew, he wanted her with him always. Perhaps, he grudgingly conceded to himself, she was right. The trouble with Kerr could last a long time. He trusted no other to watch over her the way he would. Not even the king.

"Very well." He gave a sigh of resignation and drew near to him again, his hands closing about her shoulders. "I will take you with me."

"Oh, Ronan!" She entwined her arms about his neck and stood on tiptoe to press a kiss to his cheek. "You will not be sorry!"

"Will I not?" he parried dryly. He swept her against him and gently smoothed several wayward golden curls from her face. "Now, once more, sweet lady, I will have a proper welcome."

"Aye, my lord," she murmured in a soft, seductive tone, then kissed him with such ardor that he cursed the need for them to leave right away.

They said their farewells to the king, and thanked him for his kind hospitality. He, in turn, expressed gratitude to Ronan for his loyalty, and after that, charged Analise to return for a visit as soon as possible. She assured him that she would endeavor to do so.

Sarah Beattie accompanied them outside as they prepared to leave. Analise was sorry to bid her good-bye.

"I hope you will soon be able to return to your home," she told her sincerely. Ronan, meanwhile, moved away to make certain the horses were saddled to his liking.

"I thank you," Sarah replied with an affectionate smile. "But I am well accustomed to my husband's absences. 'Tis the price we pay for wedding men of honor."

"Yes, but it is a steep price indeed." Again she was tempted to confide in someone about the intruder. Quelling the urge, she hugged Sarah warmly. "Someday, when the danger has passed, I shall accept your offer to come to Hawkfield."

"Aye. And I will come once again to Dunslair."

Analise gathered up her skirts and hurried across to where Ronan stood waiting. He lifted her up to her horse's back, then swung up into his own saddle. They rode across the grounds and out into the streets, joining the noisy, ever present bustle of the city.

The journey was mercifully uneventful. They arrived at Dunslair well before darkness. Ronan assisted Analise in dismounting. She felt light-headed, but said nothing of it as they approached the house.

"You have come none too soon!" Calum exclaimed, hastening forward to meet them. He looked very troubled and—at that moment—very young.

"What has happened?" Ronan demanded sharply.

"Angus Maxwell."

"He has come?" Ronan now asked. He had known that Angus would eventually ride to Dunslair.

"Aye," Calum confirmed. "He speaks with Dierdre in our bedchamber at present."

Ronan took Analise's arm once more. They walked

inside with Calum, their progress delayed when they stepped within the midst of the numerous Armstrongs who had gathered to dine in the baronial hall. Ronan greeted them briefly, and promised to return to speak with them once he had met with Angus Maxwell.

The trio continued up the stairs. Analise's gaze clouded with trepidation as they approached the bedchamber Calum now shared with Dierdre. She had known that Angus would be furious about his daughter's elopement, and that he would no doubt blame Ronan as much as Calum. In spite of her weariness, she would not leave her husband's side.

Angus Maxwell rounded on them as soon as they entered the room. His face reddened with anger, his eyes blazing vengefully at Ronan.

"So," he bellowed, "you have come to answer for your treachery!"

"Father!" cried Dierdre, grasping at his arm in another desperate attempt to make him see reason. He pulled away from her and advanced upon Ronan while Calum hastened to Dierdre's side.

"Well, Ronan Armstrong?" Angus ground out. "Do you now include abduction and ravishment among your crimes against us?"

"There has been no abduction," Ronan declared calmly. "Nor ravishment." His gaze locked with the other man's. "Dierdre is here of her own free will. She and Calum were legally wed. She carries his child."

"Aye, and is that not reason alone for me to strike him down?" Angus roared. He stopped mere inches away from Ronan, his expression so murderous that Analise blanched. "After *that* villainy, you gave warning of an attack by the Armstrongs. What trickery do you use against us?"

"Has Longcroft suffered a raid?" Ronan demanded in return.

"No, by—why the devil do you ask?" His eyes narrowed in wrathful suspicion. "What are you about, man?"

"I seek only to make peace between our clans." He was relieved to learn that Simon Hayward had not proceeded with his attack upon the Maxwells. Relieved and surprised. What was the English warden plotting?

"You know I opposed the marriage," Angus continued with his tirade. He jerked his head about to fling Calum a swift, bitter glare. "You yourself heard me deny your brother my blessing upon the match," he reminded Ronan. "Yet he took her anyway. And will be made to pay for his misdeed!"

"No!" Dierdre breathed, horror-stricken. "He is no more guilty than I!"

"You were led astray, girl!" her father shot back.

"You have made no mention of Ewan," said Ronan. His words had the desired effect of turning Angus's attention from the newlyweds.

"Aye, for I would hear from your own lips how you did murder my kinsman!"

" 'Twas not murder. I killed only in defense." His mouth curved into a faint smile of irony. "Even an Armstrong would hope for better odds than four against one."

"You had sworn revenge!" Angus pointed out with a scowl. "Would you have me believe that Ewan behaved dishonorably?"

"If you believed otherwise, you would not have come alone this day."

Angus opened his mouth to reply, but clamped it shut and spun about to stride angrily across to the window. He stood there for several long moments, digesting Ronan's words, while a highly charged silence filled the room. An anxious, wide-eyed Dierdre clung to Calum. Analise looked up at Ronan, and was glad when he clasped her hand with the warmth of his own.

"He was ever a wild and ungovernable one," Angus finally remarked of Ewan. He pivoted to face Ronan. "In truth, Armstrong, I always knew that he would bring about his own death. I will not claim vengeance for him. But," he added, turning his furious gaze upon Calum once more, "I cannot forgive what has been done to my daughter!"

"And what of the child?" Ronan challenged, his own eyes darkening. "Would you deny your own grandson the right to his father's name?"

"There can be no alliance between Maxwell and Armstrong!" Angus declared.

"There *can* be," Ronan dissented firmly. "Aye, if we so grant it. The time has come to set aside the blood feud. What better way to peace than through this marriage?"

"Please, Father!" Dierdre implored again. She flew across to him and raised her hands to his chest. Though pale and trembling, she was determined to have her way. "I love him. No matter what you say, I will not leave him." Pausing for a moment in order to take a deep breath and square her shoulders, she then warned, "Either offer us your blessing, or know that you will nevermore look upon my face."

"You cannot mean that, Daughter!" he protested, obviously taken aback by her threat. Her words pained him. And forced him to consider surrendering for the first time in his life.

"I do," Dierdre insisted. "With all my heart." She took her place beside Calum once more.

Angus recognized in her his own obstinance, his own single-minded resolve. Torn between love and duty, he bit out an oath and moved back to the window.

"Do you know what you say, lass?" he asked quietly. "Do you have any idea what it is to be cast out by your clan?"

"It matters not," Dierdre answered. "I am an Armstrong now. If the Maxwells shun me, then so be it."

"You would truly bring shame upon yourself?"

"What shame is there in my marriage?"

He knew the truth of her words, knew as well that he would never convince her to deny her husband. He suddenly felt very old. Heaving a sigh, he shook his head.

"What am I to tell the others of my clan?" he asked no one in particular. "That I am a softhearted fool who would place his daughter above all else?"

"You could tell them what my husband has said," Analise suggested, folding her hands together and offering him an earnest look. "It is time for peace between us, Angus Maxwell. I know you to be a fair and reasonable man. You would not wish to break your daughter's heart. 'Tis impossible, I think, for her to love one of you and not the other."

Angus turned now so that his eyes met hers. The merest spark of amusement lurked within his eyes when he told Ronan, "You are a fortunate man, Armstrong."

"Aye," Ronan agreed, capturing Analise's hand again.

"Father?" Dierdre appealed, praying that he had come to his senses at last.

"I have grown weak," he proclaimed gruffly, "for I find that I cannot bear the thought of losing you." He was rewarded with a kiss and an affectionate embrace from her. Calum approached father and daughter when they drew apart.

"I ask for your forgiveness, Angus Maxwell," he put forth in all sincerity. " 'Twas wrong of me to wed her without your consent. But I swear by all the saints, I will care for her always, and treat her well."

"Your crime cannot be forgotten so easily," Angus cautioned with another scowl. It was clear that he would still like nothing better than to give Calum Armstrong the thrashing he deserved. "Yet, for my daughter's sake, I will not seek revenge against you." He would offer no more. To Ronan, he said upon a different subject entirely, "Why have you summoned your kinsmen to Dunslair? Can it be that you expect an attack by the English?"

"No." He hesitated, then decided to reveal the truth. "Robert Kerr has declared himself my enemy."

"He is a fool."

"Aye, but a dangerous one."

"Our clans are bound together now," Angus pointed out, albeit with great reluctance. "We will stand with you against him."

"I must still honor my alliance with Simon Hayward," Ronan advised him grimly. "Though it sickens me to do so."

"The English bastard grows bolder of late." At a sudden thought, his eyes narrowed across at Ronan. "Mayhap the warning you sent was because of Hayward."

"I cannot say."

"Aye," said Angus, understanding well. "You cannot." He looked to Dierdre once more. "I bid you farewell, Daughter. And do but ask you to have a care."

She pressed another kiss to his cheek, and fought back tears while he turned and left. Ronan followed after him. Analise, sensing that Calum and Dierdre needed a moment of privacy, took her leave as well and hurried down the corridor to her bedchamber. Mairi appeared soon thereafter, ostensibly to inform Analise that she had ordered her a bath, yet in truth wanting to talk of Calum.

"So," she began with a heavy, disconsolate sigh, "Master Calum is wed."

"Yes," murmured Analise. Her eyes were full of sympathy as she turned to the young housemaid and tried to offer her comfort. "He has loved her for many years, Mairi."

"Aye, that he has." She dashed impatiently at the tears that spilled over from her lashes. "But I . . . I did not think the Maxwell would give his consent. Why could Calum not have set his eyes upon one of his own?"

"We cannot choose where we love," Analise remarked softly, then mused with an inward smile that her words were some of the truest she had ever spoken. She lifted a gentle hand to Mairi's arm and added, "I am certain that, if Calum had not already given his heart elsewhere, he would have looked to the women here at Dunslair."

"Lawrie says I have been a fool long enough," Mairi confided, still looking perfectly miserable. "He would have us marry right away." She sucked in a deep, quavering breath before meeting Analise's gaze again. "He does love me, my lady. There are none better than Lawrie Armstrong."

"You sound as though you are tempted to consider his suit favorably."

"Aye. I am past twenty. 'Tis time I was taken to wife.

And if bonny Calum will not have me, I must accept another."

"But are you—how can you think of marrying a man you do not love?" Analise queried in astonishment.

"Oh, but I do care for Lawrie," insisted Mairi. "Not the same as I did love Calum, perhaps. Still, I can think of no other man who would suit me as Lawrie does. He will not beat me ... well, not often, at least. No, nor take other women to his bed." Her mouth curved into a faint, crooked smile when she concluded, "Not all of us are as fortunate as you, my lady. Lord Ronan loves you so fierce that none could ever doubt it. Aye, and were I you, I would thank God for it." She left then, promising that the water for the bath would be brought along soon.

Alone now, Analise began peeling off her clothing. Wearing only her shift, she pulled her cloak about her shoulders again and took a seat in the chair before the fire. Her gaze fixed upon the dance of the flames, her thoughts drifting aimlessly as she waited for her bath.

She experienced a sudden wave of dizziness. Inhaling upon a gasp, she closed her eyes and waited for the light-headedness to pass. It was then that something of great significance occurred to her—she had not endured the "monthly curse" since leaving London.

Her eyes flew wide. Her mind raced to remember when she had last bled.

"Sweet heaven!" she whispered, her hand fluttering to her throat as a very real possibility made itself known to her.

A child. She might be carrying Ronan's child.

"No," she said, shaking her head while her heart pounded. " 'Tis too soon for . . ."

Her words trailed away. She told herself that, even if

her suspicions were true, it wasn't possible that her body could already be responding. Had she not heard that the sickness came after many weeks, not days? She had been married scarcely a week's time.

Yet the evidence was before her. Nausea, dizziness, a growing sense that something was different.

It was true. *She was going to have a baby.*

The thought filled her with joy and excitement—and more than a touch of apprehension. Slowly rising from the chair, she crossed her arms beneath her breasts and wandered across to sink down upon the edge of the bed.

She must tell Ronan, of course. But when? The time had to be right. Would he be pleased that it had happened so quickly? she wondered. He had vowed to get her with child. *And he was ever a man of his word.*

Still trembling with amazement, she hugged the secret close. Her cheeks were quite flushed and her eyes unusually bright when Mairi and Flora arrived with the water.

"Are you unwell, my lady?" Flora inquired, frowning with worriment at the sight of her.

"No." She smiled and declared, "No, Flora, I have never felt better."

"You are wearied from the journey," pronounced Mairi as she and her sister emptied the buckets into the bathtub. "Aye, and now you have come home to a house full of kinsmen once more. 'Tis enough to prompt any woman to illness. Please, God, they will go home soon."

"Mairi!" Flora admonished. "They are here to offer us their protection. Would you make them so unwelcome?"

"I have not done so," Mairi denied, though a bit defensively. "Yet I will be glad when they are gone. We have enough work as it is."

"Have you become lazy, then?"

"No. Not lazy. But are you not fatigued by so much extra—"

"Mayhap I should tell Lawrie of your complaints!"

"Do so, and 'twill be *you* that gets skelped this night!"

Their bickering continued as they left Analise to her bath. She washed, and afterward relaxed within the water's soothing warmth. Wishing that her husband would return and find her thus, she immediately chided herself for her wickedness. Yet she could not truly be sorry for it.

She had dried herself and donned a clean shift when Ronan finally joined her. Though he looked troubled by something, he would not speak of it.

"I have gone too long without sleep. And now would forget all else for a time," he told her. He shrugged out of his jack and tugged off his shirt. Analise found herself searching for words as she watched him sit upon the chair to remove his boots. Taking up the quilt she had left beside the bathtub, she pulled it about her and gently cleared her throat.

"Ronan?"

"Aye?" He stood and unfastened his breeches.

She opened her mouth to speak, yet said nothing. Now was not the time to tell him, she decided. He was tired, and she would not burden him further. Not that the news would be unwelcome . . . yet perhaps it would be best to wait. After all, little enough time had passed. And she was certain that, if he knew, he would be anxious on her behalf even more than he was at present. No, she would not tell him now. *But soon,* she vowed silently.

"What is wrong?" Ronan demanded. Naked now, he frowned as he drew near to her.

"Nothing," she was quick to deny. She forced a bright

smile to her lips and allowed her gaze to travel over his virile, hard-muscled form. Her face was flushed when she teasingly declared, "I cannot but think that my husband is the handsomest in all of Christendom."

"Ah, but you have little basis for comparison," he noted, then narrowed his eyes down at her in mock suspicion. "Unless you have seen other men thus."

"Indeed, my lord, at the court in London we were often in the company of gentlemen sans attire."

His only response was a faint, crooked smile. He lowered himself into the bathtub, then cupped his hands to wet his face. Analise's eyes filled with compassion at the thought of his weariness. She took a seat in the chair and watched as he began soaping his body.

"I shall have Mairi bring you some wine," she said. "It should help you to sleep."

"I have no need of the wine," he assured her.

"Then, I shall tell Calum to make certain you are undisturbed this night, and on the morrow as well."

"Would you have me remain abed like an old woman?" His gaze sparked with amusement, and pleasure at her concern.

"If such a thing is required in order to ensure your good health!" she retorted, drawing herself abruptly to her feet. She heaved a sigh and moved to kneel upon the floor beside the tub. "You have the weight of the world upon your shoulders, Ronan Armstrong," she told him, her tone soft and solicitous. "I would see you truly forget all for a time."

"You have no need to worry, lass," he replied quietly. He lifted a hand from the water and pressed it to her cheek. "Aye, for my shoulders are broad and well accustomed to the weight. I cannot run from my troubles or duties. 'Tis the way I was taught from childhood. And the way our sons will be taught."

Our sons, her mind echoed. She warmed with pleasure while a secret smile played about her lips.

"Shall I scrub your back?" she offered. Before he could answer, she had thrown off the quilt and taken the soap from the edge of the bathtub. Ronan inhaled sharply when she smoothed her hand across his back and down beneath the surface of the water to his hips.

"If you would have me sleep," he warned in a low, vibrant tone, "take care."

She merely smiled and soaped her fingers again. When she leaned forward this time, the water splashed over the edge of the tub, wetting the front of her chemise. Ronan's eyes fell to where the thin, dampened fabric clung to the rose-tipped peaks of her breasts. He groaned inwardly, his body tensing while his blood fired.

"Why, your skin is hot, almost fevered," Analise observed in surprise, her brows knitting into a frown of worriment while her fingers trailed upward once more. Unaware as yet that she herself was the cause of his heat, she raised her hand to his forehead. The scent of her was sweet, seductive. Ronan caught his breath and gritted his teeth against the desire thundering through him. "Perhaps your wound—"

" 'Tis not my wound," he ground out. He seized her wrist in a firm grip, his gaze burning across into hers. "By heaven, woman, is it your wish to torment me?"

"Torment you?" she repeated in puzzlement. Her cheeks grew warm when she realized his meaning. But, instead of contrition, she was filled with a bold and saucy intent. She smiled again, pulling free while her eyes sparkled. "Mayhap, sir, 'tis time the tables were turned."

With that, she plunged both hands into the water. Ronan suffered another sharp intake of breath when she took hold of his manhood. He grasped the edges of the tub until his knuckles turned white. Analise showed him no mercy. Her fingers teased and rubbed and caressed, her breasts taunting him as she leaned closer. They brushed against his chest once, twice, a third time. He could bear no more.

It was her turn to gasp when he suddenly tumbled her down into the water with him. She shrieked in protest, but he cradled her atop his thighs, his mouth descending upon hers with such intoxicating force that she moaned in surrender. Finally he stood from the tub and carried her to the bed, leaving a trail of water to mark his swift and determined path across the floor.

"I—I thought you were fatigued, my lord!" Analise reminded him, though not at all in complaint.

"Aye." He placed her upon the mattress and impatiently stripped the wet chemise from her body. "But I know of something better than wine to make me sleep."

"I still think, sir," she accused breathlessly while he lowered his body to hers, "that you know far too much!"

"Have you not heard it said that knowledge is power?" He grew serious then, his gaze holding hers in the firelit darkness while his hands gently swept the bright, silken tresses from her face. "I love you, Analise. More than I ever thought to love anyone. And once the danger has passed, I—"

"Speak no more of it tonight," she requested, her heart twisting anew at the thought of what lay ahead. She placed her own hand upon her abdomen, and took comfort from the certainty that a new life grew within her.

Her mouth curved into a soft, provocative smile when she whispered, "Speak not at all."

Entwining her arms about his neck, she kissed him. And knew that they would both sleep well that night. . . .

Chapter 13

Three days passed. Three days, and still no word or sign of trouble.

In spite of the awful uncertainty hanging over their heads, Analise was determined to enjoy her hours with Ronan. It seemed that a goodly portion of their marriage thus far had been spent apart. Now, however, she saw him frequently throughout the day. And slept within his arms each night.

Dierdre was equally delighted to be with Calum. Their happiness was apparent to everyone, and served to make the other Armstrongs yearn for the company of their own wives and families. But, until Robert Kerr made his move, they could not go home. Dunslair was the traditional stronghold of their clan and must not be taken.

The men occupied themselves outside most of the time, while the women had more than enough work of their own to do—cleaning and cooking, sewing, the perennial mountain of washing. None save Mairi offered any complaint. Once Flora made good on her threats to tell Lawrie of his betrothed's ill-mannered remarks, he took it upon himself to improve her humor. And though Mairi found it difficult to sit for the remainder of the week, her respect for Lawrie increased. It was clear that he would be master once they were wed.

On the afternoon of the fourth day, Analise went in search of Ronan. She flung her cloak about her shoulders and stepped out into the sunshine. Her face lifted to its warmth, for the past several days had been characteristically cold and gray and blustery. Indeed, she recalled, the wind had howled and lashed at the walls of the tower house throughout the previous night. Yet she had felt safe and secure within Ronan's strong, loving embrace.

She inhaled deeply, then gathered up her skirts and set off across the courtyard. With a smile, she responded to the many greetings sent her way as she strolled past the cottages. It was difficult to know, of course, if she had gained the people's full acceptance. In time perhaps, she told herself, they would see that she held their laird dear and would never bring shame upon him. Their affection for him could be no deeper than hers—in truth, none could love him so well as she did.

Her eyes glowed with pleasure when she discovered Ronan speaking with Lawrie near the stables. Catching sight of her, he drew away from the other man and strode forward. Her pulse leapt as she noticed the way his hair shone in the sunlight, the easy, masculine grace of his movements. She was tempted in that moment to finally tell him of the child, but was still reluctant to say anything that would cause him worry. There was plenty of time, she reasoned with herself. It would be several months yet until her belly began to swell. And surely, they would know peace long before then . . .

"Have you grown weary of woman's talk?" Ronan teased. Though he smiled, his eyes held no trace of amusement.

"Something is wrong," she noted, searching his face.

"I have received word from the king." He cursed inwardly, knowing full well that she would be troubled by the news. "I must ride again to Edinburgh on the morrow."

"No!" She shook her head in disbelief while her eyes clouded with dread. "He cannot mean to place you in such danger! What if Robert Kerr—"

"I must go, Analise." His features very grim, he took her arm and led her to the far side of the stables so that they could speak in private. "Once more, the king would have my help. And while I hate to leave you, I know that you will be kept safe here at Dunslair."

"Take me with you!" she implored him, her hands curling tightly about his powerful, hard-muscled upper arms. "Please, Ronan!"

"No," he insisted. "I cannot." He would have drawn her close, but she eluded his grasp and moved to the end of the building. Ronan's gaze followed her, his heart pained at the sight of her distress.

"How long will you be away?" she asked. Her tone was calm, distant.

"A night or two, three at most."

"I see." Furiously blinking back sudden tears, she folded her arms across her chest. "Then, I must be patient again."

"Analise."

"What else is there to be said upon the matter?"

"Analise."

She slowly turned to face him. He closed the distance between them, his eyes entreating her to reason. But her emotions were at present too raw, her fear too great.

"Tell me if you will," she said, her voice quavering.

"As your widow, shall I be expected to remain at Dunslair? Or perhaps, 'tis the custom for me to marry one of your kinsmen and—"

"By damn," he ground out, his hands closing angrily about her shoulders, "you are behaving like a child!"

"Not a child," she dissented, "but a woman who loves her husband and would not see him dead." She closed her eyes and swallowed hard before opening them again. "These past few days have been the happiest I have ever known. I would not have them end so soon."

"Och, lass," sighed Ronan, his gaze softening as he finally gathered her to him. She released a sigh of her own when his arms came about her. "Have I not told you? I will not die. Not yet. Aye, not until I am too old and feeble to lift a sword."

"How can you be so certain?"

"Are there not things you know without being told?"

Those words, above all others, gave her strength. She nodded against his chest before lifting her head to peer up at him.

"That day at Windy Gyle," she confided, "when I watched you with the others, I knew that I would love you. I knew it, and yet I was afraid to face it."

"As was I," he admitted with a quiet chuckle. He grew serious again, his eyes gazing deeply into the wide, luminous depths of hers. "We must learn to master our fears. Else we are bound to them."

"I *am* afraid," she readily confessed. "But only for you."

"I know." He drew his arms from about her, yet grasped her hand with the warmth of his. "Come. We have only this day left to us."

"Will you not at least tell me what help the king seeks from you?"

"No, for you will worry all the more."

"Is it Robert Kerr?" she persisted, hanging back when he would have led her along with him. "Does he—"

"Word has come that Kerr thinks to join forces with Simon Hayward."

"Dear heaven!" Analise breathed in horrified dismay.

" 'Tis an unlikely alliance. And one that will bring war upon the border once more." His gaze darkened, his expression one of simmering fury. "Together, they would overthrow the king. If they are allowed to try, scores of men on both sides will perish. Women and children as well. To think that Scotland could produce such a cowardly, traitorous . . ." His voice trailed away as the urge for vengeance burned within him.

"What are you going to do?"

"I am to meet with the chieftains of the other Border clans before the king. No doubt, we will be called upon to raise an army."

"And will you march upon Beauford?" she now asked, her throat constricting at the prospect. She knew her guardian to be ruthless. Ruthless and cruel and entirely without mercy.

"Aye," confirmed Ronan. "With his treachery against my king, he has broken the alliance between us. I will no longer hesitate to raise my hand against him. No, nor to make him pay for the crimes he has committed while hiding behind the protection of his office."

"Perhaps . . . perhaps I can be of use to you." She raised her eyes to his once more.

"In what way?"

"I could ride to Beauford," she offered in a rush,

knowing that he would be prompted to decline. "Indeed, I could appeal to my cousin. I could warn him against his treachery, and might—"

"No."

"But you must—"

"*No.*" This time his hands seized her arms in a firm grip. He frowned darkly. "Do you not understand? 'Tis Hayward who would make use of you. Aye, and force me to his will on threat of doing you harm."

"Am I to forever do naught, then, while you ride into danger?" she challenged indignantly. "Though I am a woman, Ronan Armstrong, I shall not accept such a . . . a mindless, damnably placid role!"

"There is honor in obedience," he decreed, the look in his eyes cautioning her against further argument.

"And madness!" Pulling away from him, she assumed an air of wounded dignity. "Were I to have a *dozen* children, I would still—"

"Children?" He grasped her arms again, regarding her closely. "What are you talking about?"

Furious at her own blunder, Analise colored and looked away. Her stomach knotted as she realized that there was no help for it now. She would have to tell him.

"Well?" he demanded, his tone sharp and his fingers tightening upon her flesh.

"I am with child." She ventured a glance up at him, only to watch as his expression turned from surprise to joy to hopeful disbelief.

"How can you be certain? We have been wed but a few—"

"I am certain," she assured him. Heaving another sigh, she fixed him with a look that was at once affectionate and reproachful. "In all likelihood, it happened the first time you forced me to your bed."

"Aye." His smile was thoroughly unrepentant, his eyes warmly aglow. "If I had not been able to claim reason enough before to stay alive, I would be able to do so now." At a sudden thought, amusement turned to anger again. "By all that is holy, you knew and yet you would have placed both yourself and the child in peril!"

"I would have my child know her father!" she shot back, her own gaze kindling.

"His," Ronan corrected, though in truth, he would be just as pleased if it were a girl.

"Son or daughter, it matters not! You will still ride away to do battle, and I will still endure the misery of wondering if you will ever return!"

"Let us quarrel no more." His hands moved from her arms to her waist. He gave her a tender smile before remarking, "Fate has been kind. There will be two Armstrongs born at Dunslair in the spring. Two Armstrongs who, if Kerr and Hayward can be stopped, will never know anything save peace."

"I want that," she murmured, then drew in a deep, ragged breath and looked up at him again. "I want that as much as you do. But at what price must it be gained?"

"No price is too dear." He drew her close, his chin resting upon the top of her head. *"No price."*

She knew that he was right. She knew it, and yet could she accept whatever was to come? Heaven help her, could she live without the tall, blue-eyed Reiver who had captured her heart?

"No," she whispered. Ronan dropped a light, gentle

kiss upon her forehead and kept one arm about her waist as they walked together toward the house.

There was a banquet within the Great Hall at Dunslair that night. Analise and Dierdre had immersed themselves in the preparations throughout the remainder of the afternoon. With Mairi and Flora to lend assistance, they had succeeded in arranging a well-deserved evening of food and drink and entertainment for their guests.

The room was ablaze with the brilliant golden light of candles and torches. One of the men had brought his fiddle, while another was a piper who was seldom without his own instrument. They began to play, filling the hall with the strains of a ballad known to all of those who heard it, save Analise. Extra chairs had been borrowed from the cottages, and had been set either around or near the long table. The table itself was laden with all manner of temptations—Dunlop cheese, roast pheasant, grouse and steak pudding, haggis, *bridies*, fresh salmon, Cock-A-Leekie, oatcakes, ale, claret, and brandy.

Analise had taken special care when dressing for the banquet. Her soft blue woolen gown had been brushed and pressed, her hair coiled and pinned loosely atop her head. Ronan, too, had cast aside his usual rough attire. He looked quiet dashing in a rich blue doublet and fitted black breeches. To Analise's eye, of course, he would have been equally magnificent in anything—*or nothing*—at all.

They mingled with their guests, happy to be among men of such honor and regard. Analise inquired after their wives and children. Ronan talked of political matters with them, and answered their questions about Robert Kerr. Calum and Dierdre took part as well, though they never left one another's side. Their marriage had been hard-won and would never be taken for granted.

Supper proved a great success. And afterward one of the younger guests proclaimed that there should be dancing. Both Flora and Mairi were pressed into service, causing Lawrie to scowl in jealousy at the sight of his future bride being whirled about the room in another man's arms. While the music swelled and the partnerless Armstrongs clapped or shouted encouragement, Ronan clasped Analise's hand and led her forward to join in the dance.

"But I do not know any of your Scottish dances," she protested.

" 'Tis a reel and easy enough to follow."

A soft gasp escaped her lips when he suddenly slipped an arm about her waist and spun her about. Conscious of the many pairs of eyes upon her, she struggled to match his steps. But it wasn't long before she caught on. Her eyes shone brightly, her mouth curving into a smile as she relaxed and danced with a gracefulness that prompted more than one onlooker to feel a twinge of envy.

"We have never before danced together," she said to Ronan, raising her voice to be heard above the music.

"Aye, but you are no novice," he replied. There was a spark of jealousy within his own eyes as he tightened his grasp upon her and frowned.

"There was little else to do in London."

"Then, I must give thanks you did naught save dance with the men there."

She smiled again as he whirled her faster. As soon as the reel had ended, a Highland fling was struck up, and she was claimed by a tall, bearded man who moved with such vigor that she grew breathless. Though Ronan would have preferred to keep her to himself, he could not deny his kinsmen the pleasure of dancing with her. Calum, however, was not so generous. He never let go of Dierdre.

The evening wore on. After the women had declared themselves too weary to dance another step, the Armstrongs gathered in front of the fire and began to tell stories. Storytelling was a time-honored tradition, Analise discovered, and one in which most Borderers were remarkably proficient. Sitting beside Ronan, she listened in fascination to the tales of battles, wooings, murders, legends, and, of course, triumphs against the English.

Finally the hour grew late. The fire burned low. Ronan and Analise bade their guests good night, as did Calum and Dierdre. Both couples retired to their bedchambers. Once they had gone from the baronial hall, Lawrie seized Mairi's hand and pulled her none too gently outside with him. Delighted by his jealousy, she offered no resistance when he swept her against him and kissed her with such fervor that all thought of Calum was driven from her mind.

Analise, meanwhile, stood at the window while Ronan placed another log upon the fire. In a few short hours, she mused disconsolately, he would be gone. A lump rose in her throat. Her hands strayed once more to her abdomen, where she knew his child—*their* child, the child conceived in a love that had taken them both by surprise, grew larger and stronger with each passing day.

"Though I know your anger will be roused by the speaking of it," she said, her gaze seeking his across the room, "I would still ride to Beauford."

"No, Analise." He drew himself upright and began

unfastening his doublet. "Even if you were not with child, my answer would be the same. The Scots do not make war with women."

"I would go to make peace, not war!"

"Aye." Taking off his doublet, he removed his shirt next and then his boots. Analise undressed as well, wearing only her shift when she approached him. He stood clad in his breeches, one hand braced against the mantelpiece while the firelight played softly over the bronzed, hard-muscled smoothness of his upper torso.

"What if I took it upon myself to ride to Beauford once you are away to Edinburgh?" she challenged, her chin lifting to a proud, mutinous angle.

"Do so," he warned in a dangerously low and level tone, "and I will give you reason to curse me."

Her eyes grew round with startled dismay. "Why, you cannot think to raise your hand to me now that—"

" 'Twas not my thought to strike you, but to confine you to the house. Indeed, to this very room if you remain so willful." He turned to face her, his hands closing gently about her waist. His touch sent a delectable tremor through her. "You will serve me best, Analise, by doing as I say." A disarming smile now tugged at his lips, while his eyes warmed with both tenderness and amusement. "I thought we had settled this quarrel. And yet you offer me debate again. Is it always to be thus?"

"Aye," she answered with a dramatic sigh. "I fear so, my lord."

"Then, I must guard my tongue well, for no doubt you will twist my words to suit my pleasure." He drew her close, his arms wrapping about her. She trembled when her thinly covered breasts pressed against the bare skin of his chest. "I will come back to you, Analise," he vowed softly. "Still, I would take the memories of this night with me." His brow creased into a sudden frown. "But the bairn—"

"Will not be harmed," she assured him. Curling her arms about his neck, she smiled coquettishly. "In truth, Scotsman, I shall never forgive you if you do not offer me a 'proper' farewell." It was difficult to turn her mind from his leaving, but she was determined to do so. And to give him the sweet memories he wanted.

"God help me, for I have married a woman who is not easily satisfied," he said in mock complaint. His voice was low, splendidly vibrant, and made her heart flutter. She gazed up into the fathomless blue depths of his eyes and knew herself to be his forever. *Forever.*

"Come," she entreated, pulling away and taking his hand. "Too soon, the morn will break."

"Aye." A shadow crossed his face, but he swiftly cast aside his disquiet and allowed her to lead him to the bed. Together they would make the night memorable. And forget, for a time at least, what the dawn would bring.

He left at first light.

Analise managed to fight back her tears until after he was gone. She sought the privacy of their bedchamber then, and wept until she could weep no more. In spite of her resolve, she could not keep the worst from her mind—thoughts of Ronan ambushed by Robert Kerr on his way to Edinburgh, or perhaps on his way home. Dear God, how could she bear it if he were killed?

The day seemed endless. Come nightfall, she was glad of the company of so many. She sat with her husband's kinsmen in the hall, listening to more blood-stirring tales, and all the while trying desperately to keep her spirits high. One of the older Armstrongs, a dark-haired man with kind, weathered features, sensed the distress she sought to conceal. He placed a warm hand upon hers and gave her a brief smile of comfort.

"You've no need to worry so, my lady," he insisted a bit gruffly. "Your husband will soon return. Aye, and with his head still upon his body."

"Do you think him truly to enjoy the protection of angels?" she asked, her tone ironic.

"Call them what you will," the man answered, "but know that he *is* protected."

"How can you be so certain?" Her eyes kindled now, her voice edging with anxiety. "Is he not a man like any other? Indeed, what makes you think him invincible?"

"He is the Armstrong."

She waited for him to elaborate, but he said nothing more. A frown of exasperation creasing her brow, she stood and wandered closer to the fire. Behind her, the storytelling continued. Someone began to sing. The fiddler, struck by homesickness, took up his instrument to offer accompaniment.

The music only served to worsen the ache within Analise. She felt a sudden need to escape. Hastening upstairs to fetch her cloak, she threw it about her shoulders and descended the steps once more. Calum's eyes followed her as she moved across the hall to the stairwell leading outside, but he made no attempt to stop her.

She passed through the two guarded gates and out into the darkness. Filling her lungs with the cold night air, she gathered up her skirts and set off across the courtyard. Her course was undecided. She eventually found herself near the mill. Recalling the intimacy she had shared with Ronan there, she heaved a ragged sigh and wandered far-

ther, toward the barmkin running along the southern edge
of the compound.

Her gaze swept across the outlying hills, bathed in pale
moonlight. She stepped closer to the wall and raised her
hands to it. The stones were cold and rough to her touch.
She shivered and drew her hands away, tugging the
edges of her cloak more securely about her. Ronan's face
swam before her eyes.

"Oh, Ronan," she whispered brokenly.

Spinning about, she leaned back against the wall and
cast a despondent look heavenward. Her heart felt so
very heavy. She closed her eyes and battled the urge to
cry again.

Without warning, a hand clamped across her mouth.
An arm slipped about her waist and tightened so that she
struggled for breath.

A scream rose in her throat, her eyes flying wide in
startlement. She fought with all her might, but it was no
use. In a matter of seconds, she was dragged over the
barmkin and hoisted up before a man on horseback.
While his arms closed about her, she tried once more to
scream. A gag was thrust within her mouth. Her terror-
stricken gaze searched for help in the darkness.

"Our patience has been rewarded at last," her captor
sneered close to her ear.

She tensed, her throat constricting. The voice was
familiar. Indeed, she recognized it as the same she had
heard when the intruder had accosted her at the palace.
She had thought little of his warning since arriving home.
But now, it returned to hit her full force.

"Silence, my lady," he cautioned, "or I will break your
lovely neck."

His tone was cruel, scornful. Filled with dread, she

could do nothing more than fling one last helpless look toward the house as the horse beneath her took flight. They rode away from Dunslair at a breakneck pace.

Ronan. Her heart cried out to him, her eyes sweeping closed again while she battled a wave of nausea and prayed that the child would not be harmed by the wild ride.

Chapter 14

To Analise, the journey seemed to last for days instead of hours. She was wearied to the bone when her captor finally reined the sweating animal to a halt. He slid from the saddle, pulling her down beside him. For the first time, her eyes lifted to the castle rising so ominously against the night sky. She gasped against the cloth in her mouth, her pulse leaping in surprise.

Beauford. Her head spun, and she felt herself torn between relief and dismay.

Her gag was finally removed. She rounded on her captor, whose face, though unknown to her, resembled another she had seen.

"Why have you brought me here?" she demanded furiously.

"Inside," he directed, his hand closing with bruising force about her arm. A dark and coarse-featured man, he was not so much taller than she. Yet she knew that he was both strong and ruthless.

She told herself that it would do little good to resist. Drawing herself proudly erect, she allowed him to lead her inside the castle. They were soon entering the cavernous hall, where a fire blazed beyond the hearth and a trio of men sat conversing with one another near its warmth.

Analise's gaze immediately fell upon Simon Hayward. He rose from his chair and advanced upon her with a smile, the look in his eyes one of malevolent satisfaction.

"Ah, dearest cousin," he drawled. "Truly, I am sorry to have kept you from your bed this night. But for too long you have made us wait. Indeed, we were beginning to think a siege upon Dunslair would be the only way to take you. How fortunate for us that your husband absented himself." He grasped her hand and raised it to his lips. She hastily jerked free.

"What treachery is this?" she accused. Her eyes strayed beyond him to the other men. Though one was a stranger, the other was not. "Robert Kerr!" she breathed in startlement, then realized that it was *he* her captor resembled. Her stomach knotting, she looked back to Simon. "Dear heaven, what have you done?"

"I have but ensured that the Armstrongs will dance to my tune."

"But this . . . this is treason!"

"Is it?" He smiled again and took her arm, compelling her forward with him. "Come and greet my guests. One is apparently known to you. 'Tis Kerr, of course, who arranged your 'visit.' I think he has longed for this moment more than I."

"We meet again, my lady," Robert Kerr remarked as he made her a gallant little bow.

"My husband knows of your alliance with my kinsman," she advised him. "If you think to—"

"Aye." His eyes were cold, his expression grave. "I fear him not," he lied.

"Your beauty has not been exaggerated to me," the

other man declared as he, too, offered her a bow. Of medium height, he was slender and pale, his face pock-marked yet undeniably aristocratic. "I am William Spencer, my lady, come from Her Majesty to lend assistance to her warden."

"The queen would have no part in this," Analise opined, shaking her head.

"Believe what you will," he replied smoothly. "Yet know that I am at your service."

"Why have you forced me to Beauford?" she demanded, turning to confront Simon again. Though so fatigued that her legs threatened to give way beneath her, she would show him no weakness. "You had no right to do so. When my husband learns of this, he will come for me!"

"That is precisely what I want him to do."

"What do you mean?"

"Only that he will pay the price of his disloyalty. You see, my dearest Analise," he explained with deceptive nonchalance, "Ronan Armstrong is of no further use to me. When called upon to join with me against the Maxwells, he declined. And now that he would ride with the king's men against me, he must be killed."

"No!" Her face blanched in horror. She clutched at the front of his expensive, brocade satin doublet, her eyes glistening with sudden tears as she implored, "Please, you cannot think to do him harm!"

"His death will serve as an example to the others who would resist me," he told her disdainfully.

"But the king will seek revenge if you dare to—"

"Do you think I care what the Scottish king would do?"

"I beg of you, sir," she choked out, "please do not turn your hand against Ronan! 'Twas you yourself who forced us to wed. And I tell you now, I do love him more than life itself. If you will but spare him, I . . . I shall do whatever you ask. I shall give you all I have. Only allow him to live!"

"Well, well," Simon remarked, his mouth curving into a smile of contemptuous amusement. "My little cousin has given her heart to one of the foul-smelling heathens across the border."

"Guard your tongue, Hayward," Robert Kerr cautioned softly. "Else *this* foul-smelling heathen will school you to manners."

"Hold your threats, damn you!" Simon shot back, glowering. "You dare to speak of manners to me? Why, you are no better than your countrymen, save for the use I can make of you."

"Mayhap our alliance was ill conceived," suggested Kerr. It was obvious that his temper was flaring. Analise hastened to seize advantage of his anger.

"You are a Scot, the same as my husband!" she appealed to him. "Would you let the English turn you so easily? Would you see your country ruled by men such as Simon Hayward?"

"Och," he growled with a gesture of disgust. "I will not listen to a woman!"

"I fear your words achieve little," William Spencer observed. He met her fiery gaze and negligently folded his arms across his chest. "Perhaps, once your grief has lessened, we can become better acquainted."

"I would see you in hell first!" Wracked with anguish and fear on Ronan's behalf, she glared murderously at her cousin and vowed, "I swear by all that is holy, if my husband suffers any injury at your hands, *I will kill you myself.*"

"Then, I must look to my back henceforth," Simon replied with another mocking smile.

He raised his hand in a signal to Lady Helena, who stood waiting at the foot of the staircase. She swept forward, flinging Analise a smug, triumphant look.

"Take her upstairs," Simon directed the woman. "And make certain the bolt is drawn." He cast Analise another sneer. "Faith, Cousin, I would not have you escape to warn your husband of his doom."

"He will strike you dead!" she cried hotly.

"Go," he reiterated to Lady Helena.

She grasped Analise's arm. And when the younger woman pulled free, she drew a small knife from a sheath at her waist and held it to Analise's throat.

"Offer further resistance, my dear little kinswoman," she warned in a silken voice, "and I will give myself the pleasure of slitting your throat."

Analise ceased her struggles. Her hands moved instinctively to where the child grew within her, and she knew that she must comply. Stiffening beneath Lady Helena's grasp, she allowed herself to be led up the stairs.

Moments later she was thrust within the bedchamber she had occupied once before. Her eyes ablaze, she watched as Lady Helena sheathed the knife and smiled.

"So you have fallen in love with the Scotsman," she jeered, lifting her head in a gesture of superiority. "He is naught but a brigand, a Border Reiver. What a fool you were to choose him over your other, far more civilized suitors."

"Ronan Armstrong is twice the man of any other!" proclaimed Analise.

"Indeed? Perhaps, then, I should find a scoundrel of my own. Simon might even consent to force *me* into wedlock with one." She began to pull the door closed behind her now. "What a lovely widow you will make."

Analise furiously blinked back another surge of bitter tears. She tensed anew at the sound of the bolt being drawn. Her hand fluttered to her throat as she stood battling despair.

"Sweet heaven, what can I do?" she whispered hoarsely. Once before, she had been imprisoned to await her husband's death. And had been equally helpless to prevent it. Simon Hayward would not be so merciful as Angus Maxwell had been. No, she realized in growing dread, he was determined to have his revenge.

She made her way to the bed and collapsed down upon it. Closing her eyes against the pain in her heart, she thought of Ronan again. He was with the king in Edinburgh . . . it would be hours yet before he knew that she had been taken . . . he would ride at once to Beauford to seek her release.

"No!" she breathed, her eyes flying wide and filling with alarm. If he came alone, he would be killed. Indeed, he would ride straight into Simon's trap.

She stood and crossed distractedly to the window. There must be a way to warn him, she told herself. Please, God, there must!

Someone was sliding the bolt free. Analise started, whirling about as a buxom, dark-haired young woman entered with a tray of food and drink.

"Meg!" she cried, her brow clearing.

"Oh, my lady, I could scarce believe it when I heard you had returned!" said Meg. She crossed to lower the tray to the bedside table, then watched as Analise hurried to close the door. "What of your husband? Did you take no pleasure in your marriage, my lady? Is that why you have come back?"

"I was forced to Beauford this night!" Analise confided. Moving back to raise her hands to the maid-servant's arms, she gave her an earnest look of appeal. "You must help me, Meg!"

"I, my lady? Why, what can I—"

"I must send word to my husband at once. Else he will meet his death here. And I know you would not wish to see my child fatherless!"

"You are with child already?" Meg asked in surprise, her gaze dropping to Analise's belly.

"Yes." She tightened her grasp upon the other woman's arms and implored, "Please, Meg, you are my only hope!"

"But even if . . . even if I *would* help you, my lady, I know not how!"

"Surely you know of someone who can carry a message to Edinburgh!"

"To Edinburgh?" she echoed in astonishment. Her eyebrows knitted together into a deep, pensive frown before she offered, "Well, there is George the stable lad. He is—" She broke off abruptly and shook her head, her eyes widening with fear. "But I cannot! The master would turn me out for certain if he knew!"

"He will not know!" Analise insisted. She forced a smile to her lips and put forth more calmly, "If you will but help me, Meg, I will take you back to Dunslair with me."

"You mean, go to Scotland?" Her tone was one of shocked disbelief, her expression almost comical. "Oh, my lady, I could not! Why, I could never live among those . . . those . . ." She vigorously shook her head again.

"They are not the savages you think them. In truth, I have found them to be men of great intelligence and honor."

"How can you say that, my lady? Did the master not force you to wed with your husband, who was himself one of the Reivers we fear so much?"

"Yes, but things have changed," Analise declared. She released the maidservant's arms and turned away. "I love my husband, Meg. More than I ever dreamed possible. And I would rather die than see him harmed!"

" 'Tis a fine mess here," sighed Meg. Frowning in confusion now, she folded her arms against her chest and asked, "Do you truly love him so much, then, my lady?"

"Truly." She wandered closer to the fire, her gaze losing itself amid the flames. "Unless he learns of my kinsman's plot against him, he will come for me. And in so doing, will be murdered." A sob rose in her throat. She sank down into the chair and buried her face in her hands.

Meg's heart stirred with compassion. She swept forward, dropping to her knees beside Analise.

"I will do it, my lady," she announced. "I will see that George rides to Edinburgh this very night!"

"Oh, Meg!" Analise exclaimed softly. She turned to embrace her in gratitude, and promised, "I shall see that you are well rewarded!"

"I seek no reward," Meg told her. A sudden, mischievous smile played about her lips, while her eyes sparkled. "Yet I *will* come to Scotland with you, if only for a time. In secret, my lady, I have longed to know if the Reivers are the devils I have always heard them to be."

"I suspect you will not meet with disappointment," Analise remarked with a brief smile of her own. She sprang from the chair and across to the writing table. Dipping the quill into the pot of ink, she quickly scrawled a message upon the parchment. And when done, she folded it, sealed it with wax, and gave it to Meg. "Tell George that he must go to Holyrood Palace once in Edinburgh, and that he must give the message to none other save Ronan Armstrong. If my husband is not at the palace, then George must ride to Dunslair. He, too, shall be rewarded!"

"Yes, my lady!" Meg secured the letter within the bodice of her gown.

"You are certain that George is trustworthy?"

"He is that, my lady," Meg confirmed, her mouth twitching anew. "And if I do but promise him a kiss, he will ride to the very gates of hell!"

She left then, closing the door behind her and drawing the bolt as she had been instructed. Analise took a seat in the chair again, physically and emotionally drained, yet holding fast to the hope that the message would get through.

Ronan. She closed her eyes, her heart twisting as his image rose in her mind.

Night gave way to morning. Another day passed. And then another.

With considerable difficulty, Analise managed to eat and sleep. She had no real appetite, of course, but knew that she must take nourishment for the babe's sake. Her thoughts were always of Ronan, her prayers always for his safety. It was agony not to know if he had received her letter. George had not returned. She began to wonder if her husband even knew yet that she was at Beauford. If he did, why, then, had he offered no response to Simon's message?

Thrown into whirl of fear and confusion, she struggled to keep hope alive.

The majority of her captivity was spent within the confines of her bedchamber, though she was required to put in an appearance in the hall each evening. She did so under protest, and offered little in the way of conversation. Simon was greatly annoyed by her proud defiance, but neither of his guests seemed to mind. William Spencer, in particular, paid her every compliment and would seldom leave her side. His attentions were loathsome to her. And though she endured them without complaint, or encouragement, she silently vowed to see him punished for his role in the treachery. She had little doubt that it was his own interests he looked to, not the queen's.

On the third night after her arrival at Beauford, she was reluctantly dressing for supper. Her fingers were unsteady upon the lacings of her emerald satin gown, and she was forced to take a seat upon the bed when another wave of nausea struck her. A faint smile touched her lips as she mused that the child, still so new within her, would be ignored no more than its father.

"My lady?" a woman's voice drew her from her reverie.

She was surprised to see Meg, for she had not heard the door opening. Color flew back to her cheeks as she stood and hastened across to grasp the maidservant's hand.

"Has George—"

"No, my lady," Meg answered. She closed the door and turned back to Analise with a frown of worriment. "I cannot think what keeps him."

"I can," Analise murmured, a shadow crossing her face. She drew away from Meg and wandered to the window, her hand entangling within the curtain there. *Dear God, when will this torment end?*

"Lady Helena bids you come downstairs. She wishes the meal to be served within the hour."

"Tell her, if you will, that I am unwell. And that I care not what she bids." Her gaze traveled over the night-cloaked countryside. She suddenly inhaled upon a soft gasp, certain that she had glimpsed movement upon the distant hills. Her eyes narrowed in an attempt to confirm her suspicions. But she saw nothing.

"It will do you no good to stay here and brood upon your misfortune," said Meg. She smiled and opened the door again. "Come, my lady. I will myself see you to the hall."

Analise was only dimly aware of Meg's words, for she had leaned closer to the panes of glass and peered outward. Still, there was nothing. She heaved a sigh and pivoted to face Meg again.

"Neither does it do me good to endure the company of my cousin and his black-hearted allies," she murmured ruefully. But she finished lacing her gown, and accompanied Meg from the room. Though she would have much preferred to spend her hours alone, she was determined to turn William Spencer's attraction for her to an advantage. It was worth a try. And, in truth, she would do anything to save Ronan. *Anything at all.*

The three men sat waiting for her in their customary place before the fire. They stood when she swept gracefully forward. William Spencer was the first to take her hand in greeting.

"If possible, my lady, you are even more beautiful this

night," he pronounced, his eyes virtually devouring her. She managed a smile, and allowed him to brush her hand with his lips.

"I thank you, sir." She smiled again, offering a slight curtsy to the other two. "Good evening, Simon. And to you as well, Robert Kerr."

"What trickery is this?" the Scot snapped, eyeing her dubiously. "You have never yet behaved with anything save an ill humor. Why do you—"

"I think, Kerr," Simon cut him off, "that my little cousin has grown weary of her solitude and would now look to her future. Is that not true, Analise?"

"Yes," she lied, adding credence with an eloquent sigh. "If I am soon to be a widow . . ." Her words trailed away, and she appeared to be close to tears. Inwardly a sharp pain sliced at her heart. She moved across to the velvet settee and sank down upon it, her hand falling to the empty place to her left. "Will you not join me, Sir William?"

"Gladly, my lady." Settling himself close beside her, he grew so bold as to draw her arm through the crook of his.

"Aye, the Armstrong has chosen himself a wife who would dance upon his grave," Robert Kerr remarked in contempt.

"She *was* forced to the marriage," Simon reminded him. Yet he, too, looked upon her with suspicion. "Is your love so inconstant, then, dearest cousin?"

"Not inconstant," she denied, keeping her tone even and her face impassive. "Since I can do naught to save Ronan Armstrong, I must accept what is to come and, as you said, look to my future." She released another long, wistful sigh before adding, "Call me heartless if you will, but am I truly so wretched a soul? I was wed but briefly, and would not spend the remainder of my years without the protection of a husband."

"And so you shall not," William decreed. Thoroughly smitten, he pulled her closer, his manner that of a possessive lover instead of a man who had known her for two days' time. "Once we are back in London, sweet lady, I must have leave to call upon you."

"I should like that, sir." Bile rose in her throat, but she kept to her purpose. "I should like that very much."

"Enough of this blethering," Robert snarled. He rounded on Simon with a deep scowl. "I grow tired of waiting for the Armstrong to come. We must ride upon Dunslair!"

"No," said Simon. "If we dare to venture across the border, we will be met by the king's army."

"By the Virgin's blood, man, he has not yet had the time to—"

"My lord!" a young footman suddenly cried as he burst into the room. All eyes turned to him. He hastened forth to Simon, making him a bow before announcing breathlessly, "The captain of your guard would speak with you must urgently, my lord!"

"On what matter?"

"I know not, my lord. He said only that you must come to him at once!"

"The fool," Simon muttered angrily. He cast a quick glance toward William and Analise.

"I will go with you," Robert told him. " 'Tis time I had a word with my men as well."

"See to Lady Analise in my absence," Simon charged William.

"With pleasure, sir."

Analise's pulse leapt as she watched Simon and Robert leave the room. Her first thought was of Ronan. Dear heaven, had he come for her at last? But no, she told herself in the next instant as both her hopes and her fears diminished. If he had done so, then there would have been little need for the captain of the guard to summon Simon. Indeed, Ronan would by now have been clasped in chains and tossed into the dungeon, *or dead . . .*

"Forgive me, dearest lady, but I can remain patient no longer!" William suddenly exclaimed beside her. Before she could ask him his meaning, he had caught her up against him and pressed his mouth to hers.

She stiffened, suffering a sharp intake of breath while battling the urge to push him away. It was all she could do to prevent herself from doing so. Though her stomach churned and every fiber of her being protested at his embrace, she knew that she must allow it. Heaven help her, she *must* suffer through it. If she could entice him well enough, he would agree to help her. *And Ronan would live.*

When William finally released her, she stood and moved closer to the fire. Her hand fluttered upward to rest upon the curve of her breasts, where they swelled above the low, heart-shaped neckline of her gown. Pretending to be breathless, and delighted, as a result of his kiss, she forced a coquettish smile to her lips.

"I am a married woman, sir," she reminded him, albeit without conviction.

"That matters little to me," he declared. His lust was all too apparent as he rose to his feet and hastened to her side. "Indeed, sweet lady, I will help you to forget your husband!" He swept her against him once more, his lips crashing down upon hers. She closed her eyes and thought of Ronan.

"Unhand her now, and mayhap live!"

Analise started at the sound of that familiar, deep-timbred voice. She hastily thrust William from her and spun about to find that her husband had somehow materialized but a few feet away. He stood with sword in hand, his handsome face thunderous and his eyes ablaze with vengeful, white-hot fury.

"Ronan!" she breathed. Overcome with mingled shock and relief, she would have gone to him then. But he gave her a fierce look that warned against it, and slowly advanced upon William.

"So, Englishman," he challenged in a voice of deadly calm, "will you live, or die this night?"

"You . . . you are the lady's husband?" William stammered, blanching with terror as the tip of the blade pressed against his chest.

"Aye. And have sworn to kill any man who dares to touch her." His fingers clenched about the hilt of his sword, and there was little doubt that he would take great pleasure in running the man through.

"Sweet mercy, Ronan, you have stepped into a trap!" cried Analise, her fearful gaze slicing toward the doorway. "My cousin and Robert Kerr—"

"Think of them no more." For a moment his eyes met hers. "I have come with an army."

"But how—" She broke off, suddenly recalling the movement she had earlier detected upon the hills. *An army.* Her head spun, her eyes widening with incredulity at what was happening. Voices raised in anger outside now drifted within the hall, along with the sound of gunfire.

"I beg of you, sir, do not think to kill me!" William entreated, stretching his arms outward. "I am unarmed, and have stolen naught but a kiss!"

" 'Tis true!" Analise confirmed. She flew to Ronan now and placed an anxious hand upon his arm. "Please, Ronan, let him live!"

Her plea only served to fuel his rage. Yet it was directed toward her as much as toward the coward before him. He muttered a blistering oath and lowered his sword.

"Go, then," he directed curtly. "Outside to join with the others." William cast him one last frightened, dubious glance before taking flight. As soon as he had gone, Ronan sheathed his sword and fixed Analise with a look that struck fear in her heart.

"By damn, Analise," he ground out, "what were you—"

"All is not yet lost!" Simon Hayward decreed, his voice echoing within the firelit cavern of the hall.

A gasp of startled dismay broke from Analise's lips. She looked to where Simon and Robert Kerr, each wielding a sword, now advanced upon Ronan.

"Indeed," continued Simon, his lips curled into a sneer, "for we have the Armstrong within our sights!"

In one lightning swift motion, Ronan drew his sword again and pushed Analise behind him.

"You have been beaten, and no doubt with little bloodshed thus far," he pointed out grimly. "It will gain you nothing to strike now."

"Aye, your men have seized Beauford easily enough," Robert conceded. "You did take it by surprise—a brilliant maneuver, Mac Ghillielaidir, and one 'tis certain the king will applaud. But you will never know his gratitude. No, for you will join me in hell this night!"

"No!" screamed Analise. She staggered backward, her skirts tangling about her legs while her gaze frantically searched for a way to help Ronan.

"Go to it, Kerr!" Simon encouraged.

Robert launched the first attack. His thrust was expertly deflected. He struck again, only to bite out a curse when the edge of Ronan's blade sliced aross his arm.

"You were ever a poor swordsman, Kerr," Ronan pointed out. "Yet a better traitor. Surrender, and—"

Robert gave a cry of rage and lifted his sword again. He aimed for Ronan's heart. But it was his own that felt the point of a blade. His weapon clattered to the floor, his eyes falling to where blood ran hot from the gaping wound in his chest.

"You have done me in!" he whispered. His pained, horror-struck gaze sought Ronan's face once more. And then he crumpled, falling heavily to the floor while the life seeped from his body.

Analise caught her breath and looked to Ronan. She saw that his features were a grim mask of determination as he turned to Simon now.

"Will you meet with same fate, Hayward?" he asked, tightening his grip upon his bloodstained sword.

"No, Scotsman, I will not." He sheathed his own sword. Then, without warning, he lunged toward Analise. Ronan started forward, but it was too late. Simon's arm clamped about her waist. He yanked her back against him and brought the point of his dagger to her throat. She gasped, her every muscle tensing in alarm while her eyes flew to Ronan's face.

"Release her," he commanded Simon, his tone dangerously low and level. His gaze held a near savage gleam.

"Pray, sir, why should I do so?" jeered Simon. He

dragged Analise along with him as he made for the door.
"My little cousin can be of use to me once again. Indeed,
she will ensure my safe passage from this place!"

" 'Tis *me* you want, then, not her," said Ronan, flinging his sword aside. He cautiously gave chase now, his
steps slow and measured. "Let her go, and none will stop
you."

"Do you think me such a fool that I would trust the
word of a Border Reiver?"

"I would have thought you a better man than to hide
behind a woman's skirts."

Analise's mind raced to think of a way to break free.
She closed her eyes for a moment, fervently praying for
deliverance from the most horrific nightmare she had
ever known.

Her prayer was answered—in the unlikely form of
John Beattie.

"Ronan Armstrong?" John called out as he neared the
hall. When he appeared within the doorway, he set in
motion the events that would finally see an end to the
standoff.

Analise hastened to take advantage of her cousin's surprise. She began to struggle violently with his grasp. A
sharp, strangled cry escaped her lips when the edge of the
dagger cut across the side of her neck, but she dropped to
her knees and rolled free.

Simon seized her arm in an attempt to pull her to her
feet again, but to no avail. His eyes, round with fear, met
Ronan's. Panicking, he spun about and raced across the
hall to the staircase.

John and Ronan started after him at the same moment.
But Ronan was the first to reach him. His hand closed
about Simon's arm. He forced him about, and brought his

fist smashing up against the other man's chin. Simon fell, tumbling down the steps. Ronan was upon him again in an instant.

John, meanwhile, hastened across to Analise. He helped her to her feet. Several tiny drops of blood fell upon her bodice, and she pressed a hand to the cut on her neck. She clung to John, watching as Ronan hit Simon again and again.

"Ronan!" she cried out, fearing that he would kill him.

Her plea had the desired affect—he ceased his attack upon Simon. Gazing down at the man who lay sprawled, bleeding, and barely conscious at the foot of the staircase, he offered him a look full of contempt.

"Aye," he decreed quietly, "you *should* live. Perhaps English justice will see you paid for your crimes."

Analise pulled away from John now and flew across the room into her husband's waiting arms. He held her tightly, burying his face in the fragrant softness of her hair while she released a long, quavering sigh.

"The castle is taken," John confirmed. Shifting his gaze to Robert Kerr's lifeless form, his features twisted into a grimace of disgust. "By all the saints, I'll shed no tears on that traitor's behalf." Looking back to Ronan and Analise, he shook his head and made haste to leave them to their hard-won privacy. He paused to force Simon to his feet, then compelled him outside into the midst of the other prisoners.

"I feared you would come alone!" murmured Analise, still pale and shaken.

"And so I would have, if the king had not ordered me against it." His eyes darkened anew when he told her, "My anger and worriment knew no bounds when I heard you had been taken. But I took comfort in the certainty that Simon Hayward would offer you no harm. You were his only hope of drawing me to Beauford."

"He would have murdered you." She shuddered, closing her eyes again.

"Never again will he threaten you," vowed Ronan.

"I sent you a message, warning you of his plan." She lifted her head and drew away a bit, warming beneath the loving steadiness of his gaze.

"Aye." The ghost of a smile tugged briefly at his lips. "Young George rode with us this night."

"I have promised him a reward for his help. And Meg—" She broke off with a gasp of startlement when he seized her by her arms and pulled her up hard against him.

"Be glad, woman, that you are with child," he ground out, his eyes hot with fury once more. "Else you would now feel the flat of my hand upon your backside!"

"What?" she breathed, staring up at him in bewilderment.

"Would the kiss have led to more if I had not come upon you when I did?" he demanded irefully. "You did not appear so unwilling a victim!"

"Oh, you—you speak of William Spencer!" she faltered, guilty color staining her cheeks. "In truth, I thought only to persuade him to lend assistance, to see you spared!"

"And how far would you have gone to do so?"

"In truth, my lord, you have a strange way of showing your gratitude!" She bristled at his reproach, her own eyes sparking with indignation.

"Am I to be grateful, then, that my wife would offer another man what I alone have the right to claim?" He swore underneath his breath and scowled down at her. "By heaven, Analise, you will yet drive me to madness!"

" 'Tis a madness of your own making!" she retorted, giving a proud and defiant toss of her head.

"Aye. It began when first I looked upon you." His temper cooling somewhat now, he gathered her close once more. His tone was laced with wry humor when he remarked, "Henceforth, lady wife, I must keep you close."

"Truly, Ronan, I would not have given myself to him," she proclaimed, heaving a sigh of pleasure when his arms came about her. "I meant only to lend him encouragement for a time."

"Encouragement? Call it—"

"What a touching reunion!"

Analise tensed within Ronan's embrace. She jerked her head about, her eyes widening in surprise at the woman who stood surveying them from a short distance way.

"Lady Helena!" The color drained from her face when she saw that her cousin's paramour held a pistol aimed directly at them.

"Lower your weapon," commanded Ronan, pushing Analise behind him again. His hand moved to rest upon the hilt of his sword. "We have the castle. You cannot hope to escape."

"Perhaps not. Yet before I am taken, I will see that Simon is avenged!" Lady Helena cried, her face ugly with rage. Slowly she began to squeeze the trigger. "You will be first, Scotsman!"

"No!" screamed Analise. She raced forward, her only thought to protect Ronan. He caught her and thrust her out of the path of the bullet. She lost her balance, and heard a gunshot ring out as she fell upon her knees.

Trembling violently, she staggered to her feet and

whirled about. Her gaze filled with surprise, then profound joy and relief.

Ronan stood over the prone body of Lady Helena, his hand grasping her pistol. She groaned while struggling to regain consciousness. A bruise already marked the spot where Ronan's fist had struck her chin.

Analise came to life again. She gathered up her skirts and sprang forward, throwing her arms about Ronan's neck.

"I—I thought you dead!"

"You English are a slow and weak-willed lot," he pronounced dryly. Her heart stirred at his teasing, and she swayed even closer.

John Beattie and a dozen other Scots hastened into the room now, drawn there by the sound of the gunshot. John, after giving orders for Lady Helena to be taken outside, approached Ronan and Analise.

"Will you not find peace, man?" he asked Ronan, his own voice full of amusement.

"Aye," answered Ronan. With his arm about Analise's waist, he smiled down at her. "I will."

He led her along with him, from the hall and out into the cold, moonlit darkness. Her gaze fell upon the scores of Borderers who had ridden to Beauford under Ronan's command. They stood in the courtyard, guarding the captured Englishmen. At a signal from Ronan, his men mounted their horses and surrounded the prisoners. They would be marched to Hexham that night, and given into the care of the magistrates there. Simon Hayward would be Warden of the Middle March no more. And William Spencer would be made to answer for representing himself, falsely, as the queen's consort.

Ronan tossed a cloak about Analise's shoulders.

"Home, my lady?" he asked softly, his hands closing about her waist.

"Aye, my lord."

He lifted her up into the saddle, then swung up onto the back of his own mount. Together they rode away from Beauford, setting a course for Dunslair and the happiness they knew awaited them there.

Chapter 15

Five years later . . .

A smile of supreme happiness touched Analise's lips as she strolled with Ronan about the grounds of Dunslair. Her gaze strayed to where their two children, under the watchful eye of a very pregnant Mairi, played together in the afternoon sunlight. Gordon, with the same unwavering confidence and chestnut-colored hair as his father, took great pleasure in teasing his younger sister. Yet tiny, blonde Catriona deserved little sympathy, for even at the tender age of two, she could hold her own against her brother and any other who dared to torment her.

"Someday she will break many a heart," predicted Ronan, his tone laced with wry amusement as he looked to his daughter.

"I fear so," Analise agreed with a sigh. "And no doubt will repay her brother for his devilment." She raised her softly shining eyes to the splendid, mesmerizing blue of his. "Oh, Ronan, 'tis so good to know that they will never have cause to look upon the English as their enemies."

"Aye. James Stewart sits upon the throne of England at last." His heart swelled with pride at the thought of his friend. "A king to reign over both countries . . . God be praised, we have waited a long time to see it done."

"And what will the Reivers do now that there is to be no more raiding along the border?"

"Turn their hands to farming, no doubt. Or perhaps learn a trade." His mouth curved into a brief smile of irony. "Their current skills will gain them little in this new age of peace."

"Well, my lord, at least I shall no longer have to bid you farewell so—"

" 'Tis a lovely day, is it not, my lady?" Meg called out as she hastened to join Mairi. She held two children by the hand—one her own son, the other the eldest of Calum and Dierdre. Soon Dierdre would give birth to a fourth, which was no true surprise to anyone at Dunslair. Even after five years' time, Calum could scarce keep his hands off his wife. And it was said that *she* was much the same when it came to the handsome, once wild rascal she had wed.

"Good afternoon, Meg!" Analise responded with a smile of genuine affection. She recalled again how the pretty young maidservant had fallen in love with one of the Armstrongs within a month of her arrival at Dunslair. Indeed, she mused silently while her eyes lit with fond humor, they were an irresistible lot.

"Shall we go to London, then, sweet lady, to pay our respects to the new king?" Ronan offered, drawing her farther along with him toward the millpond.

"No." She shook her head and told him earnestly, "Never again will I go to London. My home is here now, and I have no wish to remember my life before we were wed."

"By all the saints," he remarked in a low, vibrant tone

that made her knees weaken, "I cannot help but give thanks for *one* part of your kinsman's treachery."

"Can that night really have been so long ago?" she murmured, her brow creasing into a thoughtful frown.

" 'Tis said that fanned fires and forced marriages never did well." He paused and gave her a smile so thoroughly disarming that she felt her heart stir in a wild and rapturous manner. "But we have proved it wrong."

"We have reached the mill, my lord," she pointed out, her own voice soft and seductive now. "None are inside at present."

"What mischief is this?" he challenged, his magnificent eyes aglow.

"You are the laird, are you not? Well, then, sir, would you allow your brother's sons to outnumber your own?"

"By heaven, lass," he whispered huskily, "you *will* drive me to madness yet."

"Aye, Ronan Armstrong." She pulled away from him and gathered up her skirts, heading for the door. "I will."

He needed no further encouragement. In an instant he had closed the distance between them. A gasp of delight escaped her lips when he swept her up in his arms and carried her inside the mill.

*Lorrie Morgan was born to be
a country-western music star.*

In FOREVER YOURS FAITHFULLY,
she tells us her tempestuous story of sweet
triumph and bitter tragedy.
From her childhood as a Nashville blueblood
performing at the Grand Ole Opry at the tender
age of eleven to her turbulent,
star-crossed love affair with Keith Whitley,
a bluegrass legend she loved passionately
but could not save from his personal demons,
to her rise to superstardom,
she lays bare all the secrets and great passions
of a life lived to the fullest.

And her story would not be complete without
the music that has been her lifeline.

**A special four-song CD of
never-before-released material,
featuring a duet with Keith Whitley,
is included with this hardcover.**

FOREVER YOURS FAITHFULLY
by Lorrie Morgan

Published by Ballantine Books.
Coming to bookstores everywhere
in October 1997.

Love Letters

Ballantine romances are on the Web!

Read about your favorite Ballantine authors and
upcoming books on our Web site, LOVE LETTERS, at
www.randomhouse.com/BB/loveletters, including:

♥What's new in the stores
♥Previews of upcoming books
♥In-depth interviews with romance authors and
  publishing insiders
♥Sample chapters from new romances
♥And more . . .

Want to keep in touch? To subscribe to Love Notes, the
monthly what's-new update for the Love Letters Web site,
send an e-mail message to
loveletters@cruises.randomhouse.com
with "subscribe" as the subject of the message. You will
receive a monthly announcement of the latest news and
features on our site.

So follow your heart and visit us at
www.randomhouse.com/BB/loveletters!

Diana Palmer's
sizzling historical novels are full of soul-stirring
emotion and rich storytelling. Now she carries on her
bestselling tradition with

THE SAVAGE HEART

the fiery story of a woman with big dreams and a man
who has nothing to believe in . . . except her.

Lethal to foes and generous to friends, the enigmatic
Matt Davis can handle anything that comes his way
until Tess Meredith storms into Chicago and back into
his life. And this fearless and determined young cru-
sader is ready to wage her greatest battle . . . for a love
that will not be denied.

THE SAVAGE HEART comes to you in a brand-new
format as a lightweight, durable, elegant, affordably
priced (only $10) petite hardcover.

On sale September 2 at bookstores everywhere.

*Read on for more titles also available in this thrilling new
format from Fawcett Columbine . . .*

MURDER WILL SPEAK
by Joan Smith

Corinne, the Dowager Countess deCoventry, is wearing the magnificent deCoventry pearls one last time before handing them over to their new owner when they are stolen. Corinne's assortment of oddball friends rally to help her recover the lost legacy. The dashing bachelor-about-town Lord Luten, the elegant and aloof Sir Reginald Prance, and Coffen Paffle, the amiable bungler with a heart of gold, are all pitched into murder, mayhem, and romance as they pursue clues from the most fashionable ballrooms to the sordid back alleys of Regency London.

Don't miss this first installment of the adventures of the Berkeley Brigade,
a crew of young aristocrats-turned-sleuths in Regency England!

A PAIR OF ROGUES
by Patricia Wynn

Louisa, the Duchess of Broughton, uses the occasion of her son's baptism to make a match between his unruly new godparents. When Ned, the Earl of Windermere, an infamous rake who is trying to reform his ways, confronts the wayward Lady Christina Lindsay over the baptismal font, he discovers he has met his match—and this affair of the heart will be one of epic proportions.

On sale now!

Published by Fawcett Books.
Available in bookstores everywhere.